# BERLIN HUNGERS

# Acclaim for Justine Saracen's Novels

About *The Sniper's Kiss*: "If you've read Saracen before, she's at her finest here. Her action sequences pop, her plots are twisty, and she loves to put her heroines in the most dire of circumstances and extract them slowly."—Jerry Wheeler, *Out in Print*

*The Witch of Stalingrad* is "one of the best lesbian historical novels I've read…on the Eastern Front (not just) the night bombers, which Saracen more than excelled at portraying (but also) the conditions of POW camps, citizens who were affected by Stalin's purges that left thousands dead, and the camaraderie between strangers in terrifying situations." —*The Lesbrary*

*Waiting for the Violins* is "a thrilling, charming, and heartrending trip back in time to the early years of World War II and the active resistance enclaves…Stunning and eye-opening!"—*Rainbow Book Reviews*

"I can't think of anything more incongruous than ancient Biblical texts, scuba diving, Hollywood lesbians, and international art installations, but I do know that there's only one author talented and savvy enough to make it all work. That's just what the incomparable Justine Saracen does in her latest, *Beloved Gomorrah*."—*Out In Print*

"Saracen blends historical and fictional characters seamlessly and brings authenticity to the story, focusing on the impacts of this time on 'regular, normal people'…*Tyger Tyger* [is] a brilliantly written historical novel that has elements of romance, suspense, horror, pathos and it gives the reader quite a bit to think about...fast-paced...difficult to put down...an excellent book that easily blurs the line between lesfic and mainstream."—*C-Spot Reviews*

"*Sarah, Son of God* can lightly be described as the 'The Lesbian's *Da Vinci Code*' because of the somewhat common themes. At its roots, it's part mystery and part thriller. *Sarah, Son of God* is an engaging and exciting story about searching for the truth within each of us. Ms. Saracen considers the sacrifices of those who came before us, challenges us to open ourselves to a different reality than what we've been told we can have, and reminds us to be true to ourselves. Her prose and pacing rhythmically rise and fall like the tides in Venice; and her reimagined life and death of Jesus allows thoughtful readers to consider "what if?"—*Rainbow Reader*

"*Mephisto Aria* could well stand as a classic among gay and lesbian readers."—*ForeWord Reviews*

"Saracen's wonderfully descriptive writing is a joy to the eye and the ear, as scenes play out on the page, and almost audibly as well. The characters are extremely well drawn, with suave villains, and lovely heroines. There are also wonderful romances, a heart-stopping plot, and wonderful love scenes. *Mephisto Aria* is a great read."—*Just About Write*

"Justine Saracen's *Sistine Heresy* is a well-written and surprisingly poignant romp through Renaissance Rome in the age of Michelangelo...The novel entertains and titillates while it challenges, warning of the mortal dangers of trespass in any theocracy (past or present) that polices same-sex desire." —Professor Frederick Roden, University of Connecticut, Author, *Same-Sex Desire in Victorian Religious Culture*

**Visit us at www.boldstrokesbooks.com**

# By the Author

## *The Ibis Prophecy Series:*

The 100th Generation

Vulture's Kiss


Sistine Heresy

Mephisto Aria

Sarah, Son of God

Tyger, Tyger, Burning Bright

Beloved Gomorrah

Waiting for the Violins

Dian's Ghost

The Witch of Stalingrad

The Sniper's Kiss

Berlin Hungers

# BERLIN HUNGERS

*by*

Justine Saracen

2018

---

CREDITS
EDITOR: SHELLEY THRASHER
PRODUCTION DESIGN: STACIA SEAMAN
COVER DESIGN BY SHERI

# Acknowledgments

Moving aircraft through the skies of 1940s Germany requires a lot of technical know-how that I didn't have, and not all of it can come from books. In this case, some of it came from people like Marilee Wilson and Julie Tizard (both retired colonels) for 1940s aircraft call signs, and to Mitchell Hynes, helicopter pilot, for suggestions on how to crash a Dakota. On the production end, for this novel, as for the previous eleven, Shelley Thrasher has been a stalwart friend and editor, saving me from myself, bad grammar, and clichés, while visionary Sheri has conjured up another compelling and eye-catching cover. Sharp-eyed Stacia Seaman caught a major error, for which I am relieved and grateful. Lastly, I pay homage to Radclyffe, who created Bold Strokes Books from the wellspring of imagination. I offer my fervent gratitude for this cross-global collaboration and hope it may continue…indefinitely.

To Ahed Tamimi, age 16
Courage has no age

# CHAPTER ONE

*VE Day—May 8, 1945*

Victory! In Europe, the guns fell silent, and all of Great Britain poured out into the streets. In London, a jubilant crowd gathered in Trafalgar Square.

In its midst, Gillian Somerville stood lost in thought. Abruptly, someone seized her arm and spun her around. A soldier, obviously intoxicated, pulled her to him and pressed his mouth hard on hers. She pushed him away, then winced a smile so as not to hurt his feelings. Rebuffed, he lurched toward another young woman, who accepted his attentions more warmly.

Wiping her mouth, Gillian gazed at the conga lines, the tossed hats and easy embraces, and shared the general relief. But melancholy tainted her joy, for the Blitz was too strong in her memory, and as she swept her glance around the crowd, she kept seeing the faces of her parents.

She still bore the horror and guilt of knowing that she'd cowered in an air-raid shelter while they burned to death in their own home. Shaking with fear, she'd heard the incendiary bombs detonate and, like everyone, fervently hoped they fell elsewhere, not on her house. Her father was an invalid, and her mother would never leave him. But when she emerged to the smoke and screaming sirens of the fire rescue, she learned she'd lost this roll of the dice. Everything on her street was gone. Incinerated.

Life went on, for her as for every other survivor, but serving as a military transport pilot became her sole purpose, the closest she could come to vengeance, and for five years, she flew with a seething bitterness toward Germany and its murderous Luftwaffe.

She tugged at the hem of her tunic and brushed her fingertips over the insignia on the chest pocket. The dark-blue uniform represented her dedication, as if to holy orders. She'd learned to pilot a plane in imitation of her brother, outdid him in fact, for he'd never made it to the war, never flown anything larger than a sports plane. But once she qualified as a pilot, she'd worked her way up from simple one-engine planes to big bombers. She ferried them from the factories to the air bases and transported supplies all over the UK and later, as the Allies advanced across Europe, into Germany. Climbing out of the cockpit, then having an RAF pilot replace her for the very last leg, made her feel part of the machinery of defense, for they both wore uniforms identifying them with air power. Only hers was about to become obsolete.

Life had been both achingly difficult and morally simple. Work for freedom or die for it. The Air Transport Auxiliary had made up her whole identity, and now that it was to be disbanded, that identity was about to collapse into ashes, like London buildings in the Blitz.

"This is the happiest day of my life," the elderly man standing next to her said, pink-faced from cheering and slightly pathetic in his ill-fitting Home Guard uniform.

"I'm happy, too. Relieved," she added. "I just hate giving up air transport and the sense of doing something vital for the cause."

"Let the men take care of that, my dear." He nudged her softly with his elbow. "Pretty girl like you should go back home, marry one of the lads returning from the front, and start a lovely British family. That's the way to show your patriotism."

Was that her future? Her duty? To build a nest and satisfy the desires of some hero, instead of being one?

She shook her head to clear away the dread. It was ruining a glorious day, a once-in-a-lifetime day, that she'd want to remember. She smiled good-bye to the home guardsman and strolled toward the fountain where two young women splashed knee-deep in the water. Groups of sailors and soldiers took turns posing with them for photographs. The women got wetter and wetter, and the frolicking became more boisterous, until a man seized one of the women around the waist and they fell back together into the water.

Her feet were beginning to hurt now, though she didn't want to leave the festivities, so she edged toward the periphery of the square and its row of pubs. All were packed, but she elbowed her way inside one. When she reached the counter and called out for a beer, one suddenly appeared in front of her. "On the house," the bartender said, placing a row of bottles along the counter, where hands snatched them up within seconds. She took a gulp, and the cool liquid felt good going down.

"Bloody great day, eh?" someone next to her said. A slender, dark-haired man in an RAF uniform, someone she might have served with, though the unbuttoned jacket would have put him on report.

"Cheers," she said, tapping bottles with him. "I'm a pilot myself," she added. "Air Transport Auxiliary."

"Freight haulers, huh?" he said with faint condescension. "I'm a fighter pilot." He took another long pull on his drink and seemed to wait for some sign of admiration.

"Not just freight." Gillian felt suddenly defensive. "We flew VIP passengers, war materials, medicines, fuel, everything to keep the boys in the field going."

He wiped his mouth with the back of his hand. "Don't get me wrong, miss. The lads couldn't've done it without you. But it's not the same as combat or flying over enemy territory."

"I flew over enemy territory all the time. And along border areas where shooting was going on. I was even shot at once." She stopped. Why was she trying to impress this lout?

He snorted and leaned on one elbow on the damp counter. "I'm sure you were very brave, miss. But let's face it. You were 'auxiliary,' while we were doing the fighting and dying. I lost six of the best chaps I ever knew." He knocked back the last swallow of beer as a sort of exclamation point.

She suddenly felt small. How had the conversation become a pissing contest? He'd played the dead-comrades card, and she had nothing to counter it with.

"I'm sorry," she said, and changed the subject. "But we both know what it feels like to be up there, the exhilaration of flying a two-engine at top speed. I'll miss that, now the war's over."

"Not me. We still have bases all over Western Europe. I'm off to Germany in a few days." He leaned conspiratorially toward her. "They say the German birds are hungry for attention, with all their men dead or in POW camps." He raised an eyebrow in an obvious attempt to be lewd.

She ignored it. "Do you think they'll let women pilots fly? I mean, if I joined the women's RAF?"

He shrugged, his expression hinting at disinterest, slight ridicule. "Probably not. Plenty of good men there to do the job. But the RAF always needs…you know, secretaries and nurses." He seized another bottle from the line the bartender had set up. "You'd be around pilots and maybe meet some nice chaps."

To hell with that. She turned and began to elbow her way back through the euphoric crowd. Since the day her older brother had taken her up in his Miles Hawk and let her soar and swoop through the air, she craved no other pleasure. For the duration of the war, she aspired to be like him; she *was* like him.

Now she could already sense herself being pushed to the side of events and robbed of that identity. She grasped at only one thin straw: joining the women in the WAAF.

# CHAPTER TWO

*May 8, 1945*
*Berlin*

Erika Brandt stood for a moment paralyzed on the staircase.

"*Frau, komm!*"

She turned to flee, but the Russian soldiers rushed up and seized her, dragging her to the bottom of the steps. The largest of them, square-faced and with a wide, rapacious mouth, kicked open the door to the empty ground-floor flat. He wrestled her inside, followed by three of his mates, who grasped her legs and threw her down. She thrashed, begging in German and Russian for them to let her go, but they ignored her.

They were on their knees in a circle around her now, smelling of sweat and urine. The square-faced one who'd captured her shoved the others back and growled, "Me first." They grunted agreement, and while two of them held her down and the third waited behind him for his turn, he dropped on top of her. "*Frau gut,*" he babbled drunkenly in German as he tore at her underwear. "*Sehr gut.*"

❖

When it was over, she gathered the tattered remains of her clothing and stumbled back up the steps to her attic room. She locked the door, knowing it would keep out no one who really wanted to get in. But at that moment, she wanted to be alone and couldn't bring herself to beg at the door of the cellar where her neighbors still cowered. Then she staggered to the toilet and vomited.

She washed the best she could, using the last of her allotment of the water the boy had hauled in from the central pump the night before. Still breathless and aching, she collapsed on the sofa and huddled in a trembling cringe that wouldn't stop.

So, the reckoning had come, and it was going to be like this. For a week, as the Soviets advanced, she'd heard the shelling and rifle fire grow louder each day. Extraordinarily, the authorities had managed to provide daily reports on a one-page "newspaper" of the fall of each district—Müncheberg, Rudersdorf, Ahrensfelde—while the remaining parts of Berlin waited their turn.

The old, the very young, and the lame that made up the Home Guard had put up pathetic resistance, but the Red Army swept over them like a tidal wave. The lucky ones like Wilhelm, her white-haired neighbor from the first floor, had deserted in time, but most simply died under the unstoppable force, if the SS didn't execute them as cowards.

Now the enemy had reached the Adlerstrasse, no longer killing—for no one was left to fight—but pillaging. Shops, abandoned apartments, everything within easy reach fell to the soldiers, who snatched up anything they could carry.

Besides Erika, only three families remained in the building, and at first, they'd all hidden in the barricaded cellar. Over their heads, they could hear the invaders burst into the two ground-floor apartments. But on the second day, sixty-five-year-old Wilhelm and the boy Hanno had ventured out, unmolested, and fetched water from the one pump on the street that still functioned.

Gerda, Erika, and Hanno's crippled mother Magda had stayed behind, but Erika could not bear the damp odor and the constricting darkness any longer. When the noise from the street had quieted, she'd made a run for her upstairs apartment to grab the last of the winter apples she'd stored. It had been a grave miscalculation.

Footfall on the stairs outside her door sent a jolt of terror through her, but it was only Gerda, who normally lived on the floor below. Though she was no older than fifty, her graying hair, now as filthy as every other woman's, and the soot she deliberately smeared over her face to discourage Russian attention made her vaguely witchlike.

"I'm sorry about what happened, but you know we couldn't help you. After the soldiers left, we ran from the cellar and gathered in the Metzger apartment on the second floor, where we found some food. Come on back down. We've barricaded the door so no one can come in unless they use a cannon. You'll be safe there. I promise."

Benumbed by her ordeal, Erika followed, docile. On the second floor, Gerda knocked *dadadadum* at the door on the left, obviously a pre-arranged knock. She heard the sound of some heavy object, probably a cabinet, being dragged, and finally the door opened.

Erika crept in and looked around at her neighbors, and none of them made eye contact with her. Yet even in her stupor, she understood the advantage of moving into the Metzger apartment, provided they could keep it secure. Why hadn't they thought of it before? The Metzgers, outspoken Nazis, had fled a few days earlier, leaving a new stove, fine curtains, and a heavy, luxurious sofa. Though the second-floor apartment was only one level above the ones that had been looted, it seemed to hold no interest for the Russians, at least while others were easier to reach.

She huddled on the sofa, arms and legs tightly crossed, and Magda brought her a man's shirt to cover her bare shoulders. "The Metzgers left it, but you can put it to good use before I burn it."

Erika glanced up at the light-brown shirt of the *Sturmabteilung*. She snorted disgust but drew it on nonetheless. She had a sweater she could change into later, if someone would go down to the cellar to retrieve it.

"We found beans and canned beets in the cupboard," Gerda said. "But they won't last more than two days. Wilhelm and Hanno can fetch water, but sometime soon we have to go out and forage. That means we'll have to deal with the Russians."

Erika still held herself in a knot, sullen. "I've already 'dealt' with them, thank you. Someone else will have to do the rest."

Wilhelm sat down gently next to her on the sofa and stared at his feet. "We know that, Erika," he said softly. "But you're the only one who speaks Russian. They're not all rapists, and maybe we can find one to talk to. You can clear the way for us to enter the buildings."

"I won't. You can't make me do it." She drew up her knees and turned away. The others were silent for a while.

Magda broke the tension when she limped on her crutches to the window that looked out onto the rear court. She tilted her head as if listening. "Have you noticed? You don't hear any birds. The bombs scared them away, I suppose." She took a breath. "But the war's over. The birds will come back. We just have to hold out."

Erika closed her eyes. "With no plumbing, no lights, no food."

Magda set aside her crutches and dropped down next to her. "Look, we're sorry for what happened to you. It can still happen to us. But we have to make a plan."

Magda was right. Gerda's soot-smeared face and gray hair provided only so much protection, and Magda, although lame, was still young and attractive. With only a grizzled old man and a ten-year-old boy to protect them, their situation seemed hopeless.

Wilhelm stood up from the sofa and paced, scratching his white stubble. "Obviously, we have to avoid confronting the Russians when they're drunk and they break off into twos and threes, as Erika just found out. But when they're all together, like when they set up camp on the street yesterday, they seem calmer. They just sit around their little fires and smoke or tend their horses."

"They have nice horses." Ten-year-old Hanno spoke for the first time.

Gerda snorted. "The whole street stinks of horse manure."

"They were nice to me," Hanno said. "One of them even helped me carry the water bucket. They laugh a lot."

"A shame we can't all be ten-year-old boys," Gerda observed. "Then we could go out and dig around in the basements of the wrecked buildings in this quarter. People were hoarding like crazy the last few weeks. There's bound to be coal, at least. You just have to tunnel through the rubble."

"Yes, but we're not," Erika grumbled.

"You know…" Wilhelm stepped back and appraised her, squinting. "You could be. Not ten, of course, but your face doesn't have a bit of girlish fat left, and you have no hips, really. If you cut your hair, you could pass as a young man. Maybe seventeen, eighteen. Lots of them don't have beards yet."

"What are you talking about?" Erika ran her hand over the top of her head. Her hair was gritty, badly in need of washing. She'd always kept it blond, but now, an accumulation of soot and grime had made it dull brown. "I don't think so."

Ignoring her, Gerda marched toward the wardrobe and rummaged through the clothing the Metzgers had left. "There's an old suit here, pretty shapeless. I can take in the trousers for you on my sewing machine. It'll still be big, but everyone's clothing is too big now, and Hanno's jacket will fit your shoulders."

"Are you sure?" Erika still held on to her hair.

"Absolutely. This way, the four of us can go and forage, and if the Ruskies stop us, you can talk to them."

"I can cut your hair," Wilhelm said, warming to the idea. "I used to be a barber."

"A barber? I thought you were a violinist?"

Wilhelm laughed. "And a soldier, too. A man can be all three."

❖

"What do you think?" Wilhelm held up a mirror in front of her.

Erika peered at the glass and saw a gangly boy with uneven hair. Gerda was right. The absence of fat in her cheeks added to the masculine look, and only her slender chin gave one pause. How old was she pretending to be? If sixteen or so, she could pass for some lad from the Home Guard, though only if she could drop the pitch of her voice.

She stared at herself in the mirror. Her dark-brown, slightly hooded eyes lent her a sadness that could come as easily from military defeat as from sexual abuse. She nodded. "It might work. Maybe now they'll stay away from me."

Erika remained folded up on the sofa of the Metzger apartment, while Wilhelm fetched Gerda's sewing machine from the fourth floor, and she began to sew. The monotonous sound of the treadle soothed her, and surrounded by friends now, she was finally able to sleep.

The next morning, she awoke rested, if still sore and shaken. Gerda was already active.

"Here, try these on," she ordered, handing over the promised trousers. "Hanno and Wilhelm also donated to the outfit." She held up an old and oft-mended shirt and jacket.

Erika obeyed, stepping into the trousers and drawing on the jacket. She stared down at her feet. "The pants are too long."

"Yes, yes. I see." Gerda knelt and rolled them to the appropriate height.

"You look very convincing," Magda said. "Dashing, almost."

"All you need is this." Wilhelm handed over a large cloth bag with a shoulder strap. "And now that we have another 'man' on the team, we can forage. Gerda has the candles."

Erika was still reluctant, but hunger overrode her misgivings. She followed the others down the stairs to the ground floor, where Wilhelm pressed a bucket into her hand. "In case we don't find anything, we can at least bring back water."

They crept from the apartment, leaving Magda alone, and filed out of the building in a single line. Erika kept her eyes lowered, but in her peripheral vision, she caught sight of the soldiers squatting on both sides of her, warming their hands at bonfires, rolling cigarettes, cleaning their rifles. Their chatter died down as the group passed, and one or two looked up.

Wilhelm leaned toward her and murmured, "Take bigger steps. You walk like a girl."

"Oh," she muttered back, and lengthened her stride.

No one blocked their way as they edged toward the middle of the square. They passed the pump where old men and children stood in line to draw water for the night, and she felt a surge of confidence. In the open space, with a hundred idle men around, calm prevailed.

They marched into the next street, where the Allied bombs had reduced most of the houses to hills of rubble. Wall fragments jutted up from them like shards. Their cellars were inaccessible, deeply buried under debris and pulverized concrete, and she was almost relieved. Surely they held not only supplies but also the bodies of dead Berliners, and she had no desire to deal with rotting corpses.

Yet at the end of the street, a building still stood. Its top floor had been blasted away, and the floors below had lost the wall that fronted on the street. Erika halted, gawking. It was like an enormous dollhouse, with all its rooms open on one side. They still held furniture, and in a tiny water closet at the far end, a toilet was suspended in midair by its drain pipe.

Hanno had turned the corner ahead of them but now reappeared. "Looks better on the other side," he called out, then took off again.

They scurried after him, and when they reached the rear of the building, he was already on his knees, clearing an opening with his hands. Wilhelm joined him, scooping up the powdered brick, and after a few minutes, a cellar window emerged, its glass unsurprisingly broken.

"Why hasn't anyone discovered this yet?" Erika asked.

"Probably because people are still afraid to go out." Wilhelm used a whole brick to tap away the remaining shards of glass. "But in a few days, everyone will be doing the same thing we are."

Hanno slipped in first, and after his reassurances the others followed, dropping into near darkness. The dim light coming through the broken window allowed them to make out only the vaguest forms, of each other and of a doorway on the other side.

"Time for the candle," Gerda said, igniting it with one of her precious matches. She held it over her head, illuminating the whole space in a dull orange-gray light. It was a coal cellar with the concrete bin in one corner half full. That would be a good find, even if they discovered nothing else, and she kept the open flame at a distance.

The second door held out even more hope, and Wilhelm pushed it open. Mice scuttled away as they stepped inside with their light.

"Ah, that's more like it," he said.

Shelves lined two of the walls. One side held rows of glass jars, and closer inspection showed they contained pickled cucumbers, beets, and onions. A half dozen smaller jars were filled with fruit. Without even waiting to examine the other side, Gerda handed Erika her candle and began loading some of the jars into her sack.

"Here's a treasure," Hanno said, drawing attention to a ring of dried sausages that hung from a nail. He unhooked it and crammed it inside his sweater.

Erika spied a slab of dried bacon and tucked it into her belt, where her jacket would conceal it. The thought of the fatty meat for supper lifted her spirits for the first time.

"Hey. Come look at this." Gerda had ventured into a third room, and when Erika followed her in, melancholy seized her. An upright piano stood against a wall, with books and newspapers piled on top of it.

She set down the candle and uncovered the keys. After brushing off a layer of grit that had seeped in, she played a few bars of *Für Elise* and the opening measures of her favorite Chopin nocturne. But the piano was so dreadfully out of tune, she cringed.

"We might as well take these too," Wilhelm said, sweeping a dozen heavily sprouted potatoes into his rucksack. "We should go now, before it gets dark, and come back tomorrow for more."

Erika glanced around for anything else they could carry out. Coal could wait till the next day. But bottles on an upper shelf caught her eye, and she gingerly took one down. Schnapps.

"This could be good for barter," she said, and slipped it into her jacket pocket, though its top half jutted out under her arm.

Without further conversation, they passed through the coal cellar and clambered up through the window into the half-light of dusk. They hurried back along the rubble-strewn street, avoiding the pits and protrusions.

As they passed the pump, Hanno stopped and filled the bucket that would serve them for drinking, cooking, and a single use of the toilet, and then they covered the last distance to their building.

Emboldened by their success, Erika strode with some confidence past the soldiers camped in front of their door. As before, a few glanced up but seemed to find them harmless, and looked away again.

But not all. Erika's heart quickened when one of them, a lanky fellow with several days' beard growth, got to his feet in front of them. He stood for a moment with his thumbs in his belt, then poked Wilhelm on the chest and tapped his own wrist with one finger.

"He wants a watch," Gerda whispered.

Wilhelm pulled up his sleeve on both arms, showing he had none.

The Russian made a circle around them, obviously bent on procuring something. He touched the lumpy potato sack on Wilhelm's shoulder and grunted, glanced down at the bucket that held only water, and examined Gerda's sack full of jars. None of it interested him, but stopping in front of Hanno, he ran his hand over the lumps under the boy's sweater. His eyes brightened when he discovered the sausages, and he yanked the entire string out from under the sweater. "*Gut,*" he said and hung it over his own shoulder.

The sight of their lost dinner was too much for Erika, and she spoke up. "Please. We're starving," she said in Russian, pitching her voice as low as possible. "Let us keep the sausage and take this instead." She drew the bottle of schnapps from her pocket and held it out to the soldier.

"Ah, the lad speaks Russian," he said, accepting the bottle. "Where'd you learn that, my boy?"

"School in Saratov," she said.

He nodded understanding. "Volga Germans. I heard about your lot. I thought we moved you all to the East."

"I don't know about that. My family came back here before the war." That explained her knowledge of the language, and she saw no reason to tell a stranger that her parents had been good socialists and had died for their beliefs in a concentration camp. Conquering soldiers didn't want personal histories of the defeated.

He seemed satisfied. "Well then, since you're such a well-bred young fellow, I'll let you keep your sausages." He tossed back the ring of meat, pivoted around to his comrades who had been watching, and held up the schnapps bottle. While the soldiers were distracted, the band of scavengers slipped back into their building.

Once inside, Erika smelled again the rank odor of urine in the corridor and recalled the assault of the day before. She shook her head to dispel the memory. But her new guise seemed to protect her, and her fear lifted. It helped that they would soon all sit down to a good supper of sausage and potatoes for the first time in weeks.

And they had water for her to wash. Would she ever feel clean again?

❖

The haircut and pants were in fact liberating, and in the next days, she ventured out more often, making two more trips to the basement larder before other foragers discovered it as well. She also fetched water, along with Hanno and Wilhelm, and passed unmolested through the ranks of the Russian soldiers along the street. She never saw her four rapists again, which was a relief.

It was strange to hear the men banter with each other and talk to their horses. She still hated them, but they were becoming individuals, little different from German men. More primitive, perhaps, and they defecated like animals in empty corridors rather than in latrines, but perhaps Wehrmacht soldiers had done the same thing in the cities they'd invaded.

Once the men knew the "lad in the baggy trousers" spoke Russian, they asked for a name, and she said Erik. She was an amusing novelty, their only link to the local population. When they engaged her, she usually managed to brush them off and return to her building, but finally some of them followed her up the stairs to the Metzger apartment, setting a dangerous precedent.

The soldiers weren't much older than "Erik" pretended to be and were curious about him. "Were you in the army?" one of them asked.

She had a ready answer. "No, too young by a year. They forced me into the Home Guard, but I ran away when your troops got near Berlin. I'm not stupid."

The soldiers laughed. "Do you have a girlfriend?"

The thought amused her. "No. Nothing like that. Besides, I never see any girls. They're all hiding."

The younger soldier looked hurt. "They don't have to do that. We're all very nice. Besides, if they can love us, we'll pay. With food. Other things, too. If you know any, tell them that."

She grunted softly. Of course they could pay with "other things." They'd pillaged the entire city, and all of them had loot they could exchange.

But now they came more frequently into the building. Word seemed to have gotten out of the "boy who speaks Russian," and off-duty soldiers stopped by to investigate. The makeshift "family" kept the apartment blockaded, and the soldiers never forced their way in, but with the relaxing of vigilance, the inevitable disaster came.

Early in the morning, the street camp was usually tranquil, as the soldiers who weren't on any duty slept in. On the fifth day after her assault, when a certain normalcy seemed to have been established and the foragers had happened upon a stock of laundry powder, Erika decided to wash her coal-dust soiled trousers and shirt. She drew them off and soaked them in a washtub, while covering herself with an old dress. She craved fresh underwear, however, so risked leaving the fortress and hurrying up the stairs to her apartment.

The trip upstairs went well, but during the return, she once again faced a gang of soldiers. She recognized them from the street, and they stood aghast, seeing the boy Erik in a dress. This time there were five of them.

She fled again, and once again a soldier seized her by the arm and dragged her down the stairs. A second soldier held open the door to the empty apartment where she had been raped before. She convulsed at the thought.

Almost spontaneously, she pulled the man who held her into her arms and whispered into his ear. "You, yes. Anything you like. But not the others. Only for you."

He leaned back, obviously surprised, then seemed to conclude that exclusivity was better than sharing. Twisting sideways toward his comrades, he barked, "Go find your own. This one's mine."

A moment of tense silence followed, while the deprived men seemed to weigh his authority. Perhaps he outranked them, or perhaps they merely concluded that she wasn't worth a fight among themselves. In any case, they filed grumbling out of the building, leaving her captor to draw her into the empty apartment. He closed the door and slid a small table up against it. Then he turned around, grinning.

But her tiny victory, reducing gang rape to a single assault, gave her confidence. It was still rape, but she could negotiate it.

"Over there, on the sofa. More comfortable. Okay?"

He nodded and let himself be led. They sat down side by side, and he lunged for her, clapping his hand over her breast. She shoved him away gently. "Wait. Let me take off my clothes so you don't tear them," she said, maintaining a frozen smile.

He allowed it, removing his boots in the meantime, and then, gritting her teeth, she submitted to his clumsy, hurried lust.

❖

Afterward she sat up and drew on her dress while the soldier pulled on his boots.

"Um, my name is Stepka," he said. "What's your name? Your real name."

"Why do you care? I'm not your girlfriend."

Curiously, for a man who had just committed rape, he dropped his glance. "You're right, of course. But you're different from the others. How do you know Russian?"

"A long story, and you don't really care, anyhow." She was feeling truculent, and after all, what else could he do to her?

"I suppose not." He stared into the distance for a moment. "You know, I have a wife back in Voronezh, but I haven't seen her in four years. It's been that long since I touched a woman."

"Is that supposed to make me feel sorry for you?" She buttoned her last button, a gesture of withdrawal from him.

"No. I guess not. Only to explain. We're not all animals. Not most of the time, anyhow." He stood up and strode toward the door, sliding the table aside so he could open it.

She nodded dully. "Thank you for sending the others away."

"I did that for me," he said over his shoulder as he exited. "But maybe I'll come back tomorrow with something to eat."

The door closed behind him, and mercifully, none of his comrades burst in to claim their portion. She sat for a while, staring at the space where he had stood. How much longer would she be at their mercy? How long would rape be part of the victory?

She felt conflicting urges—to scrub herself clean, to scream reproach at her neighbors for abandoning her again, to collapse into tears. But after a moment, she realized she'd gained a slight victory. She'd learned she could negotiate.

And if she could choose where and how to be raped, she could also choose her rapist.

# CHAPTER THREE

*June 1945*

The stately Adastral House, which housed the Air Ministry in Kingsway, radiated the dignity of an earlier age that both intimidated and reassured. But the damage from the VI rocket attack of 1944 had not been fully repaired. The concrete on the exterior of the building was soot-stained and pitted, and reminded Gillian how close Britain had come to losing the war.

Inside, she located the office of recruitment where her interview was scheduled and knocked. At the "Come in," she entered and took a seat in front of the desk.

The WAAF warrant officer, a narrow-faced, no-nonsense woman, leafed through Gillian's application papers, her lips twitching slightly.

Gillian fidgeted for a few moments and then spoke. "I was a pilot in the Air Transport Auxiliary, as you can see."

The warrant officer ignored her, as if the remark didn't merit a response.

Gillian clasped her hands more tightly and pressed ahead. "Is that possible? For me to fly, I mean? Theoretically?"

The officer glanced up coolly from the application. "The WAAF offers more than fifty possible areas of service, but piloting is not one of them. We are an auxiliary to the RAF, created specifically to free the men to fly while we carry out other less critical tasks."

"I just thought perhaps there might be, well, transport, navigation, that sort of thing. Anything associated with the planes."

The warrant officer closed the application form, a gesture of forced patience. "WAAF make up some of the ground crews, electricians, signals, traffic control."

"That would be all right, I suppose. How can I qualify for one of those duties?"

The officer pursed her lips. "That would depend largely on your aptitude and performance in basic training. And, of course, what's available at the time you graduate. Since demobilization, some positions are closing, with so many women going back to civilian life to rebuild for the next generation."

Gillian fell silent. Another variation on the theme of "marrying one of the lads back from the front and starting a lovely British family."

"I'll take my chances," she said finally. "I want to be in the WAAF, not make babies."

The warrant officer scrutinized her for a moment, then seemed to soften a little. She lifted a loose-leaf binder from a drawer and began to leaf through it. "Well, then. Let's see what we can do for you."

❖

Six days later, all papers signed, all previous commitments terminated, Gillian sat in an early morning train to Gloucester, then a military bus to Innsworth Airfield.

The bus held scarcely a dozen women, suggesting that the zeal and patriotism that had brought so many women into the services had abated. What had moved the other women to enlist? Were they all as troubled as she was? She stared out the bus window into the persistent rain that seemed to conspire against any attempt at good cheer.

After mustering in a large hall, she and the other recruits marched in a line toward their barracks—a hut with some thirty beds. It was drab and damp, and had only a single coal stove at the center.

Gillian examined her assigned bunk, which had no actual mattress, but three square blocks, hard as wood, instead. Laid in a row and covered with gray blankets, they'd be her bed for the coming weeks of training. She sighed. What did she expect? She'd contracted for the military life, and this was it.

"Fall in, ladies, at the front of the barracks," a sergeant ordered them, and the motley group of recruits hurried to obey.

The adjacent hut, she saw, was a sort of medical center. Following another set of orders, she undressed to her underwear and passed through several stations, the first being a humiliating examination of her scalp and pubis.

"No sign of infection," the examining orderly said in a monotone, and her colleague noted that fact on a clipboard.

Gillian continued along the line to a chair, where a dentist poked and prodded with a spiked instrument in her mouth. "No decay," the dentist reported, and that, too, went onto the clipboard.

At the third station, she passed through a double line of orderlies, who jabbed her forcefully from both sides. Diphtheria, typhoid, and smallpox inoculations, she later learned.

A bit dizzy from the shock of multiple injections, she lurched into the adjoining room, which held shelves stacked with uniforms.

The WAAF at the counter handed her a pile of clothing. "Here's your kit, soldier. You're to change into 'regulation' right now."

Observing the women ahead of her in line, Gillian concluded that meant putting on the military bra and gray woolen knickers, beige stockings, uniform skirt, shirt with tie, and tunic. She had to reassemble the remaining articles—duplicate skirt and shirt, striped pyjamas, cap with brass badge, great coat and tin helmet—into a neat pile.

"You will now stand in your shoes, in the trough outside the hut, and then march back to your quarters for inspection," the sergeant barked.

After a puzzled glance at her colleagues, who all obeyed, Gillian stepped into the trough and cringed at the icy violation of her warm feet and brand-new shoes.

"You will wear these shoes, wet, until after the evening mess," the sergeant ordered them, and Gillian could only surmise the process would mold the stiff leather to their feet. But the shoes began to chafe immediately, and she was sure she'd wake up the next morning with blisters.

Once again in line, she marched to the canteen, as dilapidated as the barracks had been, staffed by cooks in sagging hairnets.

After the meal, they marched in their now-abrasive shoes, back to quarters for inspection—of themselves and their newly made beds, and of every article issued to them, including cutlery, mug, and toothbrush. They had to fold their towel and all parts of their uniform precisely for presentation alongside the cylindrical canvas duffel bag meant to carry them.

Instruction followed on how to knot the black regulation tie, how to polish brass buttons and black leather shoes, and how to stand at attention. Then the order came to file into a lecture hall for a talk on service history and discipline. Others followed in the next days, on current affairs, first aid, appropriate WAAF behavior, and hygiene.

The latter two were related, the instructor cautioned, for one's deportment, if it was not impeccable, could bring disaster. Specifically, careless use of public toilet seats could expose her to sexual disease or pregnancy just as much as physical intimacy with other personnel.

And, horror of horrors, fraternization with an American GI, most especially the Negro ones, could result in any number of disasters that need not be named. The instructor shuddered.

Lectures were interspersed with exercise and drills, sometimes in pouring rain, and Gillian learned the term "square bashing" for the endless marching in blocks back and forth across the parade ground.

Exhausted and largely discouraged by the apparent uselessness of it all, she was tempted to leave training. But on the third evening, as she polished her uniform buttons for the hundredth time, a voice beside her said, "Dunno about you, but I've 'ad it to 'ere with these fuckin' buttons. And all the bleedin' square bashin' has fuck-all to do wi' th'air force. I didn't join up for this shite."

Gillian glanced up, blinking toward the source of the string of obscenities, a plump and rosy-cheeked redhead in the next bunk.

Apparently seeing Gillian's shock, the woman chuckled and leaned toward her, holding out her hand. "Elizabeth Geary. Me mates call me Betsy."

Taken aback by the mismatch of coarse language and cherubic appearance, Gillian set down her can of brass polish and offered her own hand. "Gillian Somerville."

"Nice to meet you. Strange, innit? I mean how we're all thrown together here. High and low, from all over the country. Me, I'm from up north. Spent the war in the land army. Repairing bloody tractors. Four years with black fingernails. What about you?"

"I'm from London. I was in the ATA until they demobbed us."

"You were a pilot?"

"Yes. For three years. I was flying four-engines at the end." Gillian heard the boasting in her own voice and grew slightly embarrassed. Showing off was not a good way to get on with new people.

"Well done, you!" Betsy gave a single clap. "What'd you carry? Where'd you fly? Bet it was fun."

Gillian set aside her tunic with its well-polished buttons and drew up her knees, suddenly more cheerful. "You never knew what they'd assign you. Only the kind of plane, and that depended on your qualification. I started with two-engines, ferrying mostly. New craft from the factories to airfields near the front. Sometimes passengers, but not often."

"Bloody hell! Ever get shot at? I mean, like, by the Luftwaffe?" She pronounced the German word with only two syllables.

Gillian winced at the sound, and in her head she heard the word correctly. *Luft-vaf-feh*. That arm of the German military had touched her personally and always sounded like an expulsion of air ending with a soft hiss.

"Nothing like that. Hardest thing wasn't the delivery. It was getting home again. In the UK, you'd come back on a train, but taking a plane to France or even Germany meant you had to wait until someone was headed back in the other direction. Sometimes you'd have to sleep on a cot in a back room at the airport." She hung up her tunic and stowed the polish and brush.

Betsy had already slid into her bed and lay supporting herself on one elbow. "Crikey. What made you choose a job like that?"

Gillian slid under the rough covers and pulled them up to her shoulders. "My brother Alastair flew in competitions all over the world. He even took me up once to give me a taste of being airborne. But that one time was enough to make me barmy for it. Always pictured myself in jodhpurs, jacket, leather flight helmet, that sort of thing."

"Is he still flying?"

"No. He was killed in an accident. Trying to land in a fog."

"Bloody hell. I like planes, too, the way they're put together, like super-tractors, and I don't mind getting me hands dirty. I just want to be part of the RAF."

The sudden buzzer signaling lights out terminated their conversation, and Gillian settled in for the night. The twelve hours of drilling, exercise, and marching from parade ground to class, to mess had worn her down and made her blistered feet ache. She'd have no trouble sleeping.

But she lay awake for some ten minutes, watching the dull orange glow from the coke stove and listening to the coughs or snores of the other recruits. She could not have said her new comrades gave her a sense of family, or even community, but their simple presence softened her sense of homelessness.

The coal hissed softly, and as she dozed off, she thought she heard the whispered word, *Luftwaffe*.

❖

After the evening of their conversation, she and Betsy were allies in cynicism, though Betsy's foul language toned down a notch. At the end of the first two weeks of training, they received a four-hour pass and fled together down the road to the village.

The pub, or what passed for one, was a pre-fab hut left from the war and devoid of character or decoration. Its single virtue was that it offered a public space with rickety tables, a counter, and a beer tap.

After collecting their pints, they sat at their table and surveyed the room. It was as drab inside as it was outside and smelled of damp wool, cigarette smoke, and ever so slightly of urine. The noise, which Gillian remembered from pub evenings with the ATA as sometimes deafening, was subdued and consisted mainly of jeering from the far side where a circle of men played darts.

Most of the other pub visitors were civilians, the men in mud-brown trousers and shapeless jackets, the women in heavy tweed skirts and oatmeal cardigans that rose high in the back and hung low in the front. Some dozen airmen were scattered throughout the room, but she and Betsy were the only WAAF.

Gillian was about to remark on that fact when two airmen, sergeants by their stripes, joined them at the table.

The taller one, blond and dashingly good-looking, pulled out a chair and stood holding it. "Sad to see you lovely ladies all alone. We can't allow that, can we?" He waited for agreement.

"We're not alone, we're—" Gillian never finished her remark.

"Well, then," Betsy exclaimed. "You lads better sit down then, before we break into tears of loneliness."

"Righto!" the blond one said as they both seated themselves, setting their beer glasses on the table. "Jack Higgins," the good-looking one said, holding out his hand. "And this here's my mate, Nigel Katz."

The second airman, swarthier and with a narrow prominent nose that seemed to cancel out his rather pretty eyes, simply nodded, confirming he was, indeed, Nigel Katz.

Betsy took Jack's hand cheerfully. "Elizabeth Geary, but you can call me Betsy," she said, ignoring the other man.

But Nigel glanced toward Gillian. "And you are?"

"Gillian Somerville," she said neutrally, sizing up the two sergeants. They were of the same rank, but their personalities and appearances could not have been more different. She didn't particularly warm to either of them, but Nigel, at least, wasn't pushy. One of the effects of being less attractive, perhaps, or of a lifetime of rejection by pretty women.

Jack already had one arm over the back of Betsy's chair. "This is almost our last leave before deployment, so you should be kind," he said, affecting a mournful expression.

It was bait and she bit. "Where are they sending you? Or is it secret?"

"Germany," Nigel said simply, ruining the game. "In three days."

"Yes. Into the mouth of the enemy. Anything could happen." Jack stared with feigned distress into Betsy's eyes. "Can I get a kiss to remember you? In case I don't make it back?"

"You're not going into battle, silly sod. War's over." Betsy poked him on the shoulder.

He flinched theatrically. "Well, it's still dangerous over there. And lonely."

"Not with a million German women," Betsy countered. "All the men are in POW camps. It's a bloody paradise for randy airmen."

Jack persisted. "I've never been in Germany, but I bet they're nothing like our pretty English girls."

"I have," Gillian said. "Been in Germany, I mean. In the ATA. As far as Cologne and Frankfurt. You're right. They're in a pretty sorry state, and they should stay that way."

Jack seemed to see her for the first time. "You're being a little hard on them, aren't you?" He finished his beer and glanced at their still half-full glasses, seeming to consider the cost of a second glass of the unrationed but very expensive drink. Finally, he signaled the waiter for another.

Gillian snorted. "Not nearly hard enough. I lost my family in the Blitz, and as far as I'm concerned, they can all go back to the Stone Age."

An awkward silence followed, which Nigel finally broke. "I lost relatives, too. But it's not up to us to decide what happens to Germany." He scratched the side of his jaw, a gesture that rendered his remark tentative.

"Do you know where you're assigned in Germany?" she asked, and Nigel glanced toward her.

"They don't tell us. Security, of course, though I don't know who we're protecting ourselves from. Bad Eilsen, Fassberg, or Berlin.

One of the bases. We're replacing two men being discharged for bad conduct."

"Nancy boys," Jack explained contemptuously, letting his hand flop on a limp wrist. "Don't know how they got in."

Nigel glanced away and said nothing.

Everyone's glass was empty now except Jack's, his second, and Gillian didn't intend to sit idle until he finished it in front of them. She checked her watch. "Oh, dear. It's already nine thirty, and we have passes only until ten." She turned to Betsy. "We should go now. It's a long walk back."

"Righto." Betsy agreed hesitantly and stood up with her. Gillian strode toward the door, and a quick glance over her shoulder revealed Betsy planting a quick kiss on Jack's cheek.

How easy it was for some people.

❖

Basic training lasted three weeks, and in July, Gillian was summoned to report to the section officer for assignment. The door was already open, so she tapped lightly, saluted smartly, and stood until invited to sit down.

The section officer had a round face and a sort of maternal plumpness, emphasized by hair parted in the middle and drawn into a bun at the back. She ran the tip of her pencil down the page as if rereading it, then looked up. "Your aptitude, depth perception, and mechanical skills are all good," she said, "so it would be a shame to waste you in clerking, record-keeping, driving, that sort of thing, wouldn't it?"

*Dear God, don't send me to any of those.* "I was hoping for something that would connect me directly with the aircraft. Even if I can't fly them."

The section officer tapped the pencil gently on the paper, moving into the next part of her thought. "Well, given both your ATA experience and the current postwar needs of the RAF, we might assign you in several areas. Those would be as flight mechanic, radio technician, or air-traffic controller."

Gillian tried to imagine herself in any of those roles. "What would that entail, exactly. I mean, for my day-to-day job?"

"Well, they all have to do with flying, one way or another. But, to reduce them to their basics, they would mean repairing aircraft, repairing radios that talk to the aircraft, or directing aircraft by radio from the ground."

Two manual and one…not manual. It was an easy choice. "I'd like to do the air-traffic control."

The officer smiled. "I would have chosen that as well. It's an interesting field, and with the new radar, it's developing all the time. I'll do the paperwork, and we'll send you off shortly to school. Congratulations, Aircraftwoman Somerville. You have your specialty."

They shook hands and Gillian left, slightly uplifted. Directing planes from the ground was a long way from piloting them, but it kept her in the game. Fair enough.

The barracks were sweltering in the July heat, and Gillian removed her tunic immediately upon returning. Betsy was already at her bunk polishing her shoes. "So, what's the verdict?"

Gillian dropped onto her bunk and kicked off her shoes. "Air-traffic control at Watchfield."

"Watchfield. Jolly good. I asked to be assigned there, too. Engine mechanics. Someone's got to get the plane into the air so you can bring 'em down again, eh?" Betsy beamed.

"At least until the day they let us fly again ourselves."

❖

RAF Watchfield offered training programs in flying, navigation, maintenance, aerial photography, reconnaissance, and air-traffic control. In appearance, it consisted largely of one-story Nissen huts and cottages with roofs still painted in camouflage.

Accommodations were in one of the huts, where the rooms were set up for four. In spite of following different programs, Gillian and Betsy requested to house together. The third and fourth beds remained unoccupied.

While Betsy's instruction took place in a hangar, Gillian's class was in a room that held some dozen radio receivers, and wires were strung everywhere. For a teaching facility, it looked shockingly makeshift. Four of the ten students were women.

The instructor entered right after her and walked to the front table. "Good morning. I'm Flight Lieutenant Douglas, and I'm happy to welcome you to air-traffic control. We're going to teach ground-controlled approach. Radar is at the heart of it, but much of that is still secret, so you'll learn it under security. That is to say, you may not take notes or carry any materials with you out of the classroom."

"Why so much security?" one of the men asked. "How can we study without notes?"

"Because radar is a powerful defensive weapon, and every military in the world would like to have it. We share information with the United States but no one else. As far as studying, you can review it among yourselves, but not with others."

He turned toward the chalkboard, and while he drew a cartoon of a tower runway and plane, he spoke over his shoulder. "The system is rather ingenious but requires close communication between the controllers—that's you—and the incoming pilots."

"You mean we tell them what to do?" one of the women asked.

"In effect, yes. You guide them in based on information you receive from precise radar systems placed along the approach path, telling you their course, altitude, and azimuth."

"Azimuth?"

As a pilot, Gillian knew the word, but obviously not all the women did.

"In simplest terms, the aircraft's horizontal location in degrees from due north. The radar allowing those measurements is called precision approach radar, or PAR. They are set up in a van or truck along the side of the runway."

With a stroke of the chalk, he drew horizontal and vertical arrows below the plane. "Using the PAR, you can monitor descent rate and heading and, by correcting continually, guide the craft by radio to the runway."

"So the pilot doesn't even have to see?"

"Theoretically, no. Which makes the system invaluable at night and in bad weather. However, practically speaking, we want him to have the runway environment in sight, at least prior to arriving at one hundred feet above it."

"But if we have radar, can't we control the entire flight, from takeoff to landing?"

"Not in a single system. These particular antennas have a limited range, and their directional accuracy is poor. We use radar for aircraft only on their final landing track, some ten miles before the runway. The antennas measure horizontally and vertically and create a sort of cone through which we guide the aircraft."

"So we 'see' the aircraft in the radar cone, even though we can't see it in the air."

"Quite so. And sometimes, the pilot can't see the landing strip either and depends on your guidance."

"What about flight beacons, sir," one of the women asked.

"That's a different part of the story, and I'll explain all that in due time."

He drew another series of sketches on the blackboard and described the functions and limitations of the new radar. To ensure they retained the information, he made them repeat back to him what he had said in different words.

After two hours, he laid down his chalk. "You have quite enough to absorb for now. Discuss it, but only among yourselves, and we'll move on to the next level tomorrow."

Gillian left the class energized. She rather liked the scientific side of flying, though it was the polar opposite of the seat-of-the-pants method her brother had used, which had eventually killed him. Ironic to think that some little WAAF ground controller guiding in his plane could have saved his life.

At supper, she exclaimed to the other students at the table, "I'm not giving anything secret away when I say that I'm amazed that someone outside a plane can make it land."

An airman had just set down his tray at the end of the long table and overheard her. "They don't exactly make it land, you know. They just tell you how."

"Of course. That's what I meant." Gillian frowned, slightly annoyed at being contradicted.

The airman, a redhead with the inevitable freckles, leaned toward her. "I'm sorry. I didn't mean to be rude. You're right. It is amazing."

"I'm puzzled about the range," one of the women said. "But they don't give us any books to study, and I don't know who to ask, since I'm not allowed to talk about it to anyone."

"You can talk about it to me. I've been landing for weeks by ground control. You won't be giving away secrets if you simply ask questions." He glanced at both sides conspiratorially. "And I don't see any enemy agents at the table."

"Okay, then," Gillian said. "If the approach radar has such a short range, how do we locate the plane in the first place?"

"Good question." He raised orange-red eyebrows. "In fact, ground control consists of two separate radars—search radar, which sweeps around the horizon to locate aircraft coming from any point of the compass, and glide path, which is local. The traffic director in the tower contacts the aircraft first and steers it into the field of view of the landing system."

"Ah. That explains a lot," Gillian said, as the pieces began to fall into place. "Thanks for the information and for not being an enemy agent. By the way, what's your name?"

He held out his hand. "Dickie Collins. Maybe we'll be seeing more of each other."

The women at the table nodded brightly at the remark, all but Gillian, who was already drawing landing diagrams in her head.

Betsy and Gillian returned to quarters and began a nightly ritual of reciting information as a means of memorizing it.

"I have the advantage that I'm allowed to bring out notes and manuals, but it helps to be able to describe things to you. So, get comfortable while I explain the hydraulic system of the Dakota DC-47."

After she finished, Gillian recounted the principles and technology of ground-control landings, assuming that Betsy, like Dickie, was not an enemy agent. Night after night, for the next two months, they recounted the lessons of the day, until each one could—almost—do the other's job.

Betsy also seemed to have studied the aviation mechanics who worked alongside her. "Most of them are good mates, but sadly, they don't have that certain allure of the pilot."

Gillian laughed. "Did you enlist to serve in His Majesty's defense of the homeland or to find a beau?"

"How can you ask such a question, you silly bird? To find a beau, of course. What about you?"

"Well, not to catch a man, for sure. As for why, exactly, I'm not so certain. Maybe just to go back to Germany and finish what my brother started. He loved it, especially Berlin. Or maybe it's just the hunger to go up. *Per aspera ad astra.*"

"Now don't go all bloody posh on me and start spouting some foreign language."

"'Through hardship to the stars,' in Latin."

"Stars, eh? Sounds good enough for me. If you go to Germany, I'll ask to go, too. What are mates for, eh?"

# CHAPTER FOUR

*June 1945*
*Berlin*

In the weeks after the surrender, the shock of crushing defeat had dissipated, and so had the wanton brutality. Rape continued, a sort of second-degree, less-violent version in which women were no longer taken by brute force and by gangs of men. The new compulsion was subtler, essentially the exchange of two hungers: Soviet lust versus German starvation.

Erika had submitted to Stepka for several more days, for as long as his comrades knew she "belonged" to him, she was relatively safe from assault by any of them. But on the day he was to be transferred, with the cold calculation of a determined survivor, she asked him to point out his commanding officer.

Major Koslov, a barrel-chested, square-faced man, was about forty. She hoped he wasn't a vengeful or abusive sort, for the next day, gathering her courage, she accosted him on the street.

"Thank you, Major, for keeping your men in order." She gazed up at him admiringly and fingered her still-boyishly-short hair behind her ear.

At first, he seemed bemused, then grinned, revealing a gold tooth. "You speak Russian," he said, stating the obvious. When she didn't reply, he continued. "Yes, my soldiers are good men. They treat you all right?" His eyes traveled from her face down her chest to her hips, and she hoped the stains on her dress weren't obvious.

"Yes. Very well. No trouble at all," she answered, and both knew it was a lie.

"You live in this street?" His eyes went to her breasts again, though he must have been disappointed.

"Yes, in that building on the corner, on the top floor."

"Good. Perhaps I will look in on you later, to make sure you are safe," he said, cementing the arrangement. Tipping his head slightly in greeting, he went on his way. The few soldiers nearby who had been talking among themselves now fell silent, and she knew word would spread. The blanket of protection was already forming around her.

The same evening, he was there, with two tins of sardines and a sack of candles.

As she admitted him, she felt dirty, simply because she had so obviously made herself available to him. And she had no idea what he would demand of her, or how rough he would be.

But he was cavalier enough, removing his boots and tunic before lumbering over and climbing onto her bed. The act didn't take long; it never had with Stepka either. The Russian men had a no-nonsense approach, relieving the sexual urge as they did every other one, with little refinement. Afterward, he leaned back against the wall and exhaled contentment.

"I'm a lucky man. To make it alive all the way to Berlin, to experience victory, and to meet a nice woman. Yes, very lucky." He scratched his chest. "I'm not a military man, you know. In Arkhangelsk, I was an engineer. I worked on water systems. But in wartime, many men are killed, and you can advance through the ranks."

She could not imagine why he shared that information with her but thought it wise to sound interested. "Will you go back to engineering when you return home?"

"Yes. I'm sure I will. Many of our cities are in ruins, and it will be a good opportunity to modernize the water systems. I already have good ideas for that." He scratched his chin. "It's quite satisfying to develop new projects that help the people."

She thought of all the ruined cities and towns in Germany that would also need water systems but couldn't be repaired while the Russians were confiscating all the manufacturing machinery. She refrained from mentioning that fact.

Still, he seemed sincere in his zeal to work for the greater good. Societies advanced on the strength of such men. Hmm. She winced in the darkness at the discrepancy between her admiration for his individual energy and her hatred for what he and his army were doing to the cadaver that was Germany, brutalizing it economically, politically, physically.

He left near midnight, allowing her to sleep soundly in her unbarricaded apartment, confident no one would dare disturb her now. As expected, he came the next evening and the next, and each time he brought her bread, or wine, presumably confiscated from other Germans, or other little gifts, she grew more jaded. Against her will, she was getting to know him.

On the fourth evening, he actually draped his tunic and pants carefully over a chair and stood his boots in a corner, like a husband coming home from a day at the office. And in bed, to her horror, he suddenly became personal.

"A man gets lonely in the field, so far from home. I have a wife, you know. Her name is Oksana. She's dark, though, not blond like you. And more robust. You German women are so delicate."

"Probably because we're all hungry."

"Maybe. But she's smart like you. She was a teacher at the Polytechnic Institute. At the moment, she's in the army, but she will be demobilized soon. You'd like her."

"Perhaps so," Gillian said, to be polite, but smiled inwardly at the thought of him introducing them to each other. *Oksana dear, this is Erika, the woman whose body I bought every night with food, after a gang of my men raped her. Why don't you offer her a cup of tea?*

As the days passed, life improved in small increments. Suddenly one afternoon, the building had water again, though the pressure was low and didn't reach beyond the second floor. They still had no electricity, so the major's regular supply of candles remained essential. One or two tram lines were operating again, though few tram cars were undamaged and usable so they ran seldom.

One morning, she stood with Gerda at her window watching a ragtag group of stragglers amble down the street. "Wehrmacht," Gerda said. "I guess the Russians are letting some of them come home. Not worth the trouble to keep in camps, I suppose. God, they look terrible, don't they?"

Erika stared down at the men with mixed feelings. They were her fellow Germans, comrades to her late husband, but the dictatorship they had fought for had imprisoned and killed her parents. These were ordinary Wehrmacht soldiers—for the SS seemed to have evaporated from Germany completely—but even they had been held up as exemplars of German manhood while German women were relegated to home, church, and children.

Now the heroes had to slink along the streets, not daring to make eye contact with the Soviet soldiers, who ridiculed them or shoved them around.

"So much for our heroes," Erika muttered. "Broken, pathetic creatures, and just as hungry as we are."

"That reminds me. Can you ask your major for more powdered eggs? I mean more than what he just brings for you?"

Erika grimaced. "You mean you want me to whore for you, as well?"

In the end, she whored for the entire building, because the next evening, Major Koslov arrived with an armload of foodstuffs. Some, like the Russian black bread, came from the Soviet larder, but most was pilfered or confiscated. From the cellars of hoarders, she supposed. Tins of herring, several bottles of wine, dried sausages. No one asked what the sausages contained.

The next week, treating Erika's apartment as his salon, the major also brought colleagues in his wake. First behind him was another officer, whom the major introduced as Sr. Lt. Vassily Miranov. In the lieutenant's footsteps came a rather ferocious-looking Mongol, a corporal with a long Asian name, who carried an accordion of some sort under his arm. Behind him, to her surprise, a woman entered, in boots and skirt, and with a jaunty beret over thick brown hair. "Sergeant Petrova," the major said, and the woman nodded.

Erika had seen women soldiers in the street but was surprised to meet an officer. Petrova was stocky, with a flat, peasant-like face but a haughty bearing that contradicted it. For all her coolness, it was a relief to have one of the powerful people in the room be a woman.

They all set their rifles against the wall in a lineup that was an effort at decorum, but also a reminder that the guests were the occupiers and could have what they wanted.

Presumably having heard the Russians tromp up the stairs, Gerda, Wilhelm, and young Hanno arrived as well, and now the room was packed. Hanno and Wilhelm sat on the floor.

"It's almost like a party," Gerda said, nibbling her portion of sausage and eyeing the other foods on the table.

Wilhelm ate his portion quietly, as if not wanting to draw attention to his being the only adult German male in the room, but Hanno was uninhibited. "Can I have another piece of bread," he asked the major in German, and Erika interpreted.

"Of course you can, lad," the major said, rubbing the boy's hair, confirming the impression Erika had gotten in the weeks before, that the Russians loved children. It seemed the younger the children were, the safer they were from violence, protected by Russian sentimentality.

The Mongol played a tune on his accordion, and the Russians began singing. It was a melancholy song, about a Cossack who dreams about a horse. It seemed fitting, given the horses in the street that were so well cared for. The senior lieutenant called Vassily surprised her with a rich bass that reminded her of bearded male choirs she'd heard as a child in Russian cathedrals.

Other songs followed, about snow, and love, and loneliness, and the pride of being a soldier. The themes were universal and could have been sung by any army, but the melodies and the sentimentality were thoroughly Russian. All four of them knew every word and sang along emotionally, as if they were hymns, the woman an octave higher than the men.

After two hours, the food ran out, and so, mercifully, did the alcohol, for the Russians, when they were drunk, were unpredictable.

But it seemed the Mongol corporal had drunk the most, and once he'd exhausted his repertory of songs, he set his accordion on the floor, crossed his arms, and dozed off on his chair.

The female sergeant, also slightly intoxicated, leaned toward Hanno. "Such a handsome lad. I hope my boy grows up to be as handsome as you," she said, patting him on the cheek.

He rubbed the spot she'd caressed, clearly embarrassed. He'd been in the *Jungvolk*—Erika had seen him in his outfit—and now an enemy Russian was offering him sincere affection. She could sense his confusion.

With the evening's conviviality waning, Gerda and Wilhelm announced it was time for them all to go to bed, and they left, taking Hanno with them. Erika was relieved, since she no longer had to translate every remark in both directions.

As the candles began to sputter, the one called Vassily lit a third and screwed it into the neck of the empty wine bottle. "You know what I can't understand? Why a country as advanced and prosperous as Germany declared war on us."

Erika shrugged initially, then realized he actually expected an answer. "I can't say, exactly, except that with Hitler, a sickness came over the German people. I won't defend the Nazis, of course, but both our governments were expansionists."

The lieutenant leaned toward the candle to see while he rolled himself a cigarette. "But fascism has a different end—pure conquest—while communism wants to unite the working classes of the world against their oppressors."

Erika was familiar with the argument; she'd grown up with it. "My parents were good social democrats. They believed in workers' rights, and they died for that cause, in a Nazi concentration camp."

Sgt. Petrova spoke up. "Why didn't you join the resistance? We had a revolution in Russia. You could have done so also." She crossed her arms, as if to defy anyone to contradict her.

The lieutenant shook his head. "The bosses, the heads of business and industry were too strong, and the workers not miserable enough. They fell right into step."

Surprised at finding an ally, Erika was about to elaborate, but Major Koslov cleared his throat, terminating the conversation. The woman recognized the signal that it was time to leave and stood up.

"Yes, the hour is late, and we are obliged to report in the morning." She kicked the corporal's chair, waking him, and the three visitors filed through the door into the corridor.

To delay the inevitable surrender to the major's craving, Erika took up the wine-bottle candle. "It's dark on the stairs. I'll accompany them to the street."

The men led the way, with Sgt. Petrova behind, followed by Erika, who wished she had something useful to say. Nothing occurred to her. But at the foot of the stairs, Petrova halted while the men continued through the door to the street.

Glancing up toward the apartment where the major waited, she said, "You must hate us."

"I hate your army, and your victory, but not your people." Erika paused, then added, "Except for the ones who raped me."

A moment of silence passed before the sergeant spoke. "German soldiers raped me and left me for dead. So now we are even."

Erika took a breath and felt anger rising. "No, we are absolutely *not* even. We have both lost. To the brutality of men. What did you do after you recovered?"

"Returned to my unit and found the battalion of the men who hurt me. Outside Kursk."

"And then?"

"We killed them all," the sergeant said, stepping out into the street.

❖

Erika brooded on the conversation for the next week as she fulfilled her nightly obligation, thereby keeping her larder, and that of her friends, more or less full. But at the end of June, the major arrived one morning with an announcement.

"I am sorry to tell you, I am transferred back to Russia. This afternoon, in fact." The "I'm sorry" notwithstanding, he was openly cheerful, and it was obvious why.

"So, you'll see your wife again. Well, that's wonderful." Gillian's response was automatic, but she was both relieved and anxious. Her sexual servitude was over, but so was her source of provisions.

"Yes, I am very happy, but I brought you a little gift. Special for you." He placed a bulky package wrapped in newspaper on the table. "Please open it when I am gone." He executed a slight military bow and left the apartment.

She stood, nonplussed for a moment, then set the package on the table. Under the layers of newspapers lay a ring of sausage, for which she breathed relief. Food for at least a few days. But a large ball of crumpled paper was the main part of the package, and she pulled it apart.

Stupefied, she examined the object: a wooden model plane, beautifully hand-carved, with great detail. It was a sort of generic two-engine plane, with a small canopy over a one-man cockpit, wheels and tiny propellers that turned. The canopy held a minute hinge, and she flicked it open with her fingernail. Underneath in the cockpit sat a tiny pilot, exquisitely carved. The plane was painted in the light tan of the Luftwaffe, though the swastikas on the wings and fuselage had been scratched off.

She smiled inwardly. The major had obviously remembered that her husband was a pilot, though she had mentioned it only once. But where had he gotten it? She snorted faintly. It had almost certainly had been pilfered from some Berlin apartment, from the room of a child perhaps. And who knew how many hands it had passed through?

Nonetheless, it was a thoughtful gift, a piece of art, really. She'd keep it.

❖

With the reduction in front-line Soviet troops and the restoring of some public services, life became normalized. That meant order and, to a certain degree, safety. The military leaders formed a central committee to oversee the running of the city, and they did it with the help of the few German communists who came out of hiding.

Rape, even the non-violent, negotiated variety, became rare, and Erika realized she could no longer justify sleeping with Russians for reasons of safety. It was pure prostitution, and she didn't like what it made of her.

Fortunately, the new administration, which controlled rationing of food and coal, now provided another source of sustenance: the clearing of rubble. Although compulsory, it also provided a minimum of guaranteed rations.

By the month of August, Erika Brandt was one of thousands of *Trümmerfrauen*, women who crawled like ants over the piles of rubble, separating bricks from dust and splinter. She was filthy all day now, her clothes and skin grimier than they'd ever been. But it was honorable dirt from the ground, not the debasing stain of sexual servitude, and could be washed away.

Removing the mountains of rubble, some rising to four stories, seemed beyond all human capacity, even with forty-women lines, passing buckets from hand to hand. At the end of the first few ten-hour days, everyone was coughing, and nothing looked different.

Only when the authorities brought in rails and a miniature steam locomotive dragging coal cars could the rubble be carted away in reasonable amounts. The women could then work on separating out the unbroken bricks and tapping away the mortar. They piled the salvaged bricks in little walls along the street and loaded them onto horse-drawn wagons.

In spite of the persistent coughing in the dusty air, Erika noticed a sort of cheerfulness, particularly after the arrival of the British and Americans. One of the newspapers that was again appearing daily in the streets used the term "Hour Zero" to describe defeat, and people seemed to take it to mean that everything beyond zero was an improvement.

The Trümmerfrauen began to talk to each other, and the talk was optimistic. "What a difference, eh? Between the Ruskies and the Amis," one of them commented.

Another worker, tapping mortar with a trowel, spat out dust. "What do you expect? The Ruskies have nothing back home but their little villages, if any of them are left standing. Of course they want vengeance. The Amis, well, they just arrived, and look at 'em. All rich and plump, with no reason for revenge."

"And they're willing to share if you're nice to them." A third woman giggled. "If you know what I mean."

Erika knew exactly what she meant. Half the women in the line, the ones who had managed to still look desirable, flirted with the Tommies and the GIs the exact same way she had flirted with her major, with the same benefits. But she'd done it to protect herself, and now that the threat was gone, she found the thought of offering herself revolting. Even with a scarcity of soap, she washed obsessively.

By August, the streets were open again, and the remaining trams that had not been hauled off to Russia ran all day, crammed with passengers. People were still gaunt; clothing was still patched; soap, sugar, and real coffee were almost nonexistent. But Berlin was alive again. Only when a cool September arrived and the need for coal set in did the fear return.

"Are you going to the market this evening?" the woman next to her asked as she added her bricks to the pile on the horse cart.

Erika shook her head. "No. I don't have anything to sell. What about you?"

"Oh, I always find something. We gave our watches away weeks ago, but you'd also be surprised what the Amis collect for souvenirs. They'll pay for anything that looks Nazi or German military. Yesterday evening, I got rid of a military belt buckle with *Gott mit uns* on it. There must be thousands of them in the ground all over Germany, but the GI seemed very excited and gave me ten cigarettes for it. That's enough for half a kilo of butter."

On the long walk back to her building, Erika brooded on what she could sell. The Russians had stripped the empty apartments in her building of everything portable, and she and Gerda had sold everything they could from the Metzger apartment. All she had left in her own attic room were essential items for living. And the major's gift.

❖

At their sparse dinner of parsnip and potato soup, Gerda seemed to read her mind. "We need to stock up for winter," she said, wiping the last speck of soup from her bowl with a scrap of bread. "Coal, food, everything."

"How do we do that? We've sold everything we could on the black market. Books, extra pots and dishes, even my husband's dress shoes."

"We must have overlooked something." Gerda swept her gaze around the room. "What about that?" She indicated with her head the top of the empty bookshelf.

"The toy airplane?" She hesitated. "But it was a gift from the major."

"From the man who exploited you for weeks," Gerda said coldly. "I'm sure we can get a good price from some Allied soldier."

Erika shrugged. "I suppose you're right. It's just…"

"If you sell your plane, I'll sell my mother's teapot. I've kept it hidden all this time, but now I'm too hungry."

"All right. Between the pot and the plane, we should be able to negotiate a few days' food."

"Good then. We'll meet tomorrow at the Reichstag after you get off your shift. I'll have both things with me."

Before going to bed, Erika studied the wooden plane, absentmindedly stroking the smooth wood. Why was she loath to give it up? She had no sentimental attachment to the Russian who'd given it to her, and its reference to her husband also brought no nostalgia. No. She'd had enough of planes. A curse on all of them.

She set it on the floor and blew out the candle.

# CHAPTER FIVE

Her training at Watchfield completed, Gillian received a four-day pass to spend at home before being transferred to Bad Eilsen/Bückeburg, Germany.

Her leave was dreary in the extreme. She looked up friends from her air-transport days, but they were scattered all over the UK and not reachable for an afternoon tea. Finally, on her last day, to avoid another lonely walk around London, she visited her brother's grave in Brookwood Cemetery.

Holding a tiny bouquet of daisies, she stood over the marble plaque of Alastair Somerville. "Hello, old friend. I don't suppose you're listening, but I want you to know that I'm carrying on."

After a moment's thought, she added, "I mean, I've been flying, as I told you before, but now I'm in the WAAF and headed for Germany. Not Berlin just yet, but Bad Eilsen/Bückeburg. It's the headquarters of RAF Germany, and I'll be bringing in planes using radar. Of course, you don't know what radar is, do you? Anyhow, if I get a chance, I'll go to Berlin, though I'm sure you wouldn't recognize it now. We pretty much bombed it to smithereens."

She laid the flowers over his name. "I think of you a lot, especially since Mum and Dad died. You're still alive in my mind, so if I do make it to Berlin, you'll be there with me. I'll try to find out why you loved it so much."

The thought of carrying a bit of him with her lifted her spirits as she headed back to the bus stop. Germany lay ahead of her now, and perhaps something good would come of it. If not flying, at least some sort of advancement, some sense of community and purpose, because in London, she was lonely as hell.

❖

*September 15, 1945*

The flight over the channel on a Dakota DC 3 was noisy but uneventful. Gillian kept staring at the door to the cockpit, imagining what the pilot was doing. She'd flown Dakotas from factories to front-line airfields on a dozen occasions, might even have delivered the one they were flying in, but she stifled any remaining bitterness at now being hauled like so much freight.

Bückeburg Airfield, built specifically to service RAF Germany, which was headquartered in Bad Eilsen, was some two miles outside of town. The new arrivals were to be billeted in town, however, so the driver of their pickup vehicle took them on a small tour before depositing them.

Bad Eilsen was lovely, and in September 1945, less than four months after Germany's defeat, it showed few signs of the war. A stream ran through the town, with vegetable gardens along its bank. Gillian was optimistic when she climbed out and knocked on the door of the house owned by the Schneider family, where Betsy was already billeted.

Herr Schneider admitted her and showed them to the master bedroom, which had been furnished with bunk beds and cabinets for RAF female personnel.

The Schneiders were over sixty. Their manner was friendly, bordering on the obsequious, but she supposed it could be no other way. She saw no photos of children, so if they had a son in the war, the subject probably would not come up for discussion.

It took her only a few moments to unpack, and she reported immediately to the station commander.

❖

Col. Arnold Horwick appeared to be a soldier of the old school, with a bristly handlebar mustache and an upper-class aloofness. He stood up from his desk without offering his hand. "Ah, yes. Another lady has arrived," he said coolly. "I'll escort you to the ground-control van, and Jones will show you the ropes." He strode past her and held the door, then guided her back out of the terminal without speaking.

He halted in front of a bizarre construction on wheels some hundred yards away from the terminal and perhaps ten yards to the side of the runway. Two steel vans were connected to form a single structure with various fans and boxes and poles jutting from the top. It looked like a project by someone who had failed engineering school.

"This is the AN-CPN-4 ground-control-approach mobile system. It's jolly ugly, but it's just about the best in the world, and it's your workplace." He waved his hand toward the monstrosity's roof. "The antennas in the front are for the airport surveillance radar and precision-approach radar, those on the right are the VHF and UHF radio antennas, and these gadgets here are the gin poles that stabilize the trailers against the wind."

Gillian nodded, memorizing what he said.

Without knocking, he opened the door to admit her, and she climbed the two steps. Inside was a small space crowded with equipment and sporting two tiny windows at the top, presumably to minimize light and facilitate viewing of the radar screen.

Two men sat with earphones in front of their screens. One of them stood up and saluted while the other remained seated, speaking into a microphone.

The commander ignored the salute. "Jones, this is our new scopie. Would you show her the ropes?"

"Certainly sir," Jones replied.

"Carry on, then," the colonel said stiffly and without interest, and did an about-face, letting the door swing shut behind him.

Gillian took note of the man's rank and saluted. "Flight Sergeant Jones, Corporal Somerville reporting for duty."

He pulled out his own chair from the radar bench and another next to it, motioning her to sit down. "Jones will do. And you are?"

"Gillian."

"Well, Gillian, you're lucky. For the moment, traffic is light, so you can become familiar with things without risk of life and limb. We get about twenty flights in per day, though we're expecting more soon. Oh, this is Sergeant David Wilkins, by the way."

The other man waved and went back to murmuring instructions into his microphone.

"I'm sure we don't have anything you don't recognize, and you already know that our radar antennas send out radar signals that hit the planes and arrive back here, at the speed of light. These spots here are 'permanent echoes' from chimneys, buildings, and so forth. Only the ones that move and leave a little light trail are planes."

He was telling her what she already knew. "But that's the wide-sweep radar, which catches them as they approach. Where is your precision radar?"

"That's what Wilkins is staring at right now." He took a step back and stood behind the other controller, who was bringing in a plane at that moment.

Dropping his voice, so as not to disrupt the controller-pilot dialogue, he continued. "These screens are the course scope and the lateral approach. They show the landing cone and the glide path. We've set markers for optimum altitude, position, and rate of descent, and we tell the pilot if he's too far to port, too far to starboard, too high, and so forth. We're his outside eyes."

Gillian nodded, her nervousness dissipating. It was just like she'd learned at Watchfield.

"If you're ready, you can take over from Watkins there. Just slide into his seat and set on his headphones as soon as he stops talking."

Gillian followed the order and had the satisfaction of bringing in her first plane by radio. It really was just like at training, though on that day she had the safety net of a day of good visibility, so the pilots could land visually even without instruction.

At the end of her shift, she handed over her headset to her relief controller and walked away from the console like a veteran.

Jones had just come off duty as well and strode beside her to the bike shed at the main terminal. Gillian's stomach rumbled with hunger, and her single thought now was to locate Betsy and go with her to the sergeants' mess.

As they reached the terminal, a large black Pontiac pulled up, and a woman stepped out from the driver's side. An attractive woman, who leaned against the bumper and lit a cigarette. After a single puff, she began to pace, as if irritated.

"My gosh, who's that?" Gillian asked, unlocking her bike. "She looks just like Betty Grable, doesn't she?"

Jones lifted his bike from its slot and threw one leg over the seat. "Best not to say that out loud. That's the commander's wife Jean, and he doesn't like anyone talking about her. I'd wager he doesn't even like the idea of anyone *thinking* about her, because he knows the thoughts are dirty."

Jean paced nervously, circling the car, and the high heels she wore, of the sort that Gillian hadn't seen in years, caused her hips to sway. Her tight skirt emphasized the swell of her rear, and she wore real nylon stockings with seams running down the back.

The two of them stood as if hypnotized by the sight until, finally, the station commander marched past them to his wife and took the car keys from her hand. Without speaking, she crushed out her cigarette butt on the ground and swung around the car to the passenger side.

Exchanging glances, Gillian and Jones mounted their bikes, and she began the two-mile ride back to her billet.

❖

Betsy met her at the door to their room and gave her a warm hug. "Well, there you are, old sod! How'd your first day go?"

"Cracking, in fact. I have to admit, I'm jolly good at this radar thing. Brought in eight flights and not a single one crashed and burned."

"Well done! You've got the patter down, then?"

"Oh, yes. Stay calm, give every direction twice, make them trust you. Though once or twice, I forgot to say 'go ahead' and wondered why they didn't answer. What about you?"

"I don't mind it, and I quite like showing the other chaps how much I know about airplane engines. They kept telling me how to do things, but I told 'em to bog off, I could do it myself, and they soon caught on I knew my onions. We've got a couple of Jerries working there too, ex-Luftwaffe, but I avoid them."

"I know what you mean. I don't want to be chums with them either. But never mind. Have you been in the castle yet, or in town? Any good pubs?"

"Bückeburg Castle's where the big shots of RAF Germany do whatever they do, and no place for the likes of us. The pubs, on the other hand, that I can tell you about. And the lads."

"All right, then. Let's go eat, and you can give me the rundown."

❖

The days passed, and the airfield routine became familiar, as did the faces of the men and women they worked with or shared their lunch schedules with in the mess. The food was slightly better than under the rationing back home. Only the long bike ride to and from work was a bother, particularly in the rain that, in spite of their rubberized capes, drenched the hems of their uniform skirts.

But this October day began with radiant sunshine, and Gillian and Betsy pedaled confidently toward work. Their route took them along Bückeburg streets, past the castle, and into the woods. The canopy of trees pierced by beams of light, together with the birdsong, made the morning idyllic, in spite of the cold.

"Something's going on over there," Betsy remarked, riding just ahead of her.

"Villagers." Gillian craned her neck. "Wonder what they're doing here."

They halted near the circle of men and women who stood around a pit in the forest floor. The group parted, and one of the men approached them. He addressed Gillian, who was closest to him.

"A uniform. We find them all the time," he said in heavily accented English. He pointed back toward a young man who held a tunic draped over his arm and a woman with a bundle that looked like trousers. Their mud-stained condition obscured their origin, but the tall, peaked officer's cap the woman also held still retained its light-blue color. And the eagle over the bill of the cap was unmistakable.

"Luftwaffe," Gillian said coldly.

The man, who appeared to be in charge, nodded. "Ja. Bad Eilsen was Luftwaffe headquarters. When Allies come, they run away, leave guns, uniforms. You work at RAF air station?" he asked, glancing down at their uniforms. At that moment, she realized, they represented the entire RAF occupation forces.

"Yes, we do. Of course, we'll report what you've found." She tried to sound authoritative as she edged her bike away from him toward the path.

"No, not just report. Please. You take with you." He followed her. "Not good for us to keep it. Bad memories."

She halted, annoyed. "All right. Tie it to the rear of my bike."

Bearing the distasteful bundle, Gillian pedaled energetically, leading the way until they emerged from the woods and came within sight of the aerodrome. Minutes later, they locked their bikes in the shed, and she considered how to carry the filthy Luftwaffe rags to the commander without staining her uniform. She bent, grimacing, to untie the soggy bundle, then heard a voice behind her.

"Oh, my. What have you got there?"

Gillian turned to face Jean Horwick and blinked for a moment, speechless. The station commander's wife was dressed in a snug turtleneck sweater that emphasized her ample breasts. Its pristine whiteness offset with fashion-plate perfection the powder-puff blue of her skirt that seemed as tight as the previous one.

"Luftwaffe uniform," Betsy replied, unnecessarily, since Jean was already examining it. "We passed some villagers who'd found it, and they asked us to turn it in."

Jean poked it with a bright-red fingernail. "Those men, strutting around like peacocks in their plumage, flashing their stars and medals. Silly sods."

A tiny part of Gillian's brain wondered if the remark was meant to include the RAF as well. "I was about to carry it in to Commander Horwick, but it's filthy."

"Oh, don't you worry, my dear. I have just the right thing." She did an about-face and, unimpeded by her high heels, hurried over to her own car and opened the trunk. A moment later, she was back carrying a burlap sack that looked like it once carried potatoes.

"That's perfect. Thank you." Gillian deftly detached the bundle from her bicycle and dropped it into the sack. "But how can I return the bag to you?"

"Oh, don't worry about that. My husband brings them home all the time. Well, I'm off. Ta-ta!" She gave a light pat to Gillian's shoulder and strode away. Watching her for a moment, Gillian was tempted to call her walk provocative, but that seemed unkind.

❖

"Another one of those, eh?" Wg. Cdr. Horwick dropped the bag in the corner of his office. "I'll see to it that it's destroyed. We don't want the Germans collecting them as souvenirs, do we?"

Gillian waited for other instructions, but he said only, "That will be all, Corporal. Dismissed."

With an internal shrug, she saluted and left the office to report for work.

She marched the distance to the ground-control trailer and let herself in, but before she could put on her headset, Dave Wilkins leaned over her shoulder. "I came in just before you and saw you chitchatting with the wingco's wife."

She smiled at the abbreviation he'd never dare use in front of the commander himself. "Is that not allowed?"

"It's allowed, but not very smart."

"What are you talking about? All she did was give us a burlap sack."

He raised a hand as if to fend off her annoyance. "I'm just giving you some friendly advice. She's trouble."

Gillian scowled. "What the devil does that mean?"

"It means she's bored. She comes around the base because she has nothing to do at home. And she stirs things up. Just stay away from her. Word to the wise."

He tapped the current controller on the shoulder and replaced him in his seat, setting the earphones on his head.

Puzzled and vaguely annoyed at the whole matter of the damned uniform, she set her own headset on and tuned to the relevant frequency.

Air traffic was normal, well within the capacity of three controllers to handle and to take their lunch in shifts.

At 1600, Gillian went alone and slid her tray along the line in the RAF mess, receiving carefully measured portions of meatloaf and mashed potatoes. The meatloaf was more than half bread, but tasty, and the potatoes made from powder could be made palatable with salt and pepper. The carrots, locally grown and fresh, were excellent.

She stood up to leave and spotted someone standing in the doorway. His prominent nose and heavy brows over bright-blue eyes looked familiar, but she wasn't sure. Only when he smiled and marched toward her did she remember.

"Nigel. How nice to see you again." She took his proffered hand and shook it warmly.

"I'm surprised you remember me. We just had one beer in that poxy little pub at Watchfield."

"I remembered you because you were so polite, while your mate… What was his name? Jack? He was…well…"

Nigel laughed. "I believe the word you're searching for is 'arse,' at least with regard to women. But he's a decent chap in all other respects. You'll be happy to know we'll both be flying in and out of Bad Eilsen. I'll give him your love next time I see him."

She stood back as if to admire him. "I see you've been promoted to flight sergeant. Well done! Are you just passing through?"

"Yes. Taking some fancy new equipment to Gatow. They're

loading my plane out on the field right now, and I'll be flying it first thing tomorrow morning to Berlin."

"Berlin. Crikey! I've been dying to see it. I don't suppose I could go along. I'm due a day off, and I know I could get a pass."

He scratched the side of his jaw, as if weighing the hazards. "It's not strictly allowed, but it's not exactly forbidden either. I'll agree if you stay out of everyone's way. We'll only be there an hour before we turn around. I'll have you back in the afternoon."

"Sounds cracking!" In sheer exuberance, she kissed him quickly on the cheek.

❖

The next morning, she strode cheerfully next to him onto the airfield, and when the plane came within sight, she halted. "Blimey! You didn't tell me it was an Avro Anson. I flew a half dozen of those in the ATA. I can pilot one in my sleep."

He chuckled. "Well, I'm afraid I'll be doing all the flying, but with all that glass, you'll get a good view of the ground. It's the best I can offer."

She grumbled slightly but was in fact delighted to be able to go up with him, and the long, multi-paned canopy meant she could see in almost all directions. It *was* the next best thing.

They climbed in, and to avoid attracting attention to the unscheduled passenger, he started up immediately. The propeller engine seemed to cough, and then its blades turned and accelerated until they formed a blurry, transparent disk. In a few minutes, they were airborne and at cruising elevation.

At first she watched the instruments, longing to take the joystick and make a few wide swoops and dives—nothing reckless, just a bit of stretching to feel the air underneath. She'd done it so many times in the ATA, even fully loaded. The small size of the plane seemed to beg for acrobatics.

But her nostalgia gave way quickly to interest in the ground below, which she'd hardly noticed upon her arrival.

"The fields look bare," she called up to Nigel over the sound of the airplane motor. "I can't tell if they're harvested or barren."

He shouted back over his shoulder. "Barren, mostly. The Germans lost a lot of equipment, manpower, horses, everything, during the war. The whole country's living on handouts now."

She surveilled the landscape—the winding rivers, the patchwork of farms, the scattering of gray and red that identified towns, usually attached to a road or waterway, or both. Large swaths of dark green between them revealed the woodlands that had begun to recover after the land battles.

Suddenly a plane appeared from nowhere over their heads, and Gillian ducked instinctively. "Bloody hell. What was that?"

"A Yak 3, I think. We're in the Russian zone, and they like to remind us who's in charge. It's just an annoyance, though. Anyhow, we're over Potsdam now. Berlin is just to the northeast."

She craned her neck to see down to the ground, searching for signs of the war, but was disappointed. A few grayish spots showed what might have been land disrupted by bombardment, but she couldn't be sure.

From afar, Berlin looked like any large city, crisscrossed by its main thoroughfares and spotted with parks here and there. A river, which she knew was the Spree, ran from the southeast and bifurcated toward the west. It seemed a bit sooty, a bit grayish, but thousands of buildings still stood upright along the streets.

"I thought it would look worse," she said to his back.

"Just wait," he said. "I'll take us to the middle." He dropped lower, and in a few moments, she caught her breath.

The upright buildings she'd seen were hollow and roofless, ragged facades jutting up from the ground like stalagmites. Mile after mile, they passed over the devastation, over the skeleton of a city in which nothing, it seemed, could survive.

Yet the streets crawled with life. As they swooped along the wide thoroughfares, people moved like ants in both directions. Where did they live? How did they get food? If only they could see it from the ground.

They were over Gatow Airport now. Nigel spoke into his radio, identifying himself and his aircraft, obviously receiving instructions from ground control, and brought the plane to a smooth landing.

In gentlemanly fashion, he offered his hand to help her out of the fuselage and down the wing to the ground, and she saw no reason to mention that she'd climbed, unaided, out of a hundred planes before.

On the tarmac, they bent forward into the wind, and he took her by the elbow. "This part is easy. We go into the terminal, hand over the manifest, and have a coffee. The ground crew's responsible for unloading, and the mechanics will check the engine." As if to confirm his remark, two mechanics came toward them wheeling a ladder-ramp. "I notice the fuel gauge went down fast," he said to them. "It may have a leak."

"Yes, sir. We'll take a look," one of them replied, and Gillian realized they were German. Ex-Luftwaffe mechanics, like those who worked with Betsy.

After reporting briefly to his superior, Nigel returned and led her to the sergeants' mess. The promised coffee, she found, was quite good, and since it was nearly noon, he bought sandwiches for them both.

"Have you been inside Berlin?" she asked before her first bite. Cheddar cheese and mustard, she noted.

"Yes. Several times. It's a pretty lively place, considering that it was all but obliterated only five months ago. The Berliners are a tough people. They had to be, after what they went through."

"You sound like you feel sorry for them."

"It's hard not to when you see the women and children. I've carried some German passengers and have talked to a few. You have to remember, we bombed their city to smithereens, and then the Russians came in and raped all the women."

"Really? It was that bad? I mean about the Russians." She'd never heard the subject discussed before and was shocked by his candor.

"It's what they tell me, and I believe them."

She sipped her coffee, slightly shaken. Allied victory was such a cause of celebration; she'd never thought of what it meant for the women. "So, what happened to them? Afterward, I mean."

"Well, it finally stopped, when the roughest soldiers left. Now, the hospitals all over the city are treating the women for pregnancies and… um…diseases. Another form of victors' vengeance."

Morbid curiosity made her crave to see the damage up close. "Any chance we can go into the city?"

"I don't think so. We're scheduled for a takeoff in just a little while, so I—"

"Flight Sergeant, sir." It was one of the mechanics. "We checked the fuel line, and you were right. There is a problem, but it's not just a leak. It's the pump. We don't have spare parts so we have to repair it, but it will take a few hours. We have to dismantle the pump and part of the engine."

Nigel and Gillian exchanged glances. "That's fine. Do what you need to. In the meantime, I'm sure the corporal and I can occupy ourselves."

Gillian grasped him by the arm. "This is our chance, Nigel. You're not planning to come this far and not seize the moment to go into the city, are you?"

He scratched his jaw again, which seemed to aid his thinking. "It's really a question of transportation. Fortunately, the head of operations owes me a favor for bringing him real French champagne a few weeks ago. I'm sure he'll agree to our requisitioning a jeep. I'll sort the transportation, while you run over to the American PX and buy a pack of coffee beans."

"Coffee beans? Whatever for?"

"You'll see," he said cryptically, and shooed her off toward the PX.

Gillian tried not to gawk, but she was not prepared for the contradiction that was Berlin. The middle of the city was ruined beyond belief, obviously unable to support life. Yet life swarmed all over it. Somehow, in its utter devastation, it retained a sort of excitement, though perhaps that was the perverted perception of a victor, interpreting the throes of desperation as energy. But a great city retains the ghost of its greatness, even in ruin.

As the vehicle pulled into the plaza on the western side of the Brandenburg Gate, she stared up at the imposing monument to Germanic glory. The lower parts of its square columns were covered with graffiti, painted and incised in Cyrillic. With the exception of *HITLER KAPUTT*, she could make sense of none of it. Every surface from bottom to top was pitted from small-arms fire. On the far side, visible through the center archway, a young woman in a Soviet uniform directed the sparse traffic, snapping gracefully from one direction to the other and pointing with a small red flag.

"Can we pass through the archway and see it from the other side?" she asked.

"Not a good idea. It's not expressly forbidden, but the Russians are prickly about Westerners trespassing on their sector. This little trip's not exactly authorized, so we don't want trouble."

"Of course not. But now I'm sorry I don't have a camera." She gestured vaguely toward the great gate.

"Well, I know where you can get one, and if you like the Brandenburg Gate, you'll love the Reichstag."

"Isn't that where the Soviets planted a giant flag the day of victory? I'm pretty sure I saw it in *Life* magazine."

He spun the wheel and drove north past curbside rubble that still remained. In a few minutes, they were in front of the Reichstag building. He turned off the motor and sat while she gawked at the infamous edifice.

"Yes, this is where it was."

Even in total ruin, the Reichstag building held a certain dignity. It, too, was pitted from top to bottom, and its dome had collapsed, leaving a skeleton of steel girders. The ground that stretched out nearly half a kilometer in front of it was broken up and planted with vegetables. In a few places, where benches had stood, only the iron or concrete supports remained, while all the wood had been removed.

But the hundreds of people milling around at its base seemed indifferent to the cataclysm that had stormed over it.

"This is the heart of the black market," Nigel said. "The Allied leaders try to make it illegal, but no matter how often they break it up, the people come back. Soldiers too, from all four armies, come to make deals with the Berliners."

He parked the jeep at the edge of the plaza near a pile of broken brick. "Come on. Let's see if we can find you a camera."

They wandered into the midst of the crowd, and Gillian watched, rapt, as soldiers and civilians managed to negotiate, with no shared language and a minimum of gesture. Fingers were held up to show number, a nodding of the head to show agreement.

Clothing, shoes, cameras, kitchen items, war souvenirs passed from hand to hand, in exchange for other objects, for cash or, most often, for cigarettes.

"Commerce at its basic level," she observed.

Two women suddenly appeared in front of them. One was elderly, with her hair tied up in a headscarf. The other was younger, with very short blondish hair and slightly hooded eyes that made her seem dreamy. She was gaunt and subdued, though she lacked only a few good meals and a shampoo to be beautiful.

The older one proffered a porcelain teapot. *"Porzellan, bester Qualität,"* she said, confirming its quality. The younger one said nothing but simply held up a toy airplane.

Gillian was struck by her expression of defeat and longing. Yet a certain intelligence shone from the demoralized eyes. Almost unconsciously, she pointed toward the plane, and the woman placed it in her hand.

It was, in fact, a fine object, carved in wood with superb detail. The woman flicked open the canopy to reveal a tiny carved pilot. The fine craftsmanship showed it was more than a toy, and its only flaws were the patches where the paint had been scratched off. Patches that hinted of a swastika.

Gillian was torn between fascination and aversion.

"Is it Luftwaffe?" she asked.

The woman shook her head. *"Nein, nicht Luftwaffe. Nur ein Flugzeug."*

Nigel peered over her shoulder. "She says it's not a copy of a Luftwaffe plane, just a generic one. A rather nice piece, too. Would you like it?"

"What does it cost?" she asked, and the woman seemed to understand. She replied in German, and Nigel translated.

"She wants to know what you're willing to pay."

"Tell her we only have military script. Will she take that?"

Nigel shook his head. "She won't, but if you really want it, I'll get it for you." He reached into his jacket pocket and drew out a cardboard pack of Players Navy Cut.

*"Britische Zigaretten. Acht,"* he said, holding up eight fingers.

The woman seemed disappointed and glanced at Gillian with a sadness that seemed infinite. Her older friend murmured something that sounded like disapproval.

"Don't we have anything more?" she asked Nigel, frustrated. She patted her coat pocket unconsciously and felt the bulge at her side. "Oh, yes! We do!" She slid out the packet of coffee beans and held them up triumphantly. Then, out of sheer exuberance, mixed perhaps with a touch of pity, she slid out the small bar of Cadbury chocolate she'd been saving for herself.

The woman's face brightened, and she accepted coffee, chocolate, and cigarettes, concealing them immediately in her own coat pockets.

Gillian held out her hand and said the only word she knew in German. *"Danke."* The woman offered her own thin hand, and for a moment, in the cold October air, Gillian felt the warmth between their palms. Then, abruptly, the woman gave her a quick hug before turning away.

❖

"What an experience," Gillian said, still slightly awestruck as they landed at Bückeburg Airfield. "Betsy will be terribly jealous. Maybe you can take her up next time you fly out."

"Probably not. I'm going to be tied up for the next weeks ferrying people to Nuremberg. They're beginning the trials soon, and I'll be transporting staff, journalists, cameras, telephone equipment, cables, everything you can think of."

"Ah, yes. The 'trial of the century,' they're calling it. I wonder how they'll manage it, I mean, with four countries and four legal systems. I read that the defense attorneys are British and American, but the tribunal of judges will be from all four countries. Four languages! That could be a right cock-up, couldn't it?"

"Well, a cock-up is precisely what they're trying to avoid. The organizers are recruiting people to translate simultaneously into English, French, German, and Russian. Apparently, they'll be hooked up to some new technology, too. Headphones and microphones, that sort of thing."

"Who are they starting off with? Do you know?" She snorted. "Too bad the biggest fish are out of the picture. Hitler's disappeared, Goebbels was roasted outside the bunker, Himmler and Bormann are dead. Who's left?"

"There's still a couple dozen of them. Kaltenbrunner, Rosenberg, Streicher, Hess, and of course their biggest fish, Hermann Goering."

"Goering, that bastard," Gillian snarled. "I hope they hang him from the highest tree."

"Goering's no worse than the others. He started off as an ace pilot, you know."

"I don't care. He was head of the murderous scum that killed my parents and set fire to half of London." She glanced down at the wooden airplane on her lap.

Nigel laid his hand on her forearm. "It's just an airplane, Gillian. Don't let one fat Nazi ruin your love of planes and flying."

"I won't. As long as he hangs."

## Chapter Six

Erika broke off a corner of her precious Cadbury bar. "Sorry about the plane, Hanno. I know you wanted it, but we needed food more." She placed the square-inch block of chocolate in his hand.

"I understand," he said. "I'm not a baby." He bit off the tiniest corner and closed his eyes in pleasure. "And chocolate is good, too."

She distributed the rest of the bar to the others in the apartment who shared the labor of foraging and dealing.

"So, what did you get for the cigarettes?" Wilhelm asked, scratching his white beard. He'd stopped shaving after he sold his razor and sharpening block for shoes, but his new look wasn't bad. He examined his chunk of chocolate before placing it on his tongue to melt.

"Four eggs, a package of lard, and a jar of sauerkraut. We get our normal bread rations tomorrow, so we can all have fried bread and sauerkraut. And, of course, coffee." She held up the packet.

Gerda sighed. "The coffee is a prize for sure, but we ate so much better when your Russian major was here."

Erika turned away. "Those days are over. And no, I'm not going to find a nice Ami to sleep with just to improve our diet. If you're so keen on that, you can go look for one yourself."

"I'm sorry. It was just nostalgia. I remember what you went through. But the Russians weren't all bad. That one who was a teacher seemed a decent sort. And the woman, the one you said was a sniper. I wish I could have talked to her more."

"Her name's Olga," Hanno said, slipping the last fragment of his chocolate between his lips.

Erika frowned. "How do you know her name? She never told us."

He licked his fingertips. "I see her all the time, ordering people around in the Alexanderplatz."

Wilhelm laughed. "Well, well. So our Hanno has friends among the victors. Why don't you invite her to come visit again some time? And bring a ham!"

Hanno mumbled something unintelligible and slid his arms into his rucksack, preparing for another day of foraging. The boy had a real talent for it and almost always came back with something, even if it was only kindling for the stove.

Erika changed into her shabbiest clothing for her afternoon shift at work. A headscarf and a coat were absolutely necessary. After the mountains of rubble of the first weeks had diminished, so also did the lines of bucket-holders, and Erika had quickly applied to work as a mason, which paid slightly better. It was back-breakingly difficult, though, for the oncoming winter had arrived early and grew more bitter every day. Every new wall stood in the open air, and even in coat, gloves, and hat, she shivered.

December brought heavy snows. In the morning, she had to scrape ice off every surface before she could begin, and her mortar froze unless she kept it over a low flame. Her hands, that used to play the piano, were cracked and swollen.

Then, one evening in mid-December, someone knocked at the door of the attic flat Erika had reclaimed. "Who is it?" she called through the door, and a boy's voice called back. "It's Hanno."

Puzzled, she opened the door, and her eyes leapt from the blond adolescent to two Russians barely visible in the dark behind him. She stepped back in shock. What did they want? At night?

"You remember us, don't you?" the man said. "I'm Senior Lieutenant Miranov, and this is Lieutenant Petrova. We visited in the spring. Sorry we couldn't bring our musician this time."

"Uh…come in." Nonplussed, she gestured toward the wooden chairs at her table, where a single candle burned. Hanno stepped in first, seeming rather pleased with himself, and the Russians followed him.

"Hanno said you invited us to visit," Lt. Petrova said, "but we couldn't get away until now. Anyhow, we thought you might like this."

She handed over a bundle tied up in pages torn from *Red Star*, the usual Russian wrapping paper. Erika set it on the table and unwrapped it to find the familiar pickled herring and black bread.

"We also have this." Sr. Lt. Miranov held out a bottle of vodka.

Erika laughed at the cliché and relaxed. It would warm them all, for the apartment was frigid, and even drunk, these two Russians were not the raping kind. Nonetheless, after she laid out plates and knives, and glasses for the vodka, she sat down, tightly crossing her arms and legs, a posture that had become instinctive. "Do you know what happened to Major Koslov?"

Miranov filled all three glasses to the top. "He's back in Moscow with his wife. He's a career man, though, so will stay in service, but his wife will be demobilized." He held up his glass and waited for the others to take theirs.

"*Vashee zda-ró-vye*," he said, and Erika repeated the phrase. The Russians downed theirs in a single gulp, while Erika sipped at hers, but they seemed not to notice. Hanno retreated to a cushion and had none of it.

Erika turned to Lt. Petrova, who seemed less intimidating than on her last visit. Her wide peasant face bore a faint scar along the chin, which Erika hadn't noticed before. Was it the result of battle or her rape? She couldn't ask. "So, what does a sniper do when the war is over?"

Lt. Petrova wiped her lips with a knuckle and then patted one of the medals on her tunic. "Usually, she gets a medal and goes home. But not me. They promoted me to lieutenant and assigned me to occupation forces. A big honor."

"Don't you have family back in Russia?" It was a leading question. Everyone had family.

"Yes, mother, father, and a son, Yuri."

Erika faintly recalled the female soldier mentioning a child during her first visit. Obviously, for the Russians, motherhood did not exclude front-line service. "How old is he?"

The lieutenant seemed pleased that she'd asked. "He's six now. I was drafted into the army when he was two. He will not recognize me when I return to Dainegorsk."

"You haven't seen him at all for four years?"

"No. Dainegorsk is in the far-eastern part of Russia, near the Pacific. It would take too many days to go home and then return to the front. But I'll go home soon, when I am no longer needed here." She poured another serving of vodka into her own and the lieutenant's glasses. "By the way, you may call me Olga."

"Vassily for me." The senior lieutenant took another swallow of vodka. "And we know you are Erika. So how's life, Erika?"

She shrugged. "I don't have enough coal to keep warm, and this is the first herring I've had in weeks. But it could be worse. I work as a mason and get a worker's ration."

"A mason. I see. You'll have lots of work, then. But you don't look like the type. What did you do before the war? Did you have a husband?"

She shifted slightly on her chair, uncertain whether to open up to a near stranger who had only recently been her enemy. But the vodka had warmed her, lowered her resistance. "I was a musician. My husband was a commercial pilot. When the war started, he joined the Luftwaffe."

"What happened to him?" Olga asked. "He fell during the war? In the West or in the East?"

The question was fraught with potential accusation, and it would not be wise to admit one's husband had been among the invaders of Russia. Erika was relieved to be able to say he wasn't. "He crashed during an attack on Britain." She glanced over at Vassily and changed the subject. "What about you?"

"Me? I was a teacher of English. From Kursk. No wife. I'll look for one when I go back. Some good communist woman. We have to begin building the People's State."

"I wish you good luck with that. It's no easy thing to get a people to rule themselves in an enlightened way. Greed, ambition, lust for power, factionalism all seem to creep in sooner or later."

Vassily nodded. "I regret that is true. The state must rule at first, to get the machinery in motion, but when people see the benefits of egalitarianism, the state can disappear."

The vodka was making Erika deeply philosophical. "Ah, yes. The state. Therein lies the problem. We Germans couldn't agree on what kind of state we wanted."

"Yes, you wanted to be Nationalist *and* Socialist, but the two are diametrically opposed, aren't they?"

"Yes, but the Socialist part dropped away quickly, and we ended up with Fascists. That was a disaster, but we needed someone to come from outside to get rid of them. And now, the victors have to decide what to do with the ones who are left."

"You mean the trials in Nuremberg," Olga said. "What do you think of them?"

Erika shrugged. She'd been shrugging a lot lately, perhaps because she no longer had any answers for the great questions. Not even for most of the small ones either. "They are the justice of the victors, of course. They have to be. On the other hand, those men did lead Germany to ruin, and they should have to answer for it. I only object to them being seen as demons. The Allies also committed atrocities. I don't need to list them for you."

Vassily waved his hand, brushing away the subject. "Let's not talk about who is guilty of what. Can we not just admire the way they are proceeding? Surely it is the dawn of an age in which we can all talk to each other."

"Talk, yes. Far better than shooting." Erika took another drink of her vodka, which wasn't at all bad, and unclenched her arms, musing over the irony of their conversation. For months she'd lived alongside Gerda and Wilhelm, who were thoroughly practical and had no socio-political analysis, not a single theoretical thought in their heads. How curiously satisfying it was to discuss politics in the abstract with these two Russians, even if they held ideas quite different from her own.

"Will you be staying in Berlin for a while?" she asked, hoping her question didn't sound like flirtation. Intimacy was the last thing she wanted. She crossed her arms and legs again.

The winter of 1945 to 1946 was brutal, reducing the defeated Berliners to animal-like survival in which they scarcely noticed the passing of time. The days ceased to have numbers or names, were spent identically in the struggle to keep warm, clothed, fed. Private larders emptied, and precious family possessions were bartered to the victors in exchange for something to burn, wear, eat.

The Allies provided starvation rations, while eggs, potatoes, parsnips, and cabbage trickled in from the countryside, through foragers or "hamsters" who loaded up their bicycles and pockets with whatever they could acquire on any given day. They delivered the items to individual families or sold them for profit on the black market.

And then, suddenly, it was May 1946, a year after surrender, and it seemed like a miracle to Erika that they had survived.

Gerda folded the last of the clothing they had just washed with the tiny speck of soap she'd procured. Now in the second spring of their defeat, life had normalized at a level of tolerable hardship. Public transportation was running, at least along the main city lines, and rations for heavy laborers had increased.

Only the influx of refugees became more critical. They arrived in a tidal wave: returning German POWs who'd lost their homes, families expelled from Soviet-occupied lands, Poles, Italians, displaced persons, and the shattered city could not absorb them.

Most kept moving, shuffling westward in some vague hope that the Allies could help them. But some could travel no longer, and the interim administration had requisitioned every available space for them. Refugee families had been assigned to Gerda's and Magda's apartments and the one vacated by the Metzgers. Wilhelm shared his apartment with two ex-POWs. Another two families had moved into the basement that had once been the bomb shelter and prepared their pathetic meals over bonfires in the street. Erika now shared her single room on the top floor with Gerda and two Volga Germans. Trash piled up in the corridor, and the endless noise and smoke from hastily set-up wood-burning stoves made everyone irritable.

But Wilhelm had found a job giving haircuts to Soviet officers when he wasn't playing the violin for handouts on street corners. Hanno was back in Mittelschule, at least on the lower floor of the building that had remained intact. But without textbooks—for National Socialist texts were forbidden, and the Allies had not yet produced any—instruction was limited to simple science, grammar, and arithmetic written on chalkboards and miniature slates.

Erika no longer feared assault or starvation, so lesser troubles were able to emerge. The crowding was becoming intolerable, but she was sure everyone felt the same way. Her hands, after a year of handling cement, brick, and mortar, were swollen and callused. She soaked them in warm water each evening but could find no crème to keep her skin from cracking.

"I wonder if I can still play," she said, staring down at them.

"When's the last time you sat at a piano?" Gerda plugged in the iron she had just obtained on the black market and set up a wooden plank.

"Just before surrender. I played my last lesson for my teacher. He was a cellist but taught piano. It was the night before his last concert with the Berlin Philharmonic, the evening of April 12."

"I was at that concert." Startled, Erika turned to see Wilhelm in the doorway. "In the Beethoven Hall. They played Brückner's Fourth Symphony."

"And the finale from *Götterdämmerung*," Erika added. "I'm sure it was deliberate, too, since the Russians were just days away."

Wilhelm stepped inside the room, edging past the clutter of Gerda's belongings and those of the German refugees, who for the moment were out clearing rubble. "People are playing concerts again in Berlin. I plan to audition tomorrow for a chamber orchestra that needs a violin. If they accept me, we'll perform for food, whatever people can bring. You could try auditioning, too."

She glanced down at her swollen fingers. "Not with these. I need another job that doesn't hurt my hands so much. Then I'd have a chance."

"I've heard a lot's going on over at Gatow. The Brits are expanding their runway and are hiring civilian help. It's hard physical work, but maybe not as bad for hands as masonry."

"Really? Gatow? But that's in the British sector."

"If we can get work, I'd be willing to move there," Gerda said. "I'm tired of hearing people argue all day and night, and stepping over sleeping bodies just to get into this apartment."

"I would too, but where would we live?" Erika had no loyalty to the tiny room and few belongings to transport. But were things any better elsewhere?

"I have a cousin who lives in Moabit and works at Gatow. He and his wife lost their son in Poland last year and have managed to keep the room a secret, at least so far, but the housing authorities will find it sooner or later. I know he'd rather put us up in his apartment than total strangers from the East. All we have to do is ask."

❖

Gerda made the journey to Moabit to settle the arrangement, and a week later she and Erika officially relocated, registering in the British sector.

It was an easy move, for Erika had bartered away her possessions and had little left of value. She sold her paltry kitchenware and the odd piece of furniture for cigarettes on the black market and left her mattress to the refugees. When her remaining belongings could fit into two large suitcases dragged on a child's wagon, she started off with Gerda, first by S-Bahn and then by foot.

Moabit was an industrial and working-class district that Erika had long associated with German communism, though its reputation did not spare it from shelling and confiscation of its factory machinery by the victorious Russians.

"The apartment's in the Lübeckerstrasse," Gerda announced as they emerged from the S-Bahn near the Lehrter Station, and Erika was relieved to see the street had held up well. The facades were pitted from small-arms fire from the final days of the war, and everywhere windows were broken and blocked with cardboard or wood, but the walls and roofs had held.

"Your cousin, was he a communist?"

"Heinrich? Heavens, no. But he wasn't a Nazi either. His son was in the Wehrmacht. He kept out of politics and even managed to get into the Luftwaffe."

"Luftwaffe? Really? You never mentioned that."

"Just a mechanic. The only inside of a plane he saw was its engine. Probably what kept him alive through the war. That and being captured by the West."

"I see Moabit's prison's still intact." Erika gestured with her head in the direction of the Lehrter Strasse.

"Yes. Heinrich said the Allies are using it now to hold Nazis until they're tried. Ah, here we are." She stopped in front of a dark apartment building, where ragged children played, and put her shoulder against the entry door. Inside, the corridor was dark, but open, glassless windows on every landing allowed daylight into the stairwell.

Gerda stopped on the third floor and knocked. A man, who Erika presumed was Heinrich, opened the door immediately, and the smell of cooking potatoes as they stepped inside reminded her how hungry she was.

"Heinrich Dehmler," he said, offering his hand. He was fiftyish, with a mane of black hair long enough to curl around his ears. She guessed it was a way to disassociate himself from the severe officers' cut of the Luftwaffe, a look that would be a distinct liability now. A red scar sliced through his right eyebrow, and she wondered if it was a shrapnel wound or an injury from the job. In spite of his lean frame, his hands were well muscled, and his grip, when they shook hands, was warm and comforting. "Please come sit down. My wife's making lunch for us. We thought you'd be hungry."

Unusual hospitality in a city that hungered, and Erika was grateful. "How very thoughtful of you," she said, glancing around the apartment. It was spare, with well-worn furniture of no particular style. A cabinet held a row of books and photos of both Heinrich and his son in their uniforms. The only odd thing was a rope that stretched from a nail in the front doorjamb, across the living room, to a similar hook on the jamb of the kitchen door.

"My wife Charlotte does laundry and mending for the RAF,"

he explained. "It brings in a little more food. At the moment, it's all soaking in the bathtub."

Erika and Gerda set down their suitcases by the door and took a seat on the somewhat dilapidated sofa. "I'm grateful you can accommodate us," Erika said, "and of course we'll add to the household as soon as possible."

Heinrich raised a hand gently to reassure her. "Gerda has already told me you're hard workers, so I'm sure we'll manage."

At that moment, Charlotte came from the kitchen. She bore a slight resemblance to Gerda, though perhaps all malnourished fiftyish women looked the same, but her large eyes had a kindness to them. "Hello and welcome, both of you. Now please come to the table." She set down a bowl of steaming potatoes. "Our butter ration is used up, and we haven't seen meat in weeks, but I've been growing onions on the window ledge, and they're very good fried in lard."

Heinrich pulled out chairs for his two guests, while Charlotte served the potatoes and onions in four equal portions. Erika forced herself to wait for her hostess to sit down before putting the first exquisite spoonful in her mouth.

No one spoke at first, savoring the warm, high-calorie food, and when their plates were clean the conversation began.

"I see you have electricity," Gerda observed.

"In the apartments, yes," Charlotte said. "We got it back a few weeks ago. But the wiring in the corridor is damaged, and no one's been able to repair it. We have water now too, so we live in the lap of luxury."

"What about gas and heating?"

"No gas," Heinrich lamented. "We managed to lay our hands on a small coal stove and set it up in the kitchen, though it means we have to collect coal every week. Last winter, we were almost never out of the kitchen except to sleep. And then, we had to wear our overcoats."

With pleasantries out of the way, Gerda got to the point. "The last time we spoke, you said you could help us get hired on at the airport. Is that still true?"

"Yes, and you came at the right time, though I don't know if it's the sort of employment you want. Gatow is expanding its runway, and they're looking for able-bodied men and women to lay the asphalt. It's a filthy, hard job."

"As long as it's not laying bricks," Erika said. "It can't be too bad to work for the RAF, can it?"

"They pay a few marks a day, but most importantly, you get a hot meal for your labor. The alternative is to stay here and help Charlotte with the laundry for the airmen. But it's for cigarettes and candy, and it doesn't amount to much."

Erika shook her head. "Let's try first for a real job, for real pay."

"All right, then. I'll introduce you to the officer in charge. But you have to convince him you'll learn English."

"That won't be difficult. I want to do that anyhow."

"I have just the thing for you to start." Charlotte rose from the table and rummaged through a cabinet nearby. A few moments later, she dropped a pile of materials in front of Erika. "After you've worked your way through these, you'll be masters of the language."

Erika picked up one book after the other. "*A Bilingual Manuel for Repair of the Dakota C 47*. Hmm. Perhaps we'll save that one for last. *Manifesto of the Communist Party* in English, and a children's book, *See Spot Run*." She held up the last one and chuckled. "I think I'll start with this one."

"Good choice," Heinrich said. "I got that from an American at Tempelhof." He glanced toward the window that, though covered with wooden planks, revealed a dark sky through its cracks. "Well, it's getting late, so let me show you your room."

Taking up one of their suitcases, he led them along a short corridor with a large wardrobe. Scratches on the floor suggested it had been used to conceal the door and had recently been shoved to the side. Heinrich led them into a room of a good size for a child, less so for two adults, but that was better than four, as they'd been in the Adlerstrasse apartment.

A single bed stood along one wall, and at its foot was a somewhat threadbare sofa on short wooden feet. Next to it a narrow night table supported a lamp, the only light in the room. A simple pine wardrobe stood opposite the bed, and in a corner was a tiny sink.

"I don't mind taking the sofa," Erika volunteered, and Gerda looked relieved.

Heinrich closed the door behind him while they hung as much of their clothing as would fit into the wardrobe. The suitcases, still half filled, fit under the bed.

It was a luxury to be able to wash from a sink with running water. That it was cold made no difference. They could heat some on the stove for a real bath later in the week, and they were already used to the shortage of soap.

Erika kicked off her shoes, and by the light of the sofa lamp, she glanced again through their English homework. "Guess we'd better begin with this." She opened the child's book with its colored illustrations of children and animals. "'See Spot run,' said Jane," she read.

Gerda joined her on the sofa. "'See Spot run to zeh new house,'" she pronounced laboriously.

"'Come home, Spot,' said Dick," Erika replied, snickering.

"'Come, Spot, come. Come home,'" Gerda said. "My goodness. English is so easy!"

Giggling, they read through the entire chapter, repeating the phrases until they could recite them from memory. After the last run-through, Erika called a halt.

Gerda retreated to her side of the room, and Erika curled up on the moderately comfortable sofa. In just a few minutes she fell asleep, dreaming of a small dog running across the wide expanse of an airfield.

❖

The next morning, after a breakfast of ersatz coffee and plain bread, Heinrich led them to the military bus that carried workers to Gatow. All along the route, they continued to chant the tale of Spot and the house in their awkward new English.

At the airport, Heinrich introduced them to the officer in charge of labor recruitment. As it turned out, he didn't care what language they spoke, as long as they understood him.

"The job's laying asphalt," he said, barely looking up from his work. "The construction gang works from eight to six, with an hour off for lunch. You're paid at the end of each week. If you're interested, sign here and report to the construction foreman in the fourth Nissen hut. He'll tell you what to do."

Heinrich translated the information, oversaw their signing, and escorted them to the construction boss in the hut. Abandoning them to their ten English phrases, he hurried off to report for his own job in the mechanics' shed.

The foreman provided Erika and Gerda with heavy gloves and led them out onto the field, where work was already under way. Several dozen workers, almost all women, were following a mechanized scoop that evened the ground that had been dug out from the turf. The strip looked some hundred meters wide and ran parallel to the current runway, with a strip of green between them.

After miming what they had to do, and explaining something in an English they didn't understand, the foreman handed Erika and Gerda shovels and pointed them toward the other workers.

The labor was intensive, and even if they had wanted to talk among themselves, they would have had to shout over the roar of airplanes, either taking off or landing on the runway next to them.

They spent that day and the weeks that followed digging out the ground, building a gradation toward one side for drainage, and leveling the surface. When they had completed a given portion of the strip, a tractor came behind them dragging a huge drum roller back and forth over the soft soil to compact it. Working in such sections, the gang laid out a strip of compacted soil running the length of the current runway.

At the end of June, lorries arrived with crushed rock, which Erika learned was simply the fragmented bricks from all the destroyed streets and houses of Berlin. When they'd filled the entire strip to the depth of some ten inches, the tractor and drum arrived again to compact this layer as well.

They spent most of August pouring the asphalt, layer by layer, and raking it flat, then raising it slightly above the surrounding soil level so no rain could collect.

Every night they returned to the Moabit apartment filthy with grime and asphalt. Charlotte, who always seemed to be mending or knitting when they came through the door, never failed to have a steaming kettle and a tin laundry tub waiting in the kitchen. The boiling water, added to the cold water in the tub, provided a warm—if shallow—bath. And every morning and evening, they practiced English, graduating from Spot's adventures to Karl Marx's manifesto.

❖

The hot meal Erika enjoyed each noon was the high point of the day. It did her good, adding enough weight to her gaunt form to let her once again look her thirty-three years, rather than a decade older.

At the end of August, after a morning of hard labor, she tucked her gloves into her belt and strode toward the workers' end of the canteen for her meal. She tugged off her head scarf and ran her fingers through her moist hair. It had grown almost to shoulder length, and in the summer sun, the ends had gone blond again.

At the entrance to the canteen she halted suddenly. A WAAF was just coming toward her, and she also stopped. For an embarrassing moment, they stared at each other, puzzled.

"I know you," the WAAF said.

Erika smiled, remembering. "Yes. You have my airplane."

The other woman grinned back. "So I do. Well, it's my airplane now. I bought it, after all."

"For your son?" Erika was pleased to be able to use her English.

"No, for me. I used to be a pilot."

"A pilot?" Erika repeated. "Oh, very fine!" It was the only adjective she could think of. She hadn't yet learned many superlatives. But the WAAF seem satisfied with their level of conversation and in no hurry to leave.

"I didn't recognize you at first. Your hair has grown out. It looks better."

"Thank you," Erika said, draping a strand of it nervously over her ear. Strange to have a woman she didn't know comment on her hair. But very pleasing.

The woman glanced down at the heavy leather gloves and the sooty apron. "So, you work here?"

"Yes, now. On the runway. But soon we finish. I hope for a job in the canteen." She patted dust and grit from the front of her apron. "More clean."

"Well, I'll put in a good word for you. But you have to tell me your name."

"Erika. Erika Brandt. Thank you. A good word to help is very fine." She frowned at the inadequacy of her vocabulary. Surely she knew other phrases that would impress this attractive stranger. Only one thing came into her head.

"The workers of the world unite. We have nothing to lose but our chains."

The WAAF gave a wonderful warm laugh. "Ah, someone's been reading the *Communist Manifesto*."

"Yes. You know this book? Very fine." Damn, she needed to learn more adjectives right away.

"I do, but I haven't read it since my school days." The WAAF glanced back over her shoulder. "Well, my friend is waiting, so I should go now."

"You work here?" Erika hadn't learned the word for "stationed."

"No. Just visiting. I fly here from time to time with a pilot friend."

"I understand. But…your name. What is your name?"

"Gillian Somerville." She held out her hand, and Erika took it. A wave of pleasure rushed through her in the few scant seconds of their connection. Then the woman named Gillian turned and strode through a doorway and out of sight.

❖

Whether it was due to Gillian's word, or to the fact that she simply had seniority, Erika did not know. But in the middle of October, just as the weather made working on the tarmac a torment, Erika received notice that she had a position as food server in the Gatow sergeants' mess.

The October air was already bitter cold, and now the thought of being in a warm place and around food all day made her almost dizzy.

She gradually learned her way around the little bit of Britain that was the air base, distinguishing between the sergeants' and the officers' messes, as well as the functions of NAAFI—the service personnel's meeting spot and snack bar—and the American PX. She even discovered the Malcolm Club, a double Nissen hut on the apron of the airfield that was Gatow's tamer answer to the Berlin nightclubs.

It would have been pleasant to have Gerda's company on this job, too, but Gerda had found romance. Against all odds, she'd met and been courted by Fritz, a German Tempelhof mechanic twenty years older. After a month of back-and-forth, she found work at the American airfield and moved in with him.

The day Gerda had packed her things to leave the Moabit apartment, she teased Erika, saying, "Why don't you find yourself a nice British airman? You're good-looking, and now you know English. I bet you're just what those lonely boys are hungering for."

"I know, and I recognize that hunger. It's the same one the Russians had. The RAF boys are just politer about it."

Gerda tied a rope around her bulging suitcase and dragged it to the door. Together, they bumped it down the stairs to the front of the building. "What's wrong with using your best asset? Your husband died in 1940. Don't you miss sleeping with a man?"

At that moment, Fritz arrived from the tram stop and shook hands with Erika. Possibly in his sixties, or perhaps just beaten down by the war and prison camps, he was stooped. His grizzled face was friendly, but deeply lined, and he was missing all but his eight front teeth. His nails were black, worse than Heinrich's, and his handshake loose.

"Have it your own way, dear," Gerda said over her shoulder and slid her suitcase toward him. Turning back, she reached into her pocket. "Here's the address of Fritz's apartment, so if you need anything, you can find us." She pressed a folded paper into Erika's hand and gave her a warm hug.

❖

In spite of the "no-fraternization" regulation, Erika found male attention constant. One pilot was particularly persistent, a handsome blond fellow who, after several passing compliments about her English, her figure, her hair, finally introduced himself.

"Hello, lovely lady," he said one evening right after she'd finished work. He held out his hand. "Jack Higgins. And you are…?"

"Thank you. Um, Erika Brandt." She offered her hand in return, and he held it while he spoke.

"Just want you to know what a great job you're doing. Allow me to thank you on behalf of the RAF."

She smiled and nodded. She'd already thanked him; what else could she say?

"You know there's a nice club on the Kurfürstendamm, called Rio Rita. Candlelight, small band, a little dance floor. Some of the girls go there with the airmen. Perhaps you might consider joining me some evening."

She withdrew her hand. "Thank you for the invitation, but I don't think so."

His eyes twinkled. "You should talk to the other girls. They'll tell you it's jolly good fun. Just a bit of dancing. I bet it's been years since you did that with a chap. Promise me you'll think about it?"

She smiled ambiguously and walked away.

# CHAPTER SEVEN

*October 1946*

Gillian peered into the radar screen, tracing the movement of the bright dot. "Covey," she said into her microphone, using the call sign for the Airspeed Oxford eight-seater. "Covey 95. Bückeburg Ground here. Do you read? Go ahead."

A voice came back though the crackling. "Covey 95, read you fine, Bückeburg. At four thousand feet, inbound for landing. Go ahead."

Even through the interference, she recognized his voice and smiled.

"Covey 95. Aircraft ahead of you has priority. Circle at Angels three. Go ahead." She knew he understood the slang for 3,000 feet. "MOAY 7 is two miles ahead at one o'clock. Do you have visual? Go ahead."

"Bückeburg ground, descending to Angels three. Waiting for clearance. I see traffic. Go ahead."

She addressed the first incoming plane. "MOAY-7. Permission granted to approach. Winds are at one zero at five, altimeter two eight point nine four. Cleared straight in. Go ahead."

"Bückeburg ground, approaching at 1,000. Go ahead."

"MOAY 7. All clear."

She guided him down through the next several steps, until she heard the satisfying declaration. "Bückeburg, MOAY 7, on the ground." Then she returned her attention to the little eight-seater. "Covey 95, descend to 1,000. Prepare for landing. Winds are at one zero at five, altimeter two eight point nine four. Cleared straight in. Go ahead."

"Bückeburg ground. Anyone behind me? Go ahead," the pilot said.

"No. You're clear. Go ahead."

"Yes, landing now. When do you get off work? Go ahead."

She laughed out loud at the warm voice of Nigel Katz breaking radio protocol. Fortunately, no other plane was coming in that needed her instructions.

"Six o'clock," she said without using any call signs. "Over."

"Good. Jack's with me. We'll do dinner."

"Shall I call Betsy? She's free after six, too."

A long moment of silence followed, and it sounded like the pilot covered his mouthpiece to speak to someone next to him. But then he came back. "Yeah, sure. That's fine. Over."

Jack glanced around the sergeants' mess from the corner that Gillian had claimed for them. "It never gets any better," he said, lighting up a cigarette.

"Don't be so picky, old chap." Nigel raised his glass. "Me? I'm just happy to be among friends."

The others saluted back. While they all took their first swallows, Gillian glanced sideward at Nigel and felt a real warmth toward him. Over the course of the year, they'd become good friends, yet he'd never made an advance. Just as well. In spite of his pretty eyes, she felt no interest in intimacy with him. Did that apply to all men or only to the socially awkward Nigel Katz?

"So the flight report says you came from Nuremberg," she said. "Something to do with the trials?"

"Yes. We ferried in the last of the British photographers. The tribunal's done with its deliberations, and word is the verdicts and sentences could come any time."

Betsy's expression grew serious. "I hope the Nazi gobshites all get what they deserve."

Jack blew smoke out of the side of his mouth and looked bored. "Gobshites or not, the trials are simply 'victors' justice.' After all, the Russians committed many of the same atrocities the Germans did. Not to mention what we did in Dresden."

Betsy frowned. "I don't agree. Crimes are still crimes. And the Germans started the whole thing. Everything else was defensive."

"However you look at it," Gillian said, "I'm just glad they tried Goering for what his men did to London in '40. I want to see him hang."

Jack tapped the ash off his cigarette. "Everyone wants to see him hang. But some people are still calling the trials a 'high-grade lynching party.'"

Nigel shrugged. "There's some truth in that. It's no secret that the Allies themselves are guilty of plunder and killing civilians, the things we're prosecuting the Germans for. The Russians should be in the dock, too."

The background noise of the mess hall suddenly grew louder as two men scuttled in carrying a radio. "Listen up, chaps," one of them said, placing it on a table close to an outlet. He plugged it in and tuned it for a moment, then found the news frequency.

An announcer was partway through a list of names. "Karl Dönitz, guilty. Ten years. Hans Frank, guilty. Death. Hans Fritzsche, acquitted. Rudolf Hess, guilty. Life. Alfred Jodl, guilty. Death. Franz von Pappen, acquitted. Joachim von Rippentrop, guilty. Death. Hermann Goering, guilty. Death."

After that, Gillian stopped listening. Goering was all she cared about. The remaining names were just dull sounds in the background while she savored a cold satisfaction. Unfortunately, hanging was a far more merciful death than burning.

"When will the executions take place?" That was all she wanted to know.

❖

Nigel and Jack flew out again two hours later, and Gillian and Betsy resumed their shifts. At the end of the day, they met at the bicycle shed. "It's nice seeing the lads again, isn't it?" Gillian said.

Betsy bent to unlock her bicycle. "I think Jack fancies me."

"Really?" Gillian draped her security chain over her shoulder. "I thought he was rather a canteen cowboy."

"No. He's deeper than that," Betsy protested as they walked their bikes onto the paved road. "He shows off around women because, basically, he's shy and covers it up with big talk. But you know, word's going around that Gatow needs people. If I transferred, he'd see a lot more of me, and things could develop."

"You're going to ask for a transfer in the faint hope Jack Higgins will notice you? Crikey, Betsy. You can do better than that."

"Don't be silly. I wouldn't go just for him. Berlin is just more of an adventure than this place. As long as I'm in Germany, I'd be a fool not to want to go where the excitement is. Why don't you apply, too?"

"I've been wanting to be posted to Berlin, but I'll be up for promotion in a few months. I'll apply to join you after I get it."

"Well, when the time comes, I'll be the first to introduce you around to all the airmen."

❖

The day of execution of the Nuremberg convicts, Gillian reported for work. While two controllers manned the ground-control trailer for incoming planes, she joined the others gathered around the radio that still stood in the mess hall.

"Alfred Jodl, Ernst Kaltenbrunner, Alfred Rosenberg, Julius Streicher…" There were too many names, and midway through the list, she turned away. She might have savored the moment of execution of Hermann Goering, but he'd chosen the coward's way out with suicide. Now the thought of one man after another stepping forward wearing the noose, the imagined sounds of the platform dropping away, and the snap of each neck breaking—all of it suddenly made her sick.

The tribunal, she knew, would go on trying the lesser offenders, the lackeys and enablers and profiteers, in the coming months, but she was done with it.

As she was about to leave the mess, a young airman stepped in front of her. "Corporal Somerville? You are ordered to report to Wing Commander Horwick's office."

"Any idea why?" she asked as she followed him down the corridor and did a brief internal review of her recent work performance. She could find no fault.

"None whatever." He knocked, opened the door to the commander's office, and stepped out of the way.

Gillian entered, saluted smartly, and stood at attention. "Corporal Somerville reporting, sir."

"As you were, Corporal." Horwick thumbed through what looked like a two-page report, then glanced up. "Flight Sergeant Jones reports that on September 22 and again on October 4 you brought in several planes under extreme conditions, and that he has regularly asked you to take the leadership."

"Yes, sir. Flight Sergeant Jones is a good teacher."

"I'm glad to hear it. In any case, as of today, on his recommendation, I'm promoting you to the rank of sergeant. You'll have it in writing later today, and you can go immediately to pick up your new stripe." He held out his hand. "Congratulations."

The handshake done, she saluted again, stifling a sudden urge to click her heels. At his "dismissed" she pivoted toward the still-open door and marched away. But just outside the office, she came to a sudden halt to avoid a collision.

"Oh, Mrs. Horwick, excuse me," she said, attempting to circle around her.

"That's quite all right. And you are?" The commander's Betty Grable–esque wife bent forward to read the name tag on her uniform shirt. "Corporal Somerville."

Gillian grinned. "Sergeant, actually. As of one minute ago."

"Well, congratulations, dear. Aren't you the one who brought in that old Luftwaffe uniform a few months ago?" Without waiting for an answer, she rambled on. "So many lovely young women on the base. It always makes me proud when one of you rises in rank. We've certainly waited long enough."

"Thank you, ma'am," Gillian replied mechanically, puzzling slightly over the "we."

"Well, crack on, my dear," Jean Horwick said, patting her on the shoulder. "Hope to see you again some time. Ta-ta." Rocking slightly on her high platform shoes, she passed on into the commander's office and closed the door behind her.

Her head still swimming from the hanging of ten men, followed by her promotion, Gillian hurried on to the GCA trailer to do her job.

❖

The winter of 1946 was even colder than the year before, and December brought snow, to no one's surprise. In spite of the long bicycle ride in her greatcoat, scarf, and hat, and the need to wear her wellies, Gillian didn't mind. The landscape, which had looked so dreary in the October and November rains, was now enchanting. On the first snowy morning, she left her billet early.

Midway through the woods, she stopped and stood in what seemed like total silence, but for the faint hissing of the snow. It was serene, but it would have been nicer if Betsy were there, or Nigel. Or even the sultry blond woman who worked on the runway in Berlin. What was her name? Erika something.

Well, the new runway would be covered by snow now. Had the friendly word to the food-service officer helped her get a job in the kitchen? Gillian smiled inwardly. Why did she care about a total stranger, one who'd only a short time ago had been her enemy?

She sighed. In the tranquil purity of the new snow, the war seemed very long ago.

The aerodrome was also covered in white, though a team of workers was already shoveling one of the runways. Gillian locked her bike under the shed and turned toward the main building. At that moment, the commander's Austin 16 pulled up to the entrance, and Colonel Horwick stepped out from the passenger side.

She saluted him, and he flicked a casual salute back before stepping through the fresh snow toward the building, leaving deep footprints behind him.

"Hello there!" A cheerful voice rang brightly in the cold air. "It's Sergeant Somerville, isn't it?"

"Oh, Mrs. Horwick, good morning," Gillian replied, brushing snow off her shoulders. "Good Christmas weather, isn't it?"

"It certainly is, and since you mention it, I'd like to invite you to the officers' Christmas Eve party. It will be at Bückeburg Castle."

"That's very kind of you, ma'am, but isn't that only for the commissioned officers?"

"Not this year, dear. I've just decided that the most interesting people are the non-coms. And since I'm in charge of organizing it, I'll make whatever rules I want. So, you'll come, Sergeant?"

"It will be a pleasure, ma'am."

"Jolly good." The commander's wife drove off, splattering wet snow from her rear tires.

❖

On Christmas Eve 1946, the melted and refrozen snow crunched under Gillian's feet as she marched beside Jones into the castle grounds.

The entrance to Bückeburg Castle was through a magnificent red granite archway, topped by what looked like two stone griffins snarling at each other. Between them a male figure stood, who she presumed was one of the forefathers of the dynasty that owned the castle.

Once they'd passed through the archway, they reached a bridge that spanned a small lake, its surface chalky from a thin covering of ice. The castle itself was less theatrical, a central tower in yellow stone, with wings on each side attaching to outbuildings that circled the courtyard in a partial embrace. The main entrance was under a portico with four rounded columns.

A young airman acting as butler took their coats and led them to the *Festsaal* of the castle, where the party was under way. Gillian stepped in, then halted, awestruck.

The entire great hall was clad in pink marble, which provided a warm background to the heavy Baroque ornamentation. Six rounded alcoves flanked the hall on both sides, separated by Corinthian columns and topped by a gallery of recessed windows, each one fronted with a wrought-iron interior balcony. The tall bays drew her eyes upward to the painted ceiling, with its trompe l'oeil vision of angels, cherubs, and the undersides of rearing horses. Three massive chandeliers provided the festive lighting.

"Pretty impressive, eh?" Jones said, handing her a glass of punch from a passing waiter.

She nodded, speechless.

"I'm going to circulate," he added. "So you're on your own."

She nodded again and, sipping her punch, also began to meander through the crowd.

She paused to make small talk with a few acquaintances, though the many voices ricocheting off the hard surfaces made it difficult to talk without shouting. Then she spotted a familiar face and elbowed toward him.

"Jack, old scoundrel. You didn't tell me you were back in Bad Eilsen. Merry Christmas." She tapped her glass against his.

"Just popped in today, obviously when you weren't on duty scanning the skies." He sipped his punch and glanced up at the ceiling. "Posh place, isn't it? This is what the German aristocracy gets up to."

She shrugged. "No worse than ours. At least they let us have it for our RAF Germany headquarters."

"They'd damn well better. We did win the war, after all."

Gillian changed the subject. "Where'd you just come in from? You're not still ferrying people from Nuremberg, are you?"

"No. This time it was from Gatow. Always lots of traffic going in and out."

"How are things in Berlin these days?"

"Rather tense, I'd say. The Allied Control Council is a cock-up since the Russians see everything as a tug-of-war between us and them over the German spoils. All they've been able to agree on is three air corridors between Berlin and the West, and it's down in black and white."

"Corridors? Where from and how large?"

"Not very, only twenty miles wide. The southern corridor is from Frankfurt, the central one from Hanover, and the northern one from Hamburg."

"And you're the one bringing all the generals and politicians together to talk about it. You've been a busy fellow."

He ran his hand over his wavy, blond hair that no grown man deserved to have. "Not so busy that I haven't had time to socialize a bit." He puckered his lips, suggesting a risqué meaning to "socialize."

"You really are a cad, aren't you? Have you and Betsy been misbehaving?"

"Betsy?" He frowned. "Good heavens, no. Don't know where you got *that* idea. No. I've been courting a lovely German woman. Blond, intense."

"A German woman? Not enough WAAFs for you to flirt with?"

"Don't take it personally, Gillian, dear, but for me, WAAFs are a bit, well, stodgy. You know the men call them 'lumpy jumpers,' don't you? The German women, well…All their men are gone, so they're hungry for male attention. This one works in the canteen and has a nicer figure than the bony ones you see in Berlin."

Canteen? Was he talking about Erika? She glanced away for a moment so he couldn't see her dismay. Had he set his sights on the sweet woman from the airfield? Well, it was none of her business.

"Oh, there you are!" Gillian turned to see the station commander's wife approaching. Dressed in a tight forest-green skirt and a bright-red sweater, she gave the men another reason for Christmas cheer. Yet she didn't seem to notice.

"Have you seen the rest of the castle?" she asked, and her slightly giddy speech suggested she was well ahead of them on the punch.

"No, ma'am." Jack answered for them both.

"Well then, let me have the pleasure of showing you around." She grasped them by their elbows and drew them on both sides of her into a corridor.

Away from the noisy crowd, the castle was more mysterious. The family paintings had been removed, but the ornate walls still impressed, and the shortage of electrical current meant everything was in subdued light.

Dark passages branched off the corridor, and she led them along a labyrinthine route, down stone steps, then up again along a winding stairwell with tiny windows at intervals in the wall. The odor of damp stone mixed oddly with Jean Horwick's perfume.

They stopped, finally, by a wide oak door, and Jean swung it open. "Here we are, the magnificent Bückeburg Chapel." The three of them stepped in and gawked silently.

The pink marble of the Festsaal appeared again in the central platform, and so too did the series of bays, this time in gold. A carved green and gold frieze connected them with a row of golden swags. Suspended over their heads, an extravagantly carved and gilded pulpit was borne aloft by a gilt angel. Directly in front of them, an elaborately sculpted tabletop, supported on the backs of two nymphs, held a massive Bible.

"Gold, gold, and more gold," Gillian murmured. "Unbelievable."

"I'll say." Jack snorted. "Seems excessive to me. It needs toning down a bit."

Gillian glanced over at him. "You're joking, aren't you? Baroque is excess itself. If you tone it down, you're left with...um...basic church."

Jean took a step toward the roped-off marble platform. "I rather like excess. Life is short, and beautiful things are rare." She glanced meaningfully back at Gillian. "I want as much of it as I can have."

"That part I can agree with," Jack conceded. "But isn't all this worldly glitter the opposite of piety? Why have a chapel if not for piety?"

"Piety?" Now Jean snorted. "This chapel is to piety as the Festsaal is to a little get-together with friends. I suspect the people who built it weren't pious, but they knew how to have a good time."

Jack turned toward the door. "Speaking of a good time, shouldn't we return to the party? Before the punch runs out?"

"Right you are, Lieutenant." Jean touched Gillian lightly on the back, urging her away from the angels, and led them silently back to the celebration.

Reemerging in the great hall, Gillian thanked Jean for the tour and resumed her meandering, sipping punch, and wondering at the puzzle that was Jean Horwick.

Later she caught glimpses of her guide standing statuesque and silent beside her husband. The woman who an hour before had been so ebullient now seemed to fade into the background. Gillian shrugged to herself. Perhaps the nature of marriage to a commanding officer was to be ornamental.

But at the end of the evening, as Gillian was beginning to feel the effects of her fourth glass of punch, Jean Horwick suddenly stood in front of her again.

"Do you have a long way to go to get home?"

"Not so far. I have a billet with a family in Bückeburg, so it's just about fifteen minutes by bicycle. It's a lot farther from the base, though."

"Oh, dear. What do you do when you've got night duty? Do you have to ride your bike all the way to Bückeburg in the dark? That's terrible."

"Well, sometimes it's a stretch, but I'm a soldier, aren't I? If that's the worst I have to suffer..."

Jean Horwick was frowning. "You shouldn't have to suffer it at all. When's the next time you have late-night duty?"

"I volunteered to cover December 31 to let the others go out and celebrate. But as long as I'm warmly dressed, I don't mind. Keeps me fit."

The commander's wife laid a hand on her forearm. "Nonsense. On New Year's Eve especially, with drunken airman mucking about. I won't hear of it. I'm not partying either, so I'll stop by the base at midnight and pick you up. We'll put your bicycle in the back, and I'll have you back at your billet in no time."

"I...uh..." The offer was very unmilitary, but there was no regulation against it. "That's very kind of you. I accept."

"Well, then. That's settled." With a quick nod that could have meant several things, she turned and strode away.

In the meantime, Jack had been monopolizing the attention of a young WAAF who stared up at him in adoration. But he seemed to have grown bored and wandered back to Gillian.

"I'm headed to Berlin tomorrow morning. If you're off duty, you can hitch a ride again. I always like the company."

"Gosh, thanks. I'd love to go, but this time I *do* have duty. But please don't stop asking me. One time out of three I'm off duty, and I like the company, too." She realized it was true. She disapproved of him, his arrogance, and his cavalier way with women. But he treated her like a sister, and he was worth a good laugh from time to time. And a ride to Berlin was not to be taken lightly.

At ten o'clock, people began to trickle from the hall across the plaza and over the bridge. Gillian, too, requested her coat, and as she was drawing it on, Wg. Cdr. Horwick strode past her, his wife two steps behind.

Jean Horwick slowed and raised a hand to say good night. "Don't forget, New Year's Eve. I'll be waiting."

❖

The station commander's wife was as good as her word. And a good thing she was, since snow had been falling for over an hour, and pedaling a bicycle would have been difficult in the two inches that had accumulated.

The sleek, black Austin 16 was waiting right at the entrance to the base, and Gillian had to admit she quite enjoyed being escorted.

Catching sight of her, Jean stepped out and opened the rear door, and together they hoisted Gillian's bike into the rear. Then, before speaking, they climbed into the warmth of the car front.

Jean leaned toward the window and tilted her wrist to catch the light from the streetlamp on her watch. "It's only eleven fifty. You got off work early?"

"Yes. No more flights are scheduled tonight, and Flt. Sgt. Jones took the graveyard shift. Everyone else is on the ground, drinking. He'll just doze at his console with the earphones on, and the slightest noise will wake him up."

"Oh, jolly good. So, you can enjoy your own little New Year's celebration."

"Celebration?"

"You'll see."

Jean started the car and swung out of the base onto the main road. She drove at normal speed along the empty road, the wipers swishing back and forth across the windscreen. But once they entered the woods, she slowed, pulled to the side, and stopped.

"Is something wrong?" Gillian asked.

"No. Not at all. This is simply our New Year's celebration." She leaned across Gillian, popped open the glove department, and withdrew a small flat bottle.

"Sorry it's not champagne, but my husband would have noticed if I'd taken one of his precious collection. We'll have to settle for schnapps." She unscrewed the top and drew two shot glasses from the glove department as well. Holding them both in one hand, she filled them from the bottle and handed over one of them.

"Happy New Year 1947, Gillian," she said, and downed her drink in a single swallow.

"Happy New Year." Gillian swallowed hers in the same way, gagging slightly as the alcohol scalded its way down her throat. While she coughed, the little glass disappeared from her hand and returned a moment later, refilled.

"Come on, dear. We've got some catching up to do." She raised Gillian's hand until the glass was once again at her lips.

*Well, why not?* It was, after all, New Year's Eve, and everyone Gillian knew was getting drunk at just that moment. She was off duty and could do anything she wanted. She downed the second glass, and it burned slightly less than the first one.

"Ready for a third?" Jean held the half-empty schnapps bottle over her glass.

"Yes. I am." Gillian felt a bit light-headed, and correspondingly brave, even if her lips were becoming rather numb. "So, isn't Commander Horwick celebrating this evening?"

Jean snorted. "I expect he is, though I don't know which one of his birds he's doing it with tonight."

"Oh, I'm sorry. I shouldn't have asked."

"No. It's all right. We have our modus vivendi. At this point, I'm just as happy to not have him pawing at me." She took another drink, her third as well, but there seemed to be more left in the flask.

"So, do you have a gentleman friend? That handsome blond fellow you were with at the party, for example?"

"Heavens no. He's just my mate. I'm not in his league at all. He likes women with more..." She gestured with one hand under her breast.

"They're all alike, aren't they? They have one single thought, well, two, but both of them involve our body parts." Jean distributed the last of the schnapps between them. "Although to be fair, they also think of flying."

Gillian was giddy now. "Yeah, they jolly well do, but do you think those blokes would let us women do any of that? Not even an ex-pilot who's flown hundreds of hours, all over Britain and Europe. Noooo. It's all willy-waving for them, and they don't want to admit a woman can do it just as well. Well, they can just bugger off."

Jean shifted onto one hip so that she faced Gillian directly, and with her closer hand, she brushed Gillian's hair back over her ear. "Well, aren't *you* the little spitfire. But I couldn't agree more, my dear. We'd all be much better off sticking with each other and letting them see how long they can go without us, if you know what I mean."

The three and a half glasses of schnapps were definitely doing their work now. Gillian could order her thoughts, just not her speech muscles. She rubbed her mouth to prepare to say something.

"If you mean withhold our favors, I'm all for that. But unfortunately, no one's asked for my favors in quite a long time."

"Silly sods don't know what they're missing." She leaned in close. "Why don't you show me what you've got?"

"Huh?" The proximity of Jean's mouth was puzzling but not unpleasant. Her perfume now was masked by the smell of alcohol, though Gillian was certain she exuded the same aroma. But she had no idea what to do next.

"I mean a kiss for New Year's. Good luck, solidarity, all that." Without waiting for an answer, she closed the distance between them and covered Gillian's mouth with hers.

In the frigid air of the car, Jean's mouth was wonderfully warm, though closing her eyes made Gillian a bit dizzy. She remained passive, surrendering, and felt the sudden, surprising surge of arousal. She waited for the kiss to end, to ask, perhaps, what it meant, since it seemed a bit too intimate for a New Year's greeting.

But it didn't end, not for long minutes, and instead grew in intensity. In the midst of it, Jean's hand slid under her skirt and along the inside of her knee to the bottom of her knickers. Gillian recoiled and broke away with a gasp.

"No, please, don't…"

Jean released her. "Oh, I'm sorry." She clasped her hands together as if to restrain the one with the other. "It was just…New Year's… the schnapps. I'm sorry," she repeated. "You won't say anything, will you?"

"No. Of course not. It's all right. I understand. But maybe you can drive me home now." Gillian pressed her thighs together to stop the throbbing.

Jean started the motor again, and the car moved forward. "This will be our little secret, then."

"Of course. Don't worry," Gillian reassured her, though her head spun from the alcohol, and her heart still pounded from the kiss. Her only thought was to be home, in her bed, where she could figure it all out.

Neither spoke for the last ten minutes of the trip, and when the car pulled up in front of Gillian's billet, Jean helped her haul the bicycle from the rear. "Are we all right, then?" she asked tentatively.

Gillian avoided eye contact but said, "Yes, we're all right. Thank you for the ride." Without looking back, she wheeled her bicycle the rest of the way to the bike stand in front of the Schneider house. As she fumbled for her key, the car pulled away, its tires crunching on snow.

❖

Through the remainder of January, Jean Horwick made no appearance at the aerodrome, and if she picked up her husband from work, she did it while Gillian was elsewhere.

But Gillian thought of her constantly. And the new obsession caused her to postpone her plan to apply for a transfer to Berlin.

It was not so much the woman who haunted her, but the memory of the rush of excitement of being touched. Nothing had ever felt like that before, and certainly not the clumsy grappling of the boys she'd snogged with. The mixed feelings she'd experienced right after the kiss only sharpened with time: regret that she'd stopped the hand before it had crept farther, longing to experience the wicked thrill again, guilt and fear of desiring such a thing in the first place.

She'd continued to ride her bicycle home from the base, day and night, and the hard-packed snow did make pedaling somewhat easier. As before, every Friday night, she worked the six-to-midnight stand-by shift.

Abruptly, on a night in March, the black Austin 16 was there again. Gillian remained at a distance for a few minutes, thinking it might be waiting for the commander. But no. She was sure he'd left the aerodrome hours before. Cautiously, she ventured out.

The car door opened, and Jean Horwick climbed out, bent toward the rear door, and opened it. "Bring the bike," she commanded.

Gillian obeyed, lifting it into the rear of the car as she'd done two months before, then hurried around to the passenger side to let herself in. She was barely seated when they started up and swung onto the main road.

"How've you been?" Jean asked casually.

"Fine, thank you. Busy." Should she ask the same thing? Personnel weren't supposed to be interested in the wives of their commanders. But they weren't supposed to kiss them either. She decided on silence.

Jean continued driving until they reached the same spot they'd stopped at once before, a skirt of hard soil at the side of the road. She turned off the headlights and turned toward Gillian.

"At New Year's, when we were here, you didn't push me away. At least not immediately. I know I took you by surprise, but I had the impression you were…well…receptive."

"I…uh…I don't remember." It was a stupid reply, but she felt like she was in deep water and uncertain how to swim. "I'd never…been kissed like that."

"But you liked it, didn't you? I think you did." The leather upholstery creaked as Jean slid closer. "It's nice to be kissed like that, isn't it?"

"Yes, I suppose." Gillian's heart was pounding, the hot tension she'd felt at New Year's returned, and this time she recognized it. Yes, it was nice to be kissed that way. Still, she was paralyzed with fear.

"It's all right," Jean whispered, sliding one hand along Gillian's back and caressing her check with the other. "Such a sweet young thing," she murmured against Gillian's cheek, pressing little kisses and inching forward toward her mouth.

Gillian surrendered to her, letting her head drop back and moaning as the insistent tongue invaded her. A cunning hand caressed her breast, then dropped to between her knees and creeped insidiously up her thigh under her woolen knickers.

She was soaking wet and beyond caring as the relentless fingers entered her. Jean's touch, expert though it was, aroused her less than the sheer wickedness of what they did, for it was three times forbidden: furtive, adulterous, and perverse. A demon took possession of her, and she totally forgot herself as the fiendish invasion drove her to her first orgasm.

For the remainder of March, and all through April and May, the commander's wife continued to give Gillian "rides" every Friday night at midnight, always stopping at the same spot. By the fourth tryst, Gillian learned the skill herself and reciprocated, always in the cramped confines of the front seat of the Austin 16, her bicycle in the rear.

They spoke little; they had nothing to say to each other. Only once, Gillian ventured a question. "Doesn't your husband suspect anything?"

"He's far too sure of himself. Besides, on Friday nights, he visits a young lady, a WAAF like yourself, and doesn't come in until about two. I always make it home before he does."

Gillian had winced in the dark. Bad enough that she crept away at night to practice these dark arts, but the thought that it was common, that people in high positions regularly amused themselves with the younger staff, made their erotic adventure seem simply shabby.

But she couldn't stop. She had discovered lust, and now it held her captive, setting up a tension at the beginning of each week that demanded to be relieved on Friday night.

Then, one night in May, the black Austin 16 wasn't there. Gillian waited with her bicycle for fifteen minutes, then realized it was futile, and she pedaled home.

What had happened? Would Jean explain the following week? But the next week, she wasn't there again, and Gillian grasped it was all over.

Gillian arrived at the aerodrome each day, fearing confrontation, court martial, and dismissal. Jean Horwick drank too much and too often and couldn't keep the secret forever. Gillian had to leave before it got that far.

The next time Nigel flew in, she sat down with him in the mess. "I'd like to apply for a transfer to Berlin. Can you help me make the case that Gatow needs more controllers?"

Nigel chuckled. "Scopies? My dear, *all* the aerodromes need scopies. And you can thank President Truman for that. With the Marshall Plan in place, lots of money is moving around Germany, which means much more traffic in and out of Berlin. Are you sure you don't want to go to Wunstorf, Celle, or Fassberg, though? Nicer accommodations."

Gillian shook her head. "No. It has to be Berlin. I made a promise. Family honor, after all."

❖

Whether it was Nigel's influence with someone in the Gatow brass, or its pressing need for "scopies," or Wg. Cdr. Horwick's sudden desire to be rid of her, Gillian didn't care. Within a week, the application had moved through the chain of command and been approved.

The next morning, Gillian arrived at the Bückeburg terminal, suitcase and kit bag in hand. The kit bag held her other uniform, pyjamas, and regulation underwear, and the suitcase bulged with books, toiletries, and her wooden airplane. She'd said her good-byes to Jones and the others, and now she waited while Nigel's Dakota was checked and refueled for takeoff.

As she stood watching the mechanics work around the plane, a flash of color caught her eye, and she turned to see Jean Horwick a few yards away. She was with the commander and another airman, but glanced over her shoulder at Gillian. Their eyes met, but Jean's remained expressionless, and after a moment, she turned back to speak to her two companions.

*So, that's how it is. No interest, no regrets. I was her amusement, her revenge, and then I became inconvenient.* She shrugged inwardly. *Well, I have no regrets either.*

Maliciously, she wondered if the commander had also wearied of his Friday-night girlfriend?

Nigel was suddenly at her side. "Ready to go?"

"Never more ready." She hefted her kit bag and her suitcase and strode toward the plane without looking back.

# CHAPTER EIGHT

*May 1947*

Everyone called it the *Hungerwinter*, the hardest winter in memory. Erika learned that a half dozen elderly people in the Lübeckerstrasse had frozen to death in their own beds, and if she multiplied that number by every district in Berlin, the count was appalling. Rations were at starvation levels, and the bitter cold damaged much of what had been planted in the vegetable patches. Worst of all, there was no coal.

*But I've made it through.* Erika stared at herself in the mirror. Her hair had long ago grown out from Wilhelm's boy-cut, and the regular hot meal at the aerodrome had spared her the death's-head look of so many she saw in the street. Like Berlin itself, she hungered all the time but could sense herself climbing out of the abyss. And now, after almost a year working at Gatow, she spoke tolerable English.

As she emerged from her room, Charlotte called out from the kitchen. "Come have coffee while it's hot."

The coffee, of course, was ersatz, but they'd all grown accustomed to it. Erika joined Charlotte and Heinrich hovering near the stove and warmed her hands on the porcelain cup.

"Oh, sorry." Charlotte set down her cup. "I forgot to give you this." She fetched something from her knitting basket and handed it to Erika. "A young lad brought it for you yesterday, while you were working. I forgot about it."

Erika unfolded the paper. "It's from Magda, one of the women Gerda and I shared a room with in the Adlerstrasse. She has pneumonia and is asking me for help. The Russians will treat her, but only if she brings her own penicillin."

Heinrich shook his head. "She'll have to get it on the black market and pay a fortune for it."

Erika slid the note into her own pocket. "That's why she's asking for money. Or cigarettes to barter if I can get some."

"How do you plan to do that?"

"I don't know." Erika buttoned her coat and started for the door. "I'll think of something."

❖

After months of washing floors, counters, and then dishes, Erika had been promoted to serving the line of airmen who moved past her with their metal trays. The cuisine changed from day to day, within the limits of wartime availability, but the sergeant in charge of the kitchen said it was essentially what people "at home" ate. To her, the tinned meat or bacon, the cheese sandwiches, meat pies, and parsnip gravy over mashed potatoes seemed luxurious, and while she served it to the passing diners, her stomach always hurt until the moment came when she could take her own meal.

Today the menu consisted of cheese sandwiches and split-pea soup with chunks of Spam. Dessert was bread pudding, something she'd not tasted in years.

The bread was baked locally, but the cheese, called "national cheddar," was imported in blocks from the UK, and the Spam came from the United States. The smell of real coffee was dizzying, and she was allowed a cup of it each day.

"Well, well. You've been promoted to the line. Congratulations!" It was the blond airman who had invited her to a Berlin nightclub.

"Thank you. Much better than working on the runway."

"I'll bet it is. Plus, instead of overalls, you get to wear a nice dress that shows off your figure." He tilted his head. "I like your hair, too. Didn't see it under your work kerchief. Bet you get a lot of wolf whistles?"

"Wolf…?"

Before he could explain, the airman next to him shoved him along. "Come on, get a move on, eh? You're holding up the line."

Jack winked at her. "I'll be back, sweetheart. Don't run away with anyone else." He slid his tray along the counter toward his comrades.

The crowd thinned out after half an hour, and she was finally able to step away from the counter with her precious cup of RAF coffee, whitened with powdered milk. While she sipped at it, relishing the complicated coffee taste, she brooded on Magda's crisis. How could she help her? What did penicillin cost, anyhow?

"Finally, I've caught you off duty." She turned, surprised. It was the blond airman. She smiled, still not certain how she felt about him. "Only for a few minutes. I have to wash the dishes."

"Well, if you're on a break, can I offer you a cigarette?" He held out a pack of Players. A sudden memory emerged, of another airman, exchanging Players for her model airplane. And the woman he bought it for. Gillian. Her name was Gillian. She had reddish-brown hair.

"The cigarette. Would you like one?" He was waving the pack in front of her face.

"Oh, yes, thank you." She drew one out with her fingertips. When he'd dropped the flat box into his jacket pocket, he produced a lighter. A click and the flame flickered between them.

"Um. I don't smoke."

"Why'd you take the cigarette, then?"

"You offered it. I can exchange it for something later. If you don't mind."

"Ah, yes. It's like I've given you money. Well, if that's the way it is, how about I offer you even more for a kiss?" The cigarette box appeared again in his hand.

He was smiling boyishly, but it was the grin of the conqueror. She understood what was going on, and she hated it. It was prostitution in miniature. She took a breath, about to tell him that he was insulting her. But, dear God, even half a pack could still buy a lot on the black market if one traded wisely. Not penicillin, but maybe real coffee, or soap. It was more valuable than her pride.

"All right. But give me the cigarettes first."

His laughter was lewd, but he handed them to her, then slid his hand around her back, pulled her to him, and pressed his mouth hard on hers. His tongue shot into her mouth, and she could do nothing about it. Behind him, his comrades cheered.

❖

Hanno came at eight, and Erika admitted him, offering him a seat. "My gosh. You're so much taller now. I almost didn't recognize you."

She didn't add that he also looked dangerously thin, worse than he'd been in the first days of the Russian invasion. More like an old man than a twelve-year-old.

"Well, it's been a few months," he said softly. "Did you get my note?"

"Yes, and I'm so sorry to hear about your mother. I'd like to help buy the penicillin, but I don't know how much I can give. My job pays so little."

"Gerda and Wilhelm are helping, too. Anything you have that we can offer on the market. But it has to be soon. She has trouble breathing."

"I have this." Erika drew the box of Players cigarettes from her pocket and was ashamed when she caught the drop of Hanno's expression. "I'm so sorry. I don't know how to get more."

Heinrich laid a hand on Hanno's shoulder. "How many packs do you need?"

Hanno shrugged, revealing bony shoulders under his thin jacket. "I can't say. I have to make a deal. But at least twenty more of these."

"Hmm. Well, we have friends at Gatow who can buy things at their NAAFI shop. We can try to get a few more. Not twenty, though."

Hanno seemed defeated. "All right. I'll come back tomorrow and see what you've got." He backed toward the door.

"We'll scrape together what we can," Heinrich said, guiding him from the apartment. As he closed the door, he glanced back at Erika. "I hope you've got some good ideas, because I certainly don't."

Erika stared at the floor. "Maybe...I do."

❖

"Twenty packs of cigarettes?" Jack was aghast. "Just to go out with me? I can buy only two a day, even if I agreed."

Erika didn't reply. It was a purely commercial transaction, and she was aware how weak her bargaining position was. All depended on how badly he wanted her company and what he thought he could get from her in return. She wasn't sure herself what she was willing to give him.

Jack let his glance slide down her body and return to her eyes. "I could try to round some up, if my mates agree to help out. But that's a lot to ask. That would come with some...expectations. An evening at the nightclub, dancing, and...uh...whatever that might lead to."

"Yes, all right." She agreed hastily, not looking at him. "But could you have them by the end of tomorrow? They're to buy penicillin for a friend. She has pneumonia."

"You drive a hard bargain. But in the meantime, as a show of good faith…" He pulled her to him again, and she submitted patiently to the same kind of kiss he'd forced on her the day before. When he stepped back, she winced a smile.

"At the end of the day tomorrow?"

"I'll see what I can do."

At the end of the next day, when Erika went to her locker, her supervisor handed her a cloth sack. "Someone left this here for you. There's a note attached."

Erika could feel by the lumps that the sack contained the promised cigarettes, and she knew without counting there would be twenty. She tore open the sealed envelope and read the note.

*Meet me at the aerodrome entrance Sunday at 19:00. I know
you don't work on Sunday, and I'm off duty. Jack Higgins.*

Jack Higgins, so that was his name. Erika wasn't sure whether to be relieved or appalled. She was happy to try to save Magda's life, but now she'd have to spend an evening with a man who was expecting sexual favors. It was Major Koslov all over again.

Later that evening, when she handed over the bounty of cigarettes, Hanno embraced her tearfully. "I think it's enough," he said, his still-soprano voice cracking. "Wilhelm and I will go this evening to the Reichstag and make the purchase. I'll come back in a few days to tell you how she's doing." He embraced her again. "I can't tell you…"

Erika was moved to see a boy so young taking on a task many men would fail at. But Hanno had always been adult beyond his age. She touched his face lightly. "Just take good care of her and keep me informed. I can't make it this Sunday, but the Sunday after that I'll be free, and I'll come to see her."

The next few days kept her in the back of the kitchen, cooking and washing, and it was just as well. She couldn't bear to face Jack and his leering friends. How did he convince them to give him their tobacco rations? Did he promise they'd also have a chance with her? Was she going to be passed around like she'd been with the Russians? She hated them and she hated herself.

❖

On Sunday, she washed and fixed her hair as well as possible with a minute bit of soap, and as agreed, she waited in the evening at the entrance of the aerodrome. Mercifully, it wasn't raining and he appeared on time, in a jeep he'd somehow obtained. He was in top spirits, of course, and helped her into the passenger seat in a cavalier fashion.

The Rio Rita was on the Kurfûrstendamm, in one of the buildings that had survived Allied bombing. A three-piece band was playing something lively as he led her in, lightly brushing his hand across her back, and she flinched. Strange. She'd half liked him when they were just bantering in the mess, but now that she knew what he was expecting, his touch made her skin crawl.

The lights were dim, and every table seemed occupied. But when the waiter approached them, Jack pulled out a thick wad of German marks and peeled off several large bills. With a faint bow, the waiter led them to a table at the side, where two German men in civilian clothes sat. He shooed them away and pulled out a chair for Erika.

"What'll you have?" Jack asked. "They have cocktails, schnapps, brandy, or lemonade. I wouldn't trust the schnapps, though. It's locally made."

"I'll have lemonade," Erika said, gazing around the dimly lit room. Servicemen from all four armies were visible, though the majority were GIs and Tommies. The dance floor was full of couples doing a restrained jitterbug for lack of space.

The waiter returned with their lemonades, and Jack paid with another large note of German marks, receiving no change.

"Lemonade seems very expensive," she remarked.

"Everything is expensive here, but it's all in marks, so who cares? There's plenty more where these came from." He held up his wad of bills.

"How did you get so much?"

"Same way you did, by selling cigarettes on the black market."

She bristled. "I didn't sell them. I gave them to a friend, who exchanged them for penicillin."

He tapped his glass against hers. "Cheers," he said, then took a sip. "Well, whatever you did, it amounts to the same thing. Black-market deals. You can get bloody rich that way, assuming you have something to start with."

"And you do. Or you can get them from the NAAFI shop."

"Yes, indeed. Cigarettes, sugar, coffee. And if you get pound notes from home, you can exchange them for up to a thousand marks each. Trouble is, you have to spend it all here. The marks are useless anywhere else."

He reached inside his jacket and pulled out a silver flask. "Not that I care about paying, mind you, but I don't trust the liquor here. Too much is made in the bathtub. But this baby's from good old Blightly." He unscrewed the top and poured a generous portion into both of their glasses.

He continued talking while she sipped. "You know, I like you a lot and think you're really pretty. I don't want to just pay you for an evening now and then. I think we could have a good thing, you and me, over a long term. It's lonely work flying back and forth all over the country, and it'd be smashing if we could meet up when I'm in Berlin. I know someone with an apartment. We could go there and relax, be on our own. You could live well, help out your sick friends." He took her hand.

"I...uh—"

"'Scuse me." A GI stood in front of their table, rocking slightly. "I hope y'done mind, but I'ze just noticing whata lovely lady you are." He blinked slowly and licked his lips as if speaking had dried them out.

Jack raised a hand. "Move on, soldier. The lady's with me."

Ignoring him, the GI slid onto a chair on the other side of Erika. "You letting this Tommie take care of you? Just because you losta war?"

He frowned, forming a new, complex thought. "Doan gemme wrong. I got nothin' against the Brits. They got beautiful women, like you." He peered at her through half-open eyes and smiled crookedly, as if smitten. "But you can do better'n him."

Jack leaned across Erika and spoke into the GI's face. "The lady is just fine and does not want your attentions. Now move away, or I'll call an MP."

The GI seemed unimpressed but licked his lips again and spoke directly to Erika. "What's he offering, anyhow? Bet it's cigarettes. It's all the Krauts want. Well, you want cigarettes? I've got cigarettes."

He reached inside his jacket, pulled out an entire unopened carton of Chesterfields, and slammed it down on the table top in front of Erika.

She glanced down hungrily. A full carton. Twenty packs of Chesterfields. Worth three times as much as the Players she'd negotiated. Suddenly she was filled with revulsion, not only for the drunken GI, but for both men who were haggling over her body. She hated them, all of them—British, Americans, Russians—for what they'd made of her.

But before she could speak, Jack stood up, swung around the table, and seized the GI by his jacket. "I said move on, Yank." He jerked him up to a standing position. "Plenty of women to give your cigarettes to. Just not mine."

The band had stopped playing, and everyone nearby was watching the altercation. Even the two Russians stood up and wandered over.

Erika slid her chair back, alarmed, and looked around at the other women. Did they mind being bought and fought over? If so, they were silent.

"Get your fuckin' hands offa me, you limey fag," the GI snarled, knocking open Jack's grip. "I'll punch your lights out."

One of the Russian men apparently understood a little English and raised a hand. "Hey, Yank. Take easy. You go and everything good."

"Thisiz nonayo business," he shouted back, unsteady on his feet, and the waiter, who had joined them, reached out to take him by the arm.

"Come on, soldier. No more liquor for you."

"What the hell? Four against one? Notta chance!" He bent forward, lifted his pant leg, and pulled a revolver from his sock.

Soldiers and their dates within sight of the table recoiled, and when he fired a shot into the air, pandemonium broke out. Erika bolted from the table and ran for the exit, not caring whether Jack followed her. She was well ahead of him as they emerged from the club, and two MPs ran toward them.

"Hold it!" one of them shouted to Jack, seeing his uniform, but apparently no one cared about her. She kept on running, clutching her jacket around her shoulders, down the ghostly canyons of the Kurfürstendamm.

Once safely away from the club, she stopped, breathless. What was she going to do now? They'd come in a jeep, and Moabit was almost three kilometers away. It was nearly midnight. No buses or trams were running, and the streets were full of thieves and marauders.

On foot, she was far less safe in the savage, rubble-strewn streets than she was at the club, even with the wild gunfire.

She cringed when she saw three figures coming toward her and looked for a place to hide until they passed. She stepped into a doorway of a gutted building, hoping they hadn't spotted her.

But as they approached, she recognized one of them and broke into tears.

# CHAPTER NINE

*May 1947*

Even with its new airstrip, Gillian found Gatow Airfield unimpressive, and she felt no particular excitement when she landed with Nigel to begin her new duty. But it was, after all, Berlin, and if she'd had a goal beyond flying, reaching Berlin was it. Besides, she'd see more of Nigel and Betsy, who were the closest thing she had to family.

Betsy met them in the terminal and greeted them with a hug. "Welcome to our oasis. Did the Russians give you any trouble as you flew over their zone?"

"No. We kept to the corridor," Nigel said. "The weather was a bit bumpy, but nothing to worry about. So, here she is, our girl, with kit and caboodle."

"Smashing. So, when do you have to report in?"

"Tomorrow morning to the WAAF station commander."

"That's Flight Lieutenant Parsons. She's a right sort," Betsy said. "When I asked to transfer from my room to yours, she approved my request with no questions."

"Oh, no!" Gillian feigned horror.

"So I'm stuck with you again," and Betsy's elbow jab showed she got the sarcasm. "Jolly good you've got the day free to settle in. C'mon. I'll take you to quarters." She linked arms with Gillian. "I even organized a bicycle for you."

The barrack was a sturdy brick building with an entrance door that opened to another door, leaving an air space between the two.

"Nice feature," Gillian remarked. "Good way to keep out the cold."

"Not only that, but we have central heating," Betsy boasted. "No more charcoal burners in the middle of a bloody Nissen hut."

"Righto! How's the food?"

"Standard, all made from powder, just like before. The Americans get much better, I hear. But the messes are open twenty-four hours a day, since the crews come in at all hours. If you want something fancy, you can buy it yourself at the NAAFI. They also have an American PX and a Malcolm Club, so you never run out of places to go when you're off duty. It's to keep us from going into Berlin, I think."

Gillian hung up her spare uniform in her new locker and deposited her books and miscellanea in her footlocker while Betsy leaned in the doorway. "So, how do you like working here? Are you glad you made the transfer?"

Betsy's mouth twisted sideways. "Frankly, it's been a disappointment."

"Really? In what way?"

"In every way. First of all, they have no repair hangar. Gatow does only emergency repair so the aircraft can go back to its base. All of our work is outdoors, under a tarp or cover shed when it's raining, so we're wet and freezing all the time. Our crew room is just a hut at the end of the apron, with a spring bed that doesn't even have a mattress."

Gillian patted her on the shoulder. "I'm sorry to hear it, old thing. Have you at least gotten to know Jack Higgins better?"

Betsy raised a hand as if to cut off speech. "Sod Jack Higgins. Let's not talk about him, if you don't mind."

"Sure, but—" Betsy's glare cut her off.

"What time do you have to report for duty?" she continued in a new direction.

"Tomorrow at ten. They gave me twenty-four hours' leave."

"Smashing! I'm off duty at eight, and Nigel's next flight is tomorrow morning. I'll get him to organize a jeep, and we'll pick you up, say, a little after eight. Wear your civvies."

"A celebration, for me? Things are already looking up."

❖

As promised, Betsy's bike rolled up to the barrack at eight fifteen, and soon thereafter, Nigel pulled up in a jeep.

"So, where are we headed?" Gillian asked as the two of them climbed in.

"Place called Tabasco. Just a couple of smoky rooms on the ground floor of a bombed-out building, but they have a piano, and it's less noisy than the other joints."

"Well, then, onward and upward!"

As promised, the club was intimate, subdued, and cloudy with cigarette smoke. When they entered, the pianist, an emaciated old man, had just finished playing "Over the Rainbow." As they sat down and ordered their beers, several more American songs followed. "I'm in the Mood for Love," "Tea for Two," "Tumbling Tumbleweeds," "Smoke Gets in Your Eyes." Some of the clientele knew the words and sang along.

To his credit, the pianist played tunes from all four cultures. After the American show tunes, he banged out "La Vie en Rose" and, for the few Russian patrons, "Katyusha." It was pleasing to see the effect the music had on the soldiers from all four armies, eliciting an apparent basic human instinct to sing or hum along.

The last tune of the set was a song that everyone in Europe seemed to know. The German pianist began to sing *"Vor der Kaserne, vor dem grossen Tor…"* but after just a few words, his audience joined in. At the neighboring table Gillian heard, *"La vielle laterne soudain s'allume la nuit,"* while she murmured in English, "Darling, I remember, the way you used to wait." From a corner, two soldiers, a man and a woman, added their rendition of the same song in Russian.

It was intoxicating, far more than the beer, to join voices with old enemies and allies in the universally known "Lili Marlene," and to suspend national loyalties for a moment celebrating a soldier's love. "So, what happened to the 'no fraternizing' regulation?" Gillian asked Nigel.

He snorted. "Defeated by human nature. Berlin hungers, not just for food and warmth, but for all the other things people need to do, like make bread, music, love."

"And deals," Gillian added, recalling her plane purchase. "Look how fast the black market developed. Commerce just happens as soon as people have something to exchange."

Nigel shook his head. "Well, that one's gotten out of hand and is really corrupting the men. They purchase supplies from the NAAFI shop and sell them at a hundredfold profit, either to Germans, who are desperate for them, or to the Russians. Then they use the German marks to buy up jewels, silver, other things of value and send them home courtesy of the military. Or they ask their families to send a few British pounds and live like kings. It's a dirty business."

He drained his glass. "That should all come to a halt once we manage a currency change and get rid of the old mark. But the Russians are holding that process up for reasons known only to them. So, the market goes on. Like the fraternization."

"What about you?" Gillian glanced back and forth at both of them. "Have you broken the rules?" She jabbed Betsy gently with her shoulder. "I bet you have, you wild thing."

"No, nothing serious. A few cigarettes for gloves last winter. As for fraternizing, well, that's not something for a WAAF, is it? I mean, what sort of German blokes are around, anyhow? I don't know what Nigel's been doing on the sly, though." She laughed.

Nigel scratched the edge of his jaw. "Guess I'm not the fraternizing type. But what about you, Gillian? After a year in service, have you... uh...broken rules with anyone?"

The image of Jean Horwick flashed into her mind. "Uh...no. I'm just another one of His Majesty's stalwart soldiers."

The pianist left his piano and disappeared into the other room, and at that moment the two Russian officers came over to their table. "This is first time for nightclub for us," the male said in passable English. "Is possible to talk a little bit?"

"Uh, certainly," Nigel replied, and gestured toward two empty chairs. "Please sit down."

The male offered his hand. "Senior Lieutenant Vassily Miranov," he said, and the woman followed. "Lieutenant Olga Petrova."

Nigel took the lead in introductions. "I'm Flight Lieutenant Nigel Katz, and these are Sergeant Somerville and Corporal Geary."

"Is nice to talk to 'other side' sometimes, no?" Olga remarked.

"I thought we were on the same side," Betsy said.

Olga Petrova crossed her arms. "Officially, yes. I begin war as sniper and shoot same enemy you shoot. But now, with occupation, is not so clear. We have different philosophy, I think."

Nigel offered the guests cigarettes and they accepted, lighting them from handsome Zippo lighters.

Vassily exhaled smoke and inspected the cigarette. "Much better than Russian cigarette, is true."

"Are you allowed to smoke capitalist cigarettes?" Nigel teased.

Vassily went with the joke. "Is our little secret. But after New Order, when workers own production, all tobacco will be good."

It was a rare opportunity to talk to Soviets, and Gillian searched for something better to talk about. "How is it you speak English?" she asked.

Vassily brightened and seemed pleased to be asked. "I was teacher of English for one year before war. But is easy to forget, and I like to practice."

"You speak very well," she lied, but it was the standard polite response. She changed the subject. "Now that the war's over, do you have family waiting for you at home?"

Vassily replied first. "No. Military is my family. I come with first troops to liberate Germany. I was successful and have promotions. For now, new German political parties are my children."

"And you?" Gillian turned to Olga. She studied the peasant-like face with the hint of hauteur that contradicted it.

"I have son. He lives with my mother," she replied neutrally. "But now I am assistant to Marshal Zhukov in Soviet Military Administration, and Germany future is more important than play with children."

Nigel tapped his cigarette ash into the glass tray. "Political parties, hmm. You have your work cut out for you. It can't be easy finding candidates who were not Nazis. Of course, you want the parties to be communist."

"Germans are free to form parties as they choose. But we encourage workers to vote in own interests, of course."

Olga crossed her arms again as if in defiance of something, though it wasn't evident what. She spoke to Gillian. "And you? Why is RAF still here? You expect to fight again?"

Gillian smiled. The question was only half in humor. "I certainly hope not. But let's be frank. We all belong to huge forces, competing like two lions over a fresh antelope carcass. We both growl at each other over who gets to eat what."

Olga finally allowed herself a grin, an expression that changed her whole face. "More like capitalist lion and communist tiger. Siberian tiger, who wants to share carcass with all workers."

"But what about the German workers? Aren't they part of the 'workers of the world'?" Nigel asked.

"They are, but first must pay for damage they caused by following fascist leaders. Russia must rebuild entire industries Germany destroyed."

Gillian was about to reply that the destruction was mutual, when the pianist began "La Marseillaise." Two men in French uniforms rose from their table and held a salute through the entire song. They sat down, finally, just as "The Stars and Stripes Forever" began, and a dozen or so GIs shot to their feet. When the Soviet anthem came, Olga and Vassily would not be outdone and stood up to sing "Slav'sya, Otechestvo," Vassily's rich bass voice dominating the entire room.

The pianist saved "God Save the King" for last, and another table of Tommies and their ladies joined in. At its conclusion, the waiter announced in English, German, and French that the club was closing.

Nigel glanced at his watch. "Oh, bloody hell. It's almost midnight."

Vassily and Olga shook hands energetically with their new friends, but after they departed Nigel announced, "Well, I, for one, am not ready to call it a night. What d'ya say we carry on? The Rio Rita's not far from here."

Betsy stood up and saluted. "Well then, chocks away, lads!"

They bundled out to the street, emerging from the light and warmth of the club into the grotesque dark canyons. Gillian shuddered and gripped Betsy's arm. The clubs, sordid as they might be, were pockets of life in a landscape of death.

They were marching arm in arm, softly singing the famous lines of "Lili Marlene," when Nigel brought them all to a halt. "Look over there in the doorway, some woman. Dangerous place to be alone."

"A prostitute, probably," Betsy ventured.

"Not likely. No business out here." They continued walking until the woman came within clear sight.

Then it was Gillian who stopped. "That's someone from the base," she said, and suddenly recalled the name. "Erika Brandt. What's she doing out here at this hour?"

A few moments later she stood before them, visibly distraught. "Oh, I'm so glad to see you."

Gillian laid a comforting hand on her shoulder. "What happened?"

"Fighting. In the club. Guns. The police came and I ran away, but now I have to walk all the way to Moabit." She was still wringing her hands.

"No, no. It's all right," Gillian said spontaneously. "We'll give you a ride. We have a jeep." She turned to Nigel. "We can do that, can't we?"

Nigel blinked for a second, then nodded. "Of course we can. We're parked by the Tabasco, just up the street."

Making a protective circle around the hapless Erika, they returned to the jeep and followed her directions to the Lübeckerstrasse.

"So, this is where you live?" Gillian asked, glancing around at the houses on the deserted street, dark but largely intact.

"Yes, with friends. They both work for the base. Charlotte does laundry and Heinrich is a mechanic."

"Heinrich. Big bloke, thick mane of hair, scar over his eyebrow?" Betsy asked.

Erika nodded.

"I've seen him working on the planes with the other Germans. Well then, she's legit."

Erika climbed out of the jeep. "Thank you so much for rescuing me. I don't know how I—"

Nigel raised a dismissive hand. "It was nothing. But you never told us how you got to the Kurfürstendamm in the first place."

"With an airman, but he got into a fight with a GI. Over me. When the police came, I ran away. Will I be in trouble?"

"I shouldn't think so," Nigel said. "But who was the airman? What was his name? It was shameful for him to abandon you."

Erika hesitated a moment. "Really, I abandoned him. His name was Jack Higgins. A nice man, I think, but he wanted from me...more than I wanted to give." She shook hands with everyone and hurried toward the building entrance.

In the jeep, Nigel and Gillian sat, momentarily speechless. Betsy, however, muttered, "That bastard."

❖

Gillian reported to Flt. Lt. Parsons's office at ten, as ordered, in spite of a slight hangover.

After seeing the uninspiring, low block buildings of the airfield, she had few expectations, but she was surprised to discover how modern the equipment and facilities were. Not only did Gatow have two runways, but it was also equipped with high-frequency and VHF air/ground communication, directional finders, blind-approach beacons, and runway lighting, much of it brand new.

Flt. Lt. Phylis "Pip" Parsons had a commanding presence, but not an intimidating one. She was tall and, like most of the officers, spoke with a marked upper-class accent. Her cool manner seemed appropriate to leadership, but a pleasant, feminine face offset the severity she projected. She introduced Gillian to the two other controllers, one an

RAF sergeant and the other a WAAF like herself. Both were engaged and so only smiled up at her between radio communications.

As on her first day at Bückeburg, no one bothered with social courtesies. Parsons simply gestured toward the console where the WAAF controller sat. "All right, Sergeant Somerville. We've got fog coming in over the airfield. Let's see if you know your onions."

The other WAAF controller had waited until she'd just finished bringing one plane in and her radar screen showed another approaching. She handed over her headphones to Gillian, who, with a simple nod, set them on and slid into place.

"Gatow ground here. I see you," Gillian said. "Please identify, go ahead."

The pilot of the incoming craft gave his call sign. "VH-CXD-22 to Gatow ground. I'm at 1,000 feet and flying blind right. Could use assistance coming in. Go ahead."

"VH-22, you're now approaching the airfield at a heading of 279." She slid her chair a foot to the side in front of the glide-path screen. "You're a little high on the flight path. Increase rate of descent. Repeat, increase rate of descent. Go ahead."

"Gatow ground, increasing rate of descent. Go ahead."

She watched the meters that measured the craft's parameters. "VH-22, you're at 500 feet and on flight path now. Engage landing gear. Go ahead."

"Gatow ground, can't see a bloody thing. Flying on your voice alone. Go ahead."

"VH-22, not to worry. You're spot on course now, right on center line at 300 feet. Go ahead."

She watched the light that was the aircraft move along the glide path smoothly, well within the parameters required, while the pilot repeated each instruction she gave to ensure understanding.

Finally, she nodded with satisfaction. "VH-22, you are approaching end of the runway at 100 feet right in the cone. Maintain rate of descent. Go ahead."

"Gatow ground, we can see the runway lights now. Looking good. Go ahead."

"VH-22, you're almost down. Tarmac just below you. Begin braking now. Go ahead."

"Gatow ground, we've touched down. Thanks for the help. Await instructions for ground direction. Go ahead."

"You're welcome, VH-22. Watch for lorry with 'Follow me' sign and follow to hangar. Over and out."

She slid back to the larger radar screen, pleased with herself, only to see another plane coming in, and the dialogue started all over again.

The job was fatiguing, but in the course of the day, she brought in a dozen more aircraft, most of them though heavy fog. When her relief arrived, sliding onto her seat and slipping on her headset, she stretched her shoulders, noting how stiff she'd become from hunching over her microphone. But she'd acquitted herself well, and she knew Flt. Lt. Parsons had taken note of it.

Rubbing circulation back into her arms, she realized suddenly how hungry she was, and ten minutes later, she was at the sergeants' mess. At the off hour, it was surprisingly underpopulated.

"Can I get anything to eat?" she asked a German civilian wiping off a table. "I've just worked the longest day of my life."

"I'm sure we can find something, Sergeant," the man said, and disappeared into the kitchen.

A few moments later, a woman emerged from the kitchen carrying a tray with two steaming bowls of soup, and she was Erika Brandt.

"We're just between shifts now, and I've asked if I can take my supper break. Is it all right if I join you?"

"I'd love it." Gillian nodded toward the nearest table, where they sat down. "Cheers," she said, noting it was Spam and noodles, and both began to eat. After eight hours sitting in a cold trailer, she found the soup heavenly.

Finally, she shoved her empty bowl to the side. "Is everything all right after last night? You got enough sleep and made it to work on time?"

"Oh yes. I was on time. But my visit to the club was a mistake, and I have to pay for it."

"Pay for it? What do you mean?"

"The airman who asked me, Lieutenant Higgins, gave me twenty packs of cigarettes, you see," she said. "I gave them to a friend to buy penicillin. But Lieutenant Higgins gave them only if I agreed to go to the club. And let him...you know. But at the club, when the men are fighting for me, I hated them, and I hated me that I am a toy they both want to buy. So, I ran away."

Gillian nodded sympathetically. "You did the right thing."

"Yes, but Lieutenant Higgins came this morning and demanded cigarettes back."

"I see. And you can't afford to buy that many at once. What did he threaten if you didn't come up with the cigarettes immediately?"

"He tell my boss I steal from him, and I lose my job..."

"That's plain blackmail! Well, the next time you see him, you can tell him to sod off. I'll have a word with your boss myself, and what's more, I'll report him to his commander for abuse."

Erika's lovely brow wrinkled in distress. "But the cigarettes. I must to give him the cigarettes."

"Don't worry about that. Each person can buy two packs a day. Between Nigel, Betsy, and me, that's six already. We just need to do that for three days, and you've got eighteen."

"Then I must repay you." Erika snickered. "Or I belong to you."

Gillian's face warmed. "No one belongs to anyone. Some day you can return the favor."

Erika brightened suddenly. "I can return a favor now. Do you like music? I mean with...*Kammerkapelle*? I don't know this word in English."

"Chamber orchestra. Yes, I do. Though I haven't been to a concert in ages."

Erika leaned forward on her elbows, beaming. "Then I have a... chamber orchestra...to show you." She pronounced the new word carefully.

"You have an orchestra? You're a musician?" What other surprises did this woman have?

"Yes, I am a musician, but my hands are still bad from work. Only my friends play now. But, soon." She flexed her fingers, as if to test them. "I play piano. Chopin, Schubert, Brahms."

Gillian was astonished. And delighted. "When is this chamber concert? I have to apply for a pass, you know."

"Next Sunday. In the afternoon. While trams still run. You must work?"

"Yes, I do, but from two in the morning until noon. I should be able to get a pass for the afternoon."

"Very fine." They stood up and carried their trays to the kitchen door, where Erika took them. She smiled with great warmth, as if something wonderful had happened.

Gillian rode her bike away from the aerodrome as happy as she'd been for many months. She'd had a successful day, a hot dinner, and now a concert rendezvous with an interesting, attractive woman.

Finally, she was fraternizing.

# CHAPTER TEN

Jack confronted Gillian at the entrance of the terminal. "You treacherous little shite."

Shocked by the attack, she was speechless for a moment, then realized the source of his wrath. "If you mean reporting you to the commander, you brought that on yourself, Jack. It's one thing to cajole sex from hungry women with a few cigarettes. I suppose half the men on this base do that. But it's quite another to blackmail them and threaten to take away their livelihood."

He shook his head. "You have no idea what you've done."

Suddenly anxious, she asked quietly, "What happened? You were put on report?"

"Worse than that. I'm being posted back to Britain, thanks to your bloody self-righteousness."

"I'm sorry to hear that. I didn't think they'd be that harsh. But you still should not have blackmailed an innocent woman."

He didn't reply, and his unchanging expression told her the conversation wouldn't get any friendlier, so she turned to walk away.

"This is not the end of it," he called after her. "You'll hear from me again."

The hair stood up on the back of her neck.

❖

*June 1947*

By the following week, warm weather had come to Berlin, and Jack's vague threat no longer haunted her.

It was two p.m. Sunday afternoon, and with her eight-hour pass in hand, she traveled by bus to Charlottenburg for the promised concert at the Friedenskirche. The church, which Allied bombing had heavily damaged, was under reconstruction. Erika met her at the entrance and introduced her two friends, Heinrich and Charlotte.

Heinrich was an imposing fellow, with wide shoulders and large hands, and a thick head of black hair that made him seem ferocious. His manner, however, was genteel. Charlotte, whose gray hair made her look older than her husband, had a kind, grandmotherly face, and Gillian instantly liked her.

A table stood just past the entrance where guests were expected to "pay," though obviously in kind rather than cash. Various loaves of bread lay next to a carton of four eggs and a sack of potatoes. Heinrich, Charlotte, and Erika paid with two tins of Spam, and Gillian was pleased to add her own offering, two Cadbury chocolate bars purchased from NAAFI.

Once inside, Gillian gazed around at the interior. Scaffolding was erected on two sides, and the air smelled of sawdust and putty. While she studied the brickwork, three new people approached them: a fiftyish woman, a younger one on crutches, and a boy of about twelve.

"Gillian, these are my friends Gerda, Magda, and her son Hanno."

Hanno, who was rather pretty, smiled with the polite boredom of an adolescent and stepped closer to his mother, as if shielding her. Magda seemed to need shielding. A frail creature who, twenty pounds heavier and standing upright, would have been beautiful, she leaned on two crutches, and her pale face evoked mostly pity. Gillian recalled that she had just been sick enough to need penicillin and was surprised she had the stamina to attend the concert.

"Come. Let's sit where we can see," Heinrich said, and led them down the aisle to the second row. Sitting down next to Gillian, Erika seemed nervous. "I hope you like them. Every musician in Berlin is hungry to play music, but since the war, most of us have lost our edge."

"I'm sure I will," Gillian assured her. "This will be the first time I've heard live music—gosh, since my student days. I'm afraid it's mostly been radio for me."

At that moment, the musicians—with two violins, a viola, cello, large bass, oboe, recorder, and an odd-looking keyless trumpet—filed in and formed a semicircle around a harpsichord. One of the violinists addressed the audience, though Gillian wasn't able to understand much beyond "Thank you for coming, ladies and gentlemen. Tonight, we will perform Bach's Brandenburg Concertos Number 2, 3, and 4."

Gillian wasn't familiar with the Brandenburg concertos, except by name, but listening to them performed in a church raising itself out of the rubble hinted at something that transcended war and hatred. It was also a gift that Erika had invited her into her own world, the part of Germany not touched by fascism or military collapse.

Erika sat motionless next to her, but Gillian could sense her move faintly with the complicated Bach rhythms. For the first time in her life, Gillian gave her full attention to the interaction of instruments in a classical piece of music. It was a revelation.

At the end, after enthusiastic applause, Gillian stood to the side while Erika and the others exchanged pleasantries with Wilhelm, the violinist. Idly, she gazed around the church again and blinked in surprise. Standing near the doorway that opened onto the street were the two Soviet officers.

"Who are you staring at?" Erika asked her.

"Those two Russians over there." Gillian pointed with her chin. "I met them a few weeks ago in a Berlin nightclub. The night we brought you home, in fact."

Erika looked toward them, frowned, then turned away.

"You know them, too?" Gillian asked.

"Yes, but from a time I don't wish to remember. Anyhow, they're clearing out the church now. We have to leave."

They followed the rest of their group past the offerings table, now piled with food. "At least the musicians will get one or two good dinners from this," Gillian remarked. "I didn't think to ask before. How do you know them?"

"Wilhelm, the violinist, Gerda, and Magda were my neighbors in the Adlerstrasse. We foraged together during the terrible weeks after surrender. With Hanno, too. We were a good team."

They were on the Bismarkstrasse now, and she realized they were about to part ways and go in different directions. "What a shame there's no café for us to sit in and discuss the concert."

Heinrich held out one of his large hands. "Perhaps we can find another occasion to meet."

"Oh, there's our tram," Charlotte said, and quickened her pace. Erika looked indecisive. "Could we meet some time for lunch or dinner at the aerodrome?" She glanced nervously toward her friends, who were halfway to the tram stop.

Gillian waved her on. "Yes, of course. Dinner would be nice. I'll check the duty roster and see what times I have off and look for you in the canteen. Go ahead, now. Don't miss your ride."

"Wonderful," Erika said. Suddenly, she leaned toward Gillian and kissed her on the cheek. Then she took off at a run after Heinrich and Charlotte, only turning to wave as she stepped into the tram.

Touching her cheek where Erika had kissed her, Gillian turned and headed toward her own bus stop.

❖

Gillian checked the duty roster and discovered to her annoyance that she had evening duty for the next two weeks. But in the third week, she was assigned to the morning shift. Dinner would have to wait until July.

Before reporting in on the Tuesday after the concert, she stopped by the sergeants' mess for breakfast. Another one of the anonymous German women employed around the base was spooning out the scrambled powdered eggs. She asked in German when Erika was expected in.

She shook her head. "Erika doesn't work here anymore."

"What? Why not?" Gillian was incredulous. It made no sense.

"Don't know. Some trouble with RAF."

"Can I talk to the sergeant in charge of the kitchen?"

A few minutes later, a portly man came out wiping his hands on a towel. He seemed annoyed that a mere WAAF had disturbed him. Noting they were of the same rank, he didn't bother to salute.

"Someone just told me Erika Brandt didn't work here anymore. Is that true?"

"Uh-huh. What's it to you?" he asked with a noticeable Irish accent.

"I had a message for her. Why's she no longer here?"

He glanced to the side, already bored with the conversation. "Someone filed a complaint. Soliciting an RAF officer. The RAF takes a dim view of fraternizing with the likes of her anyhow. But when they go and offer themselves right here in front of our noses, that goes too far. I told her to pack it in."

Gillian was furious. "But that's simply not true. I know for a fact that the officer in question was soliciting her."

"Your word against his, miss. And he's a flight lieutenant." Before she could sputter another argument, he walked away from her. Bloody hell! Jack had managed to have his revenge after all.

In a funk, she downed her scrambled eggs and bread, and reported for work, trying to remember where Erika lived. How stupid that she'd been so drunk the night they'd dropped her off after the nightclub incident. She remembered only that it was the Lübeckerstrasse.

But Erika knew where *she* worked. Surely, if she was interested, she could send word. Any word.

Why hadn't she?

# CHAPTER ELEVEN

Erika felt drained of every emotion but guilt as she sat at Magda's deathbed. It didn't matter that she wasn't directly responsible for any of the tragedies in Magda's life. Not the polio that had shrunken one of her legs and required crutches all her life, or her brief, sad involvement with Gerhardt Brant, or the unwanted pregnancy that apparently came from it.

Nonetheless, her husband connected them. Gerhardt had seduced Magda and fathered her child, though his death had kept him from ever acknowledging it. It simply remained an understanding between Erika and Magda as Hanno grew up under the attentions of a whole building of people.

And now the poor woman lay blue and gasping in the overcrowded tuberculosis ward of the Charité Hospital. No amount of penicillin could help her this time, and the medicine Erika had provided for her pneumonia had only postponed the growth of the bacillus. Now it thrived, and she hovered at the brink of death, her feverish hand lying in Erika's.

She coughed feebly into a handkerchief, a pink, mucus-filled cough that revealed the ruinous state of her lungs. "Hanno," she whispered hoarsely, and Erika understood.

"Don't worry about Hanno. I'll look after him. Wilhelm, too."

Magda took a breath, as much as she was able. "And Gerhardt—"

"Please, let's not talk about Gerhardt. That's ancient history."

"No." She took a breath again. "Important." (Breath) "First, forgive me…(Breath)…and promise…(Breath)…not to tell Hanno."

Erika gripped the bony hand tighter. "All right. If it's so important to you. I won't tell him anything. I promise."

Magda closed her eyes in obvious relief and let her head fall back. Studying the skeletal face, ravaged by hunger and disease of all its flesh, Erika tried to recall the beauty she'd known a decade earlier. Only her physical handicap had kept Magda from arousing the lust of every male she met. One man had overlooked her lameness, and that had changed the fate of four people.

Magda was asleep now, breathing in short, shallow breaths, and it was clear the end was near. Erika brushed hair away from the sunken cheekbone. "Good-bye, old friend," she said, and kissed her softly on the forehead.

She never awakened, and the overcrowded hospital cremated her the next day.

Erika returned briefly to the building on the Adlerstrasse to make plans with Wilhelm. No one had time to mourn; she had to find work to raise herself and Hanno above the starvation rations provided to children and the unemployed. She had an idea.

Wilhelm was a godsend in both respects. Not only had he already stepped into a protective role toward Hanno years before, but he had contacts.

"Club musician? What an excellent idea. You're exactly what the soldier boys hunger for. But you need to limber up your hands and learn all the popular tunes of the British, French, and Americans. The Russians, too, if you want to do it right. I'll help you, and I even know where to find a piano that's more or less in tune."

"Wonderful. But I have to look good, too. Do you think I can manage it? I've lost so much weight." She brushed her fingertips down her hollow cheek.

Wilhelm stood back and appraised her. "You've got more flesh than many women in Berlin, my dear. Fortunately, you've always been attractive, and if you just do something nice with your hair, no manager in his right mind would refuse you. But first you have to have your musical act ready, so you can impress the owner the moment you sit down."

"All right. I can work on that. But what do you have in mind under 'something nice with my hair'? Please, no boy-cut. I have to pass as a woman this time around."

He smiled. "Trust this old man. A little judicious cutting and brushing, and you'll look like a star."

❖

Both fulfilled their parts of the bargain, and in two weeks Erika had built a repertoire of twenty popular tunes from four cultures. Finally, she sat down in front of Hanno and Gerda, and entrusted her hair to Wilhelm's scissors and comb. When she stood up again and checked in the mirror, she was impressed.

"That's not bad, you know. A little boyish but still feminine. I like it."

"You look really pretty," Hanno declared shyly. "Like an actress."

Wilhelm slid his barber's scissors back into their leather etui. "Of course she looks really nice." Then to Erika, "And since you've trusted me this far, I have a little gift for you."

He opened a drawer on the side of a cabinet and drew out a cardboard box. "I've kept them all these years in memory of my wife. The crèmes are a bit dried out, but the pencils are still good."

Erika gingerly opened the battered box, which revealed itself as a makeup kit. It held various kohl pencils in shades of black and brown, three tubes of lipstick, a jar of dried-out and rubbery face crème, tiny capsules of rouge, and a compact of face powder. All but the face crème was still useable.

Wilhelm clasped his hands in front of him. "Not to say you aren't naturally beautiful, my dear. But if you work in a nightclub, you will have to 'glamour up' to fit the aesthetic. Try it out tonight, and tomorrow, I'll go with you for your audition."

❖

Hermann Schalk, the manager of the Tabasco, was skeptical but agreed to listen as she played a selection of tunes that the patrons could either sing along with or dance to.

His expression ambiguous, he shrugged. "Very nice, sure, except we already have a piano player."

"But, Hermann, he's sixty years old and can barely walk," Wilhelm argued. "What are you going to do the first evening he doesn't show up?"

"That hasn't happened yet."

"Some night it will. You're going to apologize to your patrons, who are paying a king's ransom for your filthy schnapps, and tell them it's going to be a night with no music? The next minute, they'll walk out and head over to the Rio Rita. At the very least, you should have a warm-up and backup act."

"Warm-up and backup act? What the hell is that?"

"What it sounds like. Someone who starts the show, gets the patrons having fun, so when the main act comes in, they're all warmed up. And on those days when he doesn't make it, you have someone who can take over the entire evening." He paused and turned to Erika, drawing Schalk's attention to her. "Someone very attractive."

Hermann Schalk scratched the back of his neck. "Well, I suppose it can't hurt. I'll let her have an hour before my other guy gets in." He turned to Erika. "But it's your problem if any of the men get too free with their hands. I'm not going to play policeman."

Erika realized she'd just been hired. "Thank you, sir. I'll keep them entertained. Don't worry. When can I start?"

"Might as well be tonight. The pay is dinner. If you end up doing the whole show, it's that and a thousand marks a night." Erika cringed. A thousand marks would barely buy an egg. But then he added, "And if business is good, at the end of the week I'll add a bottle of schnapps. You can drink it or exchange it. I don't care."

That she could live with. "Thank you, Herr Schalk. I'll be here tonight at six o'clock."

❖

She played hour shifts for the month of September, but in October, Wilhelm's warning proved prophetic. Like thousands of Berliners, the old piano player came down with pneumonia, and she was suddenly fully employed. She was glad for the income, paltry as it was, but she couldn't ignore that the Tabasco Club was shabby, a radical shift in environment from the sergeants' mess at Gatow.

That thought always slipped into a recollection of Gillian, who'd been generous in helping her and who she thought might become a good friend. But that possibility had evaporated the instant she was fired. Their paths would never cross again.

October passed, and the nights became cold. Her overcoat was barely sufficient against the midnight air, and she compensated with sweaters and scarves. But returning to Moabit by bicycle at midnight every night was exhausting her.

A change in her routine occurred in November with unexpected customers. During her break, between two sets of songs, the waiter informed her that someone had invited her to their table for a drink. She acquiesced, as she was required to do, and was astonished.

"Isn't a nightclub a little capitalist for you?" she said in Russian, sitting down.

Vassily Mironov and Olga Petrova both laughed and called the waiter over. "What will you have, Erika?"

"Just lemonade," she said. "I would have thought you'd be back in Russia by now."

"Oh, no. We're part of the occupation army," Olga said. "Someone has to stay and help Germany toward socialism." She spoke in German, to show how seriously she took her job.

"Well, your German has become very good. I wish you'd help us less toward socialism and more toward prosperity. We can hardly get our economy going again when you keep shipping our factories and equipment back to Russia."

Vassily shrugged. "Sorry about that. But we wouldn't have to if your army hadn't obliterated ours."

Olga raised a hand. "Let's not talk politics. I just want to say you look quite lovely. I don't see at all that sorry creature we met that first night with Major Koslov. You've blossomed a lot."

"Not too decadent for you?" Erika touched her hair self-consciously.

"Not at all. Though you shouldn't let the club owner exploit you this way." Olga glanced over at Schalk, who sat at his table in the rear. "He's getting quite rich on the price of these drinks. And I bet, like all the capitalists, he pays you almost nothing."

"Thank you for your sympathy, but even if you're right, it's the way it is here in the West."

"Well, maybe we can help you out, as a show of solidarity." Vassily called over the waiter again. "Can you tell your manager we'd like to talk to him?"

Hermann Schalk appeared, slightly nervous, and Erika knew it was because the Soviet soldiers were unpredictable. Any offense, real or perceived, could set them off, and they weren't above breaking a few bottles, or heads. Even the Western MPs could do nothing. "How may I be of service?" he asked cautiously.

"We only want to compliment you and your establishment for the high quality of service and entertainment," Vassily said in German. "This woman is truly impressive in her musical talents, and she makes this club the best on the Kurfürstendamm. I hope you appreciate her."

Schalk seemed nonplussed. "Uh…of course we value her. Yes, great talent. Thank you for your praise."

"We just want you to know that, because the last club we were in told us they were looking for a pianist and were prepared to pay a lot. You might consider to increase her salary, for example."

"Ah, well, thank you for that information," he said noncommittally, and, tilting his head in the hint of a bow, he backed away.

"That was daring," Erika said under her breath. "But thank you. We'll see what happens."

Erika began her final set of tunes, and her Russian guests stayed until the end. They also remained at their table as Herr Schalk approached Erika at the end of the evening with a larger than usual envelope of marks. When he presented it to her, she said, "You know as well as I do, these are practically worthless. Why don't you give me a second bottle of schnapps instead?"

Schalk glanced to the side, noting that the Russians were still watching. With his lips twitching, as if in conversation with himself, he disappeared and returned shortly. She was on her feet by then, pulling on her threadbare coat, and accepted the sack with two bottles instead of the usual one. "It's a good thing you're pretty," he grumbled, and marched back to the table that was his office.

The two Russians joined her outside the club, where it had begun to snow, indifferent to the cold in their heavy military coats. Before mounting her bike, she turned to give them both a quick embrace. "Thank you again for standing by me. That was the kind of socialism my parents believed in, and died for."

"Many died for it," Vassily said somberly. "But politics and bad behavior on both sides ruin the message. Please, if things grow worse between our side and yours, remember, this is what communism is. Worker solidarity."

"Take care of yourself," Olga said, patting her on the shoulder.

Erika pedaled away with her bottles. Sensing the heavy sack on her back, now twice as rich as before, she brooded on the meaning of "solidarity." Sometimes it was just a slogan, but other times, it could mean a new winter coat. Two of them maybe, one for her and one for Hanno.

❖

Gillian stared through the barrack window at the November snow, wondering how deep it would get. Her regulation greatcoat was adequate to the weather, but not her shoes, and she always arrived with damp feet at her station. Abruptly, she thought of Erika. How was she faring in the frigid weather?

Betsy came into their room from her ablutions, toweling her hair. "Oh, that felt good. Just enough hot water for a shampoo." She glanced over at Gillian, who slouched on her bunk. "Why so glum?"

"I was thinking about Erika. You know, the woman who worked in the sergeants' mess. I was just getting to know her when she was fired, and all because of Jack. It was sheer vengeance after I reported him for blackmail."

Betsy draped her towel over the back of a chair and drew on her regulation striped pyjamas. "Frankly, I think they deserved each other. She was leading him on, and he was furious when he found out it was for nothing."

"No, you've got it wrong. Jack wanted sex, and Erika was trying to get medicine for her friend. Besides, he was the one with all the power, enough to take away her livelihood. At this point, I don't even know what happened to her."

"Erika? She's doing fine. Has a job playing piano in one of the clubs on the Kurfürstendamm. The Tabasco, I think."

Gillian blinked. "What? How in blazes do you know that?"

"Heinrich told me. He's one of the German mechanics I work with. Your friend rents a room from him and his wife."

"I know that, but it never occurred to me that you had any contact with him. So she's all right? Gosh, I'd like to get ahold of her. Do you think Heinrich would carry a message to her?"

"Why not?" Betsy slid under the covers of her cot.

Gillian rummaged through her locker until she located a pencil and a notebook. Bracing the latter on her knee, she composed a note.

*Erika,*

*I'm happy to learn you have a job with a piano and would love to hear you play some time. Please send a message through Heinrich with your schedule. Maybe we can meet for supper one evening. Gillian.*

Lacking an envelope, she folded it and used her tiny sewing kit to seal it with mending thread. She laid the note on Betsy's night table and returned to her bunk, cheered to have reestablished contact. Staring out the window again at the falling snow, she found it serene.

# CHAPTER TWELVE

Gillian's note met a series of errors and coincidences of Shakespearean proportion. Betsy carried it obediently to work, but to keep from muddying it while she pulled on her soiled overalls in the mechanics' hut, she laid it on a shelf. Distracted by an urgent summons, she left it unattended. In the comings and goings of the fitters and mechanics, the note wafted off onto the wet floor and lay there for two days, until someone swept it up as refuse.

It languished another day in the trash until Heinrich happened to rummage through it. In the past, he'd found wire, a damaged but reparable engine part, torn gloves, any number of items that he could mend or repair for his own use.

On this day, he found the folded note amidst the refuse. The melted snow had washed out its message, but he could still make out Erika's name. Strange, he thought, though his attention was immediately diverted to a dented, but not quite empty, tin of machine oil, so he slid it into his pocket. There it remained for another week, until he handed over his overalls to Charlotte for washing.

"Heinrich, while you boil the wash water I'll soak the laundry in the bathtub. Do you want this?" She held up the scrap of disintegrating paper with one hand while she shoved the overalls into her laundry sack with the other.

Heinrich hefted the full kettle onto the top of the stove. "Huh? Oh, that. Just something I found at work. It had Erika's name on it, but the rest was washed out. Silly to keep it. Just throw it away."

Erika entered just as Charlotte tossed the scrap into the stove and watched it blacken to ash. "What about my name?"

"Oh, a scrap of paper I dug up in the trash at Gatow. I saw your name on it and thought you might know what it was, even though the rest of it was blank. But then I forgot. Sorry."

Erika stared at the stove. "My name? Who would write a note to me?"

A possibility occurred to her, but she rejected it. It was too much like a wish fantasy. But still. She turned back to Heinrich, who was just lifting the steaming kettle from the stove to carry it to the bathtub.

"If I write a note of my own, would you deliver it to Gillian? You know, the one who came to Wilhelm's concert. She works in the ground-control trailer."

Heinrich frowned. "I know who she is, but I can't go near that installation. They have some kind of important equipment in there, and it's off-limits to Germans."

"She has a friend who's one of the mechanics. I'm sure you know her. Give it to her, and she can pass it on."

Heinrich was at the door to the bathroom now, carrying both the hot kettle and the sack of laundry for Charlotte to wash. "Yes, sure," he called back over his shoulder.

❖

And so it was that while Gillian sat at lunch in the sergeants' mess the next day, Betsy crept over to her table, her eyes downcast. "I… uh…I'm so sorry. I made a real cock-up of this."

"What cock-up? What are you talking about?" Gillian said, amused by the hangdog expression.

Betsy handed over a neatly folded piece of cardboard. Perplexed, Gillian unfolded it and discovered it was two sides of an empty Player's cigarettes box. The inside surface held a written message.

While Gillian squinted over the writing, Betsy explained. "The note you gave me to deliver to Heinrich…um…got lost somehow. He told me he found it later, but the writing was washed out. He only saw Erika's name on it. Somehow, they figured out it came from you and sent back a message. I'm really sorry." She stepped back, looking abashed.

Not sure whether to be annoyed at the careless loss of her note or elated at finally getting a response, Gillian snorted. "It's a good thing you're not a spy. You'd be flaming worthless."

She spread out the two sides of the cigarette box on the table and scrutinized the lines. The message was in English, misspelled in places, and the script was the strange heavily curlicued German cursive she'd heard about but never seen before. She could make sense of only about half of it.

"I think it says she wants to make sure the first note was from me, and if so, she wants to see me again." She laughed. "It's either that or 'Your grandmother eats tulips.'"

Betsy seemed relieved by the wisecrack. "I'd go with the tulips. Who would ever want to see *you* again?"

"Insult to injury, eh?" Gillian snickered, flicking a single grain of rice at her. "I'll forgive you for your carelessness if you carry back another message to Heinrich. And *this* time, make sure he gets it."

Gillian's second letter, delivered that afternoon, obviously reached its destination, for it came back the next day with a new message written on the back. She was used to Erika's curlicues now and could read the brief note in its entirety.

*Hello. I am happy you got my message. My job at Tabasco is good. Can you come and visit me there one night? I start at six. If you come at five, it is quiet and we can talk.*

Gillian wrote back, on a clean sheet of paper, that she had duty through six in the evening every day until the second week in December. But then, when she switched to morning hours, she would love to visit. Realizing that Erika had no access to writing paper, she left the back blank, a precaution that proved wise.

Two days later, the note came back with a cheerful response, and only Betsy's refusal to continue playing postman prevented the development of an ongoing correspondence.

❖

*December 15, 1947*

The Tabasco was as seedy as Gillian remembered it, but it was a comfortable seediness. Windowless, it was lit by dim electric lamps hung on the cracked walls.

Gillian arrived at five. The club had just opened, but the smoke-permeated walls and tablecloths still held the acrid smell of dirty ashtrays from the night before. Yet when Erika came out to meet her at a corner table, she no longer noticed the foul odor.

"You look...lovely," Gillian said. "I mean, in a nice dress, with your hair all done up like that. And I never saw you in makeup before. What a difference from..." She stopped, sensing she was undermining her own compliment.

Erika dropped her glance, curling a hank of hair over her ear, and sat down next to her. "Thank you. This is how I looked before the war."

Gillian swept her eyes around the club. "I hope your life before the war was better than this."

Erika laughed softly. "It was, but I don't want to talk about me when I know so little about you." She glanced at Gillian's dress. "You look nice, too, but I think of you most in your RAF uniform. Do you fly the planes?"

"I did during the war, in transport. And technically, I'm not in the RAF now. I don't exactly 'fly' planes, but in air traffic control, I help land them safely, especially in poor conditions. Someday, I'll fly again, though, no matter what I have to do."

Erika gazed at her with obvious admiration. "Is that why you bought my plane?"

"Your plane? Oh, yes, the model. Yes, I suppose so." Gillian shrugged. "Silly, isn't it? But planes were...are...my life."

"You don't have family?" The unspoken word "husband" hung in the air.

"No. Parents killed in the war, and I miss them. Not just the individuals, but the whole idea of family. The safety, the warmth." She coughed into her hand. "I'm sorry. That must sound very self-pitying. I'm sure things are much worse for Germans."

"Or maybe just the same. My parents were also killed...in Sachsenhausen."

"Sachsenhausen." Gillian knew that name. "The concentration camp?"

"Yes. Before the war, it mostly held dissidents, political troublemakers. My parents were arrested in 1936 and died in the camp a year later. Typhoid. After that I lived with my aunt and studied music until I got married, in 1938."

"And your husband was killed in the war?"

"His name was Dietrich. Yes. I'm a war widow, like a million other German women."

Caught up in her own losses, Gillian had never considered those of the enemy. "Was life difficult during the war?" she asked with sincere interest.

"No, not too bad. Life was almost normal until the last year. We even had trams until almost the end, and the bakeries were still making bread. The authorities rationed potatoes, but we still had them. Everybody went to work. Then, when we heard the Red Army was coming, everything broke apart. People said, 'Hope you enjoyed the war. The peace will be terrible.' And for a while, it was."

Gillian had heard tales of atrocities by both Germans and Russians but couldn't measure if they were true. "Terrible in what way? Forgive my morbid curiosity."

"That is all right. I like to talk to you about it. To start, the whole social structure broke down. No water or electricity, every day was a test of survival. We formed into little groups based on our buildings and the circle of friends we could reach."

"No water, light. I can't imagine. How did you manage?"

"We took water from a pump in the street, collected food in our basements and just waited in the darkness. For light, we had candles, kerosene, any oil. To be warm, we burned coal, wood, furniture, Nazi literature."

"And the Russians? Are the rumors of atrocities true?"

Erika remained silent for a moment. "How do you say, 'to steal or destroy everything in a city'?"

"Pillage?"

"Yes, it was all pillage. And revenge. For a week, two weeks. Later, they just made camp in the streets and took our furniture to make bonfires."

"So people came out of hiding?"

"Little by little. The old men and children first. The Russians are very sentimental about children and don't usually hurt them. They still took the women, but it slowly changed from violent rape to polite rape, then to business, sex for bacon and bread."

"An exchange of hungers," Gillian remarked.

"Yes. And everything was dirty like a stable. Not just from the horses. Even the men used the corridors as toilets. It stank everywhere, but it seemed a symbol of what we were, what we had done to ourselves for Hitler."

Gillian wanted so much to ask, *Were you raped?* but dared not. "Did you hide?"

"In the beginning, yes, but finally we had to come out for water, food. And I spoke Russian, so they became individuals to me. Some were brutal and some were kind, and they began to tell me their own stories. A few were quite intelligent, and we discussed politics."

Gillian rested her chin in her knuckles. Political discussion? The notion was so much at odds with the whole mindset of war. "What did you talk about? Fascism versus Communism versus Democracy?"

"Yes, though I think we had a different understanding of the words."

Just then the owner came over to their table. He spoke German, but it was clear he was calling Erika to work, and his glance at Gillian's empty glass suggested she was obliged to buy another drink.

Gillian glanced up at him, his face devoid of sentimentality. Not an evil man, she presumed, just one who knew how to make a good living in a destroyed city. She turned to Erika. "I can stay a little while. The last bus back to the aerodrome is at six thirty. But maybe we can meet again…sometime."

Erika was already standing, glancing back and forth between Gillian and her boss. "Um…you know it's almost Christmas, and I would love for you to visit us in the Lübeckerstrasse. It will be a very small *Fest*, but if we save our rations, we can make a soup or something. I will ask Heinrich and Charlotte, of course, but I think they will be very happy."

It was as if the room suddenly brightened and took on more color. "Yes. I'd quite like that," Gillian said. "If Heinrich approves, he can leave a message with Betsy. But don't worry about feeding me. Whatever they make, I'll add a few things from NAAFI, and I'm sure we'll have enough." She stood up and placed a quick kiss on Erika's cheek.

On the last bus to Gatow, she was jubilant.

# Chapter Thirteen

The air base celebrated Christmas Eve 1947 in the officers' mess, a nicer hall than the sergeants' mess she was used to. Volunteers had draped red and green streamers and a few cardboard cutouts of reindeer along two of the walls. The three-foot Christmas tree on the center table was a real fir, though it held only a few paper ornaments and tilted slightly eastward. The ad hoc band of flute, clarinet, trumpet, fiddle, and drum set had finished its first set of Christmas carols and fallen pleasantly silent, allowing people to talk.

"Punch isn't half-bad," Betsy said, knocking back her fourth. "And I'm sure the kitchen broke some rationing rules to make all that mince pie. Cheers to them."

Gillian sipped from her cup. "Actually, it tastes exactly the same as the punch we had last year at Bückeburg. The RAF must have a basic recipe."

"I bloody miss Bückeburg," Betsy said, wan. "Don't you?"

Gillian thought of the long, frigid bicycle rides and of Jean Horwick. "Not a bit. All we did was work and sometimes go to the NAAFI for a beer. Berlin is much more exciting. Different people to meet—Germans, Russians. In fact, I've been invited to celebrate a German *Heiliger Abend*. I've cadged a motorbike from the motor pool and am headed into Berlin in just a few minutes. That's why I'm in civilian clothes."

"What? You're spending the biggest holiday of the year with some grotty Germans? Sure, some of them are nice enough, but they're not like us. Why celebrate with them, trying to be understood, when we have so many dashing chaps here?"

"'Dashing chaps'? Someone must be talking about me."

Betsy pivoted around. "Oh, you cad, sneaking up on us that way. Gillian, this is my friend Lionel. Lionel, this is Gillian." An airman bearing a remarkable resemblance to Jack grinned at her, and she smiled back. He held up two red objects. "They were handing these out at the door."

"Oh, Christmas crackers!" Betsy took hold of the end of one of them while Lionel held the other. It came apart with a satisfying bang, giving up a lemon drop and a tiny metal token. Betsy held it up in front of her nose. "An airplane. Must be for all the engines I've worked on. Gillian, try yours and see what you get."

Lionel held the second cracker out to her, and Gillian obediently took hold of it. A brief tug brought another pop and yielded a cherry candy and a small enamel heart.

"I think it's the wrong way 'round, don't you?" Gillian asked. "The plane should be mine and the heart yours."

"Too late," Lionel declared authoritatively. "Fate has spoken."

At that moment, the band music started again with a dance tune, and Lionel offered his arm to Betsy. "May I have the honor?"

Betsy beamed, and they strode together onto the dance floor, created by the removal of a half dozen tables. Gillian watched them for a moment, grateful that she didn't have to spend the rest of Christmas Eve sipping punch and avoiding dance invitations. She turned away, fetched her greatcoat from where she'd hung it, and strode toward the Nissen hut that functioned as a motor pool.

It was closed and locked, but the Matchless 3GL motorcycle she'd reserved for the evening was chained directly outside, and they'd given her the key. After a few tries, she managed to kick-start it. She let it warm for a moment, then gently gripped the gas handle and started up.

Snow along the road leading away from the aerodrome had melted and refrozen, forcing her to drive with extreme caution. Although she vaguely recalled the location she'd been to the night Nigel had driven Erika home, she'd checked on the large city map posted on the base to get her bearings.

After wending her way through the Gatow district, then through Moabit, she came finally to the Lübeckerstrasse and slowed to locate the correct number. The apartment buildings looked much the same in the dark, but something new was in the atmosphere. In spite of the destitution, in every building, German families were celebrating an evening they called "holy," and though most of the windows were boarded up, light shone through many of the cracks, revealing candlelight.

With her torch, she finally identified building number ninety-eight and bumped up onto the sidewalk. Her arrival must have been noisier than she thought, for no sooner had she dismounted than the door to the street opened and Heinrich stepped out. "Merry Christmas, Gillian," he said, placing a barely discernible peck on her cheek. "You can lock your motorbike inside the corridor."

As soon as the bike was safely chained to the banister, she shouldered her canvas sack and followed him up the dark stairs to the third floor.

Charlotte stood in the open doorway and gave her a hug. Next to her, Gerda wished her *Fröhliche Weihnachten*, and behind her Wilhelm stepped forward offering his hand. She remembered him from the concert: white-haired, bearded, and avuncular. He lacked only about thirty pounds of being the perfect Father Christmas.

Only then did Gillian see Erika come from the kitchen, followed by the boy she remembered was called Hanno.

She stood for a moment before murmuring "Merry Christmas, Gillian" and kissing her cheek. "You remember Hanno, don't you? He was at the concert. Unfortunately, he speaks only German."

The boy, blond and Teutonic, bowed from the waist and repeated the holiday wish.

The warmth of their greetings did little to offset the icy temperature of the apartment, but Charlotte explained. "Every house in Moabit is as cold as this, but we're lucky to have a coal stove in the kitchen. We'll be very crowded but warm. You can even take off your coat."

Gillian set her canvas sack on the floor and slid off her greatcoat into Charlotte's arms. After laying the coat next to others on the sofa, Charlotte led everyone back into the kitchen, where a tall cast-iron cylinder stood on short feet. An elbow pipe rose from the top and made a right angle to vent through the kitchen window. A wooden plank filled the window opening, with a circular hole sawed through it for the pipe to pass through. Chairs and stools were set in a close ring around it.

"How do you like our little *Kanonenofen*?" Heinrich asked. "I installed it in September when it was clear the central heating would stay off all winter."

Gillian concealed her shock. "Oh, good solution." She held her hand an inch over it and found the heat agreeable. "It burns coal?"

"It was designed for coal, though we burn anything we can find. A lot of the neighbors have these, too, which explains why you won't find any more wooden fences in Berlin."

Charlotte gestured toward a counter, where an assortment of foodstuffs was on display. "Wilhelm brought us lovely apples from his last performance, and the cans of Spam are from the Tempelhof commissary, courtesy of Gerda. And this…" She held up a bottle of whiskey. "This also comes from Wilhelm. Amazing what people take to concerts, isn't it?"

Gillian reached into her sack. "My gifts come from the RAF," she said, drawing out a tin of bacon and five bars of Cadbury chocolate. "I hope there's enough to go around. But if not, we always have this, which our NAAFI shop was kind enough to carry." She produced a bottle of German burgundy. "Oh, and if Cadbury isn't English enough, I brought orange marmalade."

"Oh, thank you, dear," Charlotte said with genuine warmth. "Sweets are so scarce, and you brought us two kinds." She added Gillian's gifts to the others. "Now that all are here, we can start our humble Christmas dinner."

While Heinrich opened the wine, the others found places around the central stove. Charlotte handed out plates and forks and uncovered the "dinner": a single platter of boiled potatoes with tiny chunks of bacon and egg, and miscellaneous vegetable particles scattered over the top. Gillian was embarrassed to be eating the food of such desperate people, but the others seemed genuinely cheerful, especially as Heinrich poured an inch of burgundy into each person's glass.

She ate her small portion slowly, savoring the various tastes; pork, egg, salt, lard, a hint of carrot and dried mushroom. The years of austerity at home and the limited menu of the RAF cuisine had kept her expectations low, but she was surprised at how satisfying such a simple meal could be.

"How is life in the Soviet sector, Wilhelm?" she asked.

He swirled the wine at the bottom of his glass. "Tolerable, but only just. The Russians are tightening restrictions around the sector. I worry because we need to move all around Berlin to give concerts."

Erika set down her fork. "It would be terrible if they blocked you. We need music to cheer us up." She glanced over at the boy, who had cleaned his plate and was eyeing the sweets on the side cupboard. "And it would be harder to visit Hanno."

Gerda drank her wine in a single luxurious gulp. "Thank God we can move freely between the American and British sectors."

Heinrich raised a hand. "Let us talk about happier things this evening," he said, then added something in German to Hanno that seemed to have something to do with chocolate.

"Tell us about Christmas in Britain," Charlotte suggested. "Is it very fancy?"

Gillian sipped her burgundy, glad to note it was of decent quality. "It's less religious than here, and we celebrate more on the morning of the twenty-fifth. But other than that, we've stolen a lot of your traditions—the decorated tree, the Christmas songs. We even pretend to have snow, which is rare in England in December."

Charlotte collected the emptied plates. "Well, we'll try to give you some of the real thing, even under these harsh conditions."

Wilhelm turned and spoke to Hanno in German, and Gillian understood enough to know he was asking the boy to distribute the whiskey.

Out of nowhere, Charlotte produced another platter, this time with a cluster of brown cookies whose fragrance told her were gingerbread. Slices of apple and pieces of Gillian's chocolate bars were laid out in a circle around them. She took a sample of each and found they went perfectly with little sips of Wilhelm's whiskey.

When the dessert part of the meal was done, Heinrich announced "*die Bescherung*" and translated to Gillian, "the gift ritual."

At his signal, Hanno rose again from his stool and marched into another room, returning with a bucket in his arms. Sprouting from it was a fir tree of about three feet, held in place by wet sand. Erika placed it in the kitchen sink and clipped on a dozen small candles, obviously designed for such use. She lit the candles, and Heinrich cut the electricity in the room. Then, by the flickering light of the Christmas candles, they sang "O Tannenbaun," a song that even Gillian knew in German.

After the candles burned down, Erika disappeared and returned with a bulging cloth sack. "Christmas gifts," she announced. "But only if you perform a song or poem. That is the law."

Hanno was obviously long familiar with the requirement and sang a little song that began "*O, du fröhliche…*" in a sweet, pure, if slightly flat, boy-soprano voice.

After the general applause, Erika presented him with hand-knitted socks from Charlotte and a jar of preserved cherries from herself. Hanno's expression told her the cherries were of greater value, at least for the present. He kissed both women.

Heinrich and Wilhelm each recited a little poem, from Goethe and

Heine respectively, and each got a pair of wool socks. Charlotte had evidently been very busy and could knit very fast.

She had varied her output to also produce mittens, which she presented to Erika after her performance of "Stille Nacht" and a beanie with a pompom to Gerda after a song that seemed to be about snowflakes.

Gillian assumed the *Bescherung* was finished, but Charlotte commanded, "Gillian, go stand by the Tannenbaum. It's your turn."

"Me?! Uh...well...I'm not prepared."

"Oh, come on. You must know a poem or a song. Anything will do."

After a moment's thought, Gillian began to sing the last song she'd heard at the NAAFI Christmas party and that had been buzzing in her head all evening. "*Du...Du. liegst mir im Herzen, du...du liegst mir im Sinn...*" She knew only the first stanza, but it sufficed to earn a Christmas gift. Gillian tore apart the newspaper wrapping and burst out laughing. "A book called *Deutsche Kinder*. Does this mean you expect me to learn German?"

"Of course. It's Hanno's first schoolbook, and he gave me permission to give it to you." Hanno nodded at the mention of his name. "It talks a lot about the German 'Volk,' and there are a few Nazi flags in the pictures, but it's not so bad."

"Fair enough. Give me a few weeks, and I'll talk like a German child." She bent toward Hanno. "*Dankeschön,*" she said, and kissed him.

At that moment, they all heard heavy footfall on the stairs and a sudden loud knocking. Everyone froze. Frowning, Heinrich answered the door.

A moment later, he returned with his guest.

"Vassily," Erika said, apparently as surprised as everyone else, and spoke to him in Russian. In response, he reached inside his greatcoat and slid out a bottle of French wine. Almost certainly stolen, but no one minded. He switched to German and asked Erika to open it. Then he removed his coat and dropped it on the floor behind him as he squeezed into the packed kitchen.

He continued in German. "I heard singing from outside. Very nice. I sing, too."

Erika, whose job it was every night to entertain with songs in four languages, suggested "Lili Marlene," and everyone agreed.

It was comical to hear it in Russian, while she sang it in English and the others in German, but Gillian was struck again by the beauty of Vassily's rich baritone voice.

His visit, as it turned out, was brief, which was a relief, since his presence had diluted the family feeling that had been developing. As soon as the wine was drunk and the group had come up with three more songs to sing, he was on his feet again and drawing on his sheepskin coat.

Cheek-kisses for the women, including Gillian, manly hugs for the men, including Hanno, and he was out the door.

His departure seemed to mark the end of the evening, particularly since they had depleted the food and alcohol. Gillian had no idea how the others would return home, but she had a motorbike. "It's been lovely, really lovely," she said to Charlotte with sincerity. "But I must get back to quarters now."

"Yes, of course. We understand," Charlotte said as Heinrich retrieved her coat. He held it behind her while she slipped her arms in and checked the pockets for her gloves.

Erika was suddenly beside her. "I go with you to the street," she said. "So you don't fall down the stairs and break your neck." She was already out the door with a candle in hand as Gillian gave each of the others a quick farewell embrace.

They were silent as Erika led her down the stairs, and the candle she held overhead cast strange shadows on the cracked walls. When they reached the ground floor where the motorbike leaned, Erika held the candle close so Gillian could unlock the chain and tuck it into the leather pouch on the rear.

Erika set the candle on the banister post beside her, where it illuminated half of her face. By its warm yellow light, she looked curiously saintly, and they stood facing each other for an awkward moment.

"You have wonderful friends, and you're all very kind."

"Do you think so? I don't feel kind. Sometimes I feel I have nothing to give, and only need."

She seemed to peer directly into Gillian's eyes, though it might simply have been the strain to see in the flickering light.

"We all need. I've spent the whole war alone. I've had friends, of course, but that's not the same."

Erika nodded. "No, it's not the same. After my parents, I lost my husband. It breaks you, or it makes you hard."

Gillian took a step closer. "Nothing about you seems hard."

It was the darkness that enabled her, as if it could discount what happened. She slid one arm around Erika's back and held her for just a moment while their cheeks touched, and she studied the pressure of her body, her breasts, her hips. They both inhaled, their chests swelling against each other, and finally she pressed her lips on Erika's mouth.

Erika's lips were dry, unresponsive, and Gillian loosened her grip, embarrassed. It seemed she'd misjudged.

"Halloo?" The voice came from the stairwell above them. "*Alles okay?*"

They broke apart. "*Ja, ja. Alles gut,*" Erika called up the stairs. "*Ich komme gleich.* I have to go," she said to Gillian.

"Yes, me, too. But tell me, when did your husband die? Where?"

"Over the English Channel. On the seventh of September, 1940."

"September seven? You're sure?"

A voice came from upstairs again. This time it was Hanno, and the approach of a dull glow told them he was coming downstairs.

"Yes, I am sure. How can I forget that?" Erika buttoned Gillian's coat, opened the door to the street, and kissed her quickly, a meaningless kiss. "Merry Christmas," she said, holding the door open.

Spontaneously, Gillian mounted the motorbike and rolled it out onto the street. With a single furious kick, she turned the motor over and started off without looking back. Her mind was in turmoil. September seven. It was a date scorched into her mind, the night the Luftwaffe set fire to her house and burned her family to death.

# CHAPTER FOURTEEN

Shocked and confused, Erika hurried up the steps to the apartment. Her face seemed curiously warm, and she was largely silent as she helped clean up the kitchen. For lack of midnight transportation, Wilhelm bedded down in his coat on chairs in the living room, and Hanno got the sofa in Erika's bedroom.

Erika shared her bed back-to-back with Gerda and, on that frigid night, the added warmth was welcome. In any case, in her mind, she was far away, turning over the memory of Gillian's kiss, again and again.

She had to work on Christmas Day evening and on New Year's Eve, for in a city of lonely servicemen, the club offered consolation. On those days, the male attentions were correspondingly worse, from men who hadn't managed to attract women, British or German.

At New Year's, at least Gerda came to the club and sat with her during a break. Herr Schalk had even offered a schnapps on the house. "You look very nice," Gerda said. "The men must go crazy over you."

Erika sighed. "Oh, they do. They never stop pawing at me, no matter the uniform."

"It's just the way men are, dear, and after all, not all of them are brutes. Some are really nice, like my old Fritz. You just have to find the good ones."

Erika dipped one finger into her glass and placed a drop of schnapps on her tongue. You could make a glass of it last all night that way. "I'm so tired of worrying which man will help me and which one will hurt me. I can't even bear their touch anymore."

"You had some terrible experiences, I remember, but you can't give up. If you do, you condemn yourself to a lonely life."

Erika shook her head. "No. I refuse to see it that way." She hesitated, formulating a thought that shocked her as much as it would Gerda. "Men are not the only people you can love."

Gerda looked puzzled.

Erika took a breath. "I mean you can love a woman and never have to worry about her forcing you."

"Like those women who pretend to be men, who cut their hair short and wear men's clothing? The kind who used to come to the nightclubs before the war?"

"It doesn't have to be like that. At least I don't know any such women. And I wouldn't especially want women like that to make love to me."

Consternation grew on Gerda's face. "But...there are other kinds of women you *would* like to make love with?"

"I...I'm not even sure myself, Gerda. And...I have to trust you not to betray me. I need your friendship."

"Yes, of course, dear. But please tell me *what* you are talking about."

"I've met someone I care for, and I think she cares for me."

"Someone at the club? Be careful, dear. All kinds of strange people come here. Underground types who'll take advantage of you worse than a man."

"No, in fact, you already met her. The British air-force woman, Gillian."

Gerda blinked at the revelation. "She's one of *those* women, who wants you...like *that*?"

"That's just it. I can't be sure. She kissed me at Christmas, but since then, I haven't heard from her."

"You're sure it wasn't just a 'hello and good-bye' kiss?"

"It was a real one. And better than any man-kiss I ever had, even from my husband."

Gerda chuckled. "You're beginning to make me jealous." She thought for a moment. "But if she does want you, how do you know she's not another Major Koslov? Not that it would be so bad. The Brits can also be generous in exchange for—"

"No, she's not. Dear God, I hope not. Oh, Gerda, I just don't know."

Gerda reached over and squeezed her hand. "Obviously, you need to see her again, to make sure she's serious."

"I desperately want to see her again, but she hasn't contacted me. I'm afraid it might have just been a reckless moment after a little whiskey."

Gerda slapped the table. "All right. I'm losing patience with this. Just send her a damned note!"

"I don't know. Maybe. I'll think about it."

A male form appeared at the table and sat down with them without invitation.

"Oh, Fritz, it's you. You want something to drink?" Erika asked.

"No, thanks." He smiled, revealing his limited number of teeth, then elbowed Gerda. "Come on, old girl. It's almost midnight. We should go home and celebrate the New Year our way, eh?" He leered, in case she didn't get his innuendo.

After they left, Erika had three more hours of work, playing the piano and circulating, to cheer up the customers and encourage more purchases. That she was paid extra was of little solace when she was riding her bicycle through the bitter pre-dawn air.

Still bundled in her coat, she slept until almost ten, and when she awoke, her flimsy resolution had disappeared. If Gillian was interested, she would have given a sign, and she hadn't. They had nothing in common, and pursuing her would only end in humiliation.

## CHAPTER FIFTEEN

After the Christmas kiss, Gillian was crippled by uncertainty, both by the recklessness of what she'd done and by the revelation that Erika's husband was one of the murderers who had bombed London on that fatal day.

The argument simmered, barely articulated, in her subconscious. Erika was not a murderer, but she had married a murderer, for Dietrich Brandt had been in the squadron of the first blitz on London. And six years after the fact, Gillian could still not shake the memory of coming upon the glowing ashes of her home, her family, her entire past.

But even if she could reconcile her attraction to Erika with her repugnance for the Luftwaffe, what exactly was she expecting? Did Erika really want her? Even assuming the desire was mutual, how did that make her different from Jack or any other member of the occupying forces who exploited the defeated?

She buried herself in work, as if letting time pass would quiet the buzzing in her head. And for two months, she succeeded. Like nature itself, she spent the winter months in withdrawal while she became ever better at micromanaging the landings, and the calm reassuring voice she used in her guidance also soothed her personal turmoil. The tiny comets that glowed and faded on her radar screen, mere radar echoes, were all the airplanes she saw now, and she drew them in like kites on a string.

The busy days became weeks and the weeks months, and off duty, she occupied herself with her little German primer. Soon she could announce in German that she was a good child whose mother cooked soup and whose father defended the homeland.

As she labored over the strange pronunciations, she kept imagining Hanno as a six-year-old, struggling to read the words as she now struggled to memorize them. Would she one day speak well enough to have a conversation with him? She shook her head. Of course not. She would never see him again, though, curiously, his face had grown vivid in her memory.

March arrived, and she sensed a certain thaw in herself. Perhaps it was time to seek deeper connections among the other WAAFs, develop attachments among her own comrades. At the end of her workday, she turned over her screen to her relief and, bending into the cool spring breeze, hurried toward the sergeants' mess for supper.

One of the mechanics approached her on the tarmac, and as he came close, she recognized the tall, dark-haired man as Heinrich.

"Hello," she said, surprised but with genuine cheer. "It's been a long time. How is everybody?" she asked, though by "everybody" she really meant only Erika.

"We're fine. Thank you," he said. "In fact, I was looking for someone to take this to you." He slid his hand into his overalls pocket. "Erika asked me to deliver it and to wait for your answer."

Puzzled, she glanced down at the paper he'd dropped into her hand. It was folded over in three panels and sealed in medieval fashion with a spot of candle wax. Intrigued, she broke the seal and smiled. The letter was on a page torn from a child's primer, the sentences curling around the heads of two children, Jane and Sally, who played with a puppy.

She squinted over the strange German cursive and read silently.

*Sorry for the silly paper, but I have no other. I have survived another winter, and thoughts I had last year are like seeds that are emerging now in spring. I miss you and fear I said something to chase you away. Simply, I would love to see you again. Is it possible for you to come to Tabasco on Sunday when we close at ten? We can be alone for a while to talk. Please tell Heinrich yes or no. If no, I will accept I have misjudged, but if yes, I will wait for you.*
*Hopefully, Erika*

Relief and longing washed over her as she refolded the paper and slipped it into her pocket.

"Please tell her the answer is yes," she said, "and that her English has become very good. Poetic, even." She turned away and, caressing the note with her fingertips, she strode toward the sergeants' mess.

The next morning, she applied for a weekend pass, reserved the little Matchless motorbike again, and planned what to wear. How much privacy would they have at the club? Would they be alone? What should she tell Betsy when she returned to the billet near midnight?

By Saturday afternoon, she was nervous with anticipation, so she jumped when she felt a hand on her shoulder.

"Nigel, old chap." She glanced up, keeping an eye on the radar screen for any new blips. "When did you land? Why didn't I spot you?"

He bent down and pecked her on the cheek, in front of her earphone. "I came in just an hour ago, while you were at lunch, I suppose. They're unloading now, and we were scheduled to fly out right away to Braunschweig, but the landing gear's gone hinky, so we're delayed until tomorrow. Are you on duty then?"

"No. Sunday's my day off. Why?"

"Well then, do you fancy a trip to Braunschweig? We've got a space for you in the cockpit, and you can come back to Gatow by train. We'll get you to the station, where you can link up with the supply train that leaves around five. It crosses into Soviet territory at Helmstedt, then travels on to Berlin."

She frowned. "Why would I want to take a ride to Braunschweig and then spend half a day on a train? What would be the point of that?"

"The point, my dear, is the plane's an Avro Anson, 'Faithful Annie,' and the copilot is Dickie Collins. Remember him? He's fancied you ever since your Watchfield days, and he's willing to let you fly us, at least for part of the trip."

She felt her eyebrows shoot up. "You'd let me fly the Anson?"

"Sure. At least until we came in for a landing. Wouldn't do to advertise the fact on the other end."

"Quite so. Well then, I'm in. I'll put in for a twelve-hour pass instead of four, and they won't refuse. I've worked overtime shifts now for weeks. I'll meet you in the mess tomorrow morning. What time, though?"

"Can't be sure yet, but say around eight. They won't have us flight-ready before then."

"Jolly good!" She gripped his hand warmly, then caught sight of a new echo at the edge of her radar screen. "Cheerio," she said, and clicked on her transmitter.

"Gatow ground calling. I have you in sight. Please identify. Over."

❖

The next morning, she was in high spirits as she strode with the other crew members toward the Anson, which waited like an old friend on the tarmac.

The handsome two-engine reconnaissance plane with its long row of windows offered nearly 300 degrees of visibility. She'd flown more than a dozen of them, either ferrying them from factory to field or taxiing passengers and supplies all over the newly liberated war zone. She knew "Faithful Annie" like she knew her bicycle.

In war missions, it had a three- or four-man crew, but for transport flights, pilot and navigator/radio operator were sufficient, and of course its machine gun in the forward fuselage and its dorsal gun turret were removed.

They climbed inside, and pulling on the spare flight suit over her uniform, she took a seat directly behind the cockpit. She could either gaze out the window, if she wished, or lean forward and watch the pilot and control panel.

Dickie Collins had evaporated from her memory, and now she remembered why. It would have been unkind to call him homely, but his pale, freckled Irish face was easy to forget. Except for a single conversation in the mess at Watchfield, she couldn't remember ever talking to him.

Once in the air, Nigel reminded her of the hazard. "We're over the Soviet zone, and they're always buzzing and harassing us. You have to stay on guard."

As if on cue, a Soviet plane, it looked like an early Yak, swooped past them directly overhead. It circled around and buzzed across them again, this time below.

"The trick is to not make a move. It's actually more dangerous if you bank away, because he's calculated his trajectory. They get bored after a couple of passes and disappear again."

The Yak did, in fact, disappear, and Nigel took off his headset. "You can take over now." He twisted out of the pilot's seat and exchanged places with her. She buckled in, set on the radio headset, and as she took hold of the joystick, a surge of pleasure flowed through her.

The January morning sky was crystal clear, all a pilot could ask for. To test the sensitivity of the stick, she made a slight correction and felt the craft respond. She banked one way, then the other. She almost closed her eyes as the familiar joy warmed her.

"Sweet, innit?" Dickie said shyly.

"More than sweet. This is the best place in the world to be, and I just hate it that the RAF won't let me fly."

"You know, I've heard that some commercial airlines have women pilots," Dickie said, surprisingly talkative.

"Really? Which ones?"

"Central Airlines, United Aircraft. Not a lot of them, but you shouldn't give up."

"You're right. I shouldn't." At that moment, she decided two things—that she would fly professionally again no matter how long it took, and that Dickie Collins was a quite a nice chap.

To avoid unwanted questions, Gillian relinquished the controls to Nigel as they came within sight of the Braunschweig-Wolfsburg Airport, and they landed without incident. Elated from the flight, Gillian surrendered her flight overalls, hugged her friends good-bye, and cadged a ride to the train station with an hour to spare before departure.

At the station, she had no trouble identifying the Allied supply train to Berlin, where work gangs were loading sacks of coal onto one freight car and grains, flour, beans, and other miscellanea onto a second one.

Her uniform was all she needed to obtain a seat in one of the passenger cars, and after buying a *Butterbrot* at the station, she settled in for the long ride through occupied Germany to Berlin.

After less than an hour's travel, the train pulled into Helmstedt, on the frontier between the British and Soviet zones. A border guard stopped at her seat and perused her identification for several long moments. Using a German so simple even she could understand, he asked where she was traveling to. When she replied "Berlin-Gatow," he called out something to his colleague at the other end of the car, and they both laughed.

It was an ominous reaction, but he returned her identification, so she relaxed. That the train soon started up again was also a comfort, and she wondered now what the train carried. Probably military supplies, and certainly engine parts, oil drums, asphalt, replacement boots and uniforms—all the things a military force needed for maintenance. But the coal and flour she'd seen being loaded might also be for the Berliners.

Her excitement waning, she gazed out the window. The winter sun illuminated the landscape with an almost blinding brightness, and when the train passed wooded patches, ice on the trees glittered and twinkled. One could forget for long moments that the country had been ravaged by war and its people were destitute and hungry.

While the outside temperature was frigid, the interior of the sunlit train was warm, and with the sun shining on her face, she dozed off. She must have slept for the majority of the trip, for when she looked out of the window again, they were pulling into Potsdam Station.

She was nervous again. Potsdam was in the Soviet zone, and although they were only a couple of miles from the British sector of Berlin, the Russians still had the right to demand identification. She hoped the delay wouldn't be too long.

After an hour of waiting, she began to suspect it was more than an identity check. Peering through windows on both sides of the car, she saw armed guards milling around, but nothing seemed to be happening. Frustrated, she stood up from her seat and marched to the end of the car, where a guard blocked her.

"*Sitzen*," he ordered.

"Why? What do you want?" she countered in German. Surely he understood that much.

"Inspection," he said, jabbing at her with the tip of his automatic rifle and urging her back down the aisle to a seat. Obediently, she sat down.

Inspection? Would they go through every stack, crate, and bundle? Looking for what? Was that even allowed under any of the other agreements that the four powers were always making in the Allied Control Council?

She waited another hour, hearing nothing but the occasional banging of the freight doors sliding open and then shut. The other passengers, German nationals who had some job or other with the Allied forces, sat quietly. One of them, seeing her agitation, finally spoke to her in English. "They did this before. It's not inspection. It's harassment. They want you to become fed up and leave Berlin."

"How long did the last delay last?" she asked nervously.

"Five hours. Then they said we were carrying things not allowed by agreement and sent us back to Helmstedt."

"Five hours!" She glanced at her watch. Nine thirty. She was supposed to be on a motorbike on the Kurfürstendamm at ten. She fumed, then stood up and was about to argue again with the guard. But before she'd gone very far, a familiar figure appeared at the end of the aisle. She recognized him before he recognized her, but it took a moment for her to remember his name.

"Senior Lieutenant Miranov!" She quickened her pace until she stood directly in front of him, thankful that he wasn't a very large man and that, as she recalled, he spoke English. She faced him almost eye to eye. "What is this all about?"

He smiled with a curious mixture of disdain and amiability. "It's Captain Miranov now," he replied. "I'm sorry. I know you, but I have forgotten your name."

"Somerville. Sergeant Gillian Somerville. We met at the Tabasco and then again for a few minutes at Christmas. I heard you sing."

"Ah, yes. Sergeant Somerville. Pleased to see you again. Sorry about the investigation."

"What, exactly, are you investigating? You know our trains carry supplies for our bases. They aren't breaking any rules, if there even are rules."

His mouth twisted to one side. "Perhaps none in writing, but it is understood that the two sides should not block each other's efforts to rehabilitate Germany."

"How is this train blocking the Soviet Union's rehabilitation of Germany?"

"Alas, this is not a good time or place to discuss politics. But surely you can see that the very existence of your Berlin bases is a hindrance to Soviet aims."

"But the bases exist by agreement of our two governments. How do they hinder Soviet aims?"

"They do so by joining the British and American zones and by claiming authority of a city *in the middle of the Soviet zone.*"

She paused, formulating her argument in simple terms. "I thought the zones were meant to be temporary and both our sides wanted to make a strong democratic Germany."

"Not so strong that it can again invade us. We have just defeated the German monster, and now the Western powers want to resurrect it. What are we to think, we who lost twenty-seven million of our people?"

Gillian exhaled slowly, acknowledging the strength of his argument. "I can see your perspective, but I still don't understand what you hope to gain by blocking our movements into Berlin." She looked down at her watch again. "Specifically, why you are holding me, a military ally?"

He took off his cap and wiped his forehead with his glove. "We seem to have a conflict of duties, yours to the British forces and mine to the Soviet people. However, if you promise to report the substance of my argument to your superiors, I'll release you, and have a driver take you back to Gatow."

"All the way to Gatow, if I only repeat your little speech to my commander?" She glanced again at her watch. "A shame we couldn't reach this agreement two hours ago."

"Yes, a shame. I had no idea you were on board." He extended his hand and she took it. "Good luck to you, Sergeant Somerville. Let's hope we meet again one day under happier circumstances." He summoned a subordinate and gave an order in Russian. All she recognized was the word "Gatow," but that was cold comfort. Her watch said ten thirty. Erika would have already waited for her in vain, believing she was abandoned. The thought made her nauseous.

# CHAPTER SIXTEEN

Gillian hurried to the station commander's office to report the episode before returning to her billet. At the late hour, Cdr. Yarde was no longer on duty, but his adjutant relayed the information by telephone. She delivered the political message from Vassily as well but was fairly certain it would not impress him.

Having fulfilled her duty, she unlocked her bike from the bike shed and pedaled wearily back to her quarters.

"So, what happened?" Betsy asked as she entered the room and dropped onto her bed fully clothed. "Did you get a chance to fly? And why are you so late? Sorry. That's a lot of questions."

"Whew. I'm flogged, so let me summarize. Flight was aces. Train trip back was a real cock-up, though. The Russians are apparently buggered about the single British-American zone and, in revenge, have started harassment to force us out of Berlin." She struggled to a sitting position, unlaced her shoes, and tugged them off with a sigh.

"So what did they do?"

"Stopped the train at Potsdam. For three bloody hours. For all I know, it's still there. One of the officers gave me a ride back to the base." She tugged off her jacket and skirt and hung them up in her locker. In about eight hours, she'd have to put them on again.

"The Russians who stopped the train to chase us out of Berlin gave you a ride into Berlin?"

Yawning and with her eyes half shut, Gillian drew off her slip and bra, pulled on her regulation pyjamas, and slid into bed. "Can we talk more tomorrow?"

"Sure. Oh, by the way. I hope you don't mind. I've been reading your little German primer. I can now say 'German children are strong.

The German Volk is strong. Mother cooks soup. My father is a soldier,'
all in German." She clicked off the light.

"Quite all right," Gillian said over her shoulder before dropping
onto her pillow. She dozed off in just a few minutes with the words
*Mein Vater ist Soldat* ringing through her mind.

❖

On duty the next day, she sensed a change in the air, a widespread
unease, and everyone was talking about the train "inspection." Rumors
also floated around of tensions "back in the States," with President
Truman trying to push a controversial plan through Congress. Headed
by Secretary of State Marshall, it would set Europe and especially
Germany on a whole new path of development. On the other hand, it
would mean a showdown with the Russians.

The issue took up very little of her attention, for she had her own
problems. She'd left Erika standing on an empty Berlin street in the
middle of the night and ruined everything. She could only explain by
letter. During her lunch hour, she purchased paper and envelope from
NAAFI and scribbled a note.

*Deeply sorry to leave you standing. I flew to Braunschweig
and was held up by Russians in Potsdam until ten thirty. I
miss you too and still want to meet. Can we make it next
Sunday?*

She sealed it in an envelope and held it in her pocket until her
lunch break, when she marched over to the mechanics' hut. Betsy met
her at the entrance, spanner in hand. "What brings you over here to
*wom* territory?"

"I'm looking for Heinrich."

"He didn't show up at work this morning. He was looking a bit
ropey yesterday, so he's probably sick."

"Whatever he's got, it means Erika's the only one working. They
must be in terrible shape. I have to get ahold of them."

Betsy touched her shoulder. "Don't you think you're getting in too
deep with your German friends? You can't really do anything for them.
The whole country needs feeding, but they did this to themselves, after
all. Anyhow, see you tonight." She tapped the head of her spanner in
her palm and strode back into the hut.

Thwarted, Gillian stared into space for a moment, considering her choices. She wanted desperately to explain herself to Erika but had no telephone and now no messenger service. What was left? Nothing but herself. She had to show up on her next free evening and try to explain.

❖

Two weeks later, the first time she could qualify for a four-hour pass, she ventured out again in civilian clothes on the motorbike, rehearsing what she would say. Would Erika forgive her? Or had their missed connection already broken their fragile friendship? Absurdly, the image of Friar Laurence and the message that never reached Romeo leapt into her mind, and she shuddered. At least Shakespearean suicide wasn't in the twisted mix-up.

The Kurfürstendamm was a desolate place on a Sunday night, not because Berliners were God-fearing, but because the occupying soldiers who frequented the clubs had Monday-morning duty. Still, enough clients came, along with their hungry "frats" to warrant keeping the club open.

Gillian carried chocolate, too, as well as apples for Heinrich. Was she fundamentally any different from the randy GIs and Tommies? She wasn't sure.

Catching sight of the Tabasco, she checked her watch. Almost closing hour. She parked the motorbike behind a broken wall where it could not be seen from the street and chained it to some twisted steel that jutted up through the rubble.

The club was sparsely populated at that hour, so she was ushered to a table within sight of the piano. Erika was just winding up with the string of national anthems the same way her predecessor had done. Poor thing. She must be bloody sick of patriotic anthems by now.

At ten o'clock, the lights flickered, and the waiters began to collect glasses. The owner deftly urged the last patrons out the door without confrontation, however inebriated they were. Gillian didn't recognize anyone from her own air base and was relieved. How would she have explained her presence there alone?

Within fifteen minutes, the place was empty, and with a book of sheet music in her arm, Erika strode toward her. She was wearing the same dress she'd had on at Christmas, and that alone seemed a sort of reconciliation. But she sat down without speaking, her expression registering neither anger or pleasure. "Hello," she said simply.

Gillian gripped her hand, sick with guilt. "Erika, I'm so terribly sorry to leave you standing Sunday night. You must believe me that I was physically prevented from coming. I was on a train from Braunschweig, and the Russians blocked us for three hours at Potsdam. I was frantic because I couldn't get ahold of you, and I knew you'd be hurt, or furious, or…I don't know…something I didn't want you to be."

"Yes. I was hurt," Erika said softly. "Heinrich had said you would come, and when you didn't, I thought you changed your mind."

"No, no. Nothing changed. The Russians just threw a wall between us."

Erika remained silent, so Gillian rambled on. "Is Charlotte taking good care of Heinrich?" It was a rhetorical question.

"Oh, yes, you know Charlotte. She can make soup out of nails, and she fusses over him like a mother. We're lucky to have enough coal to keep the apartment warm, so he's not getting worse."

"Oh, that reminds me…" Gillian set her rucksack on the table. "I…uh…I brought these. The chocolate's for Hanno, and the apples are for Heinrich."

"That's very kind. Heinrich needs the vitamins, and Hanno, well, he was delirious to get your chocolate at Christmas. You're practically a goddess to him now."

"I remember his mother from Wilhelm's concert. It seems you've taken over her role since she died."

"Yes. I promised her we all would look after him. He stays half the time with Wilhelm and half the time with us in Moabit."

"Do you know his father?"

Erika glanced away for a moment, then said finally, "His father was my husband."

Gillian kept any hint of shock from her voice. "The one who was killed in the attack on London?"

"Yes. Magda told me, but I never got a chance to confront him about it. He was at his barrack and then was sent on the attack on Britain. He never came back."

"Ah," Gillian said, trying to absorb the disturbing new perspective on the Blitz attack that had been the bedrock of her hatred. Now the rock was crumbling.

Erika continued. "It wasn't really Magda's fault. Besides, it was wartime, and people cling together. Magda and I became friends, and I got to watch Hanno grow up."

"I think you're all very kind, to take care of each other that way."

"You said that before, at Christmas. Downstairs...in the dark, before you...before you kissed me."

The single word, acknowledged so matter-of-factly, set Gillian's heart pounding. "I've thought of that a lot. I hope you didn't think it was an assault."

"An assault? No. Not at all. It was just that...I never...with a woman. Like that."

Gillian waited for her judgment. Was it a good thing or an embarrassment? But Erika had no more to say about it.

"Well, you sort of make up a family, don't you? I envy you." She felt like she was babbling, just to keep the silence at bay. But Erika looked so lovely with her hair done up, her eyes mascaraed, her lips crimson.

"*Hey, Mädchen,*" the owner called out, and Gillian had no trouble understanding his German. He was shutting down the lights, and they had to go.

Erika asked to stay longer, promising to lock up when they left, but he shook his head. He clicked off the lamps on his side of the room to urge them out.

So much for private time. Gillian turned toward Erika. "I can take you home on my motorbike, if you like," she offered. "It'll be much faster. You can leave your bike in the club and take the bus tomorrow."

"Oh, yes. I'd like that. Let me just fetch my coat."

Gillian buttoned her own coat and hefted her rucksack onto her back. While Erika waited at the door, Gillian undid the chain on the motorbike and walked it to where she stood. The Matchless 3gl was designed for quick travel for dispatches and the occasional reconnaissance, with only a thin metal rack over the rear. But the footrests revealed it could carry a passenger.

Erika gathered up her skirt and straddled the rack. Raising her feet onto the footrests, she slid both arms around Gillian's waist and spoke into her ear. "I'm ready."

The kick-start set them in motion, and Gillian accelerated to a speed that allowed her to negotiate the pitted and irregular streets with her awkward load. She would have been happy to ride for hours in Erika's embrace, but in the March night, her bare-legged passenger had to be freezing.

When they arrived at the familiar apartment in the Lübeckerstrasse, Erika slid from her perch. "Come inside for a moment, just by the stairs where it's warmer."

Gillian dismounted and, after surveying the empty street, decided it was safe to leave the bike unlit and unchained while they stood in the doorway of the building. The broken streetlamps gave no light through the open door. Only the ambient gray cast of the street allowed her to vaguely discern Erika's form. It was a bit surrealistic, like talking to a phantom.

"After Christmas, you were silent for a long time," Erika's disembodied voice said. "Did I say something wrong?"

"No, not in so many words. It's a long story and had everything to do with me, I mean my family dying in the Blitz of 1940."

Erika leaned back against the staircase wall. "Ah, I see. The year of Dietrich's death, and you think he was part of it." Gillian's silence told her the answer was yes.

"It's true, and we Germans will carry the guilt for the Blitz and the death camps for the rest of our lives. But we suffered bombardment, too, and you can't draw a line and say this side is heroes and this other side is monsters. Many of us were victims, too. Of our own government, of the Russians, of Allied atrocities."

Gillian touched Erika's coat lapel, wanting contact in the near darkness, even through gloves. "I accept that intellectually, but emotionally, I can't forget what happened to me personally. My home, my family was incinerated."

"I understand, but the Nazis also killed my parents. And in the end, terrible things happened to me as well."

Gillian cringed at the thought of the lovely, soft-spoken woman beaten and abused. "Oh, I'm sorry to hear that." She brushed her hand across Erika's shoulder. "Makes it difficult to know who to hate, doesn't it?"

Erika's bare hand also rose, resting for a moment on Gillian's chest, then on her cheek. "I don't want you to hate me," she whispered. "I want you to...to stay."

Elated, Gillian could only smile, invisibly, she knew, in the obscurity of the corridor. She stepped in closer, pressing their cheeks together. It took only the slightest movement for their lips to meet.

It was the gentlest of kisses, unhurried, grateful, but it bridged a gulf. It was not so much passion but the promise of passion, of allegiance against all odds. Gillian understood Erika's dry lips now, that had scared her off at Christmas. They were merely the guardians of her real person. You could not force or surprise your way past them. You had to wait for desire.

"I want us to be together, too," she whispered, "but I don't know where. It can't be at my quarters. You wouldn't be allowed. And Charlotte is always in the apartment. What's left?"

"At the club, after it closes and Herr Schalk is gone. I have a key. I'll pretend to leave and then return and wait for you to come on your motorbike like you did tonight."

"Yes, we could do that. When?"

"Next Sunday? The club closes early. Do you work on that day?"

"Only in the morning. So yes, next Sunday, at the same time."

The door opened, and Charlotte called down, apparently offering a candle.

"*Nein, nein. Ich komme gleich,*" Erika called back to her, then pulled Gillian close one last time for the same dry, lingering kiss that promised "soon."

"All right. Next Sunday, at ten. Don't let them see you," she whispered, then hurried up the stairs.

# CHAPTER SEVENTEEN

The following Sunday, Gillian worked until four, obtained a pass for twelve hours, and returned to the barrack to wash and change into civvies. She killed the next few hours reading the manuals on the newest radar equipment that would soon be installed, though she found it hard to concentrate.

The corporal who signed out the motorbike to her at eight looked puzzled, obviously dying to know what the story was. It was none of his business, and she outranked him so had no need to explain, but she preferred to keep him on her side. "Even a WAAF needs to have some social life, eh?" she said, winking.

"You sure do, ma'am. And he's a lucky guy if he gets you to come to him on one of these!"

"I'll tell him you said so," and they both chortled, though at two different jokes.

Wending her way cautiously through the now-familiar streets, she arrived at the Kurfürstendamm in good time to see the last Tabasco customers stagger out in twos and threes. Some ten minutes later, all lights went dark, and the owner appeared to lock the door. The woman who stood next to him was obviously Erika.

They lingered at the door for a few moments, and then the owner hurried away on foot, apparently living somewhere close.

Erika waited until he was out of sight and reopened the club door, hauled her bike inside, and closed it behind her. Gillian started toward the club, wheeling the motorbike.

Suddenly a light beam swept across the street and caught her. "*Halten Sie, bitte!*" someone called out in an American accent.

Shading her eyes, she stood still, alarmed. She knew even before she saw the paint on the hood that it was military police, and her mind raced to concoct a story as they pulled up beside her.

With the jeep headlights no longer blinding her, she could see two beefy men in shiny helmets with the double yellow strips of the American constabulary. What were they doing in the British sector? Apparently, they wondered the same thing about her.

"*Was machen Sie hier?*" the beefier one of them asked. A torch beam slid down to her feet and up again to her face.

"You can speak English. I'm with the British forces."

"Very good. Still have the same question though, ma'am. What's a woman doing alone at this hour on the Kurfürstendamm?" She didn't know American accents very well, but this one sounded Southern.

"I...uh..." Nothing would make any sense but the truth. Or mostly truth. "I'm glad to know someone's looking out for my safety. I arrived just now to pick someone up." She glanced down at her motorbike as evidence.

"Now who'd ya be picking up at this hour?"

"A German national employed at Gatow." It was a very small lie, purely a change of tense. "She's waiting for me right now." She pointed with her head in the general direction of the club.

"Now y'all know it's past curfew."

"Curfew? Since when is there a curfew? And why are Americans patrolling the British sector?"

He leaned toward her and rested one elbow on the side of the jeep. "That's a good question, little lady. I've been asking myself that all evening. And you can bet I'd rather be tucked in my bunk right now than out here in the cold. But since the Russians've been getting all riled up over this and that, General Clay's gone and decided to get folks off the streets at night. Dunno why *we're* havin' to do it in y'all's sector, but there ya go. Military logic."

Erika now stood in the doorway of the club watching them, and the MPs spotted her, too. It was a good thing she'd told the truth.

Gillian saw no way to get rid of the police.

"I'll be happy enough to comply, Sergeant." She hoped she'd read his rank correctly. "Just let me inform my friend over there, and we'll leave immediately."

The MP cleared his throat. "Now, how're you fixing to do that?"

"On my motorbike. It carries two." She glanced down at it again.

"That piddly li'l thing? I don't think it'll hold two grown-ups."

He scrunched up his face as if thinking were difficult. "Well, now, I'll tell you what, little lady. To show you what good sports we are, we'll just load your little bike on our hood and take you both home. That way everybody's happy."

Before she could react, he'd climbed out of the jeep and taken hold of the handlebars.

"I assure you, it will hold two. It's what we planned all along," Gillian said lamely, as they tugged the motorbike from both sides. It was a hopeless cause. He was half again as large as she was and had the authority of the military police behind him, while she was an off-duty WAAF on a failed tryst.

Erika had obviously discerned what was happening and approached. The driver greeted her in German.

"I speak English," she said, presumably horrified at his accent, and he seemed relieved. He started again. "We were just explaining to your friend here that it's too dangerous for you ladies to be on the street at this hour, so we're going to take you home. Courtesy of the United States 16th Constabulary Force."

Erika glanced over at Gillian, and several expressions passed over her face: disbelief, consternation, and finally resignation. Gillian was certain they thought the same thing. *The Americans have "rescued" us from ourselves. Shit.* Gillian would never again hear the term American heroes without smiling.

Seemingly without effort, Southern Boy hefted the motorbike up to chest level and laid it over the flat hood of the jeep, securing it with cord at front and back.

"There ya go, ladies. All set. Now if y'all will just get in the back and tell us where you were headed, we'll drop you off, safe and sound."

Defeated, they climbed into the rear and sat on the narrow metal bench obviously designed more for baggage than for passengers. Erika gave the Lübeckerstrasse address and otherwise remained silent. Gillian, too, felt beaten. They couldn't even hold hands.

The jeep delivered them to the apartment in less than fifteen minutes, and they climbed out. After Southern Boy undid the motorbike from the hood and swung it down with the same easy grace as he'd lifted it, Erika touched him on the arm. "Thank you, Sergeant. You're very kind."

"You're right welcome, ma'am. I'm from Texas, and we know how to keep a woman out of harm's way." With a quick half-salute to Gillian, he hopped back into the jeep, and it took off, the roar of its motor filling the quiet street.

Erika exploded into giggles, and Gillian, straddling her motorbike once again, fell to snickering, too. "It's absurd, isn't it?" she said. "They really thought they'd 'rescued' us. If they only knew."

Erika snorted. "So stupid. First it was the Russians, and now it's the Americans. It's taken two armies to keep us apart."

"Do you suppose it's Fate trying to tell us something?"

Erika leaned toward her and brushed her lips across Gillian's cheek. "I don't care what Fate wants. I want you."

"Unless it's past curfew," Gillian murmured back, and both began to giggle again, a bright, girlish silliness until Erika grew somber. "I care for you very much, you know, and I won't let you leave until you kiss me."

"Here in the street? In front of the neighbors?"

"Silly person. It's pitch-black. No one can see." Erika took Gillian's face in her hands and pressed a slow kiss, long enough to stir the desire that Gillian had expected to have half an hour earlier in the sordid confines of the Tabasco club.

They separated for a sweet instant and had begun a second, even better kiss, when Erika seemed to hear something and pulled away.

"What's wrong?"

"Look up there. The light just went on in our apartment. Charlotte must have heard the jeep arrive, and now she's waiting for me. You have to go, I'm afraid."

"Damn. That woman must stay awake all night, knitting. So, when do you think…?"

"I don't know. Next Sunday?" Erika said weakly.

"No. My schedule changes, and I go on night duty for two weeks."

"Oh." Erika seemed defeated. "So this time the RAF is keeping us apart." She backed away, but Gillian seized her hand.

"I'm not leaving you, and there's no one else I want to be with. Just be patient. I'll come. Believe in me, please."

"Ja, ja," Erika replied in German, and Gillian knew the language enough to realize the word carried a taint of cynicism. She could think of nothing else to say, so she kissed Erika's palm and kick-started the motorbike.

As Erika disappeared inside the entryway and closed the door behind her, Gillian brooded at the forms of love she'd been offered since being posted to Germany. She couldn't decide which was worse, a surfeit of quick, emotionless sex in a parked car, or genuine, loving desire, endlessly frustrated.

Shit, she thought, and gunned the tiny motor, leaving the Lübeckerstrasse behind.

❖

The month of March passed slowly, and Gillian found the continuously thwarted romance no longer amusing. She'd been twice to visit the Lübeckerstrasse apartment in the morning during off-duty hours. Charlotte was always welcoming and appreciative of the little gifts, but always there. All Gillian and Erika could do was exchange glances or touch fingertips like Victorian spinsters. Things had to get better.

But they got worse.

On Sunday afternoon, March 28, Flt. Lt. Parsons abruptly summoned her contingent of WAAFs. She rarely called such assemblies, and when she did, they were relaxed affairs, but this time, she appeared strained.

Standing officer-like in front of the two lines of women with her hands behind her back, she announced, "Last week the Soviet representative walked out of the meeting of the Allied Control Council, effectively ending its existence as a collective authority."

"What does that mean for us, ma'am?" one of the women asked.

"Impossible to predict the ramifications, but it appears the British and Americans will now act without Soviet cooperation. In fact, just an hour ago, an announcement came by radio that the United States Congress has approved funding for the Marshall Plan. For those of you who don't know what that is, it's money. A *lot* of money to rebuild the UK and Europe."

"Even the parts of Europe held by the Russians, ma'am?" Gillian asked.

Parsons shook her head. "According to the brief report I received, most goes to the UK, then large amounts to France and Germany and a few other countries. The Americans offered it to the Soviets, but they refused it for themselves and for East Germany and Poland."

"But, for our side, things should get better, shouldn't they?" Betsy asked.

"One hopes, but the Soviets consider it an affront. They're slowing down rail traffic bringing supplies from our zones to West Berlin."

"Will that change our duties, ma'am?"

"Only to increase them, I'm afraid. We've received orders from Bad Eilsen to remain on alert because aircraft will be taking up the slack. That means more flights. Consequently, we will be on duty seven days a week, with passes limited to two hours."

Gillian's heart sank. "Does that include this evening?"

"Yes, it does. In any case, regardless of your role—mechanic, administration, signals, or traffic control—as of now, you will be on duty or on standby at all times. No one is to leave the aerodrome without official leave signed by me."

She looked around the room at her staff. "If you have no further questions, you are dismissed."

Gillian was heartsick. Now even the day visits were out of the question, and all that was left was messages. She would compose a letter as soon as possible and find out tomorrow if Heinrich would act as go-between. Would he stand for being daily postman for a relationship he wouldn't understand? It seemed a desperate thing, but what else was left?

As she left the hall, a familiar figure appeared at the end of the corridor, and she hurried toward him.

"Nigel. I'm so glad to see you. You've heard the news, I'm sure."

"Yes, I have, and it's jolly awful, isn't it? They're scrambling for pilots, too. It's a good thing we've got such good ground control now, because as soon as they've assembled enough crews, they'll be sending in planes day and night."

"Where are you off to now?"

"Orders are for Fassberg. Then Bad Eilsen. I was just coming to ask you to join me for lunch, old girl. Are you free?"

She linked her arm in his. "I'm all yours." Then, glancing down at her watch, "for forty-five minutes."

They sat down in the sergeants' mess with their trays of bean and turnip stew and shoveled in a few mouthfuls while it was still warm.

"What's new in the life of an ace pilot?" she asked, trying to be cheerful.

"What with all this Russian nonsense, we're flying in the more urgent supplies to our bases rather than letting them go by train, where they might be confiscated. They've ordered more pilots from home, too. Jack's back in Germany now, by the way. He'll be showing up one of these days."

Gillian shrugged. "I don't care about Jack. He's persona non grata, as far as I'm concerned, after what he did to Erika."

"He told me about his little blackmail of Erika and how he regrets it. Not something worthy of an RAF officer, he said. You should give him another chance. He's a decent chap, after all."

"Said by a man." She scoffed and returned to her stew.

"I'm glad I still qualify," Nigel said.

She set down her spoon. "You silly savage. You're strong, kind, attentive, exactly the kind of man millions of women would want. You just haven't noticed because you're not looking."

He shrugged. "Ironies never cease."

❖

Although they worked on different schedules, Gillian's and Betsy's orbits sometimes crossed, and on one of those nights they actually came off duty at the same time. After the evening ablutions, they hit their bunks.

"Gosh, it's been weeks since we've had time together," Gillian observed. "How's life over there with the *woms*? Or otherwise, for that matter."

Betsy sighed deeply. "Work is the same as always, but…"

"But…what? For God's sake, talk to me, quick, before I fall asleep."

"I think I'm in love."

"You're always in love. Someone new every few weeks."

"I can't help it. It's my hot blood."

"Since when do English farm girls have hot blood? It's not like you're a Gypsy or an Italian."

"Typical posh city girl's view. All farm girls are hot-blooded. Growing up with all that livestock, you learn that calves, lambs, and piglets come from big bulls, rams, and boars. I knew about fucking when I was five."

"So which bull, ram, or boar is it now?"

"His name is Maurice, and he's gorgeous. A navigator. He says I remind him of his first girlfriend, who left him for another woman. Can you imagine?"

"I suppose it does happen," Gillian said mildly into the darkness.

"It's disgusting. How does a woman go off so wrong that she wants another woman?"

"Well, maybe she was hurt."

"Maybe. In that case, I'd feel sorry for her, but I still wouldn't want to undress in front of her. I'd always have to worry about her ogling me or grabbing me tits."

"But you don't undress in front of anyone, anyhow. Do you worry about the men on base grabbing you as you walk by?"

"No, but they mostly have manners. And besides, that's natural."

"Mmm. I don't know what's natural anymore. Is rape natural?"

"What are you going on about, Gillian? We were talking about my new crush, and suddenly you're at rape."

"Sorry. I suppose I was just being…logical. I apologize. So, tell me about Maurice. What's he look like?"

After surrendering the discussion, Gillian lost interest, and after grunting agreement and approval a few times, she drifted off to sleep.

The next morning, with Betsy's condemnations buzzing at the back of her mind, she wrote a note to Erika. Briefly, she explained the increased Russian aggression and her confinement to the base as a result. She apologized for the postponement of their planned…what?

She didn't want to name it and wasn't even sure what it was supposed to be. Could they move directly from a few tender kisses into carnal knowledge? What exactly did they both imagine would happen? As time passed, and her fears had grown, it had become harder and harder to imagine anything. She finally decided on the phrase "our time alone together."

She sealed the envelope, and before reporting for duty, she marched across the tarmac to the mechanics' hut. She'd never been inside before and was shocked. No wonder Betsy complained. The place was frigid, cluttered and noisy, and held a single bedspring in the corner. For the occasional exhausted nap, she supposed, though it didn't even have a mattress.

All eyes turned as she entered. "I'm looking for Heinrich," she said to the first person she met, another WAAF. She'd never learned her name.

"He's in the loo," the WAAF replied. "Something I can tell him?"

"No. I'll wait."

After an awkward ten minutes, Heinrich emerged from a corner and waved a greeting. Now at the center of everyone's attention, including Betsy's, Gillian handed over the envelope along with a bar of Cadbury.

"The note is for Erika, and the chocolate is for Hanno."

Heinrich also seemed uncomfortable with the meeting and nodded quickly. "Sure. I'll deliver them. Thank you."

Gillian thanked him in return and fled the hut, feeling a dozen eyes on her back.

# CHAPTER EIGHTEEN

*April 5, 1948*

With their evening of "being alone together" frustrated, Gillian surrendered once again to the dullness of everyday responsibilities and reported for duty at eight in the morning.

The rain of the previous week had given way to a clear sky, so ground control, though required, was not essential. That took off much of the pressure.

Several flights had landed, and Gillian was beginning to let a small part of her mind dwell on what would be served in the mess for lunch. Then she caught sight of another spot on the periphery of her screen.

The luminous line of the scanner swung around the screen as the antenna on top of the transmitter swept across the sky. The bright dot moved slowly toward the center, and she switched on her microphone.

"This is Gatow ground control. Are you receiving me? Please identify yourself. Go ahead."

"Gatow ground, Bealine 480 here. Receiving you loud and clear. Await instructions. Go ahead."

"Bealine 480. You are entering our radar at bearing zero eight zero, range fifty miles. Go ahead."

"Gatow ground. Zero eight zero. Is that you, Gillian? Go ahead."

"Bealine 480. Yes. Who am I speaking to? Go ahead."

"Gatow ground. It's Jack Higgins. Glad you're on duty. I've got a letter I'd like you to deliver. Go ahead."

"Bealine 480. Continue on present course and remain listening."

"Gatow ground. Actually, it's for Erika. An apology. Go ahead."

Gillian's heart pounded at the mention of her name on a wavelength that a dozen other people could hear. But training kept her on message.

"Bealine 480. Reduce altitude to sixteen hundred feet and change course to two fife zero." She was careful to pronounce "fife" the radio operator's way to make it clear.

Slowly the bright spot crawled toward the center of the screen. At fifteen miles, the incoming plane was more or less lined up with the runway.

Sitting in front of the elevation and azimuth dials, the other controller called over to her, "I've got him. He's drifting slightly."

"Bealine 480. You are eleven miles from airfield. Maintain present altitude and change course to 270. Do you read me? Go ahead."

"Gatow ground, receiving you loud and clear. Changing course to 270. Did you hear what I said about the letter? Over."

"Bealine 480. Yes, I did. Wait. Another aircraft is approaching you. Do you have a visual? Go ahead." She watched in horror as a second, much smaller bright flash streamed toward him diagonally, then crossed his path. What the devil was it?

"Gatow ground. I see him. It's a Russian who keeps buzzing me. Over."

"Bealine 480. You are drifting. Change course fife degrees left. Over."

"Gatow ground, changing course fife degrees left. SHIT. He's crossed in front of me again. Over."

She could see both dots each time the radar line swept over the two aircraft, and they appeared almost joined. She wished she could shoot the Russian craft out of the sky.

"Bealine 480, you are now six miles from touchdown but drifting. Can you change course seven degrees left? Repeat, seven degrees left. Over."

"Gatow tower, changing course—Oh, Christ. He's clipped me."

"Bealine 480, you are dropping too fast. Adjust rate of descent. Over."

"Son of a—"

"Bealine 480, please respond. Do you receive? Repeat, do you receive? Adjust rate of descent. Over."

One of the other WAAF operators stood up, threw open the door of the trailer, and lurched outside to look over the airfield.

"Dear God. They're both falling!" she shouted back through the door.

Gillian refused to accept what she heard and kept repeating, "Bealine 480, please respond. Do you receive me? Over."

All she heard was the hiss of static until her colleague screamed. "Oh, my God. NO! Fire just beyond the runway. They've crashed."

A few miles to the east, Erika reported for work at Tabasco at the usual time. She played her songs without thinking, letting her hands find the familiar patterns while her thoughts wandered. Gillian's image appeared immediately, with the usual string of associations. The model airplane, the Christmas dinner—their kiss, then the comedy with the American MPs.

She had just finished a long medley when she sensed a drop in the usual background hum. A restlessness followed, and a scraping of chairs. She glanced toward the tables.

Two Soviet officers were threading their way among the tables, quietly signaling each of the Russian soldiers. She watched, puzzled, as all of them stood up and filed out of the club. What was going on?

Only after the last man had exited and one of the officers stopped to talk to Herr Schalk did she realize she knew him. Vassily Miranov now wore the shoulder bars of a captain. She stood up from her piano and approached him.

"Captain Miranov. May I ask what's going on?" she asked in Russian.

"Good evening, Fräulein Brandt. I'm afraid there's been an accident, and it is necessary to recall our personnel."

"Accident? What happened?"

"A British passenger airliner collided with one of our Yak-3s outside of Gatow just an hour ago. Unfortunately, all were killed."

"All? From a British airliner? Crew, passengers?"

"Yes, an unfortunate accident. Regrettable on all sides. And exacerbated by each plane crashing in the other's zone. Our emergency services as well as the British are at both crash scenes."

"What was the cause? Which aircraft violated airspace?"

"I cannot say, Fräulein Brandt. I am sure both British and Soviet headquarters will have a statement to make."

She touched his arm. "Captain Miranov. We've known each other for years now, and we've spoken openly. My British friend tells me your pilots harass their planes all the time. Why is that?"

He glanced around, clearly to ensure he could not be overheard. "I know your sentiments are with the West, but believe me, by combining their zones, they have broken Germany in half. Worse, they have insisted on remaining in the heart of our territory, creating a satellite city. We will urge them to leave by all means necessary."

"By blocking the trains carrying food and coal? Some of that is for us."

Seeing Schalk approach, he said quickly, "Please remember, it is all for a brighter future for Germany, and one day you will thank us for it."

As he stepped toward the door, Schalk appeared in front of her. "We've got plenty of other customers waiting. Please get on with the rest of the show."

❖

It was past midnight when Erika bicycled home, deeply troubled by the news of the air crashes. Had Gillian been at work when the accident happened? Did she know any of the victims?

Erika longed to talk to her. They'd come so close, and now it seemed like the kiss, the pledge, had never happened. She crept into the dark apartment, being careful not to wake the others.

She clicked on the little light by the sofa and spotted the object on her bed. A letter and a Cadbury bar.

The note was obviously written before the crash, for it made no mention of it, only told of the new restrictions placed on the staff because of Russian interference. But it was wonderful to hold a letter, however short, in her hand.

Tired as she was, she sat down to write a reply immediately so she could hand it to Heinrich the next morning. The English primer that Charlotte had given her still had a lot of pages left, so by the light of her tiny bedside lamp, she composed her first timid love letter.

*Dearest. I call you that because you are dear to me, and I will not use your name. We are all very sorry for the accident that killed your Englishmen. We know they came, in part, for us, and the Russians are trying to drive you out. Berlin is hungry, not only for food, but for dignity, understanding, and for the day we can rise above what our armies have done. Please say you forgive us, and please say you will stay.*

She sealed it with candle wax and went to bed.

The next morning, she rose to find Heinrich and Charlotte at the table discussing the crash.

"What happened, exactly?" Erika asked. "Do you know?"

"*Nordwestdeutscher Rundfunk* reported it yesterday evening while you were working. Apparently, the British plane was approaching Gatow when the Russian harassed it like they've been doing for months. But this time their wings touched. Both wings fell off, so the planes crashed, the British plane in the Soviet sector and the Russian plane in our sector."

It was just as Capt. Mironov had said. "Did they give any names?"

"Only that the flight crew was four RAF. No more than that."

A jumble of thoughts turned in her head. Did she know any of the passengers from her days in the Gatow kitchen? Did Gillian know any of them? Did the event touch her in any way? She had to find out.

"Heinrich, thank you for bringing the letter from Gillian. Can I give you one in return?" She held out the folded and wax-sealed paper.

He winced. "You know I can't go into the control trailer. I'll have to wait until she comes to me."

"Can't you ask one of her friends to pass it on? Please, Heinrich. I don't have any other way to talk to her." She could hear the whining in her voice and hated it.

"All right. But please don't get me in trouble with this." He slipped the note into the pocket of his overalls. "And if there are any more chocolate bars, they're for me."

After he left, Erika and Charlotte went to look for lines forming in front of the shops where they were registered. No line at all meant the store was empty. Long lines meant a hope for whatever was for sale. No shops had short lines.

They joined those waiting outside the bakery. Huddled inside her coat, Erika patted the ration coupons, hers and Hanno's, in her pocket, but the line was longer than usual, which was ominous.

"Do we still have potatoes?" she asked Charlotte.

"Yes, the powdered kind. A small bag, just enough for tonight."

"I guess we don't have much hope for carrots or turnips, do we?"

"No. Nothing in the shops for weeks, and the crops planted around the city won't produce until summer. I might have a few green beans in the window box."

Erika sighed weakly. "I asked Herr Schalk to pay me in food instead of worthless marks, but he says he can't. Though he's never missed a meal in his life."

"I'll bet he's never cold either, while I sold everything I had last winter for coal."

The woman just ahead of them in line turned around. She looked old, but since defeat, everyone did. She grimaced. "Be glad you made it through. My father didn't. Froze to death in his sleep. The house was so cold the bread froze, too. We couldn't cut it."

"They have it worse in the French and Russian zones," another woman said. "My friend Hilda says they're rationed at a thousand calories. She collects nettles to make soup."

Erika and Charlotte fell silent. At least two of their patched-together family were employed, even if only for a pittance, and that gave them a tiny advantage.

The entrance to the shop was in sight, finally. Only some ten women stood in front of them, all with eyes riveted on the door, for each time it opened, one woman stepped out, and the next one stepped in to buy her ration.

Erika counted back now. Nine, eight, seven. But then, her heart sank. Woman number six came out clutching her bread to her chest as if protecting it from attack. Behind her the door closed—she could swear she heard the lock click—and the horrifying sign SOLD OUT appeared in the glass door.

A cry of outrage rose up from the five women in front of them and the score of women behind them. Sold out. Cruel words for all, a possible death sentence for a few.

Erika stood, stupefied and defeated, but Charlotte turned to her neighbor. "Nettle soup. How do you make that?"

❖

Within a few days, *Heinrich-post* was established, with his reluctant participation. German workers were refused entrance into official buildings where they were not assigned, but he caught up with Betsy, who consented to deliver the first note. After that, she washed her hands of the system in general.

Gillian delivered her response herself, putting it directly in Heinrich's hand.

*Dearest. Yes, call me that. I love your stationery with Sally and Dick and Jane. It makes us seem so innocent. What the radio did not announce about the crash were the names of the men, and you will be shocked to know that one of them was Jack Higgins. He was carrying a letter for you in which he apologized, though of course it burned up with him. I'm sorry. It might have gotten your job back. Flights are increasing in number, and we can't leave the base now. I miss you and will write every day, with poor Heinrich as our go-between. At least I am the one who risks exposure by hiking across the tarmac each day to post or receive a note from you. Please tell me you are well and that you think of me.*

Their letter exchange lasted through the month of April, with Gillian making a daily run to the mechanics' shed every afternoon during her break.

Erika's notes continued on the blank spaces of English primer pages and told of the behavior of drunken soldiers at the club or the length of food lines, ending with terms of affection. Her German cursive was always a challenge to decipher, and so too was answering them in isolation. Betsy had shown herself to be unsympathetic, and Gillian also feared she might be curious enough to read the letters. As a precaution, she took to carrying pen and paper to the ablutions room and writing while sitting on a covered loo.

*I brought in twenty-six planes yesterday. The pilots, all strong, courageous men, trusted their lives to me. I hope you can be as sure of me as they were. I am sure of you. I trust and admire those supple, skillful hands that have made your livelihood, but also your glowing intelligence that seeps through the hindrance of a language not your own. I so much want to know more of you.*

She passed it quickly to Heinrich so as not to interrupt his work or call attention to the exchange. She tried to be discreet in the receipt or passing of a note, occasionally adding a chocolate bar or a packet of coffee, but she had no business among the mechanics and couldn't help but be conspicuous each time she arrived.

The secretive correspondence could not go on forever, and at the end of April, just as she stepped away from Heinrich, two of the station's military police confronted her. One of them reached into Heinrich's chest pocket and withdrew Gillian's letter, while the other held out a hand for the note she had just received.

"Come with us, please," he said.

As the MPs led Gillian into her office, Flt. Lt. Parsons stood up.

Gillian saluted smartly, though Parsons wasn't a stickler for military etiquette. "Am I under arrest, Commander? If so, may I ask why?"

The commander ignored her for a moment as one of the officers handed over both the letter that Gillian had just tried to send and the note from Erika that she'd not yet read. She was petrified.

The two police left, and Flt. Lt. Parsons unfolded the letter and read it silently. Puckering slightly in disapproval, she then took the smaller note from Erika and broke the wax seal. It was a quicker read.

Gillian saw the ruin of her career, preceded by a humiliating discharge for…what? Unnatural behavior? What did the military call it? Her mouth went dry, and she tried to calm the pounding in her chest.

The commander finally spoke. "These notes are only two of many, I believe. You've been seen exchanging clandestine messages and gifts with a foreign national repeatedly. At the very least, it appears to be misappropriation of military property, and at the worst, it could be construed as espionage."

"Espionage?" Gillian was momentarily speechless. "How…? You mean passing information to the enemy? But the Germans aren't our enemies anymore. And the items I gave him were from my own rations."

"So you admit to passing information?"

Gillian started to speak, then closed her mouth. Was what she wrote each night information? When did reminiscences, philosophical meanderings, vague longings become information?

"No, ma'am. They've just been letters of friendship, admiration." She had no idea what was in Erika's note, whether it was romantically explicit.

Parsons straightened her back to deliver the dreaded charge. "I'll get right to the point, Sergeant Somerville. Are you having relations with Heinrich Dehmler?"

"Relations?" Gillian blinked for a moment. "No, of course not!" she sputtered. "He and his wife are friends who invited me for Christmas, so I send part of my rations to them to help them through."

"So you are not intimate with Mr. Dehmler? He seems quite fond of you." She unfolded Erika's note and read aloud. "'I love the way the corners of your mouth curl up slightly, like you are thinking of a smile.' This is not the language of a simple friend."

It took a moment for Gillian to realize that she'd been saved from disaster by the commander's prurient imagination. Or perhaps by her lack of it. It was a buoy, and she grabbed it.

"I admit I have allowed a certain flirtation to take place between myself and Mr. Dehmler, but I can assure you, I'll take an oath if you wish, that I have never been intimate with him. I am not that kind of woman." The assertion amused the tiny part of her brain that wasn't terrified.

Parsons dropped the letters on her desk. "I know many of our airmen take advantage of the local women with those sorts of gifts, but such conduct would certainly be unbecoming a member of the WAAF."

"I see that now. But please do not punish Mr. Dehmler for my foolishness. He's a good man who's doing his best to support two other people. His wife does laundry for the men, and they take care of a boy who lost both parents. If you could see them—"

Parsons raised a hand. "I don't need to see them. They are like two million other Berliners, desperate for our help. Our government is committed to guiding the Germans to self-determination and a prosperous Europe, but our duty is to promote those goals *professionally*, by way of the chain of command, and not through personal liaisons."

"Yes, ma'am. If I'm to be disciplined, I accept that and ask only that you do not fire Mr. Dehmler."

"Fortunately for Mr. Dehmler, we cannot afford to fire any of our German fitters and technicians. They are far too valuable. But I will request that he be transferred to Tempelhof, where he can no longer dwell on the shape of your lips. In any case, Templehof has a much larger maintenance department and will be happy to have him. I will not initiate any disciplinary action, but you are to terminate all contact with this man. Is that understood?"

Gillian saluted. "Yes, ma'am."

"Then you are dismissed."

❖

Gillian marched from the commander's office, relieved that catastrophe had been averted, but anxious at losing contact with Erika.

She also felt battered. How could something that felt so uplifting and good be so despised?

More immediately, how could she let Erika know what had happened? Messages were now out of the question, and she had no telephone. All that remained was a personal trip into Berlin, at the very least, to leave a message with Charlotte.

She couldn't act right away, since that would draw attention to herself. But in the next days, she would apply for a two-hour pass, which would provide just enough time to make the bus trip to the Moabit apartment, a few minutes of talking— to Erika, if she was home, or to Charlotte, if she wasn't—and then to return. It would have to do.

But political events overtook even this plan.

On May 30, Flt. Lt. Parsons summoned her entire WAAF contingent to the officers' mess and made another, more ominous announcement.

"As you know, the Soviets have halted and searched our trains to such a degree that General Clay has canceled all rail transports. Our supplies arrive now solely by air. This will not be easy. In April, the Soviets demanded the withdrawal of American staff running communication equipment in the Eastern zone, and this has prevented the use of navigation beacons to mark air routes. In expectation of future Soviet interference, both the USAF and the RAF are stockpiling food and supplies by way of air and barge traffic. Your duties will necessarily be expanded."

"Will we still have two-hour passes to leave the base, Commander?" one of the women asked.

The commander posed defiantly with her hands behind her back, preparing to deliver unpleasant news. "Within the next week, we expect a formal announcement of the creation of West Germany as a single political entity with its own currency. Soviet retaliation will undoubtedly follow, and we must be ready for that eventuality. All passes of any duration are therefore canceled."

❖

Through the month of May, Gillian functioned on autopilot, inwardly in turmoil. She enjoyed her work, felt it was important and patriotic, but the near miss with Heinrich had shown her how precarious her situation was, how much her emotions put her at risk. Yet, without those emotions she was an automaton. Without Erika, she saw no point in staying in Berlin. And when the Western Allies wearied of challenging the Russian claim, she'd be posted home anyhow. So, perhaps it was a good thing that she and Erika were separated. It would bring them both to their senses.

Then, one evening after Gillian's usual ten hours at her console, Betsy showed up behind her singing "Happy Birthday." Somehow, it had gotten to be June 15.

"Rumor has it you're off duty in five minutes," Betsy chirped.

Gillian glanced at her watch. "As a matter of fact, I am. Do you fancy a drink at the NAAFI?"

"I can do better than that. Nigel and Dickie are in, and we're all supposed to meet at the Malcolm Club. You know where it is, I'm sure, in the huts at the far end of the apron."

"You sly dogs, you. That sounds cracking!" Gillian handed over her headset to the corporal just coming on duty and hurried from the trailer to the bike shed.

Nigel and Dickie waited with a bottle of wine and a tiny cake with a minute candle at the center. As she entered, they sang the birthday song again and handed her a greeting card.

She embraced all three of her friends, read the card, and cut the cake into four square chunks, which, with the sweet German wine they also presented her, would be just the sort of festivity she needed.

"Have you heard the latest?" Nigel asked, uncorking the bottle. "The Russians keep blocking and unblocking our transit systems— first the trains, then road traffic and barges. Now Generals Clay and Robertson want to triple our air deliveries and even start supplying the Berliners."

Nigel poured wine into everyone's glass. "Of course, no one has the faintest idea of how to do it at that scale. What's the population of Berlin? About two million? No one can provide for that many people."

"Of course not. The Luftwaffe tried it at Stalingrad for a tiny fraction of that number and failed." Dickie bit into his cake.

Gillian emptied her glass and gesticulated with it. "It's a ridiculous idea. We don't even know how much food, coal, and petrol people need, not just for themselves, but to keep the trams and U-Bahn—actually, the whole city—going."

"Calculating the food part should be easy." Dickie glanced toward the ceiling, as if using it to calculate. "Assuming a certain minimum diet of such and such grain and meat, you multiply that by two million. Coal is something else again. That fuels the electrical power plant and the factories. If the blockade goes into winter, you can double the quantity."

"It won't go into winter," Gillian insisted. "It can't."

Nigel filled everyone's glass again, emptying the bottle. "What about planes to haul all that stuff? Our Dakotas can carry only three tons. The Skymasters, Avro Yorks, the Hastings, about nine."

"The American Globemasters can carry twenty-five tons," Dickie added. "Don't know how many they could put into service, though."

"Um, what about aviation fuel? For all those planes, we'd need millions of gallons. Airplane parts, tires."

"Flight crews, many more than we've got now. And ground crews. And unloading crews. Round the clock, I suppose."

Gillian turned over her birthday card and drew a pencil from her pocket. "Okay. Let's try to calculate. Give me some rough estimates. Say, for three months, if the Russians are really stubborn." While the two men made rough guesses in each category, Gillian scribbled on the back of her birthday card. After some fifteen minutes of back-and-forth, she handed the list to them to study.

"Crikey," Dickie exclaimed. "It's bloody impossible."

Nigel agreed. "It *is* impossible. So they bloody well won't do it."

"Where does that leave us, then?" Betsy asked what they all were thinking.

"Most likely, the US and UK will be forced to concede Berlin to the Russians, and we'll go home."

Home, Gillian thought, suddenly filled with dread. She had no home but here.

# CHAPTER NINETEEN

At eight o'clock in the morning, the radio in the Dehmler household went silent, and the light in the kitchen blinked out.

"What's happened?" Erika asked, though she didn't expect anyone to answer.

She ran to the window and saw the morning tram halted at the corner. People poured out of it and out of the buildings, asking each other the same question.

Someone below snatched up a paper announcement that had been tacked on a pole during the night and waved it in the air. "Those Russian bastards have turned off the power!" The cries of anger sounded in both directions along the street.

Charlotte glanced at the wind-up clock that continued to run. "It's just after eight. I wonder if Heinrich made it to work."

"I'm sure he has," Erika said. "He left at seven on the bus. But is this going to last all day, all week? And what's the point?"

"Should I go to school?" Hanno asked. "They probably don't have power either."

"No, dear. You might as well stay here. We may need you, and I'd like for us to be together until we work out what to do."

Hanno was at the window now. "Listen. A lorry's coming. They're making an announcement."

The two of them leaned out of the window next to him trying to hear the message. A minute later the lorry was close enough for them to see RADIO IN THE AMERICAN SECTOR painted on its side.

One man drove while another spoke into a microphone that broadcast from speakers mounted on two sides. In American-accented German, he repeated the message again and again as they passed along the streets.

*Ladies and gentlemen, the Soviet Administration has cut electricity at the main Klingenberg power plant, which is in their sector. Please stay calm and be patient. Moabit and surrounding districts have auxiliary plants, and we shall endeavor to bring up some power as soon as possible. Until the situation is resolved and radio transmission is again possible, we will circulate and bring the news in this way.*

Charlotte was the first to shake herself into action. "How much water do we have? I have a full sink ready for laundry, but I can use it for cooking instead. Hanno, run and see if the baker has bread. If so, use the last of our coupons."

For the rest of the day, Charlotte and Erika combed the shops for food and candles, though every other Berliner seemed to have the same idea, and they collected little. Then they returned to the apartment and waited.

During the afternoon, Hanno wandered through the streets gathering news and seeing what measures people were taking.

"It's only in the west side, of course," he reported. "Once you cross the Bernauerstrasse, the power's on."

"What about water?"

"All the buildings I checked were dry, but pipelines in the streets have hand pumps, like when the Russians arrived." He looked back and forth at Erica and Charlotte, then threw up his hands. "Don't worry. I remember where the buckets are. Erika, can I use your bicycle to hang them on?"

"Like the good old days, huh?" she said with bitter sarcasm. "Only this time, we have no cellars to forage in. Sure. Take the bike, but please don't let it out of your sight. It's my only way to get to work."

He ambled toward the kitchen for the buckets that had saved them through the first weeks of the occupation and they'd all hoped never to have to use again.

Charlotte stared out the window, as if watching the street would provide some explanation of what to expect. The sky was blue, the weather warm, and the spring calm seemed to belie the possibility of disaster.

"It's crazy, you know," Erika said. "Thousands of us live in one sector and work in another. People move back and forth all the time, and all you need is an identity paper from your work. Very easy to counterfeit."

"I guess they'll tighten security," Charlotte mused. "Otherwise, what's the point of blocking one side of a city and not the other?"

"Even so, you can cross over in dozens of hidden places. Some buildings even have entrances in one sector and backyards in another. Didn't they think of that? And where there aren't any crossovers, we'll make some."

Charlotte nodded, but it was cold comfort.

A while later, Hanno called up from the street with two buckets of water. While he hauled them up the stairs, Erika took the precious bicycle to go to work. The club on the Kurfürstendamm was in the Western sector, but Herr Schalk had a store of candles and an even greater store of liquor. She was certain he'd find a way to stay open.

In fact, with the shock of events, few servicemen showed up to party, and after two hours, Herr Schalk decided it wasn't worth burning so many candles, and he closed.

When Erika returned to the apartment, Heinrich hadn't shown up yet. She lit only one candle, and little light came through the boarded window from the street. Hanno was sleeping peacefully, but for Erika, sitting in the quiet darkness brought dreadful memories of the first days of defeat, and when she went to bed, she slept poorly.

The next morning the RIAS news lorry swept through the sector again with further announcements, and none of them were good. The Soviet Administration that had cut the power had also permanently shut down both the main rail artery and the autobahn route from the West. Moreover, all barge traffic into the Western sector along the Havel was blocked.

Later that day the Soviets themselves posted fliers on walls and columns stating the same facts, preceded by WE REGRET WE ARE FORCED BY WESTERN RECALCITRANCE.

Twenty-four hours passed with the city in complete paralysis, and then the RIAS lorries circulated again with slightly more encouraging news.

*Auxiliary plants are now in operation to provide limited power to the western sector. Since their output is a fraction of that of the main Soviet plant, most power will be directed toward critical services: water and sewage-pumping*

*stations, bakeries, hospitals, transportation, and schools.*
*What remains will be available to private households in two-*
*hour blocks, twice every twenty-four hours, in rotation. A*
*schedule will appear soon.*

Erika stood back from the open window. "From hell to purgatory,
but at least someone on our side is taking charge."

❖

A month passed, with the Berliners adapting to the new level of
hardship. As always, Erika rode her bicycle to the club each afternoon
and back home late at night. The night air was warmer, but the few
streetlights that had functioned before, to provide her bearings, were
now dark, and her sole illumination was the friction lamp mounted on
her bike. She'd heard stories about assault, rape, and murder, from the
neighbors and from radio reports, and her only defense was speed.

Heinrich's new job at Tempelhof brought him the same hot meal
he'd enjoyed at Gatow, and in the American canteen, the food was
a step up in quantity and quality. The paltry salary was the same as
before, and so were Charlotte's tips from doing laundry and Erika's
bonuses in schnapps. Combined, however, their incomes kept them all
fed, if only just.

Still, no word came from Gillian. Had she simply abandoned
them? Nothing in her character suggested she would do that. Yet her
silence had been so very long.

The rotating two hours of electricity challenged their daily
routine. Sometimes, when Erika arrived home at midnight, Moabit's
precious two hours would be on. Charlotte would be up cooking and
washing, and everyone would be listening to the news from RIAS,
which broadcast every hour day and night. When the power went off,
they all went to bed.

At the end of July, an announcement by the Soviet Administration
appeared again on the walls and advertising columns. West Berliners
were invited to "register" as East Berliners and thus enjoy the fresh
food available through contact with farmers in the surrounding Eastern
zone.

"What does that mean?" Erika asked.

"Blackmail," Charlotte explained. "So-called 'registering' would
effectively make the population of the West defect to the East, and to

the Russians, at least on paper. It's what they want, isn't it? To turn us against the British and Americans so that they leave."

Erika's jaw set. "I'll starve to death in the dark before I surrender again to Russian demands. Things can't get any worse than they are now."

"Except in the winter," Charlotte muttered ominously.

# CHAPTER TWENTY

*July 1948*

"We're calling it Operation Plainfare," Flt. Lt. Parsons announced to her contingent of WAAFs. "The Americans are calling their end of it 'Operation Vittles,' but I suppose our people thought that sounded a bit too cowboyish. In principle, due to the land blockade, all supplies are being airlifted to Berlin from the West. As before, we'll be assisting the program in air-traffic control, administration, and mechanics. Any questions?"

"Haven't they been doing that since March?" one of the women asked.

"Yes, though at that time, the provisions were for our own stations. Now they're for the Berliners, too."

"Do we have enough men and equipment to do that?" another one asked.

"That is the question of the day, Corporal. Apparently, President Truman and Prime Minister Attlee think we do. So do the generals in charge of the occupation. It's not for us to decide, in any case. Our role is support, and to this end, I shall be drawing up a duty roster for all of you, in cooperation with Commander Yarde."

"What about passes, ma'am? Some of us haven't been off the base for weeks."

Parsons stood with her hands clasped behind her back and rocked slightly on her heels, usually a signal that she was about to deliver bad news. "Passes are canceled for the next few weeks, until General Tunner determines what resources are needed and where. After that, we will decide on a case-by-case basis, with hardships considered first."

She let her glance sweep over "her" WAAFs with an authority

softened by concern. "If there are no further questions, you are dismissed."

Gillian moped toward her post, although she had half an hour before duty began. It had been two months since she'd seen Erika. She'd counted on getting a pass, if only for a few hours, to visit her in Moabit during the hours the bus operated. But now that seemed impossible.

Betsy seemed always to be absent too, since their duty schedules were at odds, and it wasn't until the first day of August that they arrived at the same time at the WAAF barracks and dropped onto their bunks.

"How's life with the woms?" Gillian asked.

Betsy kicked off her shoes, slid off her socks, and rubbed the toes on one foot. "Dreary. We do the same things over and over again. Hydraulic failures, electrical faults. We just patch them up enough so they can limp back to their home base for actual repair. I wish I had a shilling for every hydraulic pump I've had to take out, jerry-rig, and put back in. What about you?"

Gillian hung her uniform on a hanger in her locker and sat down in her "twilights," her light-weight regulation underwear. "Bleary-eyed from staring at a radar screen for twelve hours. Traffic's so heavy now, they've put in more controllers to monitor the elevation and azimuth dials, so there's always two of us for each plane. Sometimes the echoes on the screen come in so close together, I don't know which one I'm talking to. I have to ask one of them to turn left and then check which of the dots changes position. I could really use some time off."

"Crikey. Me, too. I haven't been able to see Maurice in weeks. A girl gets lonely. You know what I mean?" She winked.

Gillian ignored the innuendo and the new name. "Yeah, lonely," she muttered, and dropped back onto her pillow as Betsy extinguished the light.

Something crackled under her head, and she sat up again and groped around her pillow. Her fingers touched something. Paper. No. An envelope.

"Betsy, turn the light on again, will you? I found something in my bed."

Grumbling, Betsy stood up and flicked on the wall switch, then dropped back into bed. "Oh, I forgot to tell you. You weren't at mail call today, so when the clerk called out your name, I said I'd deliver it."

"Crikey, Betsy. Why didn't you tell me? You're really no good at all at this mail-delivery thing, are you?"

"Well, I did deliver it, didn't I? And put it under your pillow for privacy. I didn't even know Berlin had a postal service again." Betsy pulled her pillow over her head.

The envelope held no return address, and instead of her official address, which was her military identification number, the sender had written her name and "Air Traffic Control, Gatow Airport." Gillian's heart leapt. The charming civilian address and the familiar handwriting told her it was from Erika.

*We hear the roar of your planes over our heads every day and hour and are grateful to your government for the help. I know you work very hard to bring those planes to us and hope you are well. It is a kindness like that you showed us at Christmas. Since you kissed our little Hanno, he is very attached to you and longs to see you again.*

Smiling, Gillian folded the note and slipped it into the pocket of her pyjamas. It was a coded message, a flirtation safe from censors, even after the "Heinrich incident."

She had not kissed Hanno. Only Erika.

❖

*August 1948*

The drumbeat pace of arrivals, the rush to the control trailer, then to the sergeants' mess, back to her post, and finally the return to quarters provided little time to brood. Gillian lived like a monk, focusing attention on light trails on a radar screen, though her yearning for Erika hovered like a soft mist at the back of her mind.

At the end of her duty, the August sky was still light, so she climbed one evening to the roof of the terminal and watched the stream of aircraft emerging with mechanical regularity from the horizon. How very different they were in reality from the shapeless radar echoes she stared at every day.

Even in the breeze that whispered past her ears and the roar of airplane engines, in her mind she seemed to still hear the back-and-forth between controller and pilot, the counting down of altitude, the fine-tuning of direction, the termination of each sentence with "go ahead" or "over." The rhythmic conversations recurred, barely changing, day and night, and only the voices differed with each new controller.

Out of nowhere a verse came to her from a Handel oratorio she'd sung in university choir, *The voice of him that crieth in the wilderness, prepare ye the way of the Lord,* and she smiled to herself. An airport in a hostile zone was a sort of wilderness, and while the plane was no "Lord," she did prepare its way. And in the continuous radio dialogue, she sensed a ritual incantation between heaven and earth that seemed almost a prayer.

A Dakota rumbled into a slot close by, and before its propellers stopped turning, a transfer lorry drew up next to its opening cargo door. Two men leapt inside and hefted large sacks of what appeared to be flour onto their backs, then marched the few steps to the lorry. With a deft turn-about, they dropped the sacks into the lorry bed, where another worker added them to the growing piles. The cycle repeated itself as mechanically as the arrival and departure of each aircraft.

A van marked CANTEEN swung by midway into the loading process, and the aircrew climbed out for their tea and sandwiches. She'd heard the base hired pretty girls especially for this task, so the pilots would be motivated to stay by their planes. In this case, it worked.

After scarcely twenty minutes, the unloading was completed, and the crew climbed on board again. As the lorry drove off, the propellers started again, and the plane taxied into its place on the runway in the line of aircraft waiting to depart. On one or two of the craft, groups of civilian passengers climbed inside, the lucky ones who, for one reason or other, qualified to be lifted out of the besieged city.

Then, in the warm summer evening, she rode her bike back to her quarters, where she had a leisurely hour to compose another letter to Erika. Letters through civilian post were slow and uncertain, but they were all that held them together. She had a collection of Erika's notes, full of trivia and hidden references to love, in case they were discovered. And all alluded to Hanno's deepening affection for her. Flt. Lt. Parsons could not object to that.

But in September, the letters abruptly stopped.

## CHAPTER TWENTY-ONE

*September 15, 1948*

"Is this all we have today?" Hanno glanced mournfully at the slice of bread that was his breakfast. It wasn't even buttered.

Charlotte rewrapped the remainder of the loaf in a cloth to save for Heinrich's return at the end of the day. It took all her strength to not shave off a bit of it to add to her own paltry serving, but the first little bit of theft would lead to more and would end all their trust.

"I'm sorry, dear. This is all we've been rationed. But Erika's at the black market right now exchanging her schnapps. I'm sure she'll bring back something good."

"She won't get much. She never does. That schnapps they give her at the club is trash." Sullen, he nibbled the bread, obviously trying to prolong the pleasure. "I don't understand why we don't register with our old address in the Russian sector. They'd let us go outside to the farms and get eggs, butter, ham, even."

"You know why. Erika doesn't want to live under the Russians or the government they're building in the East. We have the best chance with the West. Don't you hear the planes coming over all the time? That's for us."

"You keep saying that, but I don't see any more bread on the table. It's ridiculous for all of us to starve, just so the Tommies can claim us as part of their territory. I don't see the point." He shoved the rest of the bread into his mouth and chewed, scowling.

Charlotte laid the carefully wrapped remainder in the cupboard and attached the padlock. The lock was purely psychological, since she had the key, but it helped remind her of her responsibility to the others.

Hanno stood up from his chair. "This makes no sense. I'm an

East Berliner, and I'm going to eat like an East Berliner." With the righteousness that only a fourteen-year-old can feel, he stormed out of the apartment.

Charlotte stood helpless, for she had no good argument to hold him back. She couldn't expect a child to put principle over hunger; she could barely do it herself. If only he'd waited. Erika would have brought something, and he wouldn't have been so hungry.

Two hours later, Erika arrived with a head of red cabbage in her rucksack. Her smile of achievement faded when she saw Charlotte's face. "What's wrong?"

"Hanno's gone to the Russian side to register for East Berlin rations. I couldn't stop him."

"Oh, no! Are you sure that's where he went? To the office in Karlshorst?"

"I suppose so, but he left hours ago. He's probably been there by now."

Erika dropped her knapsack on the table and rushed out again.

❖

The Soviet Military Administration in Deutschland, or SMAD, was located in the former St. Antonius hospital in Berlin Karlshorst. Erika cringed at the sight but pedaled onward. As soon as she stopped and locked her bicycle, a guard confronted her.

She got right to the point. "My…uh…son came here earlier to register as an East Berliner, even though he lives in the West. Where would he go to do that?"

"He could have done that in several places in Berlin, but if he was stupid enough to come here, we'd have sent him to that building over there." He pointed to an adjacent building that held a sign EINWOHNERMELDEAMT. "It's the only one that's not off-limits."

She thanked him and marched over to the designated office. A soldier, whom she recognized as a corporal, looked up at her from his counter, and she repeated her question.

"What address would he have registered with?" he asked, leering, and she realized what had made her detest him at first glance. He had a square, lionish face with a wide mouth that made him look voracious. He could have been the twin brother of the man who raped her.

"With 98 Adlerstrasse, Stadtmitte," she said, avoiding his glance.

"And what is *your* address? Are you here to register as well?"

"Uh, no. I currently live in the West, and the boy is my son. He lives there now as well, so he registered by mistake."

"The address is false? It is a crime to give false information."

"No, it's not false. We used to live there, but we moved to the West when his mother died."

"You said he was your son." He stood up, his tone menacing.

She felt her face redden. "My adopted son. His mother died some time ago. But we both live now in Moabit, so you should cancel his registration."

He came around the counter and crossed his arms. "I am not in the habit of canceling anything official. And if you lived in the Adlerstrasse, you are part of East Berlin and should be registered, too."

"No, no. It's a mistake, I told you. We are registered in the West and have ration cards for the West."

He snickered. "But they're not worth much now, are they? You'll do much better with an East Berlin card. When did you move from the Adlerstrasse, anyhow? If recently, you broke the law, and I'll have to arrest you. Come on, now. Make things simple for yourself. Just sign a statement declaring Adlerstrasse as your residence." He took hold of her wrist and pressed a pen into her palm.

The memory of her pain and humiliation on the stairs on the day of surrender struck her suddenly. Without thinking, she slapped him across the face.

He slapped her back, cursing, and called in another man. Together, they threw her onto a chair.

"You made a big mistake, lady," the corporal said. "We have a place for you, where you'll learn some respect for a Soviet soldier."

Yanking her to her feet again, they hustled her down to the basement and into a crowded room. Still in shock, she spoke to only a few of the other prisoners, but it seemed they were mostly outspoken anti-communist journalists or unrepentant Nazis. She was not one of those and so felt confident that, under normalized Berlin law, sooner or later she would be heard, probably fined, or, at most, sentenced to a few days in jail for assault.

In fact, nothing happened at all for three days other than the addition of several more "offenders" to the room. Squatting on the bare floor, she fretted briefly about Hanno. Had he managed to register at the old address? If so, he would at least be safe in Wilhelm's care. If he hadn't, and simply returned to the Lübeckerstrasse, he would also be safe.

Then on the fourth day, the doors opened, and guards led them upstairs and loaded them into a covered lorry. Forced to stand for lack of room, they were chained at the wrist to a bar that ran overhead and staggered against each other when the truck started. Icy air blew in under the canvas covering.

After a ride of some three hours, they stopped, and their chains were unlocked. Climbing down from the lorry bed, she saw they were in the entryway of a camp. The sign over the gate said simply NKVD SPECIAL CAMP NR. 7, but the old, soiled brick and the mold that grew up from the wet ground onto the walls told her it had once had another purpose and another name.

She searched her memory for the names of concentration camps around Berlin that could be reached in a three-hour drive. But when their line began filing through the iron grillwork of the main entrance, she no longer had to guess. *ARBEIT MACHT FREI* was embedded in the gate in large iron letters.

"Sachsenhausen," she murmured, and her heart sank. She felt a shiver of fear. In spite of the years that had passed, the memory was all too fresh of the postcard her parents had sent.

*We are in Sachsenhausen, and doing well.*

It had proved to be a complete fake, for a year later notice came that announced their death. All for the crime of being Socialists. They had not been executed but might as well have been, for the crowding, neglect, and exhaustion had exposed them fatally to typhoid.

As she was registered, issued a number, and assigned to a barracks, it was as if she was reliving their experience of 1937. Germany's defeat had not done away with its concentration camps; it had only changed their inmates and their masters. And hearing the rules and labor assignments from the head prisoner, she was certain they were the same as those the Nazis had devised. The first night, she lay down to sleep on her hard bunk on a sack of straw, and she could not hold back tears at the futility of it all.

In spite of her misery, or because of it, she knew survival meant solidarity. The next morning as they sat over their bowls of watery porridge, Erika offered her hand to the woman sitting next to her. She'd once been blond, but now her brown roots grew out some ten centimeters, and she bore a faint resemblance to Gerda.

"My name is Erika," she said.

"Herta," the woman answered. "What you here for?"

"I'm not actually sure. I mean, I slapped a Russian corporal for groping me, but I was never officially charged."

Herta cleaned between her teeth with a fingernail. "Hmm. Not smart to smack them. Almost as dumb as me. I opened my big mouth on a tram to say the Nazis were right and the Reds are pigs. They accused me of being a state enemy, though they didn't say what state that was."

Another woman, stocky, Slavic-looking, leaned toward her. "Hi. I'm Ilse. I've been here a while, and I advise you both not to talk politics where people can hear. You never know who's listening." She looked directly at Erika. "No trial, eh? Yeah, they do that a lot. Over on the men's side, they've even got their own soldiers, Russian men who were POWs in German camps. Poor bastards. Accused of treason because they didn't die for Stalin. Right next to them, eating the same filthy food, Nazi officers the Ruskies don't know what to do with."

Herta nodded. "Almost anyone who was anybody during the war—propagandists, journalists, camp guards, secretaries, plain old Nazis like me who don't shut up."

A buzzer sounded just then, and they filed out to the central yard for roll call. After an hour standing in the cold wind, the women marched in order back to their respective barracks, where a guard locked them in. Herta and Ilse bunked some distance away, but once the doors were locked, Erika's two new "friends" of a ten-minute conversation sought her out.

"So, you're a Berliner?" Ilse asked. "I recognize the accent. What part?"

"Mostly Stadtmitte until it was packed with refugees and DPs. Then I moved to Moabit, with friends."

"Husband?" Herta asked.

"Killed in the war. You?"

"Same here. Ilse, too. We lived in East Prussia but came to Frankfurt when the war started. My husband was shipped off to the East and never came back. I've got a brother in some POW camp in the East, but I haven't heard from him in years. You got any kids? Relatives? Someone who'll miss you?"

"An adopted son, a few good friends. Even a Brit I got to know."

"You fraternized with a Tommie? Oh, lucky you. Did you get nylons from him, or is that only the Amis?" Ilse asked.

The conversation was going in a disagreeable direction, so Erika just smiled weakly and stared through the barrack window at the dull winter sky.

In the next days, the November weather grew worse, and since the camp provided no extra clothing, she was glad to be able to stay indoors. The food was minimal, but only slightly less than many Berliners ate every day anyhow. A privileged few were granted some limited occupation—sewing, light carpentry, laundry—which allowed a few hours away from confinement, but the majority had only each other.

Erika was soon drawn into the conversations and discussions that circled around the barrack. The women avoided politics but inevitably came to ask, "What did you do after surrender?" A few told tales of being violently raped or more subtly coerced by Soviet soldiers. When Herta and several others openly admitted exchanging favors for food, Erika confessed to doing much the same. In the end, the women agreed, snickering, that the Soviet men were terrible in bed.

The tiny wood-stove in the middle of their barrack gave out faint heat, and that only while the day's ration of wood lasted. In the last days of September, it made no difference, but as winter approached, the cold became biting. Erika stayed in her bunk covered by her coat, and left only to eat or use the latrine.

## CHAPTER TWENTY-TWO

Five days passed, then ten, and Gillian became anxious. She could think of no one to contact other than Heinrich at Tempelhof. A letter marked "Mechanic, Tempelhof" would probably reach him eventually but would undoubtedly pass through other curious hands first, and that might get them both in trouble again.

Yet on the twelfth day, a letter finally came to her, though it was from Charlotte. The clerk handed it to her at mail call, and she tore it open on her way to duty in the ground-control trailer.

Once again she struggled through the ornate German cursive script, but when she finally made sense of it, she was horrified.

*We are worried about Erika. Two weeks ago, she and Hanno went back to the registry office to apply for East Berlin rations. Hanno returned to Wilhelm at the Adlerstrasse, but Erika disappeared. We asked at the Russian headquarters several times, and finally they told us she was in an NKVD holding camp. They did not say the charge. Do you know someone in the military who can help?*

Gillian stood at the entrance of the trailer, stunned. NKVD camp? She was barely aware they existed. Which one? Why? What was she charged with?

"Somerville, shake a leg. We're on duty in two minutes," one of the other controllers said, passing and holding the door open for her.

She scarcely had time to absorb the dreadful news before she was seated at her screen with her headphones on, and the next bright spot detached itself from the periphery. She reacted automatically.

"Gatow Tower calling. Do you read me? Over."

❖

At the end of her duty shift, Gillian went to her commander. It was evening, and when she was admitted into the office, she could see Flt. Lt. Parsons was sliding papers into a briefcase, preparing to leave.

"Excuse my intrusion, ma'am. I was wondering, is there any way for us—I mean the British administration—to intervene for a person kidnapped by the Russians in Berlin? With your longer experience in theater, I thought you might know how to proceed."

Parsons looked puzzled. "Kidnapped? One of our soldiers?"

"No, ma'am. It's a civilian, a Berliner who resides in our sector but disappeared in the Russian sector."

"Is this your mechanic friend? I have expressly ordered you to break off ties with him."

"No, ma'am. It's a female friend, part of the family I spent Christmas with. She used to work here at the base, so I thought we might have some influence in her case."

Parsons sighed. "None whatsoever. Tracking German civilians is not the responsibility of the RAF. We're already keeping two million people in West Berlin in food and supplies, and that with a shortage of…everything. What the Russians do to individual Berliners may be unfortunate, but it is beyond our purview to intervene." She resumed packing. "Will there be anything else?"

"No, ma'am. Understood, ma'am." Gillian saluted and left the office defeated.

After a quick, tasteless supper in the sergeants' mess, she biked back to her quarters, undressed, and collapsed on her bed. Sleep wouldn't come, only images of Erika, in all the possible disasters the Russians could inflict on her. Interrogation, prison, beatings, and… She forced away the worst possibility before she imagined it.

The next morning, she dragged herself to work for another twelve-hour shift. She was bringing in mostly coal deliveries, for now, in the late October freeze, some 90 percent of incoming freight was from the Ruhr. She thought of the Christmas she'd spent huddled in a circle around a Kanonenofen and hoped Charlotte and Heinrich were getting some of the coal she was landing every day.

She considered applying for an emergency two-hour pass to visit the Lübeckerstrasse. But if Flt. Lt. Parsons guessed the reason, she would almost certainly refuse.

Fog had blanketed the entire region, slowing coal deliveries everyplace but Gatow, which had the most sophisticated ground-control system in Germany. With maximum traffic directed toward her airfield, Gillian's shift grew to fourteen hours, with an hour's break for lunch and supper, and by the beginning of November, she coughed constantly.

Finally, another letter came from Charlotte. She had contacted the office of West Berlin mayor Ernst Reuter, and even though the Russians did not acknowledge his authority, they'd provided some basic information. Erika was in NKVD camp Nr. 7, which used to be the Sachsenhausen concentration camp. It was a "holding" camp, that is, with no official interrogations or executions. Erika was alive.

❖

November brought no letup in the work schedule, but the staff was showing signs of breakdown. People were simply getting sick, and not just the mechanics, loaders, and ground crews who had to work on the icy tarmac. The signalers and indoor staff were also falling victims to colds and stomach ailments.

Gillian's chest cold worsened daily. After a week of dragging herself to her post, she woke up one morning and knew her condition was serious. Barely able to walk, she reported to the base medical office, which was a single room with a single medic. He took her temperature, listened to her lungs, and, when she fainted upon standing up, diagnosed pneumonia.

He summoned Flt. Lt. Parsons, who signed orders for her to be transferred the same morning to the RAF Hospital at Rinteln.

"Rinteln? Where's that? I don't want to leave Berlin…" She forced out the words, although every breath hurt.

"Rinteln is just a few miles south of Bad Eilsen, so we'll fly you to Bückeburg and transport you by ambulance to the hospital. Is there anyone you'd like me to inform?"

"Yes, please. Sergeant Elizabeth Geary, a mechanic, and… Lieutenant Nigel Katz." Then, her face heating from the effort and her chest refusing to provide much air with each breath, she surrendered to the medics, who strapped her onto a gurney and transferred her to the next outgoing plane to Bückeburg.

❖

Delivered by ambulance, Gillian saw RAF Rinteln's main hospital through feverish eyes, a boxy, three-story, gray, stone structure with long, single-story wings that surrounded a wide court. Physicians from the Royal Air Force Medical Corps examined her and confirmed the Gatow medic's diagnosis. Penicillin was readily available to RAF patients, and she received immediate treatment. Energetic nurses from the Queen Alexandra's nursing corps fussed over her until she fell into a deep sleep.

When she came to, one of the physicians stood over her. "You waited a jolly long time before getting medical attention. We're not at war, you know. You could have taken sick leave long before your lungs got so bad."

Gillian smiled weakly. "It might as well be war." She wheezed. "I'm with the airlift." She started coughing.

"Oh, righto." He checked her chart. "Ah, yes, they brought you in from Gatow. How is it going over there?"

"Smashing. Everyone...on fourteen-hour shifts." She took a breath. "So, how long before I'm out of here?"

The medic chuckled. "They all ask that. Except the slackers, who ask, 'How long can I stay?' I'll tell you the truth. Two weeks minimum, though with that schedule waiting for you, I'll recommend three."

"No. I'll take two." She gave a phlegmy cough and panted for a moment. "You'll see. I'll be up in two."

He patted her wrist. "Let me be the judge of that. Now get some sleep."

She tried to glare at his back as he strode away from her bed, but her heavy eyes wouldn't stay open. She fell asleep again, and when she awoke, the bed next to her was empty, which afforded a bit of privacy. She was not in a sociable mood.

Pneumonia is a cruel mistress, for in fact, her lungs began to improve within days, but her body did not follow. She could speak, and complain in an almost normal voice, but needed help to walk to the toilet. She wasn't sick enough to sleep all day, so spent most waking time alternating between boredom and anxiety for Erika.

She'd lost track of the date but knew it was sometime in late November, and through the window at the end of her ward she could see snow falling. Was Erika still in the NKVD camp? What if she, too, came down with pneumonia? Was Charlotte still sending letters to Gatow? And all being collected by Betsy? Or, worse, by Flt. Lt. Parsons?

"Nurse?" she called out when one of the Queen Alexandra's was close by. "Is there any way I can send a letter? To an address in Berlin?"

"Oh, my, yes. The lads do that all the time. I'll have one of the Red Cross girls pop by, who'll do it for you."

One of the "girls" stopped by the next morning. In a crisp uniform of fine blue and white stripes with a red cross stitched over the left breast pocket, she held a clip board and a fountain pen. "So, they tell me you want help with a letter," she chirped.

"Yes, but I can write it myself if you'll let me have that pen and paper. I just need you to put it in the mail. It's to a German address, so must go through German post."

The young woman looked puzzled for a moment, apparently having only assisted wounded servicemen to post military mail to other stations or back to the UK. "Well, I think we can do that. I'll just leave this here with you and come back in a couple of hours."

Cheered by the possibility of renewed contact, Gillian composed a brief note. Since the Red Cross nurse had not supplied an envelope, Gillian knew that privacy was not in the offing and so wrote in the vaguest possible terms.

*I just want you to know I've been transferred to a hospital in West Germany for pneumonia. I am uncertain how long I will be here and am desperate to know about our friend. Have you heard anything? Was Reuter any help? Will they let you send a message? If so, please be assured that I will find a way to help—somehow. Please write me using my military address that I gave you last time add "RAF Rinteln." Affectionate regards to all, Gillian.*

She folded the letter in three parts and wrote the Lübeckerstrasse address on the blank side. When the Red Cross nurse returned, she glanced at the letter and frowned. "You didn't say it was a civilian address in Berlin."

"Is that a problem? Surely, mail is delivered to Berlin. I saw mail sacks all the time."

"Military mail, of course, but civilian mail, I don't know." She shook off her uncertainty. "I'm sure it'll be fine." With an unconvincing smile, she did an about-face and marched out of the ward with letter and pen. Gillian felt dread fall over her again like a blanket.

At the end of the second week, she was on her feet and, except for a faint wheezing and muscle weakness, was full of nervous energy. The doctor, however, insisted she remain a third week. She lay in her bed, sullen at her imprisonment and distressed by Charlotte's silence. Had the letter gone astray?

"Excuse me, Sergeant Somerville." It was the Red Cross nurse, and she held an envelope. "This was just delivered to the hospital mail."

Gillian felt a sudden thrill of hope. But no, it was a military envelope, and her heart sank as she tore it open.

*Headquarters, Berlin Brigade, Gatow Air Base,*
*British Occupation Forces PO 2665*
*Sgt. Gillian Andrea Somerville, Service Nr. 3045001*
*Communications unit/Air Traffic Control Gatow Air Base*
*Order number 2845, November 30, 1948*
*Sgt. Somerville,*
*You will proceed on permanent change of station as shown.*
*Assigned to: Communications unit/Air Traffic Control*
*Bückeburg Air Base*
*Reporting Date: 15 December 1948—contingent upon*
*medical confirmation of health by Rinteln Hospital.*
*Transportation will be provided by military vehicle.*
*One day prior to reporting date, the contents of your*
*locker will be packed and shipped to your new quarters.*

She dropped back onto the bed, stunned. Being held hostage in a hospital while Erika was imprisoned had seemed the worst that could happen. But she was wrong. Now the combined forces of the Russian army and the RAF would separate them permanently. She threw her arm over her eyes and wept.

# CHAPTER TWENTY-THREE

Erica was the last to believe in miracles, and certainly not in the form of a Soviet officer, but at the end of November, one occurred.

It happened at roll call in the central yard one afternoon during which the Soviet Military Administration—without a shred of irony—demonstrated to official inspectors its correct and humane treatment of prisoners. Erika stood at the end of her row, pressing her arms to her sides to retain body heat. Two officers, a man and a woman, marched along the rows, their gaze sweeping over the ranks of prisoners.

Erika's eyes were riveted to the heels of the person in front of her as one of the officers strode by. She sensed the figure stop and risked raising her glance.

She was startled by the face of Sr. Lt. Olga Petrova, who appeared as astonished as she was. Only now, according to her shoulder boards, Petrova was a captain.

The expression of surprise disappeared immediately, and the captain continued marching along the line, nodding as before. At the end of the inspection, the prisoners were dismissed to their barracks.

Once inside, Erika stared at the ceiling, brooding. Had Petrova recognized her? How could she not? But of course, she was a good soldier and could not admit she knew an "enemy of the state."

At that moment, a camp guard entered, ordered her to her feet, and led her to the main building. Reaching the office of the camp commandant, he knocked, then opened the door and nudged her inside. The commandant sat at his desk, and next to him stood Olga Petrova.

The commandant cleared his throat. "Captain Petrova tells me there has been a mistake and that you are kept here improperly. Given her authority as representative of the Soviet Military Administration, I am releasing you to her custody. Please sign this statement."

He slid a sheet of paper toward her and handed her a fountain pen. The document contained a long, typewritten text in Russian. Erika signed it without reading a word. She stood somewhat nonplussed as the commander and the inspector discussed which regulations were being invoked, presumably to absolve all parties of responsibility for both the arrest and its reversal. The discussion concluded, the captain saluted and did an about-face. In passing, Petrova grasped her by the upper arm and led her from the room and along the corridor to a canvas-covered Soviet jeep. Her first words were, "I assume you need a ride back to Berlin?"

Erika exhaled relief. "Oh, yes, please. I live in the Lübeckerstrasse in Moabit and don't know how I'd get there except by foot." She glanced up at the slate-gray sky, which threatened snowfall at any moment.

Petrova nodded. "A bad time to be on foot. Come on. I'll take you home, and you can tell me what you did to be arrested." She opened the passenger door for Erika, then slid into the driver's seat.

"You can be glad there were no formal charges against you. I checked. You're just one of hundreds who ended up here for 'public disruption.' If you'd been officially charged and were on the record, I couldn't have come near you."

Erika was weak with gratitude. "Thank you for getting me out. You know, all I did was chase after a boy to stop him from going back to the East. He's like a son, and I don't want to lose him. Then this soldier laid his hands on me, like he was used to grabbing German women, and it was too much. I slapped him."

"That was unwise, my friend, especially since all he did was touch you. We've all experienced much worse." Petrova glanced over at her. "I like you, Erika, but you don't appreciate the importance of the Soviet program for Germany. It can change all of Europe for the better, and we'll never have another European war again. You are much too caught up in the personal, chasing that boy. It's your decadent Western self-absorption."

"How can you say that? You have a son, don't you?" They were in Moabit now, and Erika pointed toward the right. "Turn here."

"Yes. I do. He will grow up to be a good Communist and will understand that all the years his mother was absent, she was fighting and struggling to make a better world for him. That is much more important than coddling them over every little thing."

Erika was silent. The argument sounded familiar, though her

own socialist parents never argued it in such an extreme fashion. They would have liked Olga Petrova and admired her zeal.

"So, what will you do now?" Petrova asked.

"I don't know. The job at the club is certainly gone by now, so I'll have to find work. Perhaps I'll try again at Gatow."

"You're sure you don't want to return to the East? I could help you find work as an interpreter. Besides, other than that boy, who can obviously take care of himself, what holds you in the West? Do you have a man waiting?"

Erika studied the warm peasant face. "You are a mystery, Olga. A strong Communist, yet you take risks snatching me from the clutches of your own NKVD. Thank you for your offer, but I think I belong in the decadent West. The Lübeckerstrasse is that way." She pointed toward the left.

Petrova snickered. "Don't remind me of my weaknesses. Yes, I am a dedicated Leninist. Nonetheless, sometimes, even among the enemy, you meet a person you like as a comrade. Back home, we'd drink coffee and vodka and tell all our secrets." She fell silent for a moment. "But you didn't answer my question. Do you have a man waiting for you? That would explain a lot."

Struck by the declaration of friendship, Erika thought for a moment. Olga had just saved her life; why shouldn't she be open with her? And she yearned to tell someone.

"Not a man. A woman. A British woman."

"What?" Olga frowned in clear incomprehension. "You are returning to the West because a British woman waits for you?"

"Well, I don't know if she's still waiting after all this time, but I hope so. I care for her more than anyone else and want to see her again."

"How very strange. A woman. *And* a foreigner. And a *woman*," Olga repeated.

"Oh, come on. Don't you have women in Russia, and in the Red Army, who care for each other more than for men? I can't believe you don't."

"No, we don't. Well, not officially. Um, if you mean loyalty and comradeship, yes, I suppose so. But I think the way you mean…"

"I don't know what I mean. I don't have a word for what I feel. Can we leave it at that?"

Petrova turned sharply left into the Lübeckerstrasse. "What is the street number?"

"Ninety-eight." She couldn't help but add, "You know, falling in love isn't all that different from falling into friendship. It's just stronger."

Olga slowed and leaned forward to peer at door numbers. "I must disagree. Comradeship is a pure emotion, one that furthers the greater good, while romance is basically selfish." She pulled the jeep to the side and halted. "Here we are. Number ninety-eight."

"Thank you, Captain Petrova. I wish you much happiness in your communist *and* your personal world. I mean that sincerely." She leaned over and took hold of Olga's head, kissing her briskly on the lips. "Keep that as a souvenir from the decadent West," she said, laughing, and climbed from the jeep.

"Capitalist fool!" Olga called out and drove away.

## CHAPTER TWENTY-FOUR

*November 1948*

Inert on her hospital bed, Gillian was immobilized with despair. Happiness had seemed so close, and it had been snatched away. By what? Apparently by Flt. Lt. Parsons's suspicion she was sleeping with a German man. The irony was excruciating.

Now it made no difference when she recovered. Or even if. Bückeburg had little to do with the airlift. And without Erika, and the whole excitement of the airlift, the work she did was just employment.

Joining the WAAF had been a fool's errand, and it had come to nothing. She lay on her side the entire afternoon with her face buried in her pillow.

"Hello there," a female voice said, startling her. She awoke from half-sleep and turned her head. For a moment she was speechless, then managed to say, "How did you know I was here?"

Jean Horwick chuckled softly. "Your name was on the list of the new transfers, with the note that you were still in hospital. I thought I owed you a visit. So, how are you? You're looking good for someone who has pneumonia."

"I don't any longer. They'll probably release me in the next days."

"Why so glum, then? Don't you want to go back to work at Bückeburg? Or am I the problem?" She dropped her voice. "I've felt terrible since our friendship had to end so quickly. But my husband was catching on, and I didn't want to endanger you. He couldn't do anything to me, but he could have ruined you."

"Ah, well, thank you for your consideration. I was a little hurt, but that was eons ago. All water over the bridge."

Jean looked puzzled for a moment at the twisted cliché, then laughed. "I'm glad you're able to joke about it. I've worried about you. And you didn't answer my question. Don't you want to go back to work?"

"I do, urgently, and I've been trying to get out of here for days. But it has to be Berlin. You knew about my transfer before I did. I just got the orders yesterday, and it was a real blow."

"Good heavens, why? You're so fond of that frenzied schedule that made you sick in the first place?"

"No, it's not the work, although I do like that. It's…there are civilians in Berlin I care about, that I love. I don't want to be away from them. One of them has even been imprisoned by the Russians, and I want to help."

"Wait, wait. You mean you're personally involved with Berliners? *A* Berliner? Tell me the truth."

"Yes. Very much so. And it's killing me to be here where I can't help…them."

Jean frowned with suspicion. "Don't try to brush me off with 'them.' Are you involved with a him or a her?"

Gillian studied the ceiling for a moment, while her lips seemed to twitch of their own accord, as if undecided whether to release the words.

Jean laid a hand on her wrist. "When you make that kind of face, it has to be a woman. Dear, if there's anyone you can tell, it's me. There are a lot of women like us in the service, and we should look out for each other." She sighed. "But if you're fraternizing with a German woman, that complicates things significantly."

"Believe me, I know. It was hard enough when she was free and working in one of the Berlin clubs. But now the Russians are holding her for some reason. I couldn't do much for her while I was working on the base, but at least I was in contact with her friends and could monitor things. Now she's totally lost to me."

"Would you like me to try to reverse your orders and get you sent back to Gatow?"

"You could do that?" Gillian felt a mix of incredulity and desperation for the straw she offered. "How…?"

"A lot of things are possible when you're married to a wing commander who's good chums with a dozen other wing commanders, group captains, an air commodore or two."

"But I thought Commander Horwick was…um…indifferent."

"To me? Oh, no. That's just for the public. He doesn't want to give the impression of being under the thumb of a mere woman. But when he's between affairs, which he is now, he's very attentive. Remorseful, almost. Getting him to reverse a relocation order shouldn't be difficult."

"That would be smashing. When could you…?"

"I can set it in motion right away, but it'll take two, three days for it to go through the system, make sure Gatow still needs you, that sort of thing. If they try to discharge you tomorrow, for example, you have to have a relapse."

"I can stay sick for a few more days. And while you're making miracles, would it be too much to ask to fly back with my friend Nigel Katz?"

Jean laughed again. "You sure know how to get mileage out of your favors. But all right. I'll try."

Gillian grasped her hand. "I'm sorry for any bad thoughts I might have had about you. You're really very kind."

"I think I owe you a kindness, for the way I abandoned you." She stood up, still holding Gillian's hand. "You're an amazing person. I saw it right away."

"You too, Jean. And you're also beautiful. I never told you that."

Jean kissed her on the forehead. "Silly creature. Bet you say that to all the adulterous wing commanders' wives." She snickered and left with remarkable agility on high-heel shoes.

Elated at being free, but exhausted, Erika labored up the stairs to the third floor. Her house keys had long disappeared in the camp, so she knocked. Charlotte answered, cried out something incoherent, and dragged her inside to a tight embrace.

"Oh, my dear child. We were beside ourselves with worry. It took us so long to find out where you were, and we tried everything, even talking to the mayor, who of course was useless. No one seemed to be able to do anything."

Erika patted her affectionately on her cheek. "It's fine. I know you tried, and I'm home now. I hate to ask, but do you have any food in the house? A slice of bread, maybe?"

"Oh, forgive me. I should have realized. Just a moment."

Charlotte hurried into the kitchen and returned with a slice of dark bread.

"Your friend Gillian has been terribly worried, too. She sent me a letter from Rinteln a few weeks ago to say she was sick, but perhaps she's back to work now. I know she'll be happy to see you."

"Really?" The pleasure of being home again doubled. "When do you expect Heinrich?" she asked, changing the subject.

"Late tonight. Tempelhof keeps him working like a dog. He says they're short-handed in everything—mechanics, pilots, ground crews, cooks, cleaners. If you're strong enough to work again, maybe you could also find something."

Erika took another bite of the bread and closed her eyes at the pleasure of good news and of solid food in her stomach. "Yes, I can work, but I'd rather go back to Gatow."

"Well, with the all the pilots and crews flying day and night, I'm sure it's the same at Gatow, too. As soon as you're rested up, you can check with the military employment service."

"Yes. I'll do that first thing tomorrow. Is Hanno all right?"

Charlotte curled up next to her on the sofa. "He's with Wilhelm and he's fine. But now I want to hear what happened to you. What did they do to you for two and a half months? Finish chewing and talk!"

Jean Horwick's conspirator's skills were all she promoted them to be. Not only did another set of orders arrive two days later that reversed the first ones, but upon Gillian's discharge from the hospital, a jeep took her to Bückeburg Airport, where she was invited to wait in the operations room.

Flight 336, carrying coal, was scheduled to leave in forty-seven minutes. Impatient, she paced, which also kept her warm in the drafty building. She wore her greatcoat, but three weeks of inactivity had left her a bit weak, and she chilled easily. Finally, she huddled in the doorway to the radio room, watching the women manage ground communication.

She heard footfall, but before she could turn, someone embraced her from the rear. "So here's our little 'scopie,' back from the dead!"

"Nigel!" she exclaimed in turning. "I'm so glad it's you." She play-punched him on the chest. "But if I was so close to death, why didn't you come by and visit?"

"Sorry, ducks," another voice said. "We were saving the Berliners, and we figured you were a goner anyway." Dickie clapped her on the shoulder and gave her a hug as well.

"But seriously, we only got wind of your plight a week ago," Nigel explained. "And they kept us on a schedule that barely allowed us to sleep. We were chuffed to find out that you were tip-top and that we'd be ferrying you back to base along with our coal."

A mechanic called out through the door. "Your aircraft's almost ready, gentlemen." As soon as Nigel and Dickie had signed the duty roster, they linked arms with her on both sides and led her out of the terminal.

"So, what are we flying?" she asked as they made their way down to the tarmac where the rest of the crew waited.

"That!" Nigel pointed toward an Avro York. In its open cargo port, a gang of ground workers was loading the last of some very heavy duffel bags. "In honor of your return, we brought the big one."

She smiled at the four mighty engines hanging under the wings. "Big one, indeed."

"Think you might like to steer her a little bit?" Nigel added.

"Now don't toy with a girl's emotions unless you're serious," she said, her eyes glued to the majestic fuselage.

"Oh, I'm serious. We'll do the takeoff, and then she's all yours."

They were inside the hatchway now, and Dickie lifted something folded and bulky from the floor. "You're going to need these, of course." He held up a pair of sheepskin trousers and a jacket. "No sense in getting your nice uniform dirty, eh?"

The two men went ahead to the cockpit while she changed into the flight leathers and followed them. She looked for a place to lay her folded uniform and greatcoat, but every surface was covered with soot, so she crammed them in the space under her seat near the flight engineer.

"Sorry about the coal dust," Nigel said over his shoulder. "That's about all we've been carrying since October. Four out of five flights carry coal, and this poor machine has done a dozen deliveries already."

They taxied out onto the runway to join the line of aircraft waiting for takeoff, and in just a few minutes, they were at the front of the line. Once the tower signaled, they took off and fitted themselves into the circuit, at the required 1,000 feet above the flight before them.

Nigel called back to her. "Since you're so keen to fly, I'm going to turn over the whole job to you. You already know the signals marking the corridor, and our flight engineer's following our course on the map. I'll just catch a little kip. If you run into any problems, wake me." He surrendered his seat in the cockpit to her.

"Jolly good," she said, sweeping her eyes over the instruments panel as she sat down, making sure all the settings were satisfactory. Speed and altitude would be dictated to her, but she would have the task of adjusting for both if they moved outside the parameters.

"We're drifting north," Dickie said, and she adjusted. "Now, slow just a bit. We're gaining on the aircraft ahead of us." She adjusted again, thrilling to the power of four mighty engines under her hands, as if she were driving a whale. Four whales.

Something silvery flickered in her peripheral vision, and she flinched, but caught herself before the flinch reached the joystick. It took only a few seconds to see it was a balloon released deliberately into their flight path. She held steady, cursing softly.

"Just the Russians mucking about," Dickie said, indifferently.

The rest of the flight was uneventful, and upon their approach to Gatow, the voice of the controller came through her headset. "This is Gatow ground. I have you in contact. Are you receiving me? Over." It was Charlie, one of the new recruits.

"Hello, Gatow ground. Receiving you loud and clear. This is Avro 336, from Bückeburg. That you, Charlie? Over."

"Avro 336, yes, indeed. Who are you? You sound like a girl. Over."

"Gatow ground, I *am* a girl, last time I looked. It's Sergeant Somerville. Now give me my heading, and stop gabbing. Over."

"Avro 336, righto. Continue on present course, and remain listening on this channel." A few minutes later, "Calling Avro 336. I have you at 1600 feet. Change course to two seven zero and reduce altitude to 1500 feet. Over."

"Gatow ground. Changing course to two seven zero, dropping to 1500 feet. Over." It was strange to be acting out the ritual from the other side, but she understood now the importance of the calm voice of the controller. Her visibility was fairly good, but not all flights had that benefit, and it was supremely comforting to be guided in by someone who was confident and unperturbed.

"Avro 336, are you reading me? You are eleven miles from airfield. Maintain course. Over."

"Gatow ground, receiving you loud and clear. Maintaining course. Over."

For several moments, she heard nothing on the radio but the

weaker voices giving directions to other fights on the same frequency. She felt neglected.

"Avro 336, change course fife degrees left. Again, fife degrees left. Over."

"Gatow ground, changing course fife degrees left. Over."

Dickie was awake now and smiling with his arms across his chest, as if daring her to get it wrong. But they had already almost arrived.

"Avro 336, I see you lined up six miles from touchdown. We've got wind. Change course three degrees left. Repeat, three degrees left. Over."

"Gatow ground, changing course three degrees left. Over."

The procedure continued, and holding to the glide path, she descended, seven miles from the runway, five miles, three miles. Wheels down at two miles, one mile, and she could see the runway clearly in front of her.

She brought the behemoth York down smoothly before the end of the runway, where she caught sight of the FOLLOW ME lorry, which brought her into her unloading bay.

"Piece of cake." She sneered. "For a WAAF right out of the hospital."

"Don't say that out loud," Dickie said. "It makes the job look too easy, and we'll lose our bragging rights."

They climbed out through the passenger door, but the cargo hatch was already open, and the loading gang was clambering inside to grapple with the coal sacks. Retrieving her uniform and greatcoat, Gillian stepped out onto the tarmac, where the snack lorry waited to serve the crew and keep them close to their plane. One of the base's "pretty German girls" stood in front of the lorry holding out steaming mugs of tea. With her mind on her victory, Gillian turned to accept one, then stopped in mid-reach.

## CHAPTER TWENTY-FIVE

Gillian stood, dumbfounded, as the motionless figure came into focus and Nigel took the tea mugs from her hand. "I see you know each other." He snickered, passing one to Gillian.

"How...? What...?" Gillian sputtered, unable to form a full sentence. Then, "Erika, where the hell have you been?"

"I could ask you the same thing. I come back after two and a half months in a Russian camp and find you are gone. What happened to *you?*"

"Also a long story. But how did you know I'd be on this flight?"

"I told her," Nigel said, sipping his tea. "I happened to be in the Malcolm Club the other night after I got my orders and spotted her."

Erika bumped shoulders with him, a warm "we're friends" gesture. "I'd just started working there and asked people about you. No one knew where you were until Nigel told me he was ordered to fly you home. The first thing I did was change places with the canteen girl so I could meet you." She snickered. "I didn't know you would look like a coal miner."

"Coal miner?" Gillian glanced back at the men she'd flown with and realized they all had sooty faces. "Ah, yes. I suppose we do."

"All for king and country, eh?" Dickie said. "Uh, but do you have anything to eat?"

"Oh, sorry. Yes. Of course. Sandwiches, biscuits..." Erika retrieved a platter from the van and held it out to him and the navigator and radio operator who'd come around.

Gillian couldn't take her eyes off Erika, who seemed unfazed as she tended to the hungry crew members. Dickie leaned toward her. "You're off duty now, m'dear. But we do need our flight suit back. After that, you're on your own."

"Righto," she said, still distracted, and climbed back into the York to change. When she reemerged, the navigation jeep had arrived, and Erika's food-service van was closed.

After a quick hug to Nigel and Dickie, she climbed into the van next to Erika. "You are flying again," Erika said, starting the motor. "Will they let you be a pilot now?"

Gillian gave a helpless smile. "Afraid not. I have to report for duty at my old post. But never mind me. You scared the hell out of me, and everyone, by disappearing for so long. What happened to you? How did you get back? God, we have so much to talk about."

Erika's voice dropped to almost a murmur, although no one was nearby to hear. "When does your duty start? Will you come home with me?"

"Tomorrow morning at eight o'clock. And yes, I'd love to."

Erika smiled softly. "I finish work at five. We can meet at the bus stop."

Gillian's heart pounded. From despair to joy, in forty-eight hours. She'd have to send a letter of thanks to Jean Horwick.

❖

In a daze, Gillian dropped from the snack van at the terminal and reported to the operations officer. After formally presenting her orders and receiving his handshake, she gave a snappy salute and marched to the bike shed where, astonishingly, her bicycle still waited.

Back in her quarters, she caught sight of herself for the first time in a mirror and laughed out loud. She did indeed look like a coal miner, except for her pink lips and a line of white over her eyebrows where her flight helmet had covered her. No wonder Erika hadn't kissed her. Even her greatcoat still had a sprinkling of soot, and she shook it out over the floor of the shower in the ablutions room.

Then she laid out clean civilian clothing and showered. The water, as always, was lukewarm, but it lasted long enough for a thorough, luxurious wash with the remainder of her shampoo. Under the stream of water, she devised an elaborate plan.

❖

At five o'clock exactly, Gillian waited at the bus stop with a full rucksack on her back. It had taken all her available cash, but she wanted to do things right. She also reflected on the German she'd been struggling to learn for the last few months, hoping it was sufficient to spend an evening in conversation.

Erika appeared some ten minutes later, and now, out of her canteen uniform and wearing her own threadbare coat, she looked frail. Her face was thinner than Gillian remembered from her club days.

Gillian linked arms with her and pulled her to the side, away from the growing crowd that waited for the bus. She pressed her shoulder against Erika's. "For God's sake, tell me what happened to you during all that time."

Erika shrugged helplessly. "It was so stupid of me. Hanno just couldn't bear to go on starving when better rations were just a few districts away and all he had to do was go there and register from our old address. I tried to run after him and wasn't even sure I went to the same place he did, but in the end, it made no difference."

"You mean the Russians held you because you were originally from their sector?"

"No. Not even that. I'm sure I could have simply turned around and come back to Moabit if the man I spoke to hadn't tried to touch me. Without thinking, I slapped him, and…well…for that, they threw me into the nearest NKVD camp."

"Just like that? Without official charge or trial?"

"They do that all the time. But the worst part is that the camp they sent me to was Sachsenhausen, where my parents died."

"Dear God. How terrible." It was a pathetic reply, banal and spontaneous, but it was all Gillian could think of. "Didn't Heinrich come looking for you?"

"Yes, of course. But they lied to him at first and said they'd never seen me. It wasn't until he went to our mayor that he found out where they'd sent me."

"Oh, I'm so sorry. If only I could have helped. Or even known. How did you get out?"

"You won't believe it, but Olga Petrova, an officer I met right after surrender, helped me. She's a captain now and part of the military administration."

"I met her once, in one of the nightclubs. Interesting woman, for a convinced communist. So she got you out. And then you came home?"

"Yes. Charlotte and Heinrich were happy to see me, but they have so little food, I knew I had to work right away. Tabasco hired another musician, so I couldn't go back there. I simply tried once more here."

"And they took you back, in spite of the scandal about Jack?"

"A different supervisor was at the employment center, and the base still needed women to entertain the men when they're off duty."

Gillian bumped softly against her. "I'm sure the men loved you. You're very pretty. Even your bones are pretty."

Erika dropped her glance. "Anyhow, both Tempelhof and Gatow were hiring, so I chose to work at the Malcolm Club. It was much better than the Tabasco. Warm food, a little piano, and your friend Nigel found me there the first night."

The military bus arrived, already packed full, and they fell silent as they squeezed into it. After some thirty minutes, they climbed off again and walked the last few streets to the Lübeckerstrasse.

In mid-winter, without electric lighting, the city was alarmingly dark. They linked arms, for courage and warmth, and they could talk again.

"I brought as much food as I could get on short notice," Gillian said. "I'd like us to celebrate your return with a nice supper. Maybe Charlotte can patch something together out of the bits I'm carrying."

"Yes. A celebration of both of us coming home. You'll spend the night, won't you?"

Was that also an invitation to Erika's bed? She couldn't be sure. What would Charlotte and Heinrich think? But she was so grateful to be with Erika again, it almost made no difference if she ended on the couch. "Yes, I'd like that, though I have to report in early."

Just then an airplane flew low over their heads with a deafening roar, and Erika shouted, "You have to get used to the noise of the planes, though."

Gillian laughed and nudged her again. "You forget my job. I bring those boys in, every four minutes, fifteen of them every hour."

Erika clutched her arm more tightly. "It's a wonderful thing the Allies are doing for us. We won't forget. Ah, here we are."

At the top of the stairs, she unlocked the door, and Gillian was shocked. The cheerful room she remembered from Christmas was pitch-dark, though as soon as they arrived, Charlotte emerged from the kitchen with a candle.

The flickering light illuminated the second shock, the lines of damp laundry that hung from wall to wall.

"Hello, Gillian, dear. So nice to see you. Don't let the laundry bother you. Come into the kitchen with us and warm up at the stove."

The kitchen, in fact, was much as it had been at Christmas, with the cast-iron stove that radiated the only heat in the apartment. As before, chairs were set about it, and a kettle rested on top of it, trickling a rivulet of steam. But instead of an electric lamp, a single candle now provided the only light.

The other difference, of course, was the thunder of airplane engines that halted their conversation every four minutes.

"Come, sit down." Heinrich motioned her over to one of the chairs and fetched a fourth one for himself.

At that moment, someone knocked at the door, and Charlotte stood up. "That will be Gerda. She came by earlier to say she's had a fight with Fritz and wants to sleep here tonight. We thought she could stay with you, Erika. Is that all right?"

"Oh, don't worry," she said, turning to Gillian, "there's a place for all three of you."

Gillian's heart sank, but Erika didn't react, so perhaps separate sleeping was the plan all along. Resigned, she greeted Gerda with as much sincerity as possible, and when all five of them were seated around the cylinder stove, she opened the knapsack at her feet. "To celebrate Erika's return, I brought a few things for us to eat together. Most of it is good cold or hot. Especially this." She slid a bottle of red wine from her knapsack and presented it to Charlotte.

"I didn't come empty-handed, either," Gerda said, producing a packet of dried egg powder.

Charlotte clasped her hands. "That's wonderful. I also cooked some of the dried potatoes from this week's ration. It just needs warming on the stove." She reached into a cupboard and drew out a covered porcelain pot.

"That works out well," Gillian said. "I have a can of Spam, some tomato paste, and a tin of bacon. I also brought some dried eggs, so maybe we can keep both packets for breakfast."

"Heavenly," Charlotte exclaimed. "Though you may not want to breakfast with us." She paused while another plane passed overhead. "The power in this street comes on at five o'clock in the morning, and I use the time to iron the laundry. That way I can send it back to the base with Heinrich at seven thirty."

Charlotte sliced the block of Spam and laid the slices in a circle around the cold mashed potatoes, then added several dollops of the tomato paste. Nudging aside the hot kettle with a rag, she set the casserole on the stove top. Heinrich dug a quantity of coal from a bin in the corner with a hand shovel and added it to the interior. Through the slits in the oven door, Gillian watched the fire dim to brown, then slowly brighten to red, and finally bright orange.

"Give it about fifteen minutes," Charlotte said. "In the meantime, we can perhaps open the wine."

Erika lit a second candle and set it some distance from the first, creating two small spheres of light, illuminating their faces from both sides. The increased visibility changed the room from dismal to almost cozy, in spite of the intermittent assault on their ears.

"Do you have enough coal for the winter?" Gillian asked during the next silence, then realized that was a stupid question. No one in Berlin had enough coal.

Charlotte slid a tiny table, apparently carpentered from the same wood as the window block, next to the oven and laid out five glasses.

Heinrich filled them as he spoke. "I know the Allies are working hard to bring it to us, and we're not ungrateful, but coal is like gold."

"Let's not be so grim," Gerda said. "Tonight we have coal, and each other." She raised her glass. "To friends," she said, and they all drank. As if to underline their reason to celebrate, another transport plane thundered overhead.

When the roar faded, Gillian set down her glass. "How's Hanno?" she asked Erika. "He's stayed in the East?"

"Yes, with Wilhelm at the old address. He can ride his bike into the country to 'hamster' food from the farmers, which we're not allowed to do, so he's getting enough to eat. I think when the blockade's over, he'll come back here with us."

Charlotte shook her head. "We had no idea it would last so long." She stood up and tested the contents of the casserole with a finger. Judging it to be hot enough, she scooped out five small portions onto porcelain plates.

"Frankly, we're surprised we've held out this long," Heinrich said, handing them around.

Gillian tasted the potato-tomato-Spam mix and found it tolerable. The wine helped, and she was sorry she could afford only one bottle. She glanced around discreetly at the others while they ate, realizing she felt as much at home with them as with anyone since her own family had died. Heinrich, with his scar and mane of black hair, looked like a pirate. Charlotte looked more worn, but even gaunt from hunger, her face retained a sort of maternal softness. Only Erika, brutalized twice by the Russians, seemed fragile.

They all stared at the glowing gate of the coal stove, as if watching it could conduct the warmth to themselves, while another and another crashing wave of sound rolled over them.

After they'd eaten, and Heinrich collected the plates, they discussed music, art, poetry. By unspoken agreement, they avoided talk of the war, of who was guilty of what, or of the near future and who would control Berlin. They raised their voices as each airplane roar reached its maximum and lowered them again in the lull in between.

At last, when the coals smoldered again, Charlotte declared the evening at an end. "This is how you do it," she said to Gerda and Gillian. "You heat a brick on the stove while you take care of bathroom needs and dress for the night, and at the last moment, you carry the brick to the bed in a cloth. Then you hop in and try not to get out again until morning."

"Gerda, you'll have to share Erika's bed, and Gillian, who is our guest of honor, will get the sofa all to herself."

Gillian glanced at Erika for help. For an excruciatingly long moment, she said nothing. Then, "No. Gerda should get the sofa."

"That's not very polite, Erika," Charlotte said.

Erika held her ground. "Gerda, you're a dear and loyal friend, but you snore. At the other side of the room it's tolerable, but next to me in bed, it's…well, not. If Gillian doesn't mind sharing, it will be easier on all of us."

Gillian tried to sound detached, amenable to anything. "Oh, that will be fine. I don't think I snore."

Charlotte shrugged. "Whatever suits you all. I've put all our bricks on the stove."

With bed assignments sorted, Gillian took her turn at the toilet, where Heinrich had set two full buckets of water for flushing, then returned to put on her WAAF sleepwear. It was in no way attractive, but obviously warmth would be paramount. When all were ready, they carried their bricks back to the frigid bedroom.

Following Erika's instruction, Gillian laid her brick first at the top of the bed, where her head would lie, then shoved it down to the middle, and finally to the bottom. Erika blew out the candle, and they slid quickly into the bed to absorb the warmth before it dissipated.

For several long moments, they lay side by side, silently and awkwardly, in complete darkness. Gillian felt neither sleepy nor romantic, only cold and claustrophobic. The sheet and pillow smelled of harsh, caustic soap, and the air was so cold, the tip of her nose became numb.

Silently, Erika turned on her side and edged closer. Gillian, with the featherbed drawn up to her ears, needed no further invitation and backed up into her arms. After a brief moment of cold from the movement, she felt the beginning of warmth on her back. "How long does the brick last?" she asked.

"Never long enough."

"Are you two going to talk all night, or are we going to get some sleep?" Gerda groused from her sofa.

"Sorry," Gillian said, suppressing a snicker. She drew Erika's arms closer around her, increasing the warmth. Their embrace seemed both innocent and wicked, a forbidden pleasure with a third person close by.

When she'd finally warmed, she turned in Erika's arms until she faced her, and it seemed to be the signal that more was allowed. Though she could see nothing, she raised her hands to blindly caress Erika's neck and face, drawing her closer.

She felt Erika's mouth explore her chin and cheek with soft, soundless kisses. "My nose is frozen," she whispered, spontaneously.

"Don't worry," Erika whispered back, and pressed her lips around the tip until the moist warmth spread downward to her face. The relief was exquisite and wonderfully arousing, so that Gillian's whole body began to warm.

It took only the faintest movement for their mouths to meet, and the kiss was as it had been at Christmas—warm, silent, and lingering.

Erika still had one arm over her and one under, but she slid the upper hand under the thick pyjama top. While they explored each other with their mouths, the wandering hand moved down to Gillian's belly and slipped under the cord of her pyjama bottoms.

She gave a faint grunt of surprise and pleasure as the errant fingers edged down to stroke her thigh, then rose to brush against her pubis, causing a shock.

A curious excitement came from timing their lovemaking with the arrival of each plane. And when a moan of pleasure was mistimed, Gillian feared that Gerda, scarcely ten feet away, could hear them. Yet each "shh" that Erika whispered in her ear aroused her more.

It was a thrilling, dangerous game, but now Gillian was keen to play it, too. She also slid her hand down Erika's buttocks and around to her belly, but Erika brushed it away. If it was rejection, Gillian scarcely noticed, for Erika's hand now slipped between her thighs and sent waves of white light through her body.

Another transport rumbled past them, and Gillian allowed herself to moan into Erika's throat. The roar faded quickly, and she had to endure Erika's insidious caresses in tortured silence. Her hips wanted urgently to move and meet the stroke of Erika's fingers, but she held back, and to share the ecstasy, she reached out to caress Erika in the same way.

Erika flinched away from her again.

She puzzled faintly but was too far gone, surrendering to the exquisite torment of Erika's fingers. Passive, she let herself be drawn slowly into the dizzying tension, wound tighter by the need to remain motionless and silent.

Another plane passed, and Gillian allowed herself the briefest moan, but it seemed impossible that Gerda didn't hear her close-lipped panting.

Finally she reached it, the achingly sweet moment when the match ignites. "Oh," she called out amidst the thunder of the next plane as if it shared her climax.

She went limp in Erika's arms and lay gasping against her.

From the other side of the room, Gerda began to snore.

# CHAPTER TWENTY-SIX

At a quarter to eight in the morning and still in the pleasant daze of
the night before, Gillian saluted Flt. Lt. Parsons. "Sergeant Somerville
reporting for duty," she announced, and handed over her revised orders.

"Welcome back, Sergeant," Parsons said, giving no indication of
why she had ordered the transfer out of Gatow in the first place or how
she felt about its reversal. "Glad to see you're recovered and up to
speed again." She glanced up at the wall clock. "I believe your watch
begins momentarily."

"Yes, ma'am." Gillian saluted again, marched out to the ground-
control trailer, and let herself in. One of the operators, a young corporal,
glanced up and signaled her to wait until he finished his landing. When
he stood up a few minutes later, she slid into his seat before the radar
screen. Setting on the earphones, she began the ritual back-and-forth as
if three weeks of illness had done nothing to interrupt it.

The memories of their lovemaking had to sustain her for weeks,
for the airlift had put the airfield on a nearly war-footing. Overnight
passes weren't available, and Erika was permitted on base only for the
hours of her service. They met, literally, in passing, when Gillian took
her lunch hour at the Malcolm Club where Erika worked. But unlike
the meetings with Heinrich, which had required her to march across
half the airfield to the mechanics' shed, contact with Erika aroused no
suspicion. Watched by a supervisor, Erika continued working, passing
Gillian's table repeatedly, setting out food and smuggling notes full of
tenderness.

The intense around-the-clock flight schedule remained in effect until December 24, and so also did the no-pass policy, but on that night, bad weather reduced incoming traffic so work was at a minimum. The slowdown was welcome, since it meant the staff could turn attention to Operation Santa Claus.

The operation had elicited donations by charitable organizations, mostly American, and thousands of gift packages had arrived, to be distributed to Berlin's children from both Gatow and Tempelhof over the 24th and 25th.

Gillian worked through Christmas day, but Nigel showed up at the trailer just before ten in the evening. "Well, come on," he said from the doorway. "You're officially off duty now, and you'll miss the fun of seeing two hundred children wolfing down chocolate. I've even volunteered you to hand out some of the oranges." She didn't need to be told twice. Hanno, who at thirteen had only just still qualified as a child, would be there, accompanied by Erika.

She surrendered her place to the poor sod who was assigned to work through the rest of the night and joined Nigel outside. He linked his arm in hers. "Dickie's at the party, too, and looking forward to seeing you."

Gillian sighed. "He's an awfully nice chap. I've been hoping he and Betsy would get together, but she seems to go for the Errol Flynn types."

They entered the hall and stepped into a sphere of cheerful noise, with the sound of a Christmas carol on the gramophone seeping through the cacophony. Gillian scanned the room searching for Erika or Hanno, without success, and felt a hand on her shoulder.

"Merry Christmas," Flt. Lt. Parsons said. "Thank you for volunteering." She pressed a burlap sack of oranges into Gillian's hand. "You should hand them out as soon as the kids have sung 'O Tannenbaum.'"

"Yes, ma'am," Gillian said, trying to spot Hanno among the children, but he must have been in another line. When the moment came, she pressed an orange into each eager hand, wishing "Fröhliche Weihnachten" as each child bowed or curtsied.

"You're good with children," someone said, and she glanced up.

Gillian felt her face warm. How stunning Erika was with her hair done up and a touch of makeup. "Hello!" she chirped back, conscious of the children's glances. "I'm just done with my oranges. We can go and talk." She pointed with her head toward a quiet corner.

They found a couple of folding chairs and sat down knee-to-knee.

"You look lovely," they said to each other almost simultaneously, and laughed.

"I've missed you, Gillian. It's been so long..."

"I feel the same way, but..." She shifted her glance from Erika's face to just over her shoulder. "Ah, Hanno. I see you've got your orange. Fröhliche Weihnachten." She stood up to kiss him. "What have you been doing over in the Adlerstrasse? Do you hear a lot of music with Wilhelm?"

"Yes, a lot," he answered in English. "But more important, I learn English. What do you think?" He pointed around the room identifying objects, describing what people were doing in short sentences that were largely correct.

"What a nice surprise," she exclaimed. "You've learned English instead of Russian. I'm very proud of you."

He looked suddenly earnest. "Russians are no good."

"Really? I thought they gave you more food in the East Sector."

"We get food from the farms, not from Russians. Wilhelm cooks dinner. But Russians, they take our bicycles, our radios, are bad to women."

Erika came around behind him and threw one arm across his chest. "He's really gotten good, hasn't he? Wilhelm has enrolled him in a school that teaches English. And when he stays with me, we speak only that. It's good for both of us."

"Hello, ladies. May we join you?" Nigel and Dickie stood together, each holding a cup of Christmas punch. Nigel leaned forward and kissed first Gillian, then Erika on the cheek.

Dickie ventured a Christmas kiss to Gillian, then seemed to recognize Erika. "You were the lovely lady who brought us tea," he exclaimed.

Gillian took over introductions. "Yes, and this is Hanno, her...uh, ward. Hanno, these are my friends Nigel and Dickie. They're two of the pilots that bring in the food and coal."

Hanno held out his slender hand to Nigel, then to Dickie. "My father was a pilot," he announced.

Erika registered surprise and slight consternation but said nothing.

"It's fun to be a pilot, but it takes a lot of training," Dickie said. "And a lot of time in school, too. Do you like to study science?"

Hanno stared up at him, star-struck. "We have no science books in school, but Heinrich tells me a lot of things. He tells me about the planes you fly. Two-engine, four-engine. And you come from three towns."

Nigel pulled over one of the folding chairs and sat down, throwing one leg over the other. With his slender physique and shock of black hair that hung to one side of his narrow head, he looked quite dashing. Why had she not noticed that before?

"That's nearly true, my boy," he said. "In fact, we come from about five locations, but the Russians have left us only three air corridors. They're very narrow, too, and we have to fly in single file, keep to a certain speed and at a fixed distance from the planes before and after us."

"Do you fly by navigation beacons?"

"Oh, you know about beacons, do you? You *are* a good student." Dickie took up the lesson. "But you see, all the corridors are over Soviet land, so we can't set up navigation beams. Pilots fly by dead reckoning for hundreds of miles. Do you know what 'dead reckoning' is?"

Hanno shook his pretty blond head, bathing in the attention of the two airmen.

"It means you measure by compass and calculate according to your speed how far you think you've flown. It's very easy to make mistakes. Once we had to navigate through a thick cloud, and when it broke, we found ourselves right next to a water tower with Stalin's face on it. It meant we were way off course, so we had to return to where we started."

"But the planes usually find their way," Hanno countered, keen to show off his knowledge. "And when they're close to Gatow, Gillian sees them on her radar and helps them land." Noting their approval, he continued his recital. "The planes have to land right away, and they can't circle and wait because everything outside of Berlin is Soviet territory."

"Well done, Hanno. I think you'll make a smashing pilot." Dickie started to pat him on the head, then seemed to realize the boy was too old for a head pat. Instead, he poked him with an elbow. "Hey, fancy seeing the cockpit of a Dakota?"

Hanno seemed incredulous for a moment, then concealed his reaction with adolescent bravado. "Yes, sure." He glanced quickly around the group to ensure no one would countermand the suggestion. No one did.

"Don't keep him outside long, Collins," Nigel warned. "If you don't want anyone to notice."

"Give the boy some breathing room," Dickie said over his shoulder as he led Hanno away. "He's the son of a pilot."

❖

As they disappeared through the crowd, Betsy appeared in their place. She held a handsome young airman by the hand, more or less indistinguishable from her previous flirtations. Both wore red paper crowns from their Christmas poppers. "Merry Christmas," she called out and gave everyone a hug.

"Isn't it wonderful? All those nice gifts from America. Jolly awful we're so poor back home that we can't offer anything except a place to party. But then, one of the reasons we're poor is we're sending all our food here. Innit? Well, never mind…" She finally sat down and took a breath.

Her young man, it seemed, also had much to say about British sacrifice and German gratitude, which he thought insufficient, but what could one do? His replication of Betsy's mindset suggested they were perfect for each other.

Everyone listened politely, but after some ten minutes, Erika's expression seemed to plead "save me."

"I'm sorry," Gillian said suddenly. "I know I promised to lend you that book, but I've left it in my locker. If you'll come with me, I'll give it to you now."

Bewilderment flickered for a brief second across Erika's face, then understanding. "Oh, that would be nice. I really need it."

"Go ahead. We'll wait here for Hanno," Nigel said, also grasping the strategy.

On the bottom floor of the conning tower, a room had been set aside for storage of defunct or defective equipment, antenna parts, cables, and technicians' miscellany. Gillian steered toward it, drawing Erika with her. She flicked on the light switch and closed the door behind them.

They fell into each other's arms, breathing a sort of relief together, feeling each other's warmth. Their kisses were exquisite, wet, unashamed, as they grappled like teenagers.

Finally, Erika broke away. "Be careful, please. If someone comes…"

"I know. But this is the anniversary of our first kiss, and I couldn't let it pass. We can go back now. But wait." She rummaged hurriedly through the shelves of boxes, spools of wire, tools. "Thank God!" she exclaimed softly, tugging out a book and batting away its dust. She clapped it into Erika's hand before peering through a crack in the door. "The way's clear."

Tugging her uniform tunic back in place and dabbing at her mouth, she was glad neither of them had worn lipstick that evening. They hurried back to the main hall just as the party was ending. Hanno had returned, radiant, with Dickie, and everyone seemed to be watching for Erika's return.

"Ah, there you are. Did you get your book?" Betsy asked.

"Yes, I did." Erika held it up as proof.

"A manual for wiring and repairing a rotating antenna?"

"Um…yes. For vocabulary." Erika glanced away.

At that moment, Gen. Tunner stepped to the microphone to deliver a mercifully brief Christmas message and to announce that the buses were waiting outside. If the children would please line up, they would be taken back to their Berlin pickup points.

"I'll walk with you to the bus," Dickie said to Hanno, having obviously taken over a certain guardianship of him, and they drifted as a group toward the exit.

Outside, the visiting children and guardians lined up in the cold. Betsy and her beau wandered off, but Gillian and the two pilots stayed with the line as it edged toward the bus.

At the door, both Dickie and Nigel gave Hanno comradely hugs. Gillian gave him an actual kiss, which allowed her to also kiss Erika one more time. Erika climbed into the bus and glanced over her shoulder with a look of undisguised longing.

The next day the airlift resumed in full force, as if Christmas had never happened and Boxing Day didn't exist. Starting duty at six in the morning, Gillian sat at her screen. She was tired from the night before, but it was a cheerful sort of fatigue, and in her break time, holding a cup of tea, she reflected on her friends at the party.

Betsy was the simplest. She carried good cheer in her wake, even when she was complaining. In spite of her frequent change of beaus, she would certainly find love. It was only disappointing that she had no understanding for the love Gillian felt.

Nigel was more puzzling. He was as close to being a brother as any man she knew. He was intelligent, nonjudgmental, and affectionate, and she was sure she could tell him about Erika.

Dickie was an unexpected and pleasant addition. If he was still smitten, he never pressed his case with her, for which she was glad, and she'd come to value him. Seeing him with Hanno convinced her he'd be a wonderful father.

Erika was the miracle. Inexplicable, compelling, she made no demands and was grateful for everything. Gillian snorted inwardly. Perhaps she had the sordid affair with Jean Horwick to thank for even knowing how to be intimate with a woman.

But while she'd felt nothing but an animal itch for sex with Jean, she experienced a dizzying and complex desire for Erika. Perhaps it was the separations that filled her with so much longing. She wanted to cherish and protect her, enrich her and be enriched by her, and she also wanted to ravish her.

But Erika didn't want to be ravished.

Gillian finished her tea and returned to her screen, seamlessly taking over the flow of instructions to the incoming aircraft. A new echo appeared at the edge of her screen, and she began.

"Gatow tower calling. I have you in sight. Do you read me? Please identify yourself. Go ahead."

❖

As the winter wore on, Gillian learned patience. She parked her bike and trudged along the icy street between the entry gate and the tower building, blowing warmth onto her hands and brooding.

Like the January snow that had hardened to ice on the field outside the runway, the status quo seemed frozen in place. The Soviets refused to budge in their blockade, and the Western allies were equally adamant about their claim on West Berlin.

Her personal life was also in stasis. Erika was within sight almost daily, but she couldn't leave the base to be with her, and their last kiss had been at Christmas.

She began to understand the state of mind of Soviet soldiers who'd been separated from their wives or husbands for the duration of the war, and of Captain Petrova, who cherished her son but loved him from afar.

A handful of the other WAAF were friendly, and at meals she

laughed with them and talked about girlish things. Betsy was a stalwart companion, and when their schedules allowed, they shared an evening talking about their work and Betsy's latest beau. But Gillian sensed the subject of Erika was taboo.

So when a familiar voice surprised her just outside the breakfast canteen, "Hey, old girl. Fancy a cuppa?" her heart leapt.

"Nigel, my dear. You have a knack for showing up at the just the right moments." She gripped him by the arm. "I only have thirty minutes, but that's enough for old friends, eh? The sergeants' mess has decent buns, and at this hour, we'll have the place to ourselves."

They migrated to their favorite corner with their hot mugs and sat across from one another.

"Haven't seen you in donkey's years, old thing. Where've you been flying?"

"Oh, in and out of Tegel, Tempelhof, but when I've landed here, you were never on duty." He clown-faced loneliness and despair.

"What a ham you are. Have you seen Dickie? How's he doing?"

"I fly with him most of the time, but he's on a three-day pass right now. I think he's got a sweet young thing. He'll be returning tomorrow."

"Someone to snog with at home? Well, good for him. He deserves it."

"He does. He's so much made for domesticity. You just *know* that when this is over, he's going marry some milkmaid and have a large family of redheaded kids. He talks about marrying all the time. Sounds like a WAAF, that one."

"Not all WAAF want that, you know."

"You don't fancy marrying and repopulating Britain?"

Spontaneously, recklessly, she took a leap of faith. "Not unless I can impregnate a woman."

"You cheeky girl. What *are* you talking about?" He set down his coffee and leaned on his elbows.

She pressed her lips together for a moment, as if to hold back a flood of words that needed to come out. "Nigel, you're the only person I dare tell this to, so I have to trust you. I've only just realized that all the affection I've ever had for men was shallow."

He frowned, and she touched his cheek. "Oh, I don't mean you, ducks. You're like a brother. But passionate love, the kind you need to make babies with, the kind that warms your nether regions, that I've only felt for a woman." She took a breath. "For Erika Brandt."

Nigel squinted conspiratorially. "I *knew* something was up between you two." He laid a warm hand on hers. "Oh dear, but that's all a bit dicey-do, isn't it? Wasn't she married?"

"Yes, but her husband's dead, and it wasn't a good marriage anyhow." She shrugged. "It makes no difference. I know she cares for me."

"I don't doubt it. Have you *been* with her?" His raised eyebrows suggested he meant the question carnally.

"You mean sex? Yes, sort of, under less-than-ideal conditions. Enough for me to know it's what I want. But for that matter, you've never mentioned 'being' with a woman yourself."

He looked away for a moment. "Ah, there you've trapped me. I've never been with one in the 'nether regions' way."

"You've never had sex with anyone?"

"I didn't say that. There was that upperclassman who had his hand in my trousers at school, and a few cadets, once a chap in the loo at Paddington Station. But no, never with anyone who actually loved me."

She curled her fingers in his. "Strange, isn't it? Here I thought I was the only one in the world like me. Or that I was abnormal, with a mental illness, because I'd lost my family in the Blitz. But I keep meeting people like us, and we can't all be mentally ill."

Nigel's long eyelashes became visible when he dropped his glance somberly. "I lost both mine, too, and don't have any siblings. But that just makes you lonely. It doesn't make you a pervert." He stared at their joined hands for a moment. "It's a crime, you know. In Germany and at home, too. Everyone seems to agree about that."

She tightened her lips. "Everyone's wrong. I'm certain of that. Erika inspires the most wonderful things in me. I want to be heroic for her, and kind, and wise, and beautiful. I want to do miraculous things for her. Oh, Nigel, I'm sure you'll find someone, and it'll be the same for you."

"I hope you're right. Anyhow, you have someone, and it's only a question of finding—" The buzzer signaling the hour sounded, startling Gillian.

"Oh, sorry. I've got to report to my post." She gave him a quick hug and a peck on the cheek." I love you, old thing," she said, and left the table at a jog.

❖

Erika began work each day at eight, and on days when Gillian could avoid breakfast with Betsy in the sergeants' mess, she marched over to the Malcolm Club to eat there. At some point, she'd slip a note into Erika's pocket like a kiss.

February brought weeks of bad weather, which slowed but didn't stop the air deliveries. Inevitably, a night came when the winter storm was so severe that even Gatow closed for a few hours, and Gillian was ordered to stand down.

Gillian seized the opportunity to go to the sergeants' mess for tea and a bun, but the moment she arrived, she knew something was afoot. Several dozen people had gathered, not only officers, who ought to have been in their own mess, but airmen and ground crews seeking shelter from the rain and sleet. Then she saw what held their attention.

Gen. Tunner himself had flown in from Bückeburg that afternoon for some reason, and the storm had grounded him as well. Since Tunner was "trapped with the Brits," as he said, the base commander, Gen. Yarde, invited him to a meal and then to talk to the men and women on duty.

Yarde himself was finishing off a bun, while Tunner walked to the front of the mess and leaned against a table. He lit a cigarette, and she could smell it was American tobacco. After a long puff and exhalation, he cleared his throat. "Just want you all to know, I'm damned proud of you. When we started this, it was a real cowboy operation, running from day to day with no contingency plan."

"Tell them about Black Friday," Gen. Yarde said, sliding his thumb and forefinger in a V along his mustache to wipe away crumbs.

Tunner snorted. "Oh, yes. Last August, when every damned thing possible went wrong at Tempelhof." He took another puff and picked a speck of tobacco from his tongue.

"I had only just arrived in Germany in a terrible rainstorm. The cloud cover was almost on the ground, and the rain was so heavy, the radar was barely useful. Ours isn't as good as what you've got here. Anyhow, a C-54 crashed and burned in a ditch at the end of the runway, and a Skymaster carrying coal coming in behind it burst both tires avoiding it. A third transport swerved and landed on an unfinished runway and ground-looped. After that, traffic controllers had to stack the planes that were coming in every four minutes. I was on one of those, and I can tell you, I was not happy about it. We made a silo of circling planes, where every thousand feet, from 3,000 to 10,000 feet, each one of us was within minutes of collision with the craft in front of and behind us."

"What about radio?"

"Too many of us on the same frequency. The radio was so filled with chatter, no one could communicate. It was, as you Brits say, a real cock-up." He took a puff from his cigarette and blew smoke out sideways, then coughed with the sound of a heavy smoker.

"Anyhow, I brought the whole circus to a halt by identifying myself on the radio and ordering that every plane, starting with the lowest ring, should return to its base. After that, I required that all flights be brought in by instrument, and you only got one shot at landing. If you missed the approach, you had to return fully loaded to base and enter the circuit again."

Someone started to applaud and the others followed, but Tunner raised a hand. "No need for that. The whole point is to keep moving, bring cargo, and not crash." He glanced out the window, where the hail had stopped and rain had given way to a soft drizzle.

"I believe we can all return to duty now, ladies and gentlemen." He crushed his cigarette butt into an ashtray.

Gillian approached him and offered her hand. "Excuse me, General. I just wanted to say thank you. I work in GCA, so I appreciated your story more than anyone else here."

"Sorry. I should have mentioned the WAAF who are controlling so much of the British traffic. Well done, ladies. Have you had to deal with many emergencies?"

"One or two. The only fatal one I was involved with was the collision last summer, the one caused by the Russian pilot."

"Yes. Their damned interference. How have the pilots been handling it?"

"Very well. When they try to jam our communications, the pilots switch to another frequency. When they shine lights in the pilot's face, he pulls the shades and flies by instrument. The rockets are a problem, but a lot of the men are ex-bomber pilots and used to holding formation through flak."

"Yes, they're tough, those RAF men. The women, too. It wouldn't be possible without you." He started to walk away.

"Thank you, sir. Do you think the day will ever come when women will fly in the RAF? I mean, we were doing all the ferrying and transport during the war."

He halted. "To be honest with you, my dear, I don't care for the idea. Yes, women can and should serve, but I have to agree with my British colleagues who don't want to think of the horror of having a daughter crash and burn in some accident."

He gave a casual salute and continued walking. She stared at his back and wanted desperately to say, "But you don't mind imagining your son burning to death?"

# CHAPTER TWENTY-SEVEN

*March 1949*

The frigid days followed one after the other. Sometimes, as after a fresh snow, the cold was more tolerable, while during the damp or rainy days, it seemed to seep through every layer of clothing.

The WAAF barrack, made up of a series of four-bed rooms, had central heating, which kept the pipes from freezing and made it at least possible to sleep. But it never really warmed the rooms and certainly not the bare wooden floors.

Gillian always took a one-minute shower in the morning and hurried to dress as fast as possible. She'd laughed when she was issued the regulation "blackouts," the thick navy-blue knickers that hung halfway down her legs. But now she was grateful for them, and for the thick gray lisle stockings held up with a garter belt. On this morning, her schedule coincided with Betsy's, and so they went through the morning ritual together.

Then, barely warmed up by their greatcoats, they mounted their bikes and pedaled through the freezing air to the sergeants' mess.

"Bloody hell," Betsy groused as she blew into her steaming mug of tea. "I'm not afraid of hard work, but banging away on planes in this kind of weather is killing me." She half-sipped, half-inhaled her tea with a soft *shlurp*.

Gillian warmed her hands on her mug. "I don't see how the Berliners bear it. We at least have heating, weak as it is. Most West Berliners don't." She thought of Erika huddling in her bed trying to absorb heat from a brick at her feet.

"Very sensitive of you, Sergeant Somerville."

"Flight Lieutenant Parsons." Gillian looked up at her commander and started to rise.

"At ease. I was just grabbing a cuppa. Do you mind if I join you?" Gillian and Betsy exchanged puzzled glances. "Not at all, ma'am." Gillian stood up and slid out one of the chairs.

Parsons sat down and set her half-consumed tea on the table. "So, Sergeants Somerville and Geary, how are you holding up under the pressure?"

"We won the war, ma'am. We'll win the peace, too," Betsy said. "Just wish the mechanics' shed had some heating. It's hard on the hands working on metal in this cold."

Mindful that Parsons had already tried to transfer her away from Gatow, Gillian was cautious. "We're holding our own, Flight Lieutenant. Though I'm sure nobody ever thought we'd be doing *this*." She glanced toward the sky, suggesting the entire airlift.

Parsons nodded. "Yes, the blockade took us all by surprise. As for the cold, I saw how it had taken a toll on you, Sergeant Somerville. That's why I assigned you to a less demanding post. Rather stalwart of you to want to return nonetheless. I commend you. However, we mustn't forget, the Germans are much worse off than we are."

Betsy set down her cup. "Yes, ma'am. But we're cold and hungry back in old Blighty, too, and it's because we're giving everything to the Jerries. I understand we're bringing Germany in on our side, but crikey. Sometimes it's too much."

To Gillian's surprise, Parsons shook her head. "No, Sergeant Geary, it's not too much. What we do is imperative, politically and morally. If history judges us harshly for the firebombing of Hamburg and Dresden, the airlift will save our honor."

Betsy scowled. "If I'm allowed to speak freely, Commander, Hamburg and Dresden weren't no crimes. They was payback to the Jerries for what they done to us in London."

"Payback is a dangerous defense. We all know we fought the war for survival, but I disagree with the prime minister when he called the Battle of Britain 'our finest hour.' I think this airlift, this saving of Berlin for freedom, is our finest hour. Men have died, and will die, simply to feed people who a few years ago were our enemies. It is a testament to our nobility that we are not exacting revenge, but seeking to alleviate the general misery."

Betsy blinked, clearly stunned by the peroration the commander had just delivered. Gillian, too, gazed at her superior with new admiration.

Conscious, perhaps, of her effect, Flt. Lt. Parsons stood up with her now-empty cup, gave a casual salute to the two of them, and strode away.

Betsy had the look of someone who'd swallowed a large pill. "Well, I guess that means we should go to work."

"I dare say."

❖

Erika was less inspired. She washed dishes, made sandwiches, and banged out the same tunes she'd played at Tabasco, but she enjoyed no sense of accomplishment. She was simply grateful to have a hot meal every day.

Saturday had been particularly frustrating, for Gillian had shown up with Betsy just as she'd been called back to the kitchen. When she emerged again, the two were gone. She went home in a bleak mood, not even cheered by the thought of a day off work. It would be a hungry day, but she would visit Hanno and Wilhelm in the Adlerstrasse.

The next morning, she started out early, on the circuitous trek to the Russian Sector. It began in an empty coal cellar in a wrecked building in the Marktstrasse. Carrying an electric torch, she arrived at the opening that had been knocked through the wall into another basement that led by a cement stairway up to a garage. The garage opened to a court that led to an alley, which led to another court in the Bernauerstrasse in the East Sector. A strong March wind blew, stirring up dust into her eyes. Rain seemed likely.

After another fifteen minutes, she was at the apartment building where a half dozen ragged children played with sticks and old bicycle-wheel rims. She glanced toward the square, wincing. The pavement still bore the black stains from the campfires the Russians had made, and she could recall the smell of the ordure that lay there for weeks, from both horses and men.

To her surprise, the corridor was lit, one lamp on each landing. Obviously, the Russian Sector continued to have electricity.

At the top of the stairs, she used the coded knock, *rattatat tat tat*, and Wilhelm came to the door immediately. His white beard was longer than she'd seen it before. It made him look old.

"What a pleasure, Erika. I was hoping to see you one of these days. Come in!"

The apartment, as always, was a bit chaotic, even without the two POWs who'd moved on westward. A music stand in the corner held sheet music, but a shirt dangled from it as well. Various articles of clothing were draped over chairs, and books were piled up against the wall. The apartment smelled of male bodies and soiled laundry.

Wilhelm turned down the radio. "I was just following the reports from RIAS. Nothing new, really. I just like to have the sound."

Erika took a seat on a battered sofa that she knew was Hanno's bed. "How's work? Have the Russians given you any trouble?"

"They did, until our friend Captain Miranov bent a few rules so we could perform outside of the Russian Sector. It went well for months. But Miranov's suddenly disappeared. We think he got in trouble with someone higher up."

"In trouble? How is that possible? Vassily Miranov's a convinced Communist, one of those who stopped the trains. What could he have possibly done wrong?"

"The Russians are secretive, so no one knows, but it's rumored that he and a woman, someone named Petrova, were charged with fraternization damaging to the civil order."

"Fraternization." Erika snorted. "They were both just decent people and helped me more than once."

Wilhelm shook his head. "The Russians never trust anyone, even their own. Living under Stalin, I guess you get to be that way. And if they were charged with violating the rules to help Germans—or even worse, the West—you can bet they're in some Gulag now."

The sound of the front door opening interrupted his news. Hanno let himself into the apartment and greeted her with a hug.

"I'm sorry I have no chocolate this time," Erika said.

Hanno shrugged. "That's all right. The candy bombers flew over yesterday and dropped us sweets and chewing gum."

"Candy bombers? Whatever is that?"

Wilhelm chuckled. "It's a nice story. An American airman decided to drop treats on little parachutes for the children playing around Tempelhof. It caught on, and now several pilots are scattering them every day just before they land. You can imagine the scene. When the kids aren't in school, you can't keep them away from the airport borders."

"I saw Mr. Collins fly by yesterday," Hanno said brightly.

"How do you know it was him, dear?"

"He waved with his wings. I'm sure he recognized me and remembers that my father was a pilot. We're friends, sort of."

Erika winced. "Who told you that, dear?" She turned to Wilhelm. "Did you put that idea in his head?"

"Absolutely not. I wouldn't do that. It's not even true."

"It *is* true. My mother told me." He crossed his arms and pouted.

"She told you it was Dietrich? My husband?"

Hanno glanced away. She'd obviously told him precisely that, and he wouldn't tolerate a contradiction.

Wilhelm scratched his St. Nicolas beard. "No, Hanno, dear. I can understand why Magda would want you to believe you were the son of a Luftwaffe hero, but you weren't."

Erika stared at Wilhelm, perplexed. "What do you know that I don't?"

Wilhelm sighed. "I'm sorry I didn't come forward sooner. I knew from the beginning she wanted Hanno to think it was Dietrich. Every child needs a hero. And in fact, Dietrich did deceive you with Magda, but you know that."

"I do, but you still haven't explained why you're sure Hanno isn't his."

"Because when Dietrich met Magda for the first time, she already had her baby. Dietrich might have been unfaithful, but he wasn't that baby's father."

"Who, then…?"

Hanno glanced back and forth at Wilhelm and Erika, who'd shattered his identity.

"I don't know. And with Germany full of lost fathers and brothers, displaced and disappeared persons, I have no idea how to find out."

Hanno leapt up. "It's not true. You're both lying because you're ashamed." He lurched toward the door, slamming it behind him.

"I'm sorry," Wilhelm repeated. "I don't know what's worse, that I kept up the lie all those years or that I told him the truth now. It wasn't fair to you, but it was all he had to hold on to."

Erika's shoulders slumped. "Sometimes there's no right way."

❖

*April 30, 1949*

The Dakotas had been landing with coal since daybreak, almost a thousand pounds of it in each aircraft. Since coming on duty, Gillian and the other controllers had brought in another twelve of them smoothly, and the sturdy two-engine workhorses taxied off the runway into the line where the work gangs would unload them.

The next echo floated into view on Gillian's radar screen.

"This is Gatow ground. Do you read me? I have you in sight. Go ahead."

"This is Dakota four three Alpha Delta. Mayday, Mayday! We have fire in the aircraft. A spark someplace must have lit the coal dust. Cabin filling with smoke. Over."

She recognized Dickie Collins's voice and the sound of two men coughing. That meant Nigel was copiloting. Her heart began to pound with fear, but she forced calm into her voice, to sound exactly like she did for every other landing.

"Dakota 43, where is the fire? Can you extinguish and open vents to clear smoke? I have you at ten miles out. You can begin descent. Go ahead."

"Gatow ground, Nigel's trying, but cargo has caught fire." He coughed again. "Window all smoked up. No visibility. Need you to guide us down. Over."

Gillian struggled not let him hear her rising panic. "Dakota 43, we'll get you in. Begin descent. Change course to three zero and reduce altitude. I repeat, change course to three zero and reduce altitude. Go ahead."

"Gatow ground, changing course to three zero. Reducing altitude. Over." His voice was raw and breathless.

The bright spot that held the lives of her two best male friends was now lined up with the runway.

"Dakota 43, you are at eight miles and lined up. Right on target. We'll get you in. Go ahead."

"Gatow ground, smoke is filling cockpit. Can't see instruments. Are we on glide path? Over."

"Dakota 43, you are seven miles from airfield. Increase rate of descent. Engage landing gear. Repeat, increase rate of descent and engage landing gear. Do you receive me? Go ahead."

Flt. Lt. Parsons, who must have seen the smoking plane, rushed into the trailer and stood behind her, staring into her screen.

"Gatow ground, fire is out of control. Repeat, fire out of control." Dickie coughed violently. "Cannot read instruments, flying blind. Over."

"Dakota 43, you are now five miles from touchdown. Can you…" Just then Parsons seized another headset and bent over the microphone. "Dakota 43, you are five miles out but now above glide path. Increase rate of descent. Repeat, increase rate of descent. Over."

"Gatow…(cough) descending. Can't breathe. Get us in fast. Over."

"Dakota 43, you are three miles out, heading still good. Reduce your rate of descent. Repeat reduce your rate of descent, over."

"Gatow…" They heard only the sound of wheezing, of men trying to breathe through their shirts.

The squadron commander dropped her voice to sound reassuring. "Dakota 43, you are a mile and a half from touchdown, but glide angle too sharp. Pull up, I repeat. Pull up. Over."

"(Coughing) Trying to. Oh, God, engines…stalled."

"Dakota 43, can you restart? You are half a mile from touchdown. Use flaps and engage wheels. Over."

All that came through the radio was desperate coughing.

"Dakota 43, do you receive me? Repeat, do you receive? Over."

Gillian rushed to the ventilation windows and scanned the sky until she spotted the smoking Dakota approaching the end of the field. It was plummeting at a steep angle with little chance of gliding in on full flaps.

She watched, incredulous, as it covered some hundred meters of runway before crashing. Upon impact, the fuselage broke in two and exploded, its fireball continuing to slide forward. When it stopped, heavy black smoke poured from the mangled steel and floated out over the runway.

Riveted to the window, she gawked at the impossible sight, hearing Flt. Lt. Parson's repeating broadcast.

"Gatow ground here. All flights within range of my voice should abort landing. I say again, abort landing and return through central corridor. Accident on runway. Repeat, accident on runway. All flights return through central corridor."

Throwing off her headset, Gillian flung herself out of the trailer and watched, paralyzed, as firefighter trucks roared toward the holocaust and tried to extinguish it. Their sprays had little effect, and she heard, or imagined she heard, the crackling of the fire as it consumed the craft and crew emitting a thick, oily smoke. She staggered back to the van, and when she reached the door, Flt. Lt. Parsons stood there, ashen.

"Go home, Sergeant Somerville. That's an order."

Gillian nodded, and in a trance, she retrieved her bike and rode back to her quarters. As she pedaled, she sensed the light and the heat from the burning plane behind her. With its seven thousand pounds of coal, and the bodies of her two friends, the funeral pyre would burn all night.

❖

When Erika had arrived at the Malcolm Club that morning, she'd lit two of the burners on the field-kitchen stove to prepare the tea and buns. Only a half dozen off-duty airmen sat at the tables.

At the sound of the crash, everyone had rushed outside, halting as a group and staring, appalled, at the burning plane. The flames had engulfed the aircraft completely, and though fire trucks were rushing toward it, it was clear they would rescue no one.

"Jesus," one of the airmen had said. "I wonder who the crew was?"

"They'll tell us soon enough," a lieutenant replied. "Me, I can't stand to look at it. That could be any man here." He'd shuffled back inside the hut, and slowly the others tore their eyes away from the appalling spectacle and followed him in.

The piano remained silent the rest of the day, though some of the men occupied themselves silently and mechanically with darts. Erika served food until five thirty, then left to catch the last bus. As she passed through the guard gate of the airfield, she asked one of the men on duty if he knew yet who the crash victims were.

"Yeah. They just reported it," the guard said. "Dickie Collins and Nigel Katz, coming in from Wiesbaden. Nice chaps, those two."

Her heart sank. The loss of Nigel would shatter Gillian. The two were obviously best friends.

The loss of Dickie, Hanno's new idol, would break his heart, too. And if the guard had received the news from the RIAS radio broadcast, then all of Berlin had heard it. Hanno would simply have to bear another loss, as he had borne the death of his mother.

The bus arrived a minute early, and she hurried toward it, leaping onto the steps, where several hands helped draw her in. Pressed against the crowd, she closed her eyes. It was just so difficult to be alone.

# CHAPTER TWENTY-EIGHT

Amid the ongoing pressures of duty, bereavement was acknowledged but not indulged. The next morning, though the entire airfield smelled of coal smoke, the smoldering wreck of the Dakota had been bulldozed off the runway, and the airlift resumed at full strength.

Gillian returned to work with grief a vaporous phantom riding her back and clutching her throat. Betsy had consoled her the evening before in her own way, which managed to be both superficial and sincere. But planes still needed guidance, so she forced herself back to her post.

She had scarcely begun work when Flt. Lt. Parsons stopped by the ground-control trailer. She watched the team of controllers for several minutes, then laid a hand on Gillian's shoulder. Only that, the lightest touch. But the single gesture was enough to break Gillian's fragile calm, and she couldn't speak as the next plane appeared on the screen. She waved to a colleague to take her place and rushed outside the trailer, where she burst into sobs.

All of it poured out, her anguish and impotent rage, at the Russians, the weather, the coal, the war, and the defeated Berliners they had to feed. Her parents had been incinerated, and now two good men she'd grown to care for had been as well.

She also, unashamedly, felt sorry for herself. The loss of Nigel had robbed her of the only other soul in the RAF who was just like her. For the briefest moment, they'd formed a stalwart band of two, facing the world of condemnation and contempt, and now she was alone again.

Except for Betsy, who had a good heart but lacked all depth and sensitivity, who did she have left?

The answer was obvious and immediate. She had Erika. In a foreign land and among recent enemies, she'd found constant love.

All that kept them apart were their conflicting duties, the lack of a private place and…the airlift. She understood now that, no matter what obstacles arose, she would make a life with Erika.

Emotionally drained, she blew her nose and started back to the trailer. Flt. Lt. Parsons met her at the door and drew her back outside. "I just want you to know that I appreciate your special circumstances in this case."

"My special circumstances?"

"It's not my business to pry into personal relationships, but it has been obvious to me since Christmas that you and Lieutenant Katz were very close."

"Well, yes, ma'am. I really cared for him."

"Ah, then I was right. I'm frankly relieved to know that, especially after your unacceptable liaison with that German mechanic. It also puts to rest the ugly rumors floating around concerning Lieutenant Katz's uh…predisposition. Anyone could see, you made a lovely couple. Were you to be engaged?"

Gillian's mind raced. Where was this leading? Had Nigel been rumored to be homosexual? Could she save his reputation posthumously, with a lie?

"Uh, yes, ma'am. We weren't in a hurry, though. We thought we had time."

"Yes. We all think that. Anyhow, I ask because Lieutenant Collins's fiancée will fly here this afternoon for our memorial service. But Lieutenant Katz had no remaining family. However, I can use my discretionary authority to name you as next of kin, which means you will receive his medals and his possessions. In addition, I'll grant you three days' bereavement leave to fly back to England for some rest and recuperation, beginning immediately after the funeral."

Gillian was stupefied. Had she perjured herself? Would it come out that they were not engaged, *could not* be engaged? But no. If Flt. Lt. Parsons declared them engaged, then that was final. Betsy may have had suspicions, but only Dickie Collins knew the truth. And he was dead.

Gillian cleared her throat. "Yes, ma'am. When is the funeral?"

"The ceremony will be very brief in the officers' mess at two o'clock this afternoon, after Lieutenant Collins's fiancée arrives from Fassberg. I believe her name is Peggy. In any case, you have time to return to barracks and put on your dress blues."

"But I was about to return to my post."

"No. I'm relieving you of your duty. Your bereavement leave starts now."

Gillian was about to turn away when Parsons added, "Oh, and it would be nice if you would make a few appropriate remarks in Lieutenant Katz's memory."

❖

The Dakota from Fassberg arrived on schedule, carrying both a full load of flour and Peggy Cuthbert, who would have been Peggy Collins in two months. Flt. Lt. Parsons met her on the tarmac and guided her to the officers' mess, where the mourners were already gathering.

Gen. Brian Robertson, the military governor of the British zone, Airlift Commander Gen. Tunner, and Base Commander Gen. Yarde were in attendance, as well as whatever airmen, WAAF, and ground crew were currently not on duty. German workers were not invited.

Gillian took a seat near the front, nervous and with mixed feelings about the charade. The act of honoring the dead seemed slightly undermined by her deceit. Only the thought that Nigel himself would surely be amused kept her focused and calm.

When the higher officers were seated and it seemed the room was full, two corporals entered and slow-marched toward the table that held the podium. They halted simultaneously and set down the dress caps of the two deceased. In front of the caps they laid out flat wooden cases displaying their respective decorations.

Both men had medals for Service, Distinguished Conduct, and Victory. Nigel also had the Atlantic Star medal.

Gen. Robertson stepped up to the podium and cleared his throat, then offered the usual platitudes about bravery and sacrifice. No one would dare say how ignominious it was to die from a coal fire. Gen. Tunner spoke next, adding a few words about the special bravery of the airlift pilots, etc. A friend of both men from Fassberg added a brief tale describing what good comrades they were.

Peggy, as it turned out, was not made for public speaking, for she wept through her brief speech about Dickie's virtues, as a fiancé and as an Englishman. When she stepped down, after only two minutes, all eyes turned to Gillian.

Stiffly, she rose and strode toward the podium and allowed herself a deep breath before beginning.

"Recently, Flight Lieutenant Parsons made me realize that this airlift, supposedly in a time of peace, has called upon us to labor and sacrifice no less than at Dunkirk and Normandy and so counts with those as some of our finest hours. In that sentiment, I want to honor our fallen men with the words of a king, written by England's greatest poet and humbly adapted by me." She unfolded a piece of paper.

*Proclaim it, Westmoreland, through my host,*
*That he which hath no stomach to this fight,*
*Let him depart; his passport shall be made,*
*And crowns for convoy put into his purse;*
*We would not die in that man's company*
*That fears his fellowship to die with us.*
*This day is call'd the feast of Crispian.*
*He that outlives this day, and comes safe home,*
*Will stand a tip-toe when this day is nam'd,*
*And rouse him at the name of Crispian.*
*He that shall live this day, and see old age,*
*will strip his sleeve and show his scars,*
*And say "These wounds I had on Crispin's day."*
*And he'll remember, with advantages,*
*What feats he did that day. Then shall our names,*
*Familiar in his mouth as household words*
*Nigel Katz, Richard Collins, John Higgins—*
*Be in their flowing cups freshly rememb'red.*
*This story shall the good man teach his son;*
*And Crispin Crispian shall ne'er go by,*
*From this day to the ending of the world,*
*But we in it shall be rememb'red*
*We few, we happy few, we band of brothers;*
*And gentlemen in England now a-bed*
*Shall think themselves accurs'd they were not here,*
*And hold their manhoods cheap whiles any speaks*
*That fought with us upon Saint Crispin's day.*

She waited for a moment in the awkward silence that followed, wondering if she had made a fool of herself with irrelevant poetry, but Flt. Lt. Parson's smile and gentle nod suggested she had not.

When she stepped down, Gen. Tunner took her place and explained that the two airmen's belongings, including their awards, would be packed and transported to their next of kin, which, in the case of Lt.

Collins, would be his mother. However, in the absence of family for Lt. Katz, the beneficiary would be his fiancée, Sgt. Gillian Somerville.

The honor guard who'd brought the medals now marched in synchronized steps toward the display cases, closed and lifted them simultaneously. Continuing their matched steps, they squared the table, confronted the bereaved fiancées, and presented the cases with a flourish.

Gillian accepted the medal case and held it in front of her, nonplussed, but at that moment, the chaplain rose and enjoined everyone to bow their heads in prayer. Gillian did not pray and could not imagine what she would say anyhow to a god who had let two good and courageous men die in a coal fire, so she simply dropped her eyes. She need not have worried; the chaplain had all the necessary words, about grace and forgiveness and a better world that waited.

The prayer brought the service to a close, and everyone stood up to leave. Flt. Lt. Parsons patted her gently on the shoulder. "Here's the pass I promised you. Three days, starting today at noon. If you want to fly back with one of the transports, let me know. Two are starting out this afternoon to Wiesbaden, and from there, you can catch a flight to London."

"Yes, ma'am. Thank you." Gillian stared at the paper in her hand, the freedom Nigel had bought for her with his life, and her eyes filled again.

## CHAPTER TWENTY-NINE

Dazed and clutching Nigel's cap and medals to her chest, Gillian shuffled along the airport apron toward the Malcolm Club. The atmosphere in the entire base was somber, but crash or no crash, flights continued circulating through, crews still came on and went off duty, and the support services continued as well.

When she arrived, Erika was preparing sandwiches in anticipation of late-afternoon visitors. Gillian took a seat at a table off to the side and waited quietly, gently setting the cap and medal case in front of her.

Some ten minutes later, Erika joined her, wiping her hands on her apron. "I'm so sorry," she murmured softly, laying her hand on Gillian's. "We heard the crash, and they told us about the funeral this afternoon, but no German workers were invited. You were there, of course."

"Yes. I had to speak," Gillian replied in a monotone. "They think I was Nigel's fiancée. They even gave me these." She gestured toward the cap and medal case. "Flight Lieutenant Parsons gave me three day's leave."

"Oh, that's good. Will you fly back to England?" Erika asked with unconvincing lightness.

"No point in that. I've no one to see there. You're my family. You and Hanno, Charlotte, Heinrich."

Erika's face radiated relief and tenderness. "Then you'll spend the time with us, of course. Charlotte and Heinrich will be pleased. I work until six, and we can go home together."

"Yes. That's all I want right now. I'll go first to my barrack and get a few things, then meet you at the bus stop."

"Finally," Erika said gently, and tightened her grip on Gillian's hand before rising to leave.

Now, at least with a plan, she marched purposefully back to the bike shed near the control trailer. But reality had changed too quickly, and she was light-headed. For so many months, she'd lived in a circuit, from radar screen, to mess, to barrack, and again to radar screen. Now, the three days of freedom seemed a vast, open plain.

The ride to the barrack in the May afternoon was actually pleasant. In her room, she laid her precious inheritance in her locker, washed leisurely, and changed into civilian clothes. During the remaining hour, she went to the American PX and bought grayish buns with tasteless "national cheddar," packets of tea and coffee, miniature fruit pies, a jar of peanut butter, and a tin of bacon.

She left early for the bus stop, and when Erika arrived she embraced her lightly.

"Tell me about Nigel," Erika said, while they waited. "I know you want to talk about him."

"You're right. And I can't tell anyone but you. He was like the brother I'd lost and, do you know? He was...like us. I mean, that he would never marry, for the same reason as us."

Other passengers began to arrive for the last bus, German loaders and maintenance staff, and they fell silent.

The bus, as always, was packed, and since they were first, the crowd pressing in from behind forced them slowly into the center. Even without speaking, it was a comfort to feel Erika warm against her back.

At the Lübeckerstrasse, they elbowed their way out again. The sky was still light at six thirty in the evening, and the same thin children played in the street. The corridor of the building was dim as usual, but when Erika opened the apartment door, it was fully lit and music played on the radio.

"Gillian, hello!" Gillian embraced her warmly but was shocked at Charlotte's appearance. She was pale and haggard, the hint of grandmotherly roundness completely absent. She was also clearly ill.

"I'm happy to see you, but please excuse me. We're halfway through our two hours of electricity, and I have to make the most of it." She coughed and gestured toward an ironing board and a pile of freshly washed RAF shirts. A line still stretched across the living room with a row of men's knickers held by wooden pins. Gillian snickered at seeing so many of them up close.

"Your cold is worse, isn't it?" Erika remarked. "Why don't you stop work for the day and rest?"

"I can't." Charlotte coughed again, a dry, wheezing cough that suggested a well-developed pulmonary infection. "Heinrich has promised to deliver it all tomorrow. But I've only a few shirts left, so we can talk while I do them."

She laid one of the shirts over the board and made a sweep across the yoke with the iron. "I'm sorry to hear about the crash, Gillian," she said, her voice raw. "Erika told me they were your friends."

Gillian began to fold one of the ironed shirts. "Yes, one of them especially."

Erika unhooked all the undershorts from the line and smoothed them before folding them neatly. "They both were very kind, not always flirting like the others. Hanno simply adored Dickie Collins. He put a face on the image that Hanno had for his own father. Does he know about the crash?"

"I'm sure he does," Charlotte said. "The same way we all do, from the radio."

"He'll be shattered. I want to talk to him, reassure him that...well, I don't know what I'll say. The poor boy somehow got the idea Dietrich was his father, and I destroyed his last hope of that."

Charlotte smoothed the sleeves, then began on the front panel. "It wasn't Dietrich? Who was it, then?"

"I don't know, and I have no idea how to find out."

"If he was born in Berlin, he'd have a birth registration, wouldn't he?" Charlotte asked.

"I suppose so, but the *Standesamt* that would have it is in the Russian Sector. They won't let us rummage around in their records. With the blockade, we can't even get into the building." She added the last folded knickers to the neat pile.

Charlotte had just finished the shirt and unplugged the iron when a paroxysm of coughing struck her. She fell back onto a chair, gasping for breath.

"Look, you should go to bed right now." Erika bent over her, obviously concerned.

"She's right," Gillian said. "I've brought a few packets of tea from the PX. We'll make you a cup and bring it to you."

Charlotte took a deep breath. "You're right. I'm completely kaputt, and a cup of English tea would be lovely." With a last satisfied look at her folded laundry, she shuffled into her bedroom.

Gillian unpacked her rucksack and laid the various snacks out on a tray while Erika stoked the ashes in the iron stove to heat water for tea. "Is it always like that?" Gillian asked. "I mean two hours of frenzy in the light and then darkness?"

"For most people, yes, except Charlotte also works by candlelight. And when the power is off, she has to fetch water from the street pump. That's why she's so exhausted."

The radio was still broadcasting traditional folk tunes when they carried the tray of tea, buns and cheese to Charlotte's sickbed. Her swollen eyes brightened at the sight. "Oh, marvelous. But please set aside half of it for Heinrich. He gets home at midnight and will be hungry."

"Don't worry about him. He'll have had a big supper at Tempelhof. This is all for you."

Charlotte ate hungrily but with deliberation. Gillian had shared several meals with the Berliner couple and was always struck by the way they ate slowly, prolonging the pleasure.

After her meal, Charlotte fell back against her pillow, momentarily sated. As Erika cleared away her tray, she was already dozing. Gillian followed Erika back into the kitchen and embraced her from the rear. "It looks like we have the next hour or so to ourselves."

Erika turned in her arms and kissed her softly but broke away before it could become earnest. "We have all night, too, for wonderful things. But let's talk for a while and enjoy the light."

She guided Gillian by the hand back to the sofa in her room and drew Gillian's leg over hers. "Tell me about your family. I bet they were nice."

Gillian shifted, finding a comfortable position. "What can I tell you? I lost my parents in the war. You know that."

"Brothers? Sisters?"

"Brother. A daredevil pilot who flew in competitions all over the world. When he died in an accident, I dreamed of being just like him. He's the reason I joined the Air Transport during the war, and the RAF afterward, and ultimately why I came to Berlin."

"Pilots are a special breed, aren't they?"

"You should know. Tell me a little about the pilot you were married to."

Erika exhaled a long breath. "I don't know what you want to hear. We weren't married terribly long, but he was rather dashing. The sort of man a woman wants to show off. Maybe that was even the reason I married him."

"Do you have a picture of him? I'm curious to know the kind of man who would attract you."

"I have our wedding picture. In an album down in the basement with the rest of my books."

"Oh, I'd like to see that one." Gillian glanced at her watch. "We still have about fifteen minutes before the power goes off. Can you find it quickly?"

"I guess so." Erika slid out from under Gillian's legs, and they hurried down the stairs. At the back of the ground-floor corridor, she opened the cellar door.

Just inside, as the door clicked shut behind them, she snapped on the light switch, illuminating the single bare bulb that hung from the concrete ceiling. Battered suitcases were lined up next to a dusty perambulator. A wooden bench that had escaped smashing for firewood still stood against one of the walls. Next to the stairs, a sort of bookcase rose precariously to the ceiling. It held aluminum tubs full of unidentifiable heavy engine parts, steel rods, and hundreds of empty bottles.

"Be careful. Those shelves are unstable. One of these days they're going to topple over and kill someone." Erika stepped past them and pointed toward the corner, where a wooden crate was covered with a sheet of oilcloth. "That's it." She shoved aside the oilcloth and pried up the lid of the crate. By the overhead light, Gillian could see piles of books and sheet music.

Erika rummaged for a moment, then slid out a thick album bound in red leather. "Here it is. Come on. We can look through it upstairs."

They turned toward the stairs, and at that moment, the light went out, leaving them in complete, terrifying darkness, a blackness that was the same with open or closed eyes.

"Oh, God," Erika gasped. "The two hours. I was sure we had another ten minutes. They cut the power early."

Gillian groped to the side and found Erika's arm. "Just stay calm. We can feel our way toward the stairs. I remember roughly where they are." Gillian stepped in front of her, and while Erika kept a hand on her shoulder, she shuffled blindly forward.

She touched something wooden and grabbed hold of it to steady herself. Too late, she realized it was the wobbly shelf. She recoiled, reaching back to protect Erika, and felt the whoosh of air as it swooped past her face and crashed.

The sound of metal tubs and heavy steel objects smashing onto the concrete floor was frightening enough, but far worse was the shattering of a hundred glass bottles. In the black nothingness, she sensed shards of glass fly against her legs. And now, somewhere in front of them, lay splintered wood, aluminum bins, iron machinery, and piles of deadly broken glass.

Erika clutched her shoulder. "Are you all right?"

"Yes. I think so. I didn't feel anything hit me. What about you?" She spoke over her shoulder into the darkness.

"I'm fine. But we don't dare take another step. We'll just trip and fall onto the glass and whatever else is there." Erika tugged on her arm. "Step backward. The bench is just behind us." They shuffled back until their legs touched the reassuring surface and sat down.

"Don't worry," Gillian reassured herself as much as Erika. "How many people live in this building? Forty? Fifty? We just have to wait until someone comes through the corridor. As soon as we hear them, we'll call out. In the worst case, Heinrich arrives home in a couple of hours, and we'll hear him."

Erika slid her hand around Gillian's upper arm. "You're right. No reason to panic."

"Absolutely not. We're too old to be afraid of the dark." Gillian forced a chuckle. "Besides, we've been wanting to be alone together, haven't we?"

Erika whimpered. "I'm sorry. I *am* afraid of the dark, and of the cellar. I spent too much time sitting in one during the invasion. You must keep talking."

"I can do that." Gillian spoke in her soothing ground-control voice. "Why don't we just pretend we're in the cinema, and the screen has gone dark for a moment. We're with a hundred people, but now we have a chance to kiss with no one to see us."

"Cinema? I haven't been in one in years. What were we watching?"

"Any film you like."

Erika hesitated. "I saw a film with my husband in 1940 called *Herz der Königin*. With Zara Leander. Yes. Let's miss that one."

"*Herz der Königin* it is. And here we are waiting for the screen to light up again and finish the scene. All around us are other young people, soldiers embracing their fiancées. We can do that, too."

Gillian reached for Erika's face, then drew her closer, letting her lips creep across Erika's cheek, seeking her mouth. A strange, disembodied kiss, like kissing night itself, or the formless patches of color that swirled and flickered in her sightless eyes. Suddenly the whole of Erika was fragrance, taste, texture.

Erika's fingers slid down Gillian's ear to her throat. "Yes, this is good," she whispered. "If I can feel you, I'm not afraid. Stay by me. Not just now, later too, when we're out."

"I promise. Before I came here today, even before I lost Nigel, I already knew I never wanted to leave you."

"But when this airlift is over, however it turns out, you'll go back to Britain."

Gillian shook her head, though the gesture was invisible. "It's not like you think. First, I don't have to return right away. I can apply to stay while things get better for you in Berlin. And England's not so very far. Our pilots fly to see their families all the time and take their fiancées home."

"You want to take *me* home?" the phantom voice whispered.

"If you could see my face, you'd know how sincere I am when I say yes, I want to. I want to give you a life better than what you have in Berlin."

"It sounds wonderful, but…what about Hanno? I'm his family."

"Even though he's not really your stepson?"

"After so many years, it makes no difference. He's my son by the promise I made to his mother, and by choice. I chose him, like I've chosen you."

"Mmm," Gillian muttered, turning the idea around in her mind. A family by choice. It seemed a reasonable solution to all their loneliness. The only problems were practical ones.

"Well, you could come first, look around, get settled, and then send for Hanno. I like having him as part of the family. I know nothing about the laws of immigration, but surely that's possible."

"Yes. That would be good. In the meantime, once the crisis is over, we can keep seeing each other here." She chuckled. "Ironic that we had to be trapped in total darkness to visualize some kind of future."

Gillian took hold of Erika's hand and pressed it to her heart. "Perhaps it's easier when we can't see each other's blushes, so I can say I want so much to make love to you. Why haven't you let me do that?"

"Please don't be hurt. At the end of the war, I was forced, first brutally, and then out of fear and hunger. Then Jack tried to force me in his way. The kind of touch you want is still frightening. Surely you know now that I love you. That part of me is still alive. Only desire, at least the desire to submit, seems dead."

Gillian gripped the slender hand more tightly. "Darling Erika. I'm not some randy man who has to physically conquer you. Nothing is more intimate than to be inside your heart and your head. We can be together any way you wish. And you've already shown me how well you can *give* pleasure."

"Oh, I love to do that. I love your body and your voice and your kisses, and I love to make you excited."

"Jolly good." Gillian slid an arm around her back and murmured into her ear. "And I promise only ever to do the things you want me to do."

"You mean like cook our meals and wash the dishes after?" Erika snickered.

"Sure. If that's what makes you happy. But I insist on kisses. Like this." And with a hand to guide Erika's face, once again she let her lips creep over and cover her mouth.

It was a lovely, long kiss, that was their pledge, each to the other. So engrossed were they in its devotion, they were slow to perceive the change through their closed eyelids.

It seeped into Gillian's awareness first, and her eyes flew open. "Light," she exclaimed. She stood up and surveyed the trail of splintered wood, the overturned tubs, machine parts, and the sea of broken glass that surrounded it all. They'd have fallen and been sliced to pieces if they'd tried to plow through it blind.

"Come on, while the light's still on." But Erika was already on her feet, stepping cautiously over each obstacle, crushing glass shards with every step.

They reached the stairs and hurried up to the door. Throwing it open, they saw the corridor was also light, illuminated from one of the apartments on the ground floor.

An elderly man stood in the doorway and danced from one foot to the other. Behind him, Beethoven's *Ode to Joy* was playing on the radio.

"It's over!" he sang. "The blockade's over! The Russians just announced it." He seized their hands and shook them vigorously.

"*Gottseidank!*" Erika breathed and drew Gillian by the wrist up the stairs to her apartment. Charlotte had gotten out of bed and stood in the bright living room, seeming slightly baffled to see Erika and Gillian still fully clothed in the middle of the night. But she, too, had been awakened by the radio and, in spite of being sick, was ecstatic.

"So, what now?" she asked.

As if on cue, Heinrich came through the door at the end of his work shift. "Ah, so you know, then." He kissed each of them in turn. "What a shame we have nothing to celebrate with."

"That's all right," Charlotte assured him. "Now that the trains can come through, the rations will increase, and that's celebration enough."

"Anyhow, it's one in the morning, and blockade or no, I'm ready for bed." Heinrich ran his hand over his mane of hair. "Why don't we leave the radio on the rest of the night, so if they change their minds, it'll go silent, and we'll know."

Charlotte nodded. "Yes. We're all exhausted. And it will be wonderful to wake up to freedom, at least more of it than we've had for the last year." She took Heinrich's arm, and they ambled together toward their bedroom, apparently indifferent to Erika and Gillian's sleeping arrangements.

Shrugging, they withdrew to Erika's bedroom, where they sat down on the edge of her bed. Gillian began by undressing, glad for her civilian clothes, which didn't involve regulation knickers, but rather a slip and normal underwear. Erika followed suit and drew off her dress and slip. Shyly, they slid into bed together.

"Well, it happened sooner than we thought," Erika said, kissing Gillian lightly on her cheek and ear. "What will this mean for your job?"

Gillian grasped her hand and kissed her fingertips. "Not much, I don't think. Not for a while. I'm sure they'll continue deliveries, to build up a stockpile. You never know when the Russians will change their minds again."

"Good. That gives us some time. Once we've stocked food in the house, so we don't have to struggle each day, I'll start to track down Hanno's father."

"Tell me more about Magda," Gillian said as she huddled close.

Erika stroked her hair. "She was working class, from Wedding. She never had a real job as far as I know, since she'd had polio. But she was always beautiful. I'm sure that's what attracted Dietrich to her."

Gillian held Erika's hand against her cheek. "He must have had an easy time seducing her. I mean, a Luftwaffe pilot!"

"I'm sure he did. He did with me, too, a couple of years later. By then, the war had started, and having a child by a glamorous Aryan Luftwaffe pilot would certainly have raised her in the eyes of her Nazis neighbors, even if it was a lie."

Gillian rose on her elbow. "I don't understand how you ended up living in the same building."

Erika and traced patterns on Gillian's chest while she talked. "Dietrich and I married only a few months after we met, and he was often away on duty. I lived with my aunt. The apartment in the Adlerstrasse belonged to his mother, and he lived in barracks, but when she died, he got permission, and we moved into it. Magda and the baby were our neighbors. Dietrich was flying missions in France, so Magda and I became friends. After he was killed over the channel, she was very kind, attentive. Then one night, after too much wine, she told me that Hanno was Dietrich's son."

"And you believed her."

"Yes. Why would I not? I had no idea of the actual time they were together, and I knew before we were married, he was a ladies' man. It was possible, and I had no reason to doubt someone who was my friend."

"But as it turned out, it *was* a lie."

"Apparently so. No one knows who the father was…is."

"Where was he born? Do you know that?"

"Presumably in Wedding, where she'd lived."

"So, all we have to do is go to the Standesamt there and ask for his birth registration."

"Assuming the Standesamt is still standing, yes." Erika pulled her down under the covers again. "Come. Keep me warm. I'm too worn out to talk any longer. I just want to sleep in your arms."

"Um, yes. Sleep sounds wonderful. And tomorrow we'll wake up to electricity." She slid down into Erika's grasp, and their long, dark night was over.

They awoke at seven at the sound of Heinrich's preparations for an ordinary workday and the murmur of Charlotte's voice sending him off.

A wonderful sound, Gillian thought. The sound of long-established loyalty, domesticity, family. Could two women ever have that?

# CHAPTER THIRTY

Throughout the month of June, though the blockade was over, planes continued to deliver goods at Gatow, Tegel, and Tempelhof, though with less regularity and as a supplement to supplies arriving again by train and lorry.

Gillian's duty schedule returned to eight hours, and though she could spend the remaining time as she wished, she needed a pass to go into Berlin proper. It was at the beginning of the next off-base pass that she met Betsy at the bike shed.

"Polly and Megs and some of the other girls are getting together tonight at NAAFI. Why don't you pop by? Should be bags of fun." Betsy bent to unlock her bike just as Gillian locked hers.

"Oh, sorry. My friends are expecting me tonight in Moabit. You know, Erika, Charlotte, Heinrich. I've got a pass until tomorrow."

Betsy stood up with her lock in her hand, pouting. "Yes. I know who they are. I worked for months with Heinrich before he transferred to Tempelhof. But you've been going there every weekend, and I just don't see the attraction. I'm beginning to think you prefer the Jerries to your own people." She tossed the lock into her basket and lifted the bike off the rack.

Gillian walked alongside her as she wheeled out onto the road. "Don't be silly. We're not going to be in Berlin much longer. Don't you want to take advantage of it?"

"Not particularly. Frankly, I've had enough of this country Besides, Freddie is being posted back to Blightly, so I've applied, too."

"Freddie? What happened to Maurice?"

"Ancient history. Freddie's my true love. You have to catch up, my dear." She nodded toward Gillian's rucksack. "What are you taking them now?"

"The usual bottle of wine and my chocolate rations from the week for Hanno. Remember him?"

"Of course. Well, enjoy yourself. What are they making for your supper? Powdered potatoes?"

Gillian laughed, refusing to be made fun of. "Probably, but supplemented with wine." She patted Betsy on the back and gave her a quick kiss. "Say hello to the others for me."

Gillian's step grew lighter when she spotted Erika already at the bus stop amidst the other German workers returning home. Erika had a strange expression and glanced away, as if she held some sort of secret.

"Do you have something to tell me?" Gillian asked.

"Yes, but it can wait." The military bus arrived just then, and like an old couple, they linked arms and fit themselves into the crowd.

They arrived at six in the Lübeckerstrasse, and Gillian noted that since the lifting of the blockade, the corridor and stairwell were cleaner. Perhaps it was simply the availability of detergent, together with the renewal of energy and optimism.

Charlotte embraced her at the door, fully recovered from the chest infection that had plagued her. Heinrich took her hand, but his expression was a shade brighter than she'd seen before. Was it just the breaking of the blockade? Or the wine she'd just handed him? "Let's save this to drink after supper while we have our music," he said.

"Music?" Gillian had images of the Christmas sing-along.

"Yes. Wilhelm lent us his gramophone, and we have several disks. It'll be nice to have something other than the radio. We also moved the sofa back into the living room so we can sit out here in the evening instead of around the stove. But Hanno sleeps on it now that he's back with us, so I hope you don't mind sharing a bed with Erika."

"Oh no, not at all." Gillian glanced away and changed the subject. "How nice that you've also removed the wooden boards from the windows. It's like an apartment again, instead of a bunker." A breeze ruffled the makeshift curtains.

"Ah, there he is," Erika said as Hanno came into the apartment. Gillian had to remind herself that he was fourteen, for he seemed to have shot up during the months he'd lived with Wilhelm. He was still alarmingly thin, but his little-boy blond hair had darkened to honey-brown, and when he greeted her in awkward English, she realized his voice was changing. One or two pale hairs were emerging along his chin line. He looked less Germanic now, and she felt a certain fondness for him, wondering if he resembled his sad, beautiful mother. Or his father, whoever he was.

"Thank you for the chocolate supply. I am happy to have you in the family." His "th" still came out as "s" or "z," but otherwise his accent was tolerable.

"Oh, you're quite welcome. And I'm also happy to be in your family."

Erika smiled maternally at both of them. "He's been practicing that phrase all afternoon."

Heinrich returned to German. "He speaks for all of us, Gillian. I wish more of us knew more of you. We'd never have a war again."

At that moment, Charlotte came in from the kitchen and set a large covered bowl down on the table. "Of course it's potatoes again," she warned them. "But these are *real* ones, not that horrible powdered stuff. And we have spring vegetables from Berlin's gardens to go with the chicken I was able to buy."

"My goodness!" Gillian's exclamation was banal but sincere. She'd had so many patched-together "dinners" with the Dehmel family, enriched only by the bits and pieces she could bring from the base. To sit down to a meal that had something other than RAF canned meat was a special occasion.

But when Charlotte handed around the platter, Gillian had to smile wanly at the pigeon-sized chicken that had been carefully cut into five tiny portions. The potatoes that came steaming in a large bowl covered with carrots and green onions would make up the calorie difference, and of course no one thought of complaining.

The dinner conversation, in a mix of English and German, was lighthearted and relaxed, in a way she hadn't experienced since she'd sat at table with her parents. *Dear God. Nine years ago.*

After the meal and its cleanup by the males—Gillian was sure it was to impress her—everyone returned to the living room to hear the disks Wilhelm had sent. Their music-hungry ears heard past the scratchiness of the old needle on worn vinyl, and briefly, they lost themselves in the sublime pleasure of a Mozart concerto and the Chopin nocturnes.

"I remember my brother raving about Berlin before the war. He said there was a spirit in the city, a deep culture and creativity, in spite of the Nazis. Now I know what he meant."

Heinrich crossed his bulky arms and stared at the ceiling. "Yes, in the thirties, Berlin was electric. Something for everyone. Art, poetry, jazz, comedy, dancing, drugs. Nazis called it decadence and 'Jewish,' but that's what it looks like to people who are afraid of it."

"But if everyone was having such a great time, what happened to sweep in National Socialism? I'm just a simple English girl and never studied politics, so I'd really like to know."

Heinrich scratched his chin and thought for a moment. "It's hard to say. The economic depression, inflation, maybe. Millions without work and you had to blame it on someone. So, we blamed it on the English for winning the war, on the Jews for being too rich or intellectual, on the Bolsheviks for being too primitive, on anyone who wasn't a true German. Then came the Reichstag fire that let Hitler declare a permanent state of emergency, and in a stroke, the Republic became a dictatorship."

"Did things get better?"

"Actually, they did," Charlotte interjected. "Autocracy gets things done, and building an army and concentration camps creates jobs."

Heinrich agreed. "Yes, nationalism is a real drug. Soon we were all swept up in it. The worst were passionate Nazis, and decent people might have found it all a little ugly, but they were silent."

Gillian studied his earnest face, confident she could ask without insult, "When did you join?"

Heinrich frowned. "The party? Never. They were vulgar, stupid men. But when the war started in 1939, I was a patriot. I wanted to fly, so I joined the Luftwaffe."

Gillian laughed out loud. "Just like I did. But I didn't qualify."

Heinrich chuckled with her. "Neither did I, though in my case, it was because I didn't look Aryan enough. That, and I failed the exams. But they accepted me as a mechanic, and I got to wear the uniform after all. The girls loved it." He glanced over at Charlotte.

"It's true. You were a handsome devil," Charlotte said, then grew somber. "Our son joined, too. From the Hitlerjugend to the Wehrmacht, and was killed at nineteen before he ever had an adult understanding of what was happening." She shook her head. "Uniforms are dangerous. They make us obedient and bring our thinking into line. We lose our ability to stand back and judge."

"Let's hope that is all over now, and we can start rebuilding," Erika said.

Hanno hadn't spoken, and Gillian wondered what his memories

of National Socialism were: the ceremonial dagger and the camaraderie with other boys or the shame of surrender.

Heinrich yawned. "Well, if I'm going to rebuild Germany, I need a good night's sleep. So, if you'll excuse me, I'm off to bed." He finished his wine and stood up. It was the signal that the evening was over and Hanno could have his sofa.

"Yes, we all should do that," Erika said, clearing away glasses and avoiding eye contact.

With mumblings of "good night" exchanged back and forth, and Hanno laying out his blanket and pillow, Gillian followed Erika into her bedroom.

After they undressed without ceremony—that time in their relationship had passed—they curled up warming each other, quietly caressing and waiting for desire to grow.

Gillian was the first to nuzzle, but after a few soft kisses, Erika moved away. "I have something to show you."

"Oh, you mean the mysterious thing you talked about at the bus stop? Is it something I should worry about?"

"I don't know. That will depend on you. Remember I said I'd check at the Standesamt in Wedding for Hanno's birth registry? Well, it seems that during the bombing, they'd transferred their records to some vaults in Grünewald. I left a request there for the information, but it wasn't until just a few days ago that I got an answer."

"Oh, that sounds exciting. What did they say?"

Erika leaned away from her and reached for a folded paper on the night table. "Read this and tell me what you think."

"Ah, so that's what a German birth certificate looks like." Gillian held the paper toward the light and read out loud.

"*Standesamt Berlin-Wedding.* Record number, blah, blah. Year 1935.

"*Alle Vornamen des Kindes:* Johannes, Theodor, Bonifacius. Gosh. All those names. I wonder if he knows all of them.

"*Geschlecht des Kindes: Knabe.* A boy, obviously.

"*Geburtsdatum des Kindes*: 12 Juli 1935.

"*Geburtsort des Kindes*: Berlin, Wedding.

"*Mutter*: Magdalena Elizabeth Katherina Szabo.

"*Religion:* Katholisch.

"*Vater*—"

Gillian stopped. "What? That can't be. Or is this a joke?"

"I would never play a joke like this on you. That's the official registration they sent me, with the name Lester Somerville. But you said your brother's name was Alastair, so I didn't know what to think."

"Alastair, Lester, it's almost the same thing," she murmured, staring into space. "If she didn't know him very well, she could make that mistake."

"Then it *could be* your brother. You said he'd been in Berlin for a flying competition. What year was that?"

"Let's see. It was when we moved to London. I was just nineteen. That was the autumn of 1934."

"It's the right year. And it does all make sense. A dashing Englishman is in town for a few days for a flying competition. Flirts with a pretty girl who's desperate for affection. Things happen. He flies home and leaves behind a pregnancy." Erika smiled softly. "Looks like Hanno's father was a pilot after all."

Gillian still stared into space. "Have you told him yet?"

"No, but Charlotte and Heinrich know. I wanted to let you know first and then him. He'll have to accept he's half German, half English."

"Yes, I suppose so." Gillian struggled to grasp the implications. "And completely my nephew."

"Are you glad? I can't tell from your expression."

Gillian considered for only a moment. "Of course I'm glad. It's just a lot to absorb. It means that if you still want to come to England with me, he'll actually have priority over you."

Now Erika stared into the distance. "I hadn't thought about that. But of course I want to come. Hanno can decide for himself."

"If he decides to emigrate, which he's entitled to do, you can obviously follow as his de facto guardian. We'd be a strange sort of family, but no stranger than what you have here in Berlin."

Erika pressed close to Gillian. "A family, like husband and wife. Then I think you should make love to me."

Gillian turned on her side. "You mean that? You really want me to?"

"I do. Chance has brought us together in this extraordinary, unlikely way. I want you to be in my life and in my bed. I want you to desire me and touch me the way I touch you."

"You mean like this?" Gillian said, sliding a hand down Erika's cheek to her throat, then to her chest. It rested gently on her breast.

"Yes, like that." Erika grasped the hand and held it against her.

"You lascivious creature," Gillian murmured, entwining their legs and biting her on the chin.

"What does that mean, 'lascivious'? Is it good?"

"Oh, no. It's very bad. It means you want to do naughty things with me."

"I want you to do naughty things *to* me."

Gillian slid her hand down Erika's belly and between her thighs. "Things like this?"

"Oh, that's very naughty. I'm sure it's not allowed," Erika whispered.

"I'll show you what's not allowed, you minx," Gillian whispered back and slid her fingers along the welcoming groove.

Erika moaned appreciation. "That is minx?" She bit Gillian gently on her lips and chin. "Oh, yes. Minx is good. More minx, please."

# CHAPTER THIRTY-ONE

*September 23, 1949*

Gillian stood before Flt. Lt. Parsons, wondering why she'd been summoned. Surely she couldn't be on report. Since the official end of the blockade, half of the WAAF contingent had already been posted back to the UK, and she'd been pulling long shifts to take up the slack. Her hours were only slightly less than what they'd been at the high point of the airlift. What could the commander possibly have to reproach her with?

Parsons looked up from the dossier she'd been studying. "Sergeant Somerville, I've taken note of your extended hours in ground control and in your training of new recruits. In view of your exemplary service, I've recommended you for promotion to flight sergeant, with the concomitant elevation in pay."

"Yes, ma'am. Thank you, ma'am. Honored to serve." Gillian saluted smartly.

"Not only that, but you've probably already been informed that the last official airlift flight will be arriving at Gatow tomorrow afternoon. I'd like you to be the one to bring it in."

Gillian stiffened to attention and all but clicked her heels. "It will be an honor and a pleasure, ma'am."

"The flight is due in at 1300 hours, and we may have a photographer there to record the moment. So, try to look smart." She paused, presumably to ensure Gillian took the hint. "If you don't have any questions, you are dismissed."

Gillian saluted yet again but didn't move. "In fact, I do have a question, ma'am. Unrelated to my duties. A procedural question. I'm hoping you're more familiar with civilian law than I am."

"I don't know about that. What's your question, Flight Sergeant?" Gillian smiled, hearing her new title. "Well, I've learned that my brother's child is here. The boy's German mother is dead, and I'm his only family by blood, so I'd like to take him back with me to Britain. A family friend has cared for him since the mother's death, and I'd like to take her back as well. How can I do that?"

Parsons frowned, clearly incredulous. "You have a nephew here? How is that possible?"

"It's a long story, ma'am, but not so strange if you know the background. My brother was a sports pilot who flew a flight competition in Berlin in the '30s. He was my inspiration both for flying and for coming to Berlin. He met a young German girl, and, well, nature took its course."

"And how did you find out about this...um...act of nature?"

"During my trips into Berlin with Lieutenant Katz, I became friends with people who were caring for a boy whose mother had died and whose father was unknown. When the blockade was lifted, they went to the registry in the Russian sector and obtained his birth certificate. The father's name was listed as Alastair Somerville, and the birth date corresponded to nine months after the competition."

Parsons squinted, following the extraordinary tale. "I see." She cleared her throat. "Well, I don't think we've ever dealt with a situation like that. The RAF Legal Branch will have to advise us." She drummed her fingers on the desk.

"I do know, there are different classes of immigrants, and the child would have the strongest case, as long as you can document that he's the son of a British subject. The female caretaker will take a little longer, but it should be possible, provided she has no Nazi affiliations."

"She is the widow of a pilot in the Luftwaffe, ma'am. Would that count against her?"

"That in itself need not prevent her entry. She'll just have to show that neither of them was active in the party. In any case, to leave Germany, both of them will need an exit permit and an entry visa from the UK. And in order to work, the woman will have to apply for a labor permit as well. As the de facto guardian of your nephew, she would qualify for domestic service, as his caretaker."

"She speaks English, if that helps."

"I'm sure it does. Once established, she could find work in other areas. I'll check with the RAF lawyers and let you know. In the meantime, you better prepare for your final airlift call-down. Perhaps a bit of makeup for the photograph?"

Gillian saluted for the third time and did an about-face. As she passed through the door, she confronted a group of Berliners, two adults and two little girls in party dresses. The children fidgeted nervously, and one of them held a dachshund puppy.

Intrigued, she stepped to the side and watched from the doorway as the girls made a little speech thanking the women for all their help in the airlift. Then, with a curtsy, they presented the puppy to Flt. Lt. Parsons.

By then a half dozen other WAAF had gathered next to Gillian, and they all filed into the office, each one petting the obviously bewildered dog.

"Oh, how absolutely delightful," Parsons said. "I am happy to accept this gift from the people of Berlin on behalf of the women of the RAF." She glanced at the ceiling for a moment, seeming to deliberate, then announced, "We'll call him Dakota, for all the sturdy Dakota planes that have served us this last year."

An RAF photographer arrived just in time to take a photo of the station commander and her new mascot.

Smiling at the scene, and at her pending assignment, Gillian marched back to her post. The day was going very well, and it was only ten o'clock in the morning.

❖

The next afternoon, the final delivery arrived from Lübeck right on schedule, and although the sky was clear, Gillian went through all the steps of the ground-controlled approach until the aircraft touched down on the tarmac.

At that moment, she laid down her headset for the last time and hurried out of the GCA trailer to join the entire ground-control staff and a row of photographers and journalists on the apron. She posed for press photos with GCA colleagues while they waited for the plane to taxi into place for unloading.

On cue, the coal truck pulled up, and the gang of loaders leapt out, and while Gillian watched the activity under the flicker of flashbulbs,

Erika emerged from the crowd. "Well done, my dear. Not just this landing, of course, but all of them."

Slightly dazed by the mix of relief and nostalgia, Gillian took her by the arm. "Thank you, but come. Let's get out of the way." They wandered around to the far side of the plane, away from the unloading gang and the press. Someone had painted the numbers 21:11 in amateurish fashion on the nose of the plane. "What do you suppose that is?" Gillian asked one of the ground crew next to her.

"No idea," he said.

"From the Bible. Psalm 21:11," one of the German laborers said. He recited it in German and Erika translated. "*For they intended evil against thee; they imagined a device, which they could not perform.*"

Gillian snickered. "No, they couldn't, but it took them long enough to realize it."

Erika linked arms with her again and strode alongside her back to the terminal. She, too, seemed somber in spite of the festivities. "How much time do you still have left here in Berlin?"

"I haven't received any orders yet, but I'm guessing it's not much." Erika winced, and Gillian took her hand.

"You shouldn't worry, darling. I've already spoken to my commander about immigration, and it looks quite good. She's checking with our legal officers, but she let me believe we'll have no great problem. Even if it takes a few weeks or even months for the process to run its course, that's not a bad thing. I'll need time to find a new job and a place for us to live. We'll be three, after all."

"You won't stay in the military?"

"Only until I can get a position flying. London has small private companies, and I'll try every one of them until someone hires me. Then we'll build from there. People back home were always pestering me to 'start a new family for England,' and now I will, with you and Hanno."

Erika gazed at her solemnly. "He loves you, you know. His mother was sick for so long that Charlotte and I became the women in his life, but you're the first one who's given him a real identity. Pride, even. He talks about you as much as he does about his 'father the pilot.'"

"That pleases me to hear. But we all want to have something to be proud of. I want to be his 'auntie the pilot,' and I hope you'll be his 'auntie the pianist.'"

Erika brushed an invisible speck from Gillian's uniform, a

domestic touch. "It's peacetime, the blockade's over, and we're free. We can do that."

They glanced out over the airfield. In the distance, a small plane was just taking off into the bright afternoon sky, indifferent to the closing celebration on the ground. It seemed a good sign.

## CHAPTER THIRTY-TWO

*November 1949*

Gillian banked the Avro Anson to starboard, and the midday sunlight reflecting off its nose momentarily dazzled her. A quiet elation filled her, as after a great and successful labor, for she was at both the end and the beginning of something wonderful.

The airlift had ended, aid was pouring into Germany, and West Berlin was stirring once again to rebuild itself. Gillian had flown home with the Gatow WAAF contingent to the same acclamation the RAF men received, with a parade and royal inspection at Buckingham Palace. King George himself had shaken hands with Flt. Lt. Parsons, and they'd all been invited to a banquet.

Ironically, just as the name Women's Auxiliary had been changed to Women's Royal Air Force, Gillian had herself finished her enlistment and joined a civilian airline. Nothing had seemed more natural than the transition from traffic control of transport to the transport itself, in a plane she could fly in her sleep. It hardly mattered that her pay was only two-thirds of what the men received. She'd been underpaid as a WAAF as well, and it was simply the way of things.

The thrice-weekly flights to Italian and Spanish ports were not only a pleasure, but they also let her smuggle in a few bottles of fine liquor, to sell discreetly to Covent Garden merchants for a small but regular profit.

Now her uniform hung in her closet, and the memories of the airlift were only half of her joy. The other half was what the rest of the day would bring.

The Croydon airstrip came into sight, and she brought the Anson smoothly in to the British Eagle freight terminal. Patting her navigator on the shoulder, she made her way from the cockpit back to the cargo hatch and watched as the ground crew unloaded the crates of fruits and vegetables from Italy. It was a scene much like what had unfolded countless times at Gatow, but now salaried Englishmen, rather than starving Berliners, did the work. And this time, of course, she was the pilot.

Leaving the men to their work, she headed into the terminal.

"Good flight?" the operations officer asked, pro forma. She suspected he was onto her little business, but as long as the deliveries came as ordered, undamaged and on time, he didn't care.

"A doddle," she replied, handing over the flight manifest. Inside the freight-terminal staff room, she changed out of her flight overalls and sheepskin jacket and secured them in her wall locker. With a grunt, she hefted her rucksack, loaded with six bottles of Amaro Montenegro and Toshi Nocello, onto her back.

As she hurried back into the main hall of the terminal, she glanced up at the clock. One o'clock. It had been a good idea to spend the night at the freight terminal at the Verona airport and make it a morning delivery. She had plenty of time now to meet the train.

"Hey, there!" she called out, spotting Hanno on one of the benches. "Did you have to wait long?"

He smiled like he was dying to tell some good news. "I came early and talked to someone about flying lessons. They said Croydon has a flying school and I can start when I'm sixteen." Without asking, he took the rucksack from her and swung it around onto his own back. "I just have to come up with the money."

"Very ambitious. You want to start already next year?" She took his arm, and they strode together from the terminal to the bus stop.

"Of course I do. That gives me a year to save the money from my dishwashing job."

She hugged his arm. "Erika always said you were brilliant in the hard days after the war. I see now what she meant. And I'll make you a deal. We're going to have a lot of expenses in the coming year, but if you can come up with two-thirds of the cost, I'll provide the other third."

He glanced down at her, for he was already two inches taller. "Thanks, and I'll accept if I need it. The restaurant said I could work full-time in the summer, so maybe I can manage the whole amount."

"Well, the offer still holds, though I know you've always been able to take care of yourself."

"Not just myself." He grinned. "I did the shopping you asked me to do this morning. All you have to do is cook it. Oh, and I got us some pastry."

"Pastry? Oh, well done, my dear. Now let's just hope the trains run on time."

❖

At Victoria Station, the trains did run on time. At 4:40 p.m., while they waited at the beginning of platform four, the train from Dover Priory steamed into the station and hissed to a halt. A few moments later, the doors on one side opened and disgorged the passengers like so many ripe peas from a long string of pods. She watched, straining to separate out the individuals in the mass that flowed toward them.

As the minutes passed and the oncoming crowd grew thin, she began to chew her lip, impatience evolving to anxiety. Why was she not there? Erika's letter, which was still in her pocket, said it would be this day and this train.

"I see her!" Hanno's greater height let him spot her first, and he rushed to meet her. Taking her battered valise, he led her by the arm back to Gillian.

They halted three feet in front of her, and she gazed, grinning, at the object of her longing. Two months of—for Berlin—relative prosperity, had put flesh on Erika's thin body and smoothed out her face. Her hair was blonder than before and carefully coiffed, and, in spite of the four-day journey across Germany and Belgium and the steamer trip from Ostende over the channel, she looked stunning.

"I had forgotten how beautiful you are," Gillian murmured finally, and then they were in each other's arms.

"I'm sorry we couldn't meet you at Dover." Gillian spoke into her hair. "I had to make a delivery, and the Immigration people said you'd be tied up in formalities anyhow. You must be exhausted."

"Come on, you two." Hanno stood impatiently under the double weight of rucksack and valise. "You can exchange news at home."

"Home," Erika said. "What a nice word."

Gillian took her by the arm. "You'll like it, I think. We have a two-bedroom flat in Soho. A little like Charlotte's, but with glass windows and without the iron stove. We're over a restaurant, where Hanno has a job after school, so it often smells like cooking oil, but you get used to it. I've found a job for you, too."

"I know. My immigration application said I was working for you, as housekeeper."

Gillian laughed. "Much as I'd love to have someone to clean up after me every day, that was only for the work permit. In fact, one of the schools nearby needs a piano teacher. You'll have only a few students at first, and as a German, you'll have to win them over, but it's a start. And Soho has clubs and theaters that always need pianists in the evening."

They were outside Victoria Station now, and darkness had set in. They stood for a moment while Erika gazed at the bustle of people, the density of buses, and the tall buildings all around them.

She laughed brightly. "Just like Berlin. Before the destruction, I mean."

"Yes. It's a bit like it. I think you'll feel at home."

"I know I will. And after all, Berlin isn't so far."

"Not when you fly," Hanno remarked. "And when I have my license, I'll take us back to visit Wilhelm and the others."

"Oh, my. Two pilots in the family." Erika tugged on both their arms. "Won't that be lovely. But first let me get to know London."

"We'll work on that first thing. I don't have to fly tomorrow, so we'll go to Covent Garden to sell the liqueur I brought in from Italy. Then I'll show you around Soho and introduce you to the music director of the Spence School. By the end of the day, you'll be an old Londoner."

"That sounds wonderful. But I'm very tired from the journey, so tonight, I'd like to go to bed early. If that's all right."

"Of course. Everything's ready. We even have a bathroom in the apartment, with lots of hot water."

Erika turned toward Gillian and hugged her arm. "Smashing," she said, in her new language.

# BERLIN HUNGERS: POSTSCRIPT

**ATA-Air Transport Auxiliary**
A British civilian organization based at White Waltham Airfield during World War Two. Employing pilots considered unsuitable for the RAF by virtue of age, physical handicap, or gender, the ATA maintained fourteen ferry pools all over the UK. They flew new, damaged, or newly repaired military aircraft—and occasionally personnel—to maintenance units, scrap yards, and in-service airfields. The ATA employed 166 female pilots (one in eight of all ATA pilots) from ten different countries, and from 1943 they received pay equal to that of their male coworkers, a first for the British government. They flew every type of aircraft used by the RAF except the flying boats. The ATA was disbanded in November 1945, three years before the Blockade/Airlift.

**Berlin Airlift: British "Plainfare," American "Operation Vittles"**
Cargo flights from the West to Berlin initially supplemented trains and trucks to supply the American, British, and French military installations. After the blockade began (June 1948), planes began provisioning the civilian population, but in a disorganized manner. The acquisition of significantly more aircraft and crews, and the arrival of Maj. Gen. Tunner, turned the ad hoc operation into a smooth-running circulation of cargo planes four minutes apart from West German airfields along three corridors to American Tempelhof, British Gatow, and (later) French Tegel airports. While the blockade officially ended on May 12, 1949, the deliveries continued until September, guaranteeing a stockpile in the event of future interference.

**Berlin Blockade: June 1948–May 1949**
The blockade arose out of a conflict in policies regarding spheres of influence in defeated Germany. Lacking natural borders, such as the US and UK have, and having been invaded twice (by Napoleon and Hitler), Russia was obsessed with keeping a large buffer zone to the west. This fear, coupled with an expansionist ideology and a general bitterness toward Germany, conflicted with the more conciliatory policies of the West. Two sore points were the presence of the Western allies in Berlin, deep inside the Soviet zone, and the introduction of a new currency in the West without Soviet agreement. By March 1948, cooperation in the Allied Control Council had ceased. Over the next two months, in an attempt to force the West out of Berlin, the Soviet Union first harassed, then, in June, blocked all Western rail and road transportation into the city. The response was the Airlift.

**Candy Bomber**
American pilot Col. Gail Halvorsen became known as the "Berlin Candy Bomber" after he began without authorization to drop candy and gum with miniature parachutes to children on the periphery of Tempelhof airport. His fellow pilots began to do the same, and when word spread, donations of candy came from all over the United States. Candy bombardments expanded over Berlin with other pilots, and Halvorsen became a national hero. After the Airlift, Halvorsen received the Congressional Gold Medal, and in the following decades, he promoted candy drops in Bosnia-Herzegovina, Albania, Japan, Guam, and Iraq.

**Crash of April 5, 1948**
As described in the story, on April 5 a Soviet Yak-3 fighter plane buzzing a BEA Vickers Viking airliner lost control and struck its wing. Both planes crashed. The Soviet pilot and all ten passengers and four crew on the airliner were killed. Each plane crashed in the other's zone. The incident did much to further animosity.

**Division of Germany**
After the German surrender (May 1945), the Western allies and the Soviets had conflicting aims with regard to what to do with defeated Germany. After an initial division into four zones under the control of Soviets, Britain, the US, and France, the latter three joined their

zones into a single bloc and wanted to rebuild Germany as a Western democracy and buffer zone against communism. Russia—economically devastated by the Nazi invasion—wanted huge reparations and a Germany under Soviet influence. Cooperation in the Allied Control Council disintegrated quickly, and the insistence of the Western powers to retain control of part of Berlin—deep inside the Russian zone—led to the Blockade and ultimately to the Cold War. Germany was not reunited until 1990.

**Ground Control Approach**
Radar developed right after WW2 was still evolving and very secret but by 1946 was already used to position incoming aircraft so as to guide them by radio to the runway, even at night and in poor visibility. The British at Gatow were particularly advanced in this technology. Two radar systems were used simultaneously: Airport Surveillance Radar (ASR), a wide-ranging radar to detect an aircraft and direct it to a specific airfield, and Precision Approach Radar (PAR), for monitoring and control of landing. The system depends on continuous radio contact between ground control and pilot. Currently, in most civilian airports, GCA has been replaced by the instrument landing system (ILS) and GPS-based approaches, which can serve many aircraft at the same time.

**Kurfürstendamm**
Berlin's Broadway or Champs-Elysees. Although damage from Allied bombardment was considerable, the Kurfürstendamm remained the street of the postwar nightclubs, which soldiers from all four occupying armies frequented. The club names in the novel are authentic. Once rebuilding started, it once again became a prominent and prosperous commercial avenue.

**Nuremberg Trials**
A series of military tribunals that ran from November 1945 to October 1946 in Nuremberg prosecuting surviving leaders of Nazi Germany, the most famous of which are listed in the story. Subsequent trials prosecuted Nazi doctors, judges, and lesser criminals. The trials were ground-breaking, first in the use of multinational judges and legal counsel, and multilinguistic testimonies aided by simultaneous translation via headphones. They also introduced the concepts of "war crimes," "war of aggression," "crimes against humanity," and international criminal

courts in general. However, critics have called the trials "victors' justice" and legally and morally questionable, since the Allied accusers were guilty of some of the same crimes as the accused.

## Phylis (PiP) Parsons

WAAF Station commander at RAF Gatow during Berlin Airlift, 1948–1949. For this service, King George VI personally thanked her and her contingent of WAAFs at Buckingham Palace. At the end of the Airlift, the citizens of Berlin presented Flt. Lt. Parsons and her team with a dachshund, which she subsequently named Dakota. She kept the dog for the rest of its life, even after it became partially paralyzed.

## Psalm 21:11

I found no pictures of the final air-lift plane, and the account may be apocryphal, though it is sufficiently strange to probably be authentic. The actual King James quote is this: *For they intended evil against thee: they imagined a mischievous device, which they are not able to perform.* Presumably the psalm and verse numbers were not recognized until some journalist (not a ground-crew member) looked them up.

## Russian entry into Berlin, May 1945

The Russian entry into Berlin was notoriously marked by widespread looting and rape. However, this phase was fairly brief, and as soon as a governing military body was formed, theft and sexual predation took a subtler form. The nonfiction book *A Woman in Berlin* gives an excellent account of the plight of women during this period.

## Sachsenhausen

A Nazi concentration camp in Oranienburg, Germany, used primarily for political prisoners from 1936 to the end of the war in May 1945. After the war, since Oranienburg was in the Soviet Zone, the Russians renamed the camp NKVD Special Camp Nr. 7 and used it to incarcerate their own "enemies." These were suspected Nazis, anti-Stalinists, holders of "illegal" print and broadcasting devices or weapon deposits, Social Democrats, and "spies" suspected of "anti-Soviet activities" or for contacts with organizations in the Western zones. Among the alleged Nazis were some 10,000 youths and children. In 1946 only 10 percent of the inmates had been tried, and in early 1950 still only 55 percent. In 1950, the camp was handed over to the East German government, which tried the remaining inmates.

**WAAF/WRAF**

Created in June 1939, WAAF served as parachute packers, barrage-balloon handlers, caterers, weather reporters, flight mechanics/fitters, radar operators, code-breakers, reconnaissance/intelligence analyzers, flight mappers, and medical orderlies. In 1949, greatly diminished in number, the force was renamed the Women's Royal Air Force (WRAF). Women were gradually admitted to fields in the RAF, and in 1994 the *W* was dropped. At Gatow, WAAF worked in administration, mechanics, and, above all, radar and ground control. In spite of the critical shortage of pilots, I could find no record of any woman piloting any of the thousands of flights during the Airlift.

**Woms**

RAF slang for mechanics.

# About the Author

A recovered academic, Justine has twelve novels under her literary belt, all setting lesbians in the historical landscape. After dallying with ancient Egyptian theology and the Crusades, she moved to Italy with *Sistine Heresy*. *Sarah, Son of God* took us through Stonewall-rioting New York, Venice under the Inquisition, and Nero's Rome. Then came *Beloved Gomorrah*, an LGBT version of Sodom and Gomorrah, channeled through modern scuba divers, while the next, *Dian's Ghost*, honors the memory of Dian Fossey and her mountain gorillas.

Saracen's recent preoccupation has been World War II, viewed from unfamiliar perspectives. *Tyger, Tyger, Burning Bright* follows the lives of four lovers during the Third Reich, *Waiting for the Violins* focuses on the French and Belgian Résistance, *The Witch of Stalingrad* is an homage to a real female Soviet pilot, and *The Sniper's Kiss*, based on actual female Soviet snipers, lets us see the war through Russian eyes.

Having won numerous Golden Crown and Rainbow prizes through the years, in 2016, Saracen was awarded the high-profile Alice B Readers medal for her entire body of work. She lives in Brussels where she enjoys good wine, chocolate, baguettes, and socialized medicine. Occasionally, she travels to exotic locations like the United States, or to Egypt to scuba dive. She can be reached by way of www.justinesaracen.net, through FB as justinesaracen, and at Twitter as JustSaracen.

# Books Available From Bold Strokes Books

**A Call Away** by KC Richardson. Can a businesswoman from a big city find the answers she's looking for, and possibly love, on a small-town farm? (978-1-63555-025-2)

**Berlin Hungers** by Justine Saracen. Can the love between an RAF woman and the wife of a Luftwaffe pilot, former enemies, survive in besieged Berlin during the aftermath of World War II? (978-1-63555-116-7)

**Blend** by Georgia Beers. Lindsay and Piper are like night and day. Working together won't be easy, but not falling in love might prove the hardest job of all. (978-1-63555-189-1)

**Hunger for You** by Jenny Frame. Principe of an ancient vampire clan Byron Debrek must save her one true love from falling into the hands of her enemies and into the middle of a vampire war. (978-1-63555-168-6)

**Mercy** by Michelle Larkin. FBI Special Agent Mercy Parker and psychic ex-profiler Piper Vasey learn to love again as they race to stop a man with supernatural gifts who's bent on annihilating humankind. (978-1-63555-202-7)

**Pride and Porters** by Charlotte Greene. Will pride and prejudice prevent these modern-day lovers from living happily ever after? (978-1-63555-158-7)

**Rocks and Stars** by Sam Ledel. Kyle's struggle to own who she is and what she really wants may end up landing her on the bench and without the woman of her dreams. (978-1-63555-156-3)

**The Boss of Her: Office Romance Novellas** by Julie Cannon, Aurora Rey, and M. Ullrich. Going to work never felt so good. Three office romance novellas from talented writers Julie Cannon, Aurora Rey, and M. Ullrich. (978-1-63555-145-7)

**The Deep End** by Ellie Hart. When family ties become entangled in murder and deception, it's time to find a way out… (978-1-63555-288-1)

**A Country Girl's Heart** by Dena Blake. When Kat Jackson gets a second chance at love, following her heart will prove the hardest decision of all. (978-1-63555-134-1)

**Dangerous Waters** by Radclyffe. Life, death, and war on the home front. Two women join forces against a powerful opponent, nature itself. (978-1-63555-233-1)

**Fury's Death** by Brey Willows. When all we hold sacred fails, who will be there to save us? (978-1-63555-063-4)

**It's Not a Date** by Heather Blackmore. Kade's desire to keep things with Jen on a professional level is in Jen's best interest. Yet what's in Kade's best interest…is Jen. (978-1-63555-149-5)

**Killer Winter** by Kay Bigelow. Just when she thought things could get no worse, homicide Lieutenant Leah Samuels learns the woman she loves has betrayed her in devastating ways. (978-1-63555-177-8)

**Score** by MJ Williamz. Will an addiction to pain pills destroy Ronda's chance with the woman she loves, or will she come out on top and score a happily ever after? (978-1-62639-807-8)

**Spring's Wake** by Aurora Rey. When wanderer Willa Lange falls for Provincetown B&B owner Nora Calhoun, will past hurts and a fifteen-year age gap keep them from finding love? (978-1-63555-035-1)

**The Northwoods** by Jane Hoppen. When Evelyn Bauer, disguised as her dead husband, George, travels to a Northwoods logging camp to work, she and the camp cook Sarah Bell forge a friendship fraught with both tenderness and turmoil. (978-1-63555-143-3)

**Truth or Dare** by C. Spencer. For a group of six lesbian friends, life changes course after one long snow-filled weekend. (978-1-63555-148-8)

**Children of the Healer** by Barbara Ann Wright. Life becomes desperate for ex-soldier Cordelia Ross when the indigenous aliens of her planet are drawn into a civil war and old enemies linger in the shadows. Book Three of the Godfall Series. (978-1-63555-031-3)

**A Heart to Call Home** by Jeannie Levig. When Jessie Weldon returns to her hometown after thirty years, can she and her childhood crush Dakota Scott heal the tragic past that links them? (978-1-63555-059-7)

**Hearts Like Hers** by Melissa Brayden. Coffee shop owner Autumn Primm is ready to cut loose and live a little, but is the baggage that comes with out-of-towner Kate Carpenter too heavy for anything long term? (978-1-63555-014-6)

**Love at Cooper's Creek** by Missouri Vaun. Shaw Daily flees corporate life to find solace in the rural Blue Ridge Mountains, but escapism eludes her when her attentions are captured by small town beauty Kate Elkins. (978-1-62639-960-0)

**Twice in a Lifetime** by PJ Trebelhorn. Detective Callie Burke can't deny the growing attraction to her late friend's widow, Taylor Fletcher, who also happens to own the bar where Callie's sister works. (978-1-63555-033-7)

**Undiscovered Affinity** by Jane Hardee. Will a no-strings-attached affair be enough to break Olivia's control and convince Cardic that love does exist? (978-1-63555-061-0)

**Between Sand and Stardust** by Tina Michele. Are the lifelong bonds of love strong enough to conquer time, distance, and heartache when Haven Thorne and Willa Bennette are given another chance at forever? (978-1-62639-940-2)

**Charming the Vicar** by Jenny Frame. When magician and atheist Finn Kane seeks refuge in an English village after a spiritual crisis, can local vicar Bridget Claremont restore her faith in life and love? (978-1-63555-029-0)

**Data Capture** by Jesse J. Thoma. Lola Walker is undercover on the hunt for cybercriminals while trying not to notice the woman who might be perfectly wrong for her for all the right reasons. (978-1-62639-985-3)

**Epicurean Delights** by Renee Roman. Ariana Marks had no idea a leisure swim would lead to being rescued, in more ways than one, by the charismatic Hudson Frost. (978-1-63555-100-6)

**Heart of the Devil** by Ali Vali. We know most of Cain and Emma Casey's story, but Heart of the Devil will take you back to where it began one fateful night with a tray loaded with beer. (978-1-63555-045-0)

**Known Threat** by Kara A. McLeod. When Special Agent Ryan O'Connor reluctantly questions who protects the Secret Service, she learns courage truly is found in unlikely places. Agent O'Connor Series #3 (978-1-63555-132-7)

**Seer and the Shield** by D. Jackson Leigh. Time is running out for the Dragon Horse Army while two unlikely heroines struggle to put aside their attraction and find a way to stop a deadly cult. Dragon Horse War, Book 3 (978-1-63555-170-9)

**The Universe Between Us** by Jane C. Esther. Ana Mitchell must make the hardest choice of her life: the promise of new love Jolie Dann on Earth, or a humanity-saving mission to colonize Mars. (978-1-63555-106-8)

**Touch** by Kris Bryant. Can one touch heal a heart? (978-1-63555-084-9)

**A More Perfect Union** by Carsen Taite. Major Zoey Granger and DC fixer Rook Daniels risk their reputations for a chance at true love while dealing with a scandal that threatens to rock the military. (978-1-62639-754-5)

**Arrival** by Gun Brooke. The spaceship *Pathfinder* reaches its passengers' new homeworld where danger lurks in the shadows while Pamas Seclan disembarks and finds unexpected love in young science genius Darmiya Do Voy. (978-1-62639-859-7)

**Captain's Choice** by VK Powell. Architect Kerstin Anthony's life is going to plan until Bennett Carlyle, the first girl she ever kissed, is assigned to her latest and most important project, a police district substation. (978-1-62639-997-6)

**Falling Into Her** by Erin Zak. Pam Phillips, widow at the age of forty, meets Kathryn Hawthorne, local Chicago celebrity, and it changes her life forever—in ways she hadn't even considered possible. (978-1-63555-092-4)

**Hookin' Up** by MJ Williamz. Will Leah get what she needs from casual hookups or will she see the love she desires right in front of her? (978-1-63555-051-1)

**King of Thieves** by Shea Godfrey. When art thief Casey Marinos meets bounty hunter Finnegan Starkweather, the crimes of the past just might set the stage for a payoff worth more than she ever dreamed possible. (978-1-63555-007-8)

**Lucy's Chance** by Jackie D. As a serial killer haunts the streets, Lucy tries to stitch up old wounds with her first love in the wake of a small town's rapid descent into chaos. (978-1-63555-027-6)

**Right Here, Right Now** by Georgia Beers. When Alicia Wright moves into the office next door to Lacey Chamberlain's accounting firm, Lacey is about to find out that sometimes the last person you want is exactly the person you need. (978-1-63555-154-9)

**Strictly Need to Know** by MB Austin. Covert operator Maji Rios will do whatever she must to complete her mission, but saving a gorgeous stranger from Russian mobsters was not in her plans. (978-1-63555-114-3)

**Tailor-Made** by Yolanda Wallace. Tailor Grace Henderson doesn't date clients, but when she meets gender-bending model Dakota Lane, she's tempted to throw all the rules out the window. (978-1-63555-081-8)

**Time Will Tell** by M. Ullrich. With the ability to time travel, Eva Caldwell will have to decide between having it all and erasing it all. (978-1-63555-088-7)

**Love After Hours** by Radclyffe. When Gina Antonelli agrees to renovate Carrie Longmire's new house, she doesn't welcome Carrie's overtures at friendship or her own unexpected attraction. A Rivers Community Novel. (978-1-63555-090-0)